Once Again I Fear

By Lyn Sellers

PublishAmerica
Baltimore

© 2007 by Lyn Sellers.
All rights reserved. No part of this book may be reproduced, stored in a retrieval system or transmitted in any form or by any means without the prior written permission of the publishers, except by a reviewer who may quote brief passages in a review to be printed in a newspaper, magazine or journal.

First printing

All characters appearing in this work are fictitious. Any resemblance to real persons, living or dead, is purely coincidental.

At the specific preference of the author, PublishAmerica allowed this work to remain exactly as the author intended, verbatim, without editorial input.

All scripture quotations are from the King James Version(KJV) of the bible.

ISBN: 1-4241-5442-1
PUBLISHED BY PUBLISHAMERICA, LLLP
www.publishamerica.com
Baltimore

Printed in the United States of America

Dedication

I wish to dedicate this book to my sweet Jim, who has always been supportive of me in all my endeavors as a writer.

Acknowledgements

I wish to acknowledge those who offered invaluable aid, in researching my book.

The Saratoga, California, Chamber of Commerce

The Palo Alto, California, Chamber of Commerce

Amy Walker, of Hornblower Dining Yachts, who gave me lots of information and pictures,

Officer Jim Diegnan and Inspector Ron Kern (now retired) of the San Francisco Police Dept., without whose help I could not have developed my character of Lucas Dayton.

Linda, at the Union Square Association

Joel Riggs of Been There Aerial Photographers, whose maps helped me to keep my bearings.

Any errors are my own.

Also, I hope the people of San Francisco will not be too upset that I have inserted fictional buildings into their treasured streets.

Chapter 1

I had not seen him in six years, but there he was! Six years in which I had begun to feel safe, the constant dread of a hovering, dark shadow gradually ebbing from my consciousness. It had been a false security, for now I saw the all too familiar figure, lounging nonchalantly against the lamp post, not a full block from my apartment.

Fortunately, I had seen him in time to duck into a doorway feeling my stomach drop sickeningly and my knees turn to water. Why was he here now, after all this time?

A young, red-haired woman came to the doorway, and I stepped aside, flattening my body against the wall. The woman stared at me curiously, and I, weakly, tried to smile at her. The door closed after her, leaving behind her the scent of hair spray and White Diamonds. Still I stood frozen against the cold, gray stone, praying that God would help me to know what to do.

Cautiously, I peeked around the wall. The figure of my great fear was walking away from me, his gray trench coat ballooning in the wind that was a near constant in San Francisco.

I watched him disappear among the after-work crowd, feeling that he was an alien among them. He didn't belong here; he was a nightmare persona that my mind had willed to stay away, never to return.

Shaking violently, I left the doorway and hurried to my apartment building.

Only when I had closed my apartment door, locking it behind me, did I realize I had been holding my breath much of the last few minutes. Letting out a ragged gasp, I burst into tears.

I stood in my familiar surroundings, seeing the white walls, carpet and furniture, splashed with warm, bright colors in throw pillows, accent rugs, floral arrangements and pictures, all the things that I had chosen to complement the furniture that I had brought from my family home. I smelled the potpourri in decorative pots on white-washed tables, and heard the soft whir of heat being blown through vents just above floor level. But, now, the dark shadow had returned, filling my serene life with a deep, paralyzing fear. My mouth was dry and tasted bitter, as if I had tried to swallow a quinine pill without water.

My tortoise shell cat, Tache, came scampering toward me, her tail held high. She reared up, resting her tiny paws on my leg, and mewed imploringly. Picking her up, I held her close, smelling the clean aroma of her soft fur, and her kitten breath, so warm, and so like that of a human baby. But her nearness could not still the storm that raged within me.

My mind was filled with images of Judson Edward Bard III, my former fiancé, my enemy.

He had fled to Europe before his trial for murdering my mother and trying to murder me. On occasion, he had been seen in trendy European nightspots, sidewalk cafes, and on the sands of the Riviera, no doubt being supported in his fugitive life by his fabulously wealthy father. Though living in the public eye, he had proved to be elusive, evading capture by any foreign law enforcement entity that chose to make a feeble attempt to bring him to justice. Maddeningly, there were those police forces that shrugged off the pleas of the U. S. officials to find and return him for trial.

Month after month I persevered, but to no avail. It took a long, long time for me to realize that everyone, except me, had lost interest in my cause. Sightings of Judson had tapered off and then stopped entirely.

"Miss Atherly, he's gone; there's nothing more we can do. He will remain on the wanted list, but I'm afraid he's made a new identity for himself or, perhaps, he's dead." I had heard some version of this speech at least a dozen times. The wall between me and the justice I sought had grown to an unscalable height, so, reluctantly, I had gone about putting my shattered life back together.

I had thought I could never be free from fear again, but as the years passed, I became immersed in my work as a department store buyer. The debilitating fear had given way to an acceptance, broken only by momentary mental images of the snarling face of Judson Bard, the screams of my mother blending with my own, and the blood, always the blood.

The flashes had diminished to the point that I could, at times, feel that the horror was a dream. I was awake; I could go on and live.

I had almost convinced myself that Judson was either dead or had lost interest in me. Now, I had to reassess. He was alive, he was nearby, perhaps knowing where I lived, and, I was sure, had arrived to renew his pursuit of me.

I stood in the growing darkness and, suddenly, the terrifying past swept into my memory, so real that it seemed to be happening now.

My heart pounded against my chest wall, and cold sweat drenched my whole body as I gave way to the memories and relived what had led up to the end of what had been my secure, hopeful world.

Chapter 2

I grew up in Saratoga, California, originally a small lumber town, and then an arty village, scrunched up against the redwood-covered foothills of the Santa Cruz Mountains. Serene, trendy, Saratoga was named for the nearby mineral springs which resembled those of Saratoga Springs, New York. In addition to the springs, Saratoga became known for its wineries, which dotted the hillsides, with vineyards reminiscent of France and Italy.

Tourists came to enjoy the ambience of a village so different from the traffic-choked cities surrounding it. Homes were built here by those who were drawn by the beauty of the mountain setting and the Mediterranean-like climate.

Then, white-collar workers in the Silicon Valley built more and more spacious homes in and around Saratoga. Gradually, prune and apricot orchards surrounding the town gave way to upscale subdivisions, shopping centers and elementary schools. However, the downtown stayed virtually the same, since it had little place to go except into the forests above it, and those were reluctant to budge. The result was a small town atmosphere in the middle of sprawling progress.

Our home was nestled into the woods on the side of the mountain south of town, a two-story, wood house, painted light gray, and decked across the back in warm redwood. The inside was open and airy, with vaulted ceilings and professionally decorated rooms; the grounds expansive, with a swimming pool and tennis courts. My father had worked his way up the corporate ladder until he had became the CEO of

ONCE AGAIN I FEAR

a computer manufacturing company in San Jose, providing the luxurious life we enjoyed, but spending little time with my mother and me. Therefore, my mother became my world.

It was she who came to the school programs, attended teachers' conferences, took me to dance classes, and came to my recitals and all the other things that parents should share or do together. My fifth grade teacher had once remarked that my father seemed to be the invisible man, since she had never seen him at any time. I assured her that he was truly flesh and blood, but he was BUSY. Somehow, in my mind, I always saw the word "busy" in all caps and boldfaced print, rather like the tone in which my father always used the word to excuse his absences from my life.

I suppose children usually take their parents' word as gospel and accept what is handed them in life. The only time I questioned whether or not these were normal circumstances was when I saw other children's fathers attending functions for which my father had no time. Sadly, though, I knew quite a few friends who also had absentee fathers, either through divorce or, as in my case, the fathers being BUSY.

I say all this to emphasize how my life was wrapped around my pretty, petite mother, Annabel Prince Atherly.

She had been a nineteen-year-old ballet student, with great promise for a professional career when she met my father. Her teacher at a dance academy in Los Gatos had arranged for her to have an audition with the San Francisco Ballet. It was her dream come true, since this was America's oldest ballet company and one of its finest. But, three weeks before it was to be held, Stan Atherly had appeared on the scene at a party given by one of Annabel's friends.

Stan and Annabel had clicked instantly and, within two months, Stan had persuaded Annabel to marry him and give up her career. They were married six months after they first met. I grew angry every time I thought of it. I felt it was pure arrogance for a man to think a woman should drop all her plans just for him, particularly when he thought nothing of spending so much time on his own career that she was pushed to the back burners of his life. Dad seemed to want a beautiful, graceful wife who could entertain his clients, throw large, elegant parties and accompany

11

him to endless company functions, always smiling and saying the right things. I, who had not yet known the power of love, had vowed that would never happen to me.

It was clear to me that Mom sometimes thought longingly of the career she had let pass her by, but she put a good face on things, passing it off as not worth thinking about. She, from time to time, attended an advanced ballet class, just to keep from getting rusty, but always was far beyond the other students. The instructors called on her sometimes to fill in as a teacher, when there was an illness or family crisis among the staff members. She graciously, and skillfully, taught the classes, but never gave in to their pleas to join the staff permanently. I knew that my father would not have approved, thinking it was not what the wife of a young executive, and later, a CEO, should be doing.

She enrolled me in the same academy but, unfortunately, I lacked that poetic grace and strength that my mother had.

So I grew up in the lavish home, with a loving, devoted mother, but with too little quality contact with my handsome, brilliant father, though I loved him intensely. I knew Mom was, in some ways, very lonely, but she never complained. On a few occasions, I heard her crying, when she thought I was out of earshot. I never intruded on her pain, because I knew there was nothing I could do to help her, except love her.

I know Mom enjoyed her time with me, perhaps reliving some of her own young days in ballet. One year, when I was fourteen, I was to perform in *The Nutcracker* at Christmas time. The dance academy, being the area's premier training school for dancers, joined with the Santa Clara Ballet Company to present the colorful, exciting classic. It was staged at the San Jose Civic Auditorium for four performances on a weekend before the holiday. Even the Beginner-One students had parts, those not requiring too much technical skill—toy soldiers, mice, etc.

Since I had studied for nine years, I was on pointe and was able to dance in several roles, including one of the snowflakes with the Snow Queen. Mom had agreed to appear as the Snow Queen, since she was one of the most gifted dancers associated with the academy. I was thrilled to death to be able to be on stage with my beautiful mom, and knowing that I was the envy of the other girls for having a mother like her.

ONCE AGAIN I FEAR

At one point, during the final rehearsal, when we were not on stage, she and I sat in the auditorium, watching the toy soldiers fighting the mice with wooden swords. It was always fun to get a chance to watch some of the show from the audience's perspective. Mom was laughing heartily at the action on stage.

"Do you know that Nureyev danced on this stage?" she asked me.

"Did he? Really?"

"Oh, yes. I heard that he got down on hands and knees and went over every inch of this stage, before he would set foot, or I should say, ballet slipper, on it. He wanted to make sure there were no sunken spots on the floor. Apparently he was satisfied, because he went ahead with the performance. It was to a sold-out house, as you can imagine.

"I remember *The Nutcracker* one year when I was a teenager," she continued. "Half the cast ended up with the mumps. It was perfectly awful. Even the Nutcracker, himself, was ill. And the poor Snow Queen! By the Sunday matinee, she was starting to swell under her jaws, but she went on, anyway, and did a superb job. All the sick ones did. No one was going to keep them off that stage. I was one of the lucky ones; I didn't start getting sick until three days after the last performance."

She glanced at the stage as the King of the Mice was defeated. "I remember one tiny soldier, probably eight-years-old. By Sunday afternoon, she was glassy-eyed with fever, but she wielded her little sword as if there were nothing wrong with her in the least." Mom smiled at the memory. "Today, that little soldier is Jineane Wiedermann of the New York City Ballet."

I sat up and stared at my mother. "You knew Jineane Wiedermann? I didn't know that! I've seen her picture dozens of times in dance magazines. And I've seen her perform on PBS a few times. Wow!"

Mom laughed at my astonishment. "Yes, I watched Jineane grow up, as a person and as a dancer. It was obvious, early on, that she was something special, as graceful as a swan, but strong as a lion. She studied here until she was sixteen, when she went to New York to the Performing Arts School. She finished high school there and studied with Helena Bartoloni. This academy has produced some of the best." She fingered the crisp tulle of her snow-white tutu and stared at the stage. It was then that I saw a deep sadness in my mother's beautiful green eyes. She had been one of the best and still was.

It was only rarely that Mom allowed anyone to see the sadness of her lost dreams. Even with me, she was upbeat and turned her enthusiasm onto my training. She never, even for a moment, made me feel she was disappointed in my lack of that essential quality that is termed greatness. I was good, I knew that, but I did not have that greatness.

It was not as important to me, though, as it had been to her. I loved ballet, but my dreams actually revolved around being something connected with the fashion world. From early childhood, I had sewn dresses for my dolls and made accessories out of bits of faux leather, feathers, ribbons, beads and whatever else I could find to serve the purpose. Mom's eyes shined when she saw my creations, exhibiting as much pride as if I were dancing the Sugar Plum Fairy role. "You've got a real sense of fashion, Rachelle," she would say. "I'll bet you'll end up being a fashion designer."

However, I soon became fascinated by the stores in which we shopped, marveling at the layouts of merchandise and the beautifully clad mannequins in the windows. I could have spent hours just roaming the aisles, taking in the wonders on display. Before long, I knew that I wanted to work in that world.

After watching fashion shows on television, and seeing buyers in the audience, taking notes on clipboards, I felt that that was what I wanted to do: choose the wonderful merchandise for the stores.

At Saratoga High School, I took as many business courses as I could, as well as every sewing class offered. Through these, I learned about fabric and workmanship, knowledge that, in later years, became vital in my chosen profession. Soon, I was wearing an extensive wardrobe that I had created for myself. Mom encouraged me every step of the way.

When it came time for college, nearby Stanford was my first choice as the college where I would pursue my business degree. I was totally elated the day I received my acceptance letter. "I knew you would be accepted," Mom rhapsodized, "since you are ranked second in your class and scored higher than anyone at Saratoga High on your SAT. With that and all your

ONCE AGAIN I FEAR

extracurricular activities, you couldn't miss. Stanford wants students with those kinds of accomplishments." She hugged me and grinned glowingly. I was doing some glowing, myself.

Chapter 3

I will always remember my years at Stanford; they were both exciting and rewarding. The academic standards were high, but I had no real difficulty with living up to those standards. Perhaps I had been blessed with superior intelligence to make up for what I lacked in ballet artistry. Mom would always laugh, when I said that to her.

At the end of the first semester, it was announced that I would be on the Dean's List. I remained on that coveted list all through my four years at The Farm, the affectionate nickname of the school which had been established on Leland Stanford's farm.

I felt so much a part of this sprawling institution, with its landmark Hoover Tower, crowned with red tile, the exquisite Memorial Church, with Biblical murals and stained glass above graceful arches. It was a joy to stroll the Inner Quadrangle, which is joined by arcades to the twelve original classrooms, the Memorial Church and the Outer Quadrangle. The sandstone buildings are a melding of Romanesque and Mission Revival architecture, with red clay roofs, and connecting arches and long arcades.

Many times I thought of the grief that Jane and Leland Stanford must have felt when their son, Leland Jr., had died of typhoid in 1884 when he was fifteen and on a European tour. The University which sits on the site of the old Palo Alto Stock Farm, where Stanford bred world-famous horses in the late nineteenth century, had been designated as a memorial to the Stanfords' son.

ONCE AGAIN I FEAR

The Stanfords had collaborated with Frederick Law Olmsted, who designed New York's Central Park, to produce the plans for the University. Olmsted's belief in the connection of people and the environment is strongly stated in his plans for the campus.

The rest of the university had grown up around the original buildings, maintaining the same ambience and grace. It was always a thrill to stand in the Quad, imagining the origination of the school and thinking of all the other feet that had walked through this area, and the thousands upon thousands of degrees that had been bestowed, since the school's opening on October first, eighteen ninety-one, almost one hundred years before my coming to the campus.

Though there were ten sororities on campus, I decided not to pledge. I was, however, inducted into an academic fraternity, and proudly wore the gold pin signifying my membership.

During my first two years, I participated in the campus dance theater, including a superbly staged "Sleeping Beauty". In my junior year, though, I decided to concentrate as much of my energy as I could to my studies, so dropped out of the theater group.

During one summer, I took an intense course in fashion design and merchandising at The Fashion Institute in San Francisco. In those two months, the school had crammed in studies that would have taken a full year at most schools. Only the most dedicated could survive it and absorb what they taught. I was in my element, soaking up everything I could.

I, at one time, considered taking advantage of the University's Overseas Studies program. A few months, or a year, at the Stanford campus in Paris, the home of the great fashion houses, would have been wonderful. However, I decided to stay in Palo Alto all my four years, partly because I wasn't yet ready to be that far from my parents.

My other extracurricular activities at Stanford included various community service projects and serving on the Freshman Advisory Committee in my junior and senior years. I also attended every football home game that was played in the old stadium, which was set in among magnificent eucalyptus trees. Also, I became the number one supporter, in my estimation, of the Cardinal basketball team. When they made the

Sweet Sixteen in the NCAA tournament in my junior year and the Elite Eight in my senior year, no one was more joyful than Rachelle Atherly.

In the spring of my senior year, my roommate in Donner Hall, Stephanie Kulin, asked me to go to a track meet in which Stanford was hosting Cal Berkley and San Jose State at Angell Field. Stephanie was dating one of the sprinters and never missed a meet in which he ran.

Most Stanford students bicycle everywhere, sometimes creating pedal-driven traffic jams. I enjoyed the challenge of avoiding a two-wheeled smash up. But, that day, as Stephanie and I threaded our bicycles through a myriad of other cyclists, I did not foresee that going to one sports event would change my life forever. It was there that I met Judson Edward Bard III.

Judson was the anchor man on the four-by-one-hundred relay and also ran in the eight-hundred and fifteen-hundred races. I first noticed him as he deftly took the baton from his teammate, with the Stanford team in second place, slightly behind Cal Berkley. His long, lean body took on the quality of a deer in flight, covering long distances with each step, his slightly long, dark hair flowing behind him. He overtook the Cal runner, soon leaving him far behind. As Judson crossed the finish line, a roar went up from the crowd and he jauntily sprinted a few more yards before turning to join his teammates in celebration. I had never seen anything more beautiful, even on the ballet stage.

After the meet, Stepanie's boyfriend, Rick, ran toward her, with Judson closely behind.

Judson caught sight of me and whistled. "Hey, Steph, who's this luscious female you've brought to see Rick run—and Judson, too?" He grinned at me, his gray-blue eyes sparkling mischievously. Stephanie introduced us, and then he grabbed my hand and squeezed it. "Rachelle Atherly, this is my day! Where have you been hiding all these years at Stanford? Wait until we get changed, and we are going into town to O'Connell's for something to eat. You and I are going to get acquainted."

That was Judson, self-assured, never doubting that I would go along with anything he suggested.

At the beginning, it had seemed so right that he should be that forceful. It was just his nature, I reasoned. I accepted strong men, men like my

ONCE AGAIN I FEAR

father, as being the norm. Little did I know that Judson's pattern in our relationship would be just that, force! At that moment, however, I was stunned by the beauty of the man, overwhelmed by the fact that he had decided instantly that he wanted to know me better. I grinned happily and agreed to wait for him.

That was the beginning of a relationship that would take me to fantastic heights and, later, drag me down to the depths of grief and despair.

Chapter 4

Judson Bard became totally involved in my life from that point on. I was completely smitten the moment he turned those compelling eyes and the warm smile on me. He seemed to take over my existence, and I felt powerless to protest the preemptory way he told me what we were going to do, never asking. Judson always did it in a charming way, with words of love and extravagant compliments. He also showered me with expensive gifts and romantic notes.

Why did I succumb so easily, in spite of being a strong, intelligent young woman with a clear goal in life? Why couldn't I see that this was clearly a pattern of control, a pattern that would only escalate into far worse manipulation and abuse? Who can explain anything the human heart leads one to do, even if it is totally contrary to what a person believes is right.

I did take one stand against him, though. That was in the area of a more intimate relationship. At times, I came very near to giving up my resolve to remain pure until marriage, but something deep in my inner core of strength rose to save me from making that mistake. Judson wasn't happy about that, to put it mildly, and continued to pressure me to give in, telling me that he loved me and wanted me to be completely his. There were times when he would get angry and tell me that if I really loved him, I would make love with him. Those were the rare times when I became angry, too, because I believed that I loved him more than anything in the world, and how dare he use such shoddy tactics on me?

ONCE AGAIN I FEAR

I suspected, sometimes, that he sneaked around with other, more compliant girls, to get his pleasure. Even that, however, was not enough to break the emotional hold he had on me.

I look back now and wonder why Judson didn't drop me, as I had heard he did with some other girls who resisted his advances. Perhaps, I was a real challenge to him. It is possible that he had assured himself that no girl could keep saying "no" to Judson Edward Bard III forever. He certainly did make every effort to wear me down.

Three weeks after I met Judson, I took him home to meet my mother. I was very nervous, because I wanted her to like him. Judson was his usual charming self, holding my mother's soft, white hand for a moment too long, when they were introduced, and smiling his most brilliant smile. "Mrs. Atherly, I am so happy to meet Rachelle's lovely mom. I can see where she got her beauty."

It was an old, ingratiating line, but Mom smiled graciously and said, "I'm happy to meet you too, Judson. Rachelle tells me you are quite a runner for Stanford."

She couldn't have said anything that pleased Judson more; he liked nothing better than being able to strut his stuff in front of a beautiful woman. "Oh, I have won a few in my time," he answered, in mock humility.

"Well, I'm sure you will make the school proud. I understand that the Pac-Ten Championship meet will be held in the Stanford Stadium this year. Perhaps you'll be able to win the championship in at least one of your events, and do it at home."

"I'll certainly do my best. There's only one guy in the Pack-Ten who gives me any concern in the eight-hundred meter, and that's a guy at Arizona. Actually, I think I can take him, though." He smiled more broadly and winked at me.

"You should see him run, Mom," I said. "He is a cross between a deer and a cheetah. It is just breathtaking."

"Perhaps I'll come up to the next home meet and see for myself," Mom promised as she led us to the right of the foyer into the game room where pool and table tennis tables sat on opposite ends. Another room, opening from the far end was our dance studio where an exercise *barré* ran

21

along one mirrored wall, and a stereo was set up to provide the music for our practices. A cabinet, built around the stereo, held an enormous collection of tapes and CDs of almost all the great ballet music available

Without even thinking, I walked quickly toward the dance room, pushed the play button on the stereo, and took off my white running shoes. Dressed in white shorts and an aqua knit top, my waist-length, light brown hair banded into a pony tail, I moved easily around the smooth, polished wood floor. My feet, clad only in white tennis socks, automatically traced the familiar steps that I had known most of my life. My arms curved and flowed, following each position of my feet, my mind hearing the beautiful music that was a part of my very being. I did a series of leaps and then turned in a graceful pirouette before kneeling on one knee in a deep bow, my hands and arms sweeping up softly, like the wings of a swan.

Judson and Mom clapped heartily and Judson yelled, "Bravo!" I stood and smiled at them. It was at that moment, despite his smile, that I caught the faintest flicker of something in Judson's eyes that I could only feel was anger. Why? Was he jealous of anyone who took center stage away from him, even for a moment? Or was it that he did not want me to have any talent that came even close to his own?

I did not recognize the fact, then, that any time I started to shine, he felt he would lose control over me, and he couldn't stand that. It is too bad I didn't recognize that look for what it was; perhaps it would have saved my family from the misery that came later.

I mentally shrugged off my momentary twinge of fear, and went to hug my mother, telling her how happy I was to be home. I am five feet six, so I could see the top of her head as she hugged me with strength beyond her five feet three size.

After releasing me, mom turned quickly, her waist-length, light brown hair, so much like mine, swirling around her, headed toward the door of the game room. "I'll get us some cold drinks; I'm sure you're both thirsty. Why don't you play some pool or something?"

After she had gone, Judson became his usual self, showing nothing of the darkness I had seen in his eyes. "Hey, a game of pool sounds great. How about it?"

ONCE AGAIN I FEAR

"Sure, but I've gotta warn you, chum; I'm pretty good at this game," I answered, picking one of the cue sticks out of the rack and starting to chalk the tip. At that moment, my big, gray cat, Cleo, trotted into the room, and rubbed against my leg, purring loudly. I bent and picked her up, holding her close as I nuzzled her neck.

Judson selected a cue to his liking and also chalked the end with great enthusiasm. "You'll never see the day you can beat Judson Bard, lady."

I set Cleo down, and then the game began. I soon sensed that I was far better than he was, and it was a real temptation to beat the socks off him. But would I see that terrible look again, perhaps even worse? I purposely started missing a shot here and there or making a bad decision on which ball to put in which pocket. For my own dignity, I was not going to let him beat me by much, so when the game ended, he was the winner by only a small margin. I think he knew, too, that I was good at the game, and was extremely smug when he declared himself the winner.

I had always been a highly competitive person, so it was hard to watch him swagger around the table, when I knew I could easily have won the game. I refused another game, not being able to stand purposely losing again, so he took it as my being afraid of his "superior" ability. Let him think what he would; I didn't want to make him unhappy with me.

Mom returned with iced tea and chips and salsa. I was happy to sit next to Judson on the leather sofa in one corner of the game room, with Mom in a chair facing us, the snacks and drinks on a table between us. Judson launched into an amusing and charming anecdote about something that had happened at track practice the day before.

Mom, an excellent conversationalist from long practice, asked just the right questions and drew out a lot of things about Judson that I didn't know yet. I learned that he had a married sister, Gwynneth, who lived in San Francisco, and the family had a dog named Sugar. For some reason, he had never told me anything except that his father was the owner of a fleet of freight liners. Also, he had said the family lived in Sausalito, across the Golden Gate Bridge from San Francisco. It was unsettling to realize suddenly that I actually knew very little of real importance about this man for whom I had come to care so deeply. It struck me as odd, also, that he had never invited me to visit his home and meet his family. Nevertheless, again, I mentally shrugged it off.

I caught Mom eyeing him thoughtfully from time to time and wondered what she saw, perhaps that I didn't. She was, however, extremely sweet. A casual observer would not have guessed, as I did, that she wanted very much to see beneath this charming, clever exterior of the young man that I thought was next to God.

All during the evening, while we had dinner, watched a video, and played a game of table tennis, at which Judson was definitely my superior, Mom kept up her bright banter with the two of us and I began to relax, thinking that she liked him very much.

Dad, as usual, didn't come home until late, so he had only a few very distracted minutes to meet Judson.

He shook his hand absently, and then went upstairs to change clothes. He had already eaten dinner, so simply disappeared from view, probably to his computer in this upstairs office. How like him.

I didn't get a chance to talk to Mom alone that evening. Judson and I had classes the next day so we left for Palo Alto at eight thirty. Mom kissed me warmly, holding me an extra few seconds, and shook Judson's hand. "Drive carefully, kids," she admonished us as we headed toward Judson's bright red Corvette.

I waved to her as I slid into the low seat and then threw her a kiss. My heart swelled with love for the slender woman in the lighted doorway.

Chapter 5

It was the last week in April when Judson proposed to me. I felt happy beyond words and answered, "Yes!" without even having to think. Any misgivings I might have about Judson were pushed to the farthest recesses of my mind, displaced by the certainty that everything was going to be wonderful, everything I had ever dreamed of.

My giddiness was short-lived, though, for, now, Judson seemed to feel that he really owned me. He rushed out and bought me an enormous diamond solitaire, and, before long, I came to feel that that ring was a ball and chain on my life.

Of course, he had taken it for granted that I would now go to bed with him, and was furious when I reiterated my firm no. "We aren't married yet, Judson," I told him, "and I won't do it until we are." How did I have the courage to refuse him still? I can only guess, now, looking back, that it was the hand of God on me, although I didn't know Him then.

From the point of my first post-engagement refusal, Judson became more and more manipulative and controlling of me. He demanded to know everywhere I went and everything I did. And, most importantly, he wanted to know to whom I talked. I didn't dare mention I had had a conversation with another guy, because he would accuse me of all ridiculous things that implied I was unfaithful to him. That was very hurtful, in view of the fact, now known to me, that he had done the very same thing to me quite a few times.

There was no reasoning with him. We usually ended up in a shouting match, and he was far better, and louder, at shouting than I was. Invariably, I would start to cry in hurt and frustration, and he would either stomp off or sit and pout like a child. It is embarrassing to me to think about it, but I would usually be the one to apologize and try to set things right between us.

The first time he hit me was shortly before graduation. On a Friday night, we had gone out to an informal, pre-graduation party with a group, including some of his track teammates and some fraternity brothers.

The evening had gone quite well at first. I shared everyone's exhilaration that four years of hard work were finally going to get us our coveted diplomas. Mixed with this delight, were feelings of sadness that, soon, many of us would say good-bye, probably never to see each other again.

The party was held at a college hangout, a local bar and grill on The El Camino Real, in north Palo Alto, near Menlo Park. The booze was flowing and loud music made conversation almost impossible without shouting. Judson led me through the smoke-dimmed crowd, holding tightly to my arm, until we joined two of his friends and their dates at a table near the back.

I had known both of the guys, Bobby Deets and Sean McConnell, from track meets, and had briefly met the two girls, Jody and Kim—I never caught their last names. They all seemed amiable enough. Judson ordered us each a beer, which was brought in icy-cold, brown bottles, moisture droplets running down the sides. I detested beer, but, characteristically, Judson didn't even ask what I wanted. There was so much noise that it was hard to protest, even if he would have been willing to listen. So, I sat idly twirling the bottle, taking tiny sips, more to cool my dry tongue than anything, and longing for a Coke or a Dr. Pepper.

At the beginning, I joined in the conversation as well as possible under the conditions. After a while, despite great effort to stay focused on the people around me, my mind began to wander as the noise numbed my ears, the heavy smoke burned my nose and lungs, and the sour smell of stale beer brought me to the verge of nausea. I sat thinking of the plans I had for job hunting after graduation. I was roused out of my near-trance by Judson poking me in the ribs. "Rachelle, Kim asked you a question!"

ONCE AGAIN I FEAR

"Oh, I'm sorry, Kim," I apologized. "I was thinking of something else. What did you ask me?"

Kim asked something about a final we had both had in an advanced math course, though we each had the class at different times. I tried to concentrate on my answer and make her hear me above the cacophony that assailed my senses.

Judson was totally engrossed in discussing his victory in the eight-hundred at the Pac-Ten finals, even to notice that I wasn't drinking much of the beer which he kept ordering for me. I finally got the attention of a waiter, asking for a Coke with lots of ice.

Toward midnight, I became so restless that I knew I had to get up and walk around. The effort to carry on conversation was wearing me to a limp rag, although it seemed to stimulate my companions. No one seemed inclined to mingle with the rest of the party or to dance. What was a party worth, when we just sat at a table and shouted at each other?

"I've got to get out of here," I said to Judson.

At first, I didn't think he heard me, but soon realized he was ignoring me. I finally shook his arm and repeated, "I have to get out of this noise and smoke. It's getting hotter and hotter in here, and I'm having trouble breathing."

He turned and glared at me, but realized I was determined to leave. Reluctantly, he got up and followed me out into the cool night air.

He said nothing until we were standing by the passenger side of his Corvette. At that moment, he grabbed my arm, digging his fingers into my flesh, and snarled, "You are a real joy to be with, lady! What's the matter, couldn't you get Bobby's attention? I saw you ogling him all evening, staring across the table, trying to get him to look at you!"

"What are you talking about, Judson?" I cried. "I didn't look at Bobby any more than I did at Sean—or Jody or Kim, for that matter. For your information, I was getting bored to tears with the lot of them!"

"In a pig's eye, you were bored!" he yelled, shaking me harder than ever. "I oughta beat the crud out of you for making such a spectacle of yourself right in front of me!"

"Judson, no! Don't say that! I did not stare at Bobby Deets. He's nice, I guess, but I think he is really immature." My voice was cracking because

I was rapidly becoming frightened of this dark Judson that I did not know, his face contorted with rage, and sparks almost literally flying from his eyes.

"Immature? You talk about anyone being immature! A grown woman wouldn't act like a floozie with her fiancé's closest friend!" At that moment his hand landed hard against my cheek, jerking my head back, and throwing me against the car. I grabbed the door handle to keep my balance, tears smarting in my eyes, and a searing pain burning my cheek.

I wanted to yell at him or fight back. Anything, to express my hurt and outrage, but I knew he would hit me harder if I did. I simply started to cry and held my cheek in my hand. Judson sullenly released my arm and opened the car door; I hoped his anger was abating.

I crawled into the seat, edging as far to the right hand door as I could, not wanting even to feel the warmth of his body near me. He went around and folded his long frame into the low car, jamming the keys into the ignition. He peeled out of the parking spot, throwing me toward the dash. Quickly, I fastened my seatbelt, knowing I was in for a frightening ride.

Judson drove down the El Camino like a wild man, swerving in and out of traffic, which, even this late at night, was quite heavy. He said nothing, but, in the sporadic light, I could see his jaws clenched. At full speed, he took the turn off The El Camino onto Galvez St., by the football stadium, screeching the tires and fishtailing the Corvette. I breathed easier as, just beyond the stadium grounds, we curved south and turned onto Campus Drive, heading toward the main university campus. Towering eucalyptus trees shaded the road, and strips of bark from their massive trunks were strewn everywhere. Their ever-present, pungent scent filled the air. The arboreal giants, usually so familiar, and even comforting, now seemed to hover menacingly above me.

When Judson stopped the Corvette in the parking area beside my dorm, he sat with his hands on the steering wheel, his head tucked toward his chest. I fumbled with the seatbelt release, but, then, to my amazement, he began to cry. "Rachelle, I'm sorry. I can't believe I did that. I'm so sorry."

I sat stunned as he wept and then finally stopped, taking a tissue from a box in the console and blowing his nose. Then, he turned and looked at

ONCE AGAIN I FEAR

me imploringly, "Say you'll forgive me, Rachelle, please! I'll never do that again, I promise. I love you so much; you drive me crazy when you look at another guy."

"But Judson, I wasn't looking at Bobby more than I would in any normal conversation. I swear it."

"I know, baby, I know. It's just that I'm so crazy about you. Please forgive me."

My heart melted, and then I was in his arms. When his kisses became too insistent, I pulled away and said, "Judson, honey, I'm so tired; I've got to go to bed. There are so many things waiting to be done tomorrow to prepare for graduation. We can talk again tomorrow afternoon, when you finish your meeting at the frat house. Okay?"

I was afraid for a moment that his rage was returning, but, then, he took a deep breath and said rather mildly, "My Rachelle, the perennial virgin. One of these days..." He trailed off, his meaning perfectly clear to me: the day would come when he wouldn't take "no" for an answer.

I got out and started toward the sidewalk that ran at a right angle to the walk leading to the front door; Judson made no move to get out and accompany me. Looking back, I saw him back his car into the street and, then, head south, turning onto Campus Drive. He headed northward, the opposite direction of the Sigma Alpha Epsilon house. I had a feeling I knew what he was going to do for the rest of the night.

Chapter 6

On Sunday, Judson had more meetings, probably all-day, with a committee of his fraternity, so I decided to go to Saratoga. I hadn't seen Mom and Dad for a couple of weeks and I missed them. I also needed to pick up my graduation dress, which had been altered after Mom and I chose it in San Jose.

I left the campus, taking Campus Drive East to Junipero Serra Blvd., then to Page Mill Road. From Page Mill, I turned onto the Junipero Serra Expressway. My small, white Mustang convertible purred its way eastward to Saratoga-Sunnyvale Road, and then headed south.

My thoughts were still a jumble from what had happened on Friday night. Yesterday, Judson had been so attentive and so sweet, that I had difficulty associating him with the maniac that I had faced in that dim parking lot. The pull of his attraction for me was still powerful, but, now, I sensed a tiny breech in my numbed spirit through which light shown, a feeble ray of sense and wisdom.

What was this man really like? Was he the charming Judson of yesterday, or was he the dark Judson of Friday night? Was he someone with whom I wished to spend my entire life? Was I rushing into a permanent relationship which would bring me heartache and even danger? What lay ahead for me if I made that final commitment to him? The diamond solitaire lay heavy on my left hand. Tears threatened behind my tight eyelids, but I determined not to cry. In weeping lay the danger of

ONCE AGAIN I FEAR

weakness and lack of resolve to solve the dilemma in which I was imprisoned.

Did I really love Judson, or was I just mesmerized by his charm and strong personality? I had had my share of fascinations with other guys, some very strong, some resulting in pain, but this was different. No man had ever so taken over my life before, become the center and moving force of my being. My complete attachment to him was part excitement and part fear, even though I had denied the latter until Friday night. I could now see that there were other times when he had come close to striking me, but I had been too besotted to admit that I recognized it.

I drove through Saratoga, past the little plaza surrounded by quaint shops on the west and the fire department on the east side, and headed southeast on Saratoga-Los Gatos Road. Our house sat on the side of the mountain about a mile south of town, a half mile off the main road. I turned off on the familiar road which wound through the closely-growing trees, mostly tall, strong oak, live oak and pine. At that instant, I felt the hard, cold worry, which had taken control of me, begin to soften and then to melt into the pleasure I always felt when I drove up this road to my home, now my refuge. A smile broke through the frown that I knew had puckered my brow and drawn my lips into a thin, firm line.

I smoothly turned my sleek, little Mustang into the circular drive in front of our sprawling gray house, stopping at the steps which led up to a cobblestoned area. Sliding out of my car, I stood for a moment admiring the graceful, yet powerful, lines of the house that my father had planned, making initial sketches, himself, from which the architect worked. Beyond the cobblestoned area, a portico, supported by redwood columns, and edged by redwood railings, hugged the entire front of the house. The portico roof, consisting of redwood beams and wooden shingles, overhung the heavily carved, double doors set in an arch of mountain stone. The doors had been retrieved from an old winery in France.

Breezes blew through the tall, stately oak and pine trees, singing a sweet song to my spirit, filling me with hope that this house would always be here, always be my sanctuary.

31

When I opened the front door, Cleo was waiting to greet me. She had obviously recognized the sound of my car, because she would usually hide from visitors she didn't know. I picked her up, holding her warm, soft body close to me.

"Mom! Dad!" I called, but my call was answered by silence. "I guess Dad is playing golf, Cleo, and Mom is probably at church."

Mom had started going to church during the last three months, and I had seen her reading her Bible with rapt attention. "I really feel there is something I need," she had told me about six weeks ago, "here, deep inside." She had placed her hand over her heart. "Our Saviour Community Church has something—something powerful and deep that I want."

"I think we all feel an emptiness sometimes," I told her. "I know I do. I've done so many satisfying things in my short life, but I always feel I want something beyond that, something more important. What do you think that is, Mom?"

"Could it be God? I'm beginning to think it is. You know I've never been very religious, but I came to think that maybe religion was worth a try." Her eyes begged me to understand.

"You could be right. I honestly never thought much about God, that is until you started talking about church and the Bible. In all my educational years, no teacher, no professor suggested we read the Bible. Isn't that strange? I guess it has been around longer than most of the literature we read, but so many people act and speak as if it is some book that is totally irrelevant to education."

"I've wondered the same thing," Mom said thoughtfully. "And the strangest thing is that there are so many great institutions in this world that are built on its principles, hospitals, schools, colleges, crisis pregnancy centers, missions for the street people—oh, so many of them. I have no doubt all the intellectuals would praise most of these works, but, yet, they even sneer at the Bible and religion, behind those institutions. It baffles me. I can say, for myself, I never was negative to religion; I just ignored it, I think."

I could see that she was thinking deeply, searching for answers within her own spirit. "Well, anyway, I turned on the television one day and saw

ONCE AGAIN I FEAR

the pastor of Our Saviour Community church preaching, and I was very impressed with what he said. It seemed to strike a chord in my heart. I wanted to know more of what he had to say. Thus, my excursion into religion." She laughed her merry little laugh and then continued. "Pastor Harrington is amazing. He knows the Bible frontward and backwards, and he believes it all without question. I don't know if I am ready to accept it all yet, but I'm willing to consider it. I guess that is a good start."

"I'm glad for you, Mom. You haven't had everything easy, as I well know, and, if this makes you happy, I'm very pleased. Perhaps I'll do some research into it, too."

Standing here in the foyer of our home, I remembered saying that to my mother. Research. How like me. As if it were a scientific project. After talking to Mom about the Bible, I had gone to the University library and found that there were several Bibles in the religion section, one in the language of King James, intricate, poetic, and sometimes baffling. Another one, called *The Living Bible*, suited me better; it spoke in everyday language that I better understood. It, too, however, had some sections that I did not grasp fully, but I did continue my study, feeling a response in my heart.

I carried Cleo upstairs to my room, and stood looking out the window which faced down the hill. Saratoga-Los Gatos Road was visible in bits and pieces through the trees so I caught glimpses of cars on their way southeast. Perhaps they were headed to I-17 and then south to Santa Cruz, sprawled along the northern curve of Monterey Bay, to spend the day at the beach. My friends and I had spent so many warm, lazy days at the Santa Cruz beach and boardwalk, coming home sunburned, our clothes filled with sand.

I could picture it now: The Boardwalk, fronted by the roller coaster, built in 1924, a tame ride by today's standards, and the magnificent 1911 Carousel. Beyond, to the west, the long wharf pointed into the bay. Gulls and pelicans hovered overhead, swooping down, hoping to snatch a fish from a fisherman's catch. We would walk the long wharf, hearing the cry of sea lions beneath it and the slap of surf against the wooden pilings. The smell of salt and fish, mixed with the aroma of food being cooked in restaurants along the wharf, assailed our nostrils.

Here in my pink and white room, I smelled the scent of floral perfume, soap and lemon furniture polish. I stood surveying the room in which I had spent so many happy hours since we had moved here when I was twelve. A pair of pink toe shoes hung by their ribbons from the mirror of my oak dresser, and framed pictures of ballerinas hung over my bed, which was covered by a frilly white spread. On my desk in one corner, stood a photograph of my mom and dad, together on a rare vacation in Hawaii, my mother's head thrown back in laughter and Dad smiling his wide, white-toothed grin. Why couldn't they always have been like that, together and laughing?

Sighing deeply, I returned downstairs and decided I would go down to the village. Some of the small shops were open on Sundays, shops that held an endless array of treasures unlike any other stores anywhere.

Cleo was distinctly disappointed when I set her down by the door and went outside. She ran to a window and looked out at me, mouthing a silent meow through the glass. I waved to her as I got into my car and pulled away.

Chapter 7

Even on this Sunday morning, the village was cheerfully alive, with people wandering unhurriedly, a collage of color and sound. Passenger vehicles of every sort lined the streets, but I hit it lucky and found a parking place on Big Basin Way, right in front of one of my favorite shops.

I knew that I had a couple of hours before my parents returned home, so I went from shop to shop, exploring, savoring my time alone with no demands on my attention. My only purchase was a pair of silver earrings, set with amethysts, for Mom. They looked like her, lovely, dainty, but strong in character.

The village is built on the side of a hill, with the rear shops dropping down behind the ones facing the street. A walkway led between two buildings with steps leading to the level below. I followed the steps, humming along with the folk music which issued from a gift shop. Below, on the lowest level, I came to a small cafe which, in my estimation, served the best bagels and coffees in the world. After choosing a bagel, topped with sun-dried tomatoes and fresh basil, and a cup of Mocha Latte, I took them to a small table by the window.

Through the window, I watched people leisurely walking down the steps, laughing and chatting in unhurried pleasure, and entering shops along the way. Then my mind began to drift, reluctantly returning to my problem with Judson. What was I going to do? Could I trust him again after what he had done Friday night? My thoughts went round and round in circles, so that I didn't even taste the food and drink as I consumed it.

I was startled by a voice at my elbow. "Rachelle? Rachelle Atherly?" It was a female voice and I turned to see a beautiful, slender girl with shoulder-length black hair and sapphire-blue eyes in a creamy-white face. She was dressed in a short, azure-blue linen dress with a gold cross necklace around her neck and gold posts in her ears. "You are Rachelle Atherly, aren't you?" she asked.

Puzzled, I studied her, feeling that I had seen her before, but not being able to attach a name to her. "Yes, I'm Rachelle. I don't believe I know your name."

"I'm Colleen McConnell, Sean's sister," she answered, sitting down in the chair opposite me. I sensed she didn't intend just an idle chat; an intense expression clouded her lovely face.

"Oh, yes, I know Sean. And I think I've seen you. I know I've heard him mention that he has a sister."

I waited to see what she was going to say, not knowing how to prompt her. "I used to go with Judson; did you know that?"

I was rather surprised that she would be so blunt, and, again wondered what she had in mind.

"It's very hard for me to approach you like this. I've wanted to many times, but I was always afraid you would get the wrong idea, perhaps think I'm jealous of your relationship with Judson, or something. Nothing could be further from the truth. It would please me if I never had to lay eyes on him again. He's a monster, or have you already found that out?"

I tried to hide my shock at her words, but I'm sure she read the look on my face. "You do know, don't you?" she asked, looking me directly in the eye. "He's already slapped you around, hasn't he?"

Heat rapidly rose up my neck and into my face; my tendency to blush violently when upset had been the bane of my life, but, right now I didn't care. "I'd like to hear what you have to say," I told Colleen, warily.

"You didn't answer my question with words, Rachelle, but you didn't have to. Judson started out being so sweet and gallant with me, telling me that I was the most beautiful girl in the world, and that he wanted to marry me. He even wanted to buy me a ring." She glanced down at the huge stone on my left hand. "I told him I wasn't ready to make that kind of commitment, but that I did love him. I begged him to be patient. Well,

ONCE AGAIN I FEAR

patience was never Judson's strong suit, as you probably know. He kept after me constantly, and, of course, pressured me to go to bed with him. For some reason, I just couldn't, even though I wanted to in the worst way."

This was a very familiar scenario, except for the fact that I, unlike Colleen, had agreed to marry Judson.

"So, what happened?" I asked.

"Well, one night, we'd been out to a bar with some other people. Finally, I told him I had to leave to go do some studying at the library. He made a big fuss, but, then, took me to the library and let me out. I was there about an hour and a half, and, then, started to walk back to my dorm. I live in Wilbur Hall. When I had gotten almost to the walk of my dorm, I saw Judson's car pulling out onto Escondido Rd. coming from the far end of Wilbur hall. Tiffany Feldon was sitting beside him. She was snuggled up to him like glue! Tiffany Feldon has a certain reputation, if you know what I mean.

"You can't know how hurt I was—or perhaps you do," she continued, still observing my responses. "The next day, he was good old Judson, same as always. That evening we went out for a ride up in the mountains. He pulled off the road and, again, started his usual come-on. I pushed him away and yelled at him, 'How can you do this when you were with Tiffany last night?' He looked stunned, but, then belted me right up the side of the head. I nearly lost consciousness, but hung on.

"Before I could say anything, he, of all things, started crying! Judson Bard, crying! I couldn't believe it. He then begged my forgiveness and promised he would never do it again. Like a fool, I believed him, and was even willing to forget about Tiffany. That's how crazy I was about him. He seemed so sincere, but I was soon to learn that Judson is a consummate actor; he can bring on the tears at a moment's notice. Yeech!" She hit her open palm against her forehead, and frowned at what, apparently, was a painful memory.

"Did it happen again? Did he ever hit you again?"

"Not more than two days later. Again, he had parked up on a dark road. Then he started accusing me of looking at some other guy in the cafeteria. I hadn't been! And, do you know, when he hit me that time, it

37

knocked my blinders off. For the first time, I was able to see that, from the moment we had met, he had run my life, telling me where I was going, what I was going to do, and even ordering my food and drinks for me. How blind can someone be? The pain of that slap dissolved all the love I had thought I had for him and replaced it with a deep, burning disgust. I told him to get out of my life and stay out."

"How did he take that?" I had wondered what he would do if I gave him that ultimatum.

"Very badly! He slapped me again, so hard that my head snapped back. Without even thinking, I got out of the car on that dark road and started walking. He tried to get me back into the car, but I refused. I jog several miles a day, so I knew I could get back down by myself, and, at that moment, I was too angry to be afraid of the dark. He finally gave up.

"I ran two miles to the highway, where I flagged down a Sheriff's patrol car and asked the officer to call me a taxi. I told him what happened, and he said I could press charges; he could see the red marks on my face. He gave me a ride back to the campus and I spent most of the night seething with fury. It is now a mystery to me why I didn't press charges. I've heard he has done the same thing to at least two other girls. Now there's you, and I felt I had to warn you."

I didn't know what to say, so remained silent. "Judson Bard is dangerous, Rachelle. After I told him to get out of my life, he stalked me for weeks, suddenly appearing everywhere I went, staring at me. He would call me at the dorm and at home, send me flowers and notes, some sweet and loving, and others containing veiled threats, nothing that I could really prove anything by. Once, after I'd spent the previous evening with another guy, I found my tires slashed. Again, I couldn't prove it was Judson who did it. It was only after I threatened to go to the Dean of Students that he finally left me alone."

"I can't believe that he and Sean are still friends after all that."

"I never told Sean anything that happened. In fact, I kept it to myself completely. I just wanted to forget it and go on with my life. Maybe I should have told Sean, but I figured Sean would probably challenge him, and then there would have been a big fight. Sean, along with Judson, could have been thrown out of school, and, as you probably know, my brother is going on to law school."

"Thank you for telling me this, Colleen. It's cleared up some of my thinking. I really love Judson, or at least I think I do. But I, too, am troubled by his temper, the pressure for more intimacy and his reaction to being rejected. It's comforting to know some other girl refused his advances." I laughed lightly, then, feeling a deep relief. "I do have to make some decisions about Judson. Think some good thoughts for me."

"I'll do more than that; I'll pray for you. I've found prayer is a great healer." She smiled and stood up. "I really must go now. I promised to go to a late church service with a friend here in Saratoga. I wanted to buy her a gift at the shop over across the way. You be very careful, Rachelle, and remember what I said. I think Judson is capable of much, much worse than punching girls in the jaw."

She turned and walked out without any further words. I was left full of my worries over Judson and with a deepening fear of this man that had been such an important part of my life.

Chapter 8

The sunshine of the early morning had started to fade into the shadows of impending rain as I maneuvered my car back up the hill to home. As I slid out of the driver's seat, I noticed clumps of gray clouds, heavy with moisture, gathering into dark masses over the mountains to the west, the wind moving them slowly in our direction. This was perhaps one of the last storms of the season, since rain seldom fell in California after May and before November.

Dad pulled into the driveway and was getting out of his long, silver-gray Lincoln as I shut the door to my car. He heaved his golf bag out of the trunk and walked up the steps beside me. "How's my baby?" he asked, putting an arm around me.

"I'm feeling great, Dad," I answered, managing to smile in spite of the sadness about my situation that remained in my heart. I knew my reply to my father was at least partially a lie, but I couldn't bring myself to talk to him about my problems.

Just as Dad inserted his key into the lock, Mom's powder-blue Buick turned into the drive. She came up behind us, looking exquisite in a beautifully cut navy blue suit, adorned by a pearl necklace and earrings. She wore her long hair in a French twist, held in place by a gold comb. Her green eyes were shining with a happiness that I had not seen in my mother before. How beautiful her eyes were, I thought. I had inherited her hair color, but, instead of her green eyes, I had been given my father's brown ones.

ONCE AGAIN I FEAR

"My darlings," she said with a huge smile, "it is so wonderful to have you both here with me. Let's make this a great, family day. There is a standing rib roast in the oven, and I made a cherry cheese cake for dessert."

That day was the best I could ever remember, a rare event with both my parents at the table with me, talking of the events in all our lives and about my plans for graduation. I still eyed Mom speculatively, wondering at the change in her. She seemed so at peace, so full of delight about her life. Gone was the tiny crease between her brows that always told me of her tension and underlying unhappiness. I noticed Dad watching her with interest, also.

I helped Mom put the dishes in the dishwasher and the pans in the sink. "We'll leave these for Lorraine to do tomorrow," she said. Lorraine was the sweet, grandmotherly woman who came twice a week to help Mom care for this huge house. "I don't want to waste a minute of this pleasant day with my two favorite people."

We spent the afternoon in the game room, playing pool and just talking, while we listened to a new album by The Boston Pops Orchestra.

At around five o'clock, Dad excused himself to go up to his office. "I've got some stuff I have to get on the computer before I forget all the details," he said. "Ralph and I came up with some new ideas about the buyout we are trying to achieve, and I want to make notes of them while they are fresh in my mind. Then, of course, I'll have dozens of e-mails to answer"

When he had gone, Mom and I sat on the sofa in the formal living room, a spacious, vaulted-ceiling room with a glass wall looking out onto the back deck and the view beyond. Rain had begun to fall about an hour earlier and now blew in sheets against the windows. We had brought glasses of iced tea and sat in companionable silence for a few minutes, with Cleo between us. She had carefully washed her nether parts and then curled into a ball, falling into a comfortable snooze.

I could hold out no longer before asking Mom about her changed demeanor. "You seem so happy, Mom," I told her.

She laughed merrily and patted my knee. "I've never been happier in my life, honeybunch. Last Sunday, I came fully to understand what Pastor

41

Harrington was trying to get across from the pulpit. I didn't need religion; I needed Jesus. It was that simple. All this time, my Lord was waiting, with open arms, for me to just come to Him. I feel as if a massive load has been lifted from me, and, for the first time, I see this big, beautiful world is full of miracles, things that I either overlooked or took so for granted. For instance, a family. What is more wonderful than people loving each other and being together, even for a few minutes at a time? I love you and Stan so much and thank God for you every day. Even when we aren't together, I feel your presence here in the house, in my heart. I'm totally overwhelmed at what the Lord has done in me." I saw tears glistening on her lashes, but knew they were happy tears.

"I'm so thrilled for you, Mom," I reached over and squeezed her hand. "It must be so awesome to feel that way."

"It is, and you can have that, too." She looked into my eyes and I saw that she was urging me to take the same step she had. I wanted that, to have the peace she had; my heart was so full of fear and anxiety that it would have been total relief to let go of it. There was, however, something blocking my ability to come to the place my mother had. I couldn't quite accept the fact that the same thing could happen to me, as much as I wanted to believe.

"I wish I could have what you do, Mom," I admitted, knowing sadness could be heard in my voice. "I've always envied people who could have a deep religious faith. They always seem so at ease with circumstances. I'll certainly do some thinking about it."

I think Mom was very wise to just smile and say, "I'll be praying for you, honey." She seemed to sense that I needed to come to faith in my own way and time, and that Jesus had begun, already, to deal with her daughter's heart.

The drive back to Palo Alto was through a driving rain, accompanied by winds that threatened to push my small car off the highway. Mom had been concerned about my starting out in such a storm, but I had to get back. I assured her that I was a very careful driver and would take the utmost care. She responded that it wasn't my driving that she worried about, but that of the other people on the road with me, especially the "crazies".I reminded her that I had my cell phone, so could call for help, if I needed it.

ONCE AGAIN I FEAR

I was never afraid to drive in rain; in fact, there was always the excitement of adventure, when I had to match my wits against nature's forces. Rain had always been a comforting phenomenon to me, the rhythm of the elements touching some answering note in my spirit.

As soon as I arrived back at my dorm, I gave Mom a quick call to alleviate her fears for me. Then, I changed into a sweat suit, hanging my damp clothes on hangers to dry. Since Stephanie was out, and most likely would not return until the wee hours, I looked forward to a quiet evening to put the finishing touches on a term paper I had to turn in the next morning. All that was left to do was to put it into a binder and stick on the title label. I had to hand it in and take one more final and I would be done with my academic responsibilities at Stanford University.

I was startled by the sound of loud knocking on my door. Outside, I found, Lizzie, the woman who worked behind the information desk in the lobby. "Someone wants to see you downstairs, Rachelle. He says it's important."

"Who is it?" I asked, puzzled. Usually, anyone wanting to see me would merely come up and knock.

"It's that young man who comes over here to see you quite a bit— Jason? I'm not sure I caught his name."

"You mean Judson?"

"Oh, yes, that's it. He said he didn't want to come up because he's wet. He just wants you to come down and talk to him."

"Okay, I'll be right down," I told her and she went out the door. I put on a pair of sneakers, took my key and descended the stairs to the lower level.

Judson was standing by the front door, his trench coat and his folded up umbrella dripping all over the floor in the entry hall. "Judson, what's up?" I asked immediately, with no preliminary conversation. The look in his eyes told me he wasn't here to cheer up my evening.

"Come outside; I want to talk to you," he demanded through clenched teeth. The sound of his voice struck fear in me, although I told myself it was silly to think he would get violent right here where he could be seen.

"I really don't want to go out in the rain," I demurred, willing myself to put firmness into my voice. "We can talk in the lounge."

43

"I'll hold the umbrella over you. Come on, I really have to talk to you about something and I don't want a bunch of people around."

I'll just bet you don't, I thought, but then shrugged and followed him out the door, partially out of curiosity. He held the umbrella over my head, but the wind was blowing wet gusts against my legs, rapidly dampening my sweat pants. The scent of wet eucalyptus and pine filled the night air

Judson took my arm and led me down the steps and around the side of the building facing the parking area. He then pushed me up against the vine-covered wall that ran along side the building. I quickly glanced around, but there was no one in sight; few people wanted to be out in this weather. I sensed I had been a fool to come out here with Judson.

"Where were you today? I looked all over for you when I got out of my meetings, and you were nowhere on campus!" In the dimness I could see his eyes glinting, and, again, fear gripped me.

"I went to Saratoga and spent the day with my parents. I had to pick up my graduation dress. What's the big deal?" In spite of my resolve, I heard my voice quaver.

"The big deal is that I expect you to let me know where you are at all times!" he shouted at me.

"Judson, that is absurd! I don't ask you to tell me everywhere you go, every minute of the day. For your information, you don't own me!" I was getting angrier by the minute.

"I own you, woman, and don't you forget it. You're wearing my ring, and that says I have the right to know where you go and who you're with every minute of the day and night!"

"I can't believe you are saying something that is so off the wall! Nobody can own anyone else, not anyone. If that's the way you feel, you can have this ring back and get out of my life!" I pulled the heavy diamond off and thrust it at him, thumping him in the stomach.

He threw the umbrella on the ground and grabbed my arm, twisting it cruelly. "You're going to keep that ring and I'm always going to be in your life. Is that clear?"

Wincing with pain, I kept my voice level. Rain dripped off my hair and ran down my nose. "The only thing clear to me, Judson Bard, is that you're a nut case. I don't know how I ever could've been so mistaken

ONCE AGAIN I FEAR

about you. As of this night, you and I are no longer engaged, and I don't ever want to talk to you again. Now, take the ring and let go of my arm!"

A low growl rose from his throat, and he twisted my arm around behind my back. The ring fell to the ground. Then, with his other hand, he grabbed my long hair, pulling it so hard that tears smarted in my eyes. He rammed my head against the wall and then, letting go of my hair, punched me with his fist. My jaw felt as if it were broken.

From somewhere inside me, strength began to well, a product of fear and anger, or could it have been my mother's prayers? From all my years in ballet, I had extremely strong legs, and I now used them as weapons. I kicked him with all my strength in the shin and then brought a knee up into his groin. He groaned and loosened his hold on me.

At that moment, I broke free and ran down the walk and up the steps, bursting through the front doors. Lizzie stared at me from behind the desk. I'm sure I looked disheveled and wild-eyed, but I didn't care; I just wanted to get to my room and lock the door.

I was shaking so badly that I had trouble getting the key in the lock, but finally managed to do so and get into the safety of my room.

I stood leaning against the door for a few minutes, trying to regain my breath. How could Judson do such a thing to me? Was he mentally ill? A sudden image of Colleen McConnell running down a dark road to escape just such an attack came into my mind. She had told me Judson was dangerous. How right she was.

What should I do now? Should I prefer charges against him? I had no witnesses, and I knew the idiosyncrasies of California law in such a case; I would probably be required to go arrest him myself, accompanied by an officer, of course. How in the world could I do that?

In the bathroom, I saw an unpleasant sight in the mirror, a girl with wet, tangled hair, a bruise, rapidly turning purple, on her jaw, and wide, brown eyes full of pain and anger. She didn't look like the Rachelle who usually looked back at me. I promised my mirror image that I would never allow Judson Bard back into my life.

After a long, hot bath, I sank into bed, assuming that I was in for a night of tossing and turning. Surprisingly, I almost immediately sank into a deep dreamless sleep.

Chapter 9

The early hours of the following day went smoothly. I took my exam at eight o'clock, feeling assurance that I had done well. I hoped no one noticed the bruise on my chin through all the makeup I had caked on it. Apparently, no one did, because I got no comments. I had also covered the bruises on my arm with a long-sleeved blouse.

When I went to deliver my finished term paper, I ran into Kim outside the classroom. We chatted a few minutes and then she asked, "Where's your gorgeous diamond ring? You didn't lose it did you?"

"No," I answered. "Judson and I are no longer engaged."

I saw a tiny light of pleased surprise in her eyes, before she composed a look of sadness on her face. "Oh, I'm sorry, Rachelle. Guys are pretty awful, aren't they? You give them your deepest devotion, and then they dump you."

Although I didn't think it was any of her business, I had caught that "Oh, the-stud-is-fair-game-for-me-now" look in her eye, and it infuriated me. However, I kept my temper and said mildly, "It isn't always the guy who does the dumping, Kim. I gave Judson back his ring." I wanted very much to warn her about making any attempt to get mixed up with Judson, but couldn't bring myself to do it. Anyway, I figured that, with school ending, she would have little chance. Perhaps, also, Sean would keep her mind off Judson.

After lunch, I drove over to the low, rustic Town and Country Village Shopping Center across the El Camino from the football stadium. I needed to buy some pantyhose, and a small boutique there had a brand that I particularly liked. After making my purchase, I walked toward my car, noticing, at that moment, a bookstore at the end of the complex. I had never paid much attention to it, but now noticed that there was a sign over the door that read, "Christian Book Store".

Curious, I entered and stood looking around. It was a surprise to me what an extensive array of merchandise the store contained. There were not only books and Bibles, but framed pictures and mottos, T-shirts with religious slogans or Bible verses on them, greeting cards, jewelry, and so many other things, that I had a hard time taking it all in.

I really don't know what I expected to find that would interest me. In the book sections, though, I was amazed at the various titles on a multitude of subjects: Marriage relations, teenage problems, parenting, psychology, fiction, science, all from a Christian perspective. I even found some murder mysteries, again written from a Christian standpoint.

Before long, I had picked up three fiction books that looked interesting, including one by Catherine Marshall, and a book by an astronomer concerning creation. Then, I spotted one that stopped me in my tracks. The title: *Abuse in the Name of Love*. A short summary on the back indicated clearly that it was about women in abusive relationships like I had had with Judson—still had? My hand shook as I thumbed through it. Subtitles on chapters seemed aimed directly at me and what I had suffered at Judson's hands.

As I stood scanning the book, a tall man with thinning gray hair and kind eyes, behind rimless glasses, appeared next to me. "Is there anything I can help you with, miss?" he asked smiling.

"Oh, this is my first time in this store," I told him. "I'm getting ready to graduate from Stanford, and I think I'm finally going to have time to do some reading."

He noticed the book I was holding. "That was written by a man I know, personally. He had a daughter that was in an abusive relationship, and, sadly, she ended up being killed by her boyfriend. The father wrote this out of the depths of his sorrow, and with his experience as a psychologist. He notes in the introduction that the book is his 'twenty-twenty hindsight'."

"I just broke up such a relationship," I found myself confessing to the very pleasant man. "I wonder if it's possible that he could have ended up killing me." I had never allowed myself even to think such a thing, but, now, I felt sure that Judson was entirely capable of reaching the point of doing just that. Tears started streaming down my face before I could stop them.

The man patted me on the shoulder, in a fatherly manner, and then, said, "I know that breaking up is not always the end of these relationships. The other party, many times, does not want to accept that breakup as final. Would you like me to pray with you about your situation?"

He had voiced my own fears. I nodded and answered, "Yes, I think a prayer would be helpful." I caught a glance from him, which I would later grasp was his realization that I probably did not have a true relationship with the Father to whom he wished to pray.

It should have seemed awkward to have someone praying for me in a store, but, strangely, it did not. Instead, it was infinitely comforting. I felt this man had a very big heart, full of the greatest of love. In coming years, I returned often to the store to talk with this merchant, who not only sold things, but gave so much away.

I returned to my dorm and immediately started to read the book about abuse. Although I didn't fully comprehend the religious side of it, the common sense psychology that poured from the pages told me so much about Judson that I felt the author knew him. A man who had done what Judson did to me was indeed dangerous. I became so engrossed in the book that I forgot all about dinner and was still reading when Stephanie arrived back at midnight.

Quickly closing the book and sliding it under a pillow, I greeted her. We exchanged some small talk about her evening with Rick, and then went to bed. I would liked to have stay up and read until I finished the book, but I turned out my light and lay thinking about what I had read. Could God help me to deal with Judson? I really didn't understand God that well, so I didn't know how to ask Him to help me. In my heart, though, I felt there was an answer somewhere and I would continue to look for it.

Chapter 10

I had always prided myself in being a quick study in school and in ballet, but, when it came to spiritual things, I believe I was incredibly dense. Such a long time it took me to come to a personal relationship with Jesus and with so much grief in the interim.

During those last few days at Stanford, I felt I was being hunted like prey in a forest. Everywhere I went, Judson turned up, staring at me across a room, or just happening to brush against me. Once, in the cafeteria of Tresidder Union, he plopped himself down next to me, starting to carefully arrange his lunch in front of him, and turning to smile at me. I know my face turned red with anger as I tried to ignore him.

"Nice day, isn't it, baby?" A stranger sitting nearby might have thought he and I were close friends, but I was seething.

"What are you doing here?" I asked under my breath. "I told you I don't want to see you any more. Now, put your stuff back on your tray and get out of here!"

"Oh, come on; this is a public dining room. I have the right to sit in this empty seat. Anyway, you and I have a lot to talk about. I do hope you're over your little snit."

"Snit? You are beyond belief!" I found my voice rising and noticed curious glances from nearby diners. "I should have had you arrested, you big baboon! I've still got bruises."

"Now, you know you weren't going to do that. What are the police going to do about a lovers' spat?"

49

"We aren't lovers, in any sense of the word, Judson, and besides, lovers don't beat up on their loved ones. You are a monster, and I'm just glad I woke up to that fact before it was too late. I have nothing to say to you, so leave me alone!"

I rose, picking up my half-eaten lunch, and hurried out of the building. As I hurried out the west side of the building, through the shaded outdoor eating area, with its round white tables with attached red chairs, I halfway expected him to follow me. I glanced around and saw him standing near the entrance, watching me, a grin on his face. I wanted to go back and slap that grin off him, but I knew that, then, I would be stooping to his level.

In mid-afternoon, I returned to my dorm and Lizzie hailed me from her desk. "Oh, Rachelle, these came for you." She got up and brought me an enormous bouquet of yellow roses. An alarm went off in my head, so, before taking them, I looked at the card. As I had suspected, it was signed by Judson, beneath words of love.

Enraged, I tore the card to shreds and told Lizzie she could keep the roses. Her plain, round face broke into a delighted grin. "Are you sure? They certainly are beautiful!" She sniffed the blooms.

"Yes, I'm sure, Lizzie. You enjoy them."

I sat in my room the rest of the afternoon and read the books I had gotten at the Christian Book Store. I had finished *Abuse in the Name of Love* and, then, had delved into the fiction, which I found I enjoyed very much.

At six o'clock, I had a meeting of a committee on which I had served. We needed to wind up the year's business and organize all aspects of the committee's work for the next year. Leaving my dorm, I walked along north of the School of Law, around the post office, and onto Santa Teresa Mall toward Old Union, where the meeting would be held. My heart was light with anticipation of my coming graduation. I knew, too, that the positive messages in the books I was reading had contributed to my mood.

The mood was not to last long. As I neared Old Union, Judson was standing by the door. How did he know I was coming here? I glared at him and silently walked toward the door. He grabbed my arm and growled, "Hey, don't you walk past me without speaking. Who do you think you are, the Queen of Sheba?"

ONCE AGAIN I FEAR

Then he suddenly smiled and let go of my arm. "How did you like the roses, sugar?" It flashed into my mind that his dog was named Sugar.

"I gave them to Lizzie, if you want to know. At least she can enjoy them without wanting to throw up!"

I saw the darkness return to his face, and he grabbed for my arm again. I jerked it away and fled into the building.

He didn't follow, but, when I came to the door an hour and a half later, he was still there. Fortunately, I saw him before going out, so retraced my steps to the meeting room, asking two of the guys on the committee to walk out with me. When the three of us came out, I saw Judson's retreating back, moving in the opposite direction of my dorm.

On Friday, the day before graduation, I packed up my belongings in the dorm, making them ready for my father to pick up after the ceremony. He had a Plymouth Voyager van, in addition to his Lincoln, and that would hold all the multitude of belongings I had accumulated in my dorm during the year. There was an undercurrent of sadness in my heart as I removed the pictures, posters, and bulletin board off the walls and emptied drawers into boxes. My clothes in the closet would be carried out on their hangers, so I didn't need to pack them. Clearing out the medicine chest, I found things that I had forgotten and didn't need. The same was true of my desk. How strange that people who, otherwise, are so well organized, can keep so much junk that is long past the day when it was needed, or thought to be needed. It was rather fun sorting through my belongings, being reminded of so much that had happened to me this last year of my college.

I picked up a University catalog for graduate students, a picture of Hoover Tower, viewed through an arch in a nearby building, on the front. Eventually, I would start studying for my MBA, but not now. I was drained from the four years through which I had already come, focusing on my training for a career, and letting nothing deter me.

How weird, that after more than three and a half years of smooth sailing, I had hit a giant iceberg, his name being Judson. Oh, how I wished I had never met him! It would have been such a joy to sit here thinking back over four complete years, with only pleasant memories. Each time I tried to concentrate on happy thoughts of fulfilling days here, Judson's handsome, but malicious, face superimposed itself over my vision.

51

My jewelry box sat on top of a small dresser. Inside were a collection of earrings, brooches, bracelets, necklaces and gold and silver chains. My eyes immediately fell on a gold pendant, glittering with a half-carat diamond. Judson had given this to me the week after we started dating. Now, it gave me a sick feeling in the pit of my stomach. Picking it up, I laid it aside, along with a fire opal ring, a pair of silver and turquoise earrings, and a diamond tennis bracelet, all gifts that I now abhorred.

My memory was jogged about two more of Judson's gifts, which hung in my closet. I pulled out an ivory cashmere cardigan and a fringed jacket in butter-soft beige suede. So beautiful, and yet so distasteful to me now. I put the jewelry into the box in which I had purchased my panty hose, and placed it, the sweater and jacket into a shopping bag. I would give them to Sean to return to Judson. I didn't want them.

I quickly stuffed the rest of my collection of papers and books into boxes and taped them with clear, exceedingly sticky, tape. I'll bet I could tape a freight train together with this stuff, I thought, pressing the tape into place with my thumb and ignoring the oblique wrinkles that always managed to mar my otherwise neatly packed boxes.

Chapter 11

That night, a party was being held in the dining room of Tresidder Union, and I had promised my friends from the committee that I would attend with them.

I quickly showered and put on white duck pants, a pink oxford cloth button-down shirt and white canvas deck shoes. My jewelry was a simple gold pendant and gold post earrings. I pulled my long hair into a white scrunchy and applied concealing foundation, blush, mascara and pink lip gloss. In the mirror, a still-troubled Rachelle returned my assessing stare. She looked rather pretty though, I thought, with her heart shaped face, so like Annabel Atherly's, but with brown eyes, a firm nose, with a slight rise in the bridge, and an overall subtle strength like Stan's.

I had the best of both my parents, my mother's sensitivity and my father's drive, but nowhere, in either of them, could I see the weakness that had gotten me into this terror-filled situation with Judson Bard. But, then, could it possibly be that my mother's willingness to give in to my father's wishes, discarding her dreams to marry him, was manifesting itself in me in this way? Is that why, though I had promised that I would never do as she did, I had allowed Judson to take over my life for so long?

No, that didn't seem to fit. Mom was in no way obsequious, in her relationship with Dad, and he, in turn, showed no proclivity toward abuse in any form. I suspected that Dad loved Mom deeply and devotedly, only not being able to place her as his first priority. Last Sunday, I had seen something between them that, before then, I had not been able to see, perhaps because I had so long ago formed such negative ideas about their state of affairs.

My nerves were strung tight as I made my way toward Tresidder. What would it be like to be able to go wherever I pleased without being afraid of being accosted?

A large crowd of students had already arrived and were milling around the outdoor area on the east side of the building. The ubiquitous bicycles thronged Santa Teresa Mall as I hung close to the edge of the pavement and turned up the walk.

If I could only get through this one evening without any unpleasant incident, perhaps the whole miserable saga would be over. However, what I had read in the book about abuse did not give me cause to believe that would be so. In the book, the ex-boyfriend had never given up, pursuing the girl until he had finally shot her in the head. I shuddered at the thought of that happening to me. Could it? I had a firm conviction that it could.

For a while I forgot my fear of Judson and enjoyed my final party with the friends I had come to love here at Stanford.

My committee friends were people I liked a lot, but they weren't the most scintillating conversationalists. I was pleased, therefore, when some of the people who had been in the dance theatre with me gathered around to wish me well in my future.

I was asked many times that evening what I was planning to do now that school was about over. Actually, I had not finalized my choice of a job. I had been offered four interviews. One at Neiman Marcus, in the Stanford Shopping Center, I had vetoed immediately, because it was a business position, having nothing to do with buying. One was in Los Angeles, one in Seattle and one in San Francisco. Though the one in San Francisco appealed to me most, partly because it was at my favorite store, Devon's, and partly because it was close to home, I still wasn't completely sure that would be my choice.

Lethargy had settled over me in the last weeks, smothering the excitement that I had always had in anticipation of finally being able to do that for which I was trained. With the emotional turmoil, which I had endured lately, had also come a feeling that I just wanted to run home and

ONCE AGAIN I FEAR

hide away, for God only knew how long. I wanted the love of my mother and the safety of my own room.

A recurrent dream lately was of me, lying in my bed, with Cleo curled up against my body, while the music from *Swan Lake* played endlessly, soothing my troubled soul. I would wake, sure that I could hear the final, lovely notes, and catch glimpses of tutued dancers bowing gracefully in finale.

When asked about my plans, I would lightly evade any extensive discussion, just saying I would know in a short while.

Sean McConnell arrived with Kim hanging on his arm. Sean noticed me and came over, smiling, but a bit shy, perhaps not sure what to say to his good friend's ex-girlfriend.

"Hi, Rachelle; haven't seen you in a while, girl." He touched me on the arm as he said it, and I found myself flinching away. His presence reminded me too much of Judson.

Immediately, I felt ashamed, because Sean had nothing to do with Judson's behavior. I casually laid my hand on his arm for a second and tried to make small amends. "Haven't we all been swamped with last minute loose ends to tie up?" I smiled as warmly as I could. "And, Sean, I heard you were accepted into the Law School here. Congratulations. By the way, what area of law are you planning to pursue?"

"Tax law, I think. With all the constant changes with the IRS, I think I'll be kept busy in that field."

I thought, then, of Judson, wondering if he still planned to go into his father's business. Just as quickly as the thought appeared, I dismissed it, knowing I didn't care what he did. Actually, I would have been delighted to hear he had secured a position in Saudi Arabia or Borneo.

I then turned to Kim. "I suppose you're all set to start your career, Kim."

"Oh, yes, I have a job as a Computer Software Engineer at Stanford Linear Accelerator. I'm just thrilled to be able to stay here in Palo Alto, and SLAC is a great place to work."

"I'm sure you will be very successful." Kim sometimes seemed like an utter airhead, but I had learned that she was, actually, a brilliant girl. Perhaps many of us lacked common sense in some area of our lives. I had to plead mea culpa to that.

Kim and Sean wandered off, and I returned to my dance theater friends. Bebe Scheuster suddenly announced, "Rachelle, we're going to leave pretty soon and go up to San Carlos. The Lloyd Wayman Dance Troupe is performing there tonight. One of our guys came down with some awful bug, so we have an extra ticket. Want to come?" She glanced at Jeremy Sikes, her steady boyfriend, for affirmation of her invitation, and he nodded.

It sounded like heaven, and I was about ready to accept the invitation. At that moment, however, I felt a firm grip on my arm, and, turning came eye to eye with Judson Bard. A shudder ran through me, draining strength out of me. I glared at him and tried to shake loose from his grip. He held fast as my friends' eyes widened in surprise, as they realized something unpleasant was about to happen.

"Let go of my arm, Judson, and I mean it," I said, through clenched teeth.

"No way, sugar, you're coming with me. No trip to San Carlos for you tonight. This is our last night on campus and we're going to spend it together." My nostrils were assailed by the strong smell of beer, mixed with his expensive men's cologne.

I again was totally flabbergasted at the audacity of this man. "I am not going with you, Judson. There's no way I want to spend even a minute with you." I tried to keep my voice as low as possible, knowing that everyone nearby already was staring at us with curiosity.

"Hey, don't argue with me, Rachelle. I've had enough of your temper, and it's going to stop now." He started to pull me toward the door, but two of the guys from the dance theatre stepped on each side of him.

"Let go of her, Judson," Jeremy stated, firmly, and Eric Murphey took another step, indicating his support of Jeremy's demand.

"What're you going to do if I don't? I could whip a couple of sissies like you with one arm." Judson stared at them with a sneer on his face.

I knew something that Judson didn't. Eric and Jeremy were dancers, which, in itself, made them extremely strong, but they were also black belts in Karate, the gracefulness of ballet flowing seamlessly into the ancient martial art. "You really don't want to mess with these guys, Judson," I said quietly, feeling the strength rush back into my body.

ONCE AGAIN I FEAR

Judson laughed maliciously and shoved me aside. I knew he was ready to fight Eric and Jeremy, but, before he had a chance to make a move, Jeremy had him in a choke hold and, slowly, he slid to the floor, unconscious. There were nervous titters from the bystanders, but, then, a cheer arose.

Eric and Jeremy took Judson outside, half carrying him. Sean ran out after them. I knew he would handle Judson when he awoke, no doubt furious, but humiliated.

I was still trembling a bit, but, as I watched Judson's strong runner's legs dangling like those of a marionette, I suddenly felt totally inappropriate laughter bubbling up inside me. Unable to hold it in, I laughed, feeling the laughter contained a note of hysteria. It was, no doubt, the release of the strain of dealing with such a horrendous situation. Soon, others standing around were laughing, too, and coming over to pat me or hug me.

"Now," I said to my friends, as Jeremy and Eric returned, "let's go to San Carlos. After this little, uh, complication, I can't wait to be exposed to something uplifting."

Eric threw an arm around my shoulders, motioned to where Judson had just exited, and whispered in my ear, "You had a real winner there."

I grinned up at him. "Yeah, if it were a contest for the biggest jerk on campus, he'd be the winner, alright."

Chapter 12

After I had given Judson back his ring, I had phoned my mother, telling her only that Judson and I had split up. There was no doubt in my mind that I heard a definite note of relief in my mother's voice. I am positive that she had seen something of Judson's arrogance and potential for violence that I could not grasp, in spite of being in his company much more than Mom had been.

Mom and Dad were scheduled to arrive at noon to take me to lunch before the afternoon ceremony. Great pride in my accomplishments swelled up in me. I was graduating Magna Cum Laude, a reward for four years of hard, hard study.

I slept late, awakening at nine o'clock. Stephanie was putting on her shoes, preparing to leave to meet Rick for brunch. She had been such a blessing as a roommate; she moved so quietly, that she never disturbed me when arriving after I was asleep or rising earlier than I did. I looked at her through one half-opened, bleary eye. "You look absolutely beautiful, Steph," I told her.

She grinned at me as I sat up rubbing my eyes. "You are a dear to say that, Rachelle. Let's hope Rick thinks so, too."

"Steph," I said slowly, "I do want to tell you something. I have loved every minute of these last four years, sharing a room with you. You're probably the best roommate I could have gotten. Do you realize that you and I have never had an argument all these years?"

ONCE AGAIN I FEAR

Stephanie laughed softly and looked at me for a long moment. "Yes, I'm fully aware of that amazing fact. I honestly don't have words to express my gratitude for you, Rachelle. I mean that. You've become like a sister to me, and that's precious, since I have only brothers. We're never going to lose touch with each other, and that's a promise. As you know, Rick and I are going to be married in August; we're both from Colorado, and we're going to have the wedding there. I'm asking you right now to be my maid of honor."

My eyes were wide-open now. I jumped up and hugged her. "Wild horses couldn't keep me away, Stephie." I had no way of knowing then that I would not be able to keep that promise to my dear friend.

A frown crossed Stephanie's face. "I have only one regret, Rachelle, and that is that I introduced you to Judson Bard. Oh, don't look so surprised that I feel that way; I've talked at great lengths with Colleen McConnell. It's too bad I didn't talk to her, before you got involved with that jerk. I know you haven't told me everything that happened between you two, but I have eyes. There were even times that I thought I should intervene, but I couldn't bring myself to intrude on your privacy. It wasn't hard to pick up clues as to what was happening between you and Judson. And right now, I can see the bruises on your face."

Involuntarily, I touched my chin which was now turning frightful shades of green and yellow; sleeping in concealing foundation had been out of the question. I had tried to keep the bruised chin turned from my roommate until I could hurry to the bathroom to apply the cover-up. Today, I had forgotten.

"Steph, you really weren't responsible for my entanglement with Judson. Besides, you had no idea about his real character at that time. I haven't told anyone what he did to me, and perhaps I should've. I just couldn't bring myself to do that. I felt really ashamed that I'd gotten into that predicament, thinking sometimes that I should've done something to prevent it. That's the usual victim mentality, isn't it?"

"Yes, it is, Rachelle. I didn't earn a degree in psychology without learning a few things about spousal abuse and date abuse. You did nothing to provoke this abuse and you could not have prevented it, since you had no idea what kind of person he really is. He's a perfect gentleman to everyone, except girlfriends. Someday, it may be his wife. I'm going to go on and get my doctorate in Psychology, and my emphasis is going to be on counseling abuse victims. Knowing what you have gone through, and being unable to help you, gave me the impetus to pursue that specialty."

Tears formed behind my eyelids and I leaned my head against Steph's shoulder. "You watch yourself, Chelle; Judson is not through with you yet. I would advise you talk to the police or a lawyer, and, definitely, go for some counseling. Promise me you will!" She stared directly into my eyes, waiting for my reply.

"I'll think about it, Steph. I'll promise you that."

"And Rachelle, tell your parents what happened. You may need their help more than you realize right now."

Chapter 13

After Stephanie had gone, trailing the sweet, delicate scent of Anais Anais, I lay back on my pillow, thinking about our conversation. I knew, now, that Stephanie had known, or at least guessed, for a long time, what I had tried so hard to conceal from her. Being the good friend that she was, she hadn't felt she could interfere. Now, after seeing my bruises, she had been compelled to speak firmly to me about it.

What was I going to do? Could I tell my parents all the sordid details? I still felt shame every time I thought of that frightening episode in the rain. There was also fear, and I didn't know if I could easily convey to them why I felt such anxiety about Judson's future intentions. Would he continue to pursue me even after today's graduation?

I got up and showered, washing my long hair with scented shampoo. Then, wrapped in a large, fluffy towel, I began the long process of blow-drying my hair, trying to keep my mind on pleasant things. Today was such an exciting day; I would not allow thoughts of Judson Bard to ruin it for me.

After I had finished with my hair and make-up, I donned my aqua silk dress. Then, as I smoothed the long sleeves at the wrists, delighting in the texture of the exquisite fabric, loud knocking, which I recognized as Lizzie's, sounded, startling me. She stood smiling her usual room-lighting smile and announced, "Rachelle, there's a young man to see you in the lounge."

My heart sank. Not Judson!

Lizzie caught my look and winked. "I've never seen this young man before. He sure is a cutie." I think she had figured out that something dreadful had happened that night with Judson.

"Did he give you his name?" I asked.

"No, he just said he was a friend."

Well, if it wasn't Judson, that left quite a few people it could be, but no other to fear. "Ok, Lizzie, tell him I'll be right down. I just have to put on my shoes."

When I entered the spacious lounge, there were perhaps a dozen people there, huddled together in groups, talking excitedly. How I wished my heart could be that light, with no cloud of dread hanging over me.

Sean McConnell stood near a window, looking out at a flock of English sparrows chattering in a pyracantha bush outside the window. When I entered, he caught sight of me peripherally, and turned, smiling. Sean is a tall man, slender, as are most runners, with black hair and azure-blue eyes, like his sister, Colleen. Today, he bore signs that there was something disagreeable that he wished to discuss, a certain indefinable agitation.

He twisted his hands together as he said, "Hi, Rachelle. You look pretty, as usual." He cleared his throat and added, "You have the most beautiful hair of anyone I know."

It was obvious that Sean was groping for a way to say what he had come to say. "Thank you, Sean, that's very sweet. Now, to what do I owe the pleasure of this visit?"

"Let's sit down; I want to talk to you." He motioned to two chairs near the window.

When we were seated, he finally came to the point, as if, by plowing ahead, he wouldn't lose his nerve. "Rachelle, I had no idea that Judson was capable of abusing you, or anyone, when you met him that day at the track. I swear it. After what happened last night, I had a talk with Colleen, insisting she tell me what had happened between her and Judson, if he had ever been abusive with her. I learned she had talked to you in Saratoga recently, and what she had told you about Judson. I'm just sick that, before now, my own sister couldn't tell me what had happened to her."

"She wanted to protect you from doing something foolish. That's only natural, don't you think?

ONCE AGAIN I FEAR

Sean raised troubled eyes to look into my face earnestly. "That about kills me, do you know that? She took all the crud that sicko dished out and kept it all to herself for a year. She's right, though; I'd like to beat the living daylights out of him."

I reached over and took Sean's hand and held it lightly in my own, willing some of my own calmness into this very distressed young man. "Sean, you can't take all this upon yourself; you had no way of knowing what Judson was doing when you weren't around to see it."

"I don't know if that is really true, Rachelle. I can look back now, and see any number of subtle clues indicating his inclination to obsess where women were concerned, and the dark moods into which he would fall when a relationship broke up. Of course, he would lie to me, telling me that he had broken up the relationship. He would pass off his moods as anger, saying the girl had been unfaithful or had embarrassed him in public, any number of reasons.

"One thing that strikes me now is that he would suddenly disappear during an evening, not telling any of the guys where he was going. Now, I know he probably was out stalking his latest victim. I remember one afternoon, at the beginning of this year. He had been dating Julia Hightower for a short while, but he had told me he broke up with her, because she had dated someone else. I was walking through the Quad and saw him standing on the north side of the Main Quad, across from the Memorial Church, behind a palm tree, half hidden from view. When Julia, with another girl, emerged from the first classroom to the west of the church, Judson ran across and caught up with them, grabbing Julia's arm. She turned and said something that I couldn't hear, but it must have enraged Judson. He said something to her, his eyes blazing, and his finger stabbing at her chest. Julia slapped his hand down and quickly walked away with her friend.

"Later, I asked him about it and he claimed Julia had kept a jacket of his, and he wanted it back. Now, I can only guess that was an outright lie. It was perhaps two weeks after that that he started dating Jessica Daniels. Needless to say, that didn't last long either. That was always hard for me to understand; this good-looking guy, with a great personality, couldn't keep a girlfriend for more than a few months. I should have guessed, Rachelle, especially when it was my sister last year.

"Another thing I have to tell you, Rachelle. Last night, after I got Judson back to his room, he sat seething about what Jeremy had done to him. Then he started cursing you, calling you names I couldn't even repeat. Then, the most frightening thing: He raged, 'I'll make that b——— wish she had never been born! Just wait and see.'"

My heart lurched so hard that I felt somewhat faint. However, I kept my voice steady, hoping to comfort Sean. "You can't keep worrying about it. Judson will be leaving Stanford after today, and you have to concentrate on law school. What an exciting future you have. Judson will get his one of these days, mark my word."

"But how many other women will he hurt between now and then?" Sean asked.

A cold chill swept over me, and I shivered. Could it have been a foreboding of what was going to happen? Could something, Someone, have been trying to warn me that an unspeakable horror lay in my future because of Judson Bard?

Chapter 14

My parents arrived, as they had promised, at noon, taking me to a Chinese restaurant for lunch. For those hours that day, I forgot about Judson Bard, concentrating on the love I felt with my parents, and the anticipation of actually having my degree in hand.

Mom looked pretty and spring-like in a soft pink voile dress, her hair drawn high on the back of her head with a matching pink clip. She looked much too young to be my mother. Daddy was handsome in a gray suit, tailored especially to fit his tall, broad-shouldered body. With it, he wore a pale yellow shirt and a gray and yellow patterned silk tie. Never had I been more proud of my parents. For this great occasion, Stan Atherly was definitely not the invisible man.

The actual graduation went smoothly and without any overtly unpleasant events. There was only one rather disquieting instance, when, standing in line to receive our diplomas, I glanced over someone's shoulder and met the blue-gray eyes of Judson Bard. I suppose it was to be expected that I would see him; we were in alphabetical order and my name was in the last of the "A's", his at the beginning of the "B's". He smiled his deceptively sweet smile, and I quickly looked away.

The festivities were finally over; the class of 1989 was launched into the world. Mom sat in the passenger seat of my small car, as I followed Dad's tightly-packed Voyager on the trip to Saratoga. Mom had had to ride with me since even the front seat of the van was full. I found myself chatting gaily with her, at last being able to feel that, just maybe, Judson Bard was out of my life for good.

As we sped down the Junipero Serra Freeway, Mom suddenly was solemn and thoughtful. She finally turned to me and said, "Tell me what happened between you and Judson. I don't want to pry, but I feel there is something you haven't told me." Her eyes implored me to tell her the truth.

"Well," I began slowly, "I learned that Prince Charming wasn't even a frog, but a rattlesnake. It's hard, even now, to realize he had me so fooled."

Mom remained quiet, but her eyes showed her surprise at my statement.

"It really isn't any fun to have a boyfriend who likes to use you for a punching bag."

At that, Mom gasped and swiveled in her seat to look at me more squarely.

"He beat you? Rachelle, honey, why didn't you tell me? And why didn't you report it to the police?" I had never heard such alarm in my mother's voice.

"He hit me a couple of times, yes. I have a dandy of a bruise under this makeup and another under my right sleeve. I'm happy to say I got in a couple of licks, one where it hurts worst, if you get my drift." I managed to laugh then, and Mom smiled, half a smile, at least.

"How did he take your breaking up with him?" Mom asked. Strange, that was the exact question I had asked Colleen.

"I have to admit, not too well. Judson doesn't like to be told to get lost. He has harassed me a bit." I tried not to make it sound too important, but I suspect I failed to convince the person who knew me best in the entire world.

"What has he done, Rachelle? Tell me." There was a definite firmness in her demand.

I told her of the occurrences since I'd given Judson his ring. I finished by telling her that I'd given his gifts to Sean to return to him.

"That will do one of two things, Rachelle: Cause him to give up the hunt or, as I fear, exacerbate the situation. Can you think how infuriated he will be when Sean hands him that bag of gifts?

ONCE AGAIN I FEAR

"I suppose I can't worry about that, since it's already done, can I? Let's just hope for the best."

Mom sighed deeply. "I just pray that it will all be over, now that school is out. Sausalito is a long way from here, so maybe Judson won't find it worth his time to come down here to give you trouble."

My hands tightened on the steering wheel, as another chill swept over me. I really didn't believe that, and neither, I suspected, did my mother.

Chapter 15

I settled in at home, feeling it to be a safe refuge from all the pain and fear that I had endured during the last weeks. A part of me admitted it might be a false sense of security, but I was desperate to grasp even the smallest thread of hope at this point.

Mom asked my permission to tell Dad of my experiences with Judson, to which I agreed. I couldn't bring myself to go over it again. Later, Dad sat me down in his office and told me that I couldn't keep living under this cloud of anxiety where Judson Bard was concerned. He insisted that I should report what had happened to the police. I told him I would think about it, the same thing I had said to Stephanie.

Dad then reached and took my hand, gently pressing it. "Rachelle, I know I haven't been the best father and husband I could have been, and, believe me, I am trying to make some amends. A few months ago, my life suddenly felt so empty, in spite of my success, and it came to me that my absence from my family was the cause. My success was like sawdust in my mouth. I have been making a real effort to be at home more with your mother. I really love you two; you are my life. I hope you know that. Now, it hurts me deeply to see you going through something that I have so little power to make right. I will be here for you, though. That may be hard for you to accept, but you can count on that."

I leaned over and kissed my father on the cheek and smiled at him through tears that had started to form. "Thank you, Daddy. You don't know what that means to me. I love you, too, very, very much."

ONCE AGAIN I FEAR

Dad's declaration to me gave me a sense of wholeness that I had never had before. I believed, then, that everything was going to turn out okay, in spite of Judson Bard.

Cleo was delighted to have me home, following me every step I took, and jumping on my lap every time I sat down. She was so comforting and familiar. I had had her for twelve years, so she and I were deeply bonded.

Neither Mom nor Dad pressed me about my future plans. They sensed my ambivalence, wanting to work, but still afraid of that hovering threat.

Mom continued to go to church, but I, as yet, hadn't agreed to accompany her. I don't know why, really. There were just so many things I didn't understand about God, and I harbored a great many doubts. Mom left me to find my own way, but I suspected she was spending a lot of time praying for me that I would come to the Lord and that I would be physically safe.

One Sunday when Mom was again at church and Dad playing golf, I sat in the living room reading the book on creation that I had gotten at the Christian Book Store. It was difficult to understand all the scientific information, but I grasped enough to get some understanding of what the man was trying to say. It was beyond my comprehension that I had studied for four years at Stanford, taking some of the required science courses, but had never heard some of the things this man wrote about. His arguments that God created everything made so much sense. I had always blindly accepted evolution as a fact, but now realized that it was a mere theory, one so full of holes that a Greyhound bus could drive through them.

I was so deeply engrossed in the book that the phone rang twice before I was aware of it. I picked up the extension on the table at my elbow and rather absently muttered, "Hello."

The voice at the other end shocked me into full awareness. "Hi, baby," said Judson Bard. There are no words to express my anger at hearing that voice, which I had hoped I would never hear again.

"Why are you calling me, Judson? I have nothing to say to you."

I started to hang up, but, anticipating this, he said quickly, "Don't hang up, Rachelle. I want to talk to you in the worst way. We never did talk this thing out."

"Do you really think there is anything you and I have to discuss?" I was furious. "Don't you ever call me again, and I mean it, Judson. You are a sick, evil person, and I want nothing whatever to do with you!" I slammed the phone down, my whole body shaking.

I didn't tell Mom and Dad about the call when they came home; perhaps he would not call again. I know that sounds naive, but I kept trying to convince myself that he would eventually get the point.

My faint hopes were shattered within twenty-four hours, for about the same time the next afternoon, Judson called again. Dad was at work, and Mom was at a meeting.

I picked up the phone, again hearing Judson's voice, so normal-sounding, so confident. "Rachelle, how are you, sugar? What's going on with you? Any job prospects yet?"

I could have screamed. Frustration held me frozen, unable to even answer him.

"Rachelle, are you there? Chelle, talk to me." It was more than I could stand. Again, I slammed the phone down, and leaned my head against the sofa arm.

It took me a full fifteen minutes before I could control the seething rage within me and start to think clearly. I knew now I had to do something about Judson. The first thing being to tell my parents of his calls.

My father's immediate suggestion was to change our phone number. I refused to let him do that, because a lot of his business connections had the number, and it would cause him a great deal of difficulty. Reluctantly, he agreed to wait a while, but we all concurred that, from now on, I would never answer the phone, if one of them were there. When they weren't, I was to hang up the second I knew it was Judson, giving him no time to say anything to me.

It was an uneasy agreement. Dad still wanted to change the number, and I know Mom felt the same way.

I don't think that any of us seriously considered that Judson might try to come to the house. He would not be able successfully to break in, since we had a state-of-the-art security system in the house, one that would signal the police immediately if any breach of the system occurred. Right now, though, we concentrated entirely on keeping his voice from invading our home.

Chapter 16

The first week of July, I had finally scheduled my job interview at Devon's Department Store in San Francisco. The opening was for the middle of August, so the company was just now getting around to making the interview appointments. I had put off looking for any other jobs, but now felt I had to get my life moving. It would be a wonderful job, an associate buyer at this exciting, upscale department store, just what I had hoped to get.

The day before the interview, I was home alone when the phone rang again. "Hi, Rachelle, this is Sean McConnell," said the voice at the other end. "How are you?"

I thought it unlike Sean to greet me in that breezy way, but I answered, "Oh, I'm okay, Sean, just taking it easy."

"Do you have a job yet?" he asked.

"No, not yet, but I have an interview for one in San Francisco tomorrow morning."

"Hey, that's great Colleen and I have been wondering about you."

It was at that moment that I knew that it wasn't Sean. He had pronounced Colleen's name with a short "o", when I knew she pronounced the vowel long. Sean did, too. "Judson! Is that you?" I nearly screamed at him, only to be answered by hysterical laughter.

Something Colleen had said flashed into my mind: "Judson is a consummate actor." He had mimicked Sean's voice perfectly.

Now he dropped the pretence and said, "Hey, so you have a job interview in San Francisco. Great! I wish you the best of luck. Now, how about going out to lunch with me after the interview? You know, if you get a job up here, we can see each other often."

I don't know why I had hung on and listened to him, but, now, I had had enough. I hung up and burst into tears of rage.

When my parents came home, I told them about the call, and Dad asserted, "That's it. The number is being changed immediately." The time was before five o'clock, so he went to call the phone company at once.

The next morning, Mom wanted to drive up to the city with me, but I refused to let her give up her plans for me. "I'll be okay, Mom. There will always be people around me everywhere, so don't worry." I sounded more confident than I felt. After all, Judson had accosted me in a crowd once; he was not above doing it again.

"Okay, honeybunch, but you be extremely vigilant at all times. I'll pray for you all the time you're gone." She kissed me and held me for a few minutes before releasing me.

The drive up the Bayshore Freeway was the usual hassle with heavy traffic. I could imagine what it would be like at rush hour, bumper to bumper, stop and start. It was something I would never endure on a daily basis.

I had always loved San Francisco, with its streets that climbed almost straight up and then dropped so suddenly that it was impossible to see over the hood of the car for a few seconds. People walking the streets were such a wide assortment of types that it would be great fun to sit on a corner people-watching. There were the usual perfectly attired business people, students in baggy pants and t-shirts, scruffy hippy-types, still stuck in the sixties Haight Ashbury days, stoned out of their skulls, tourists from all over the world and even some very ordinary-looking people. I wondered if I would become a member of this diverse populace. It would be an exhilarating possibility, that is, if I didn't have to worry about Judson Bard's proximity in Sausalito.

ONCE AGAIN I FEAR

The Union Square area was a fantastic place to see. It included many square blocks of tall buildings, housing shops of every genre and many major department stores. The massive Westin Saint Francis Hotel bordered the west of the Square, facing onto steeply-climbing Powell Street, which aimed upward toward Nob Hill.

The area centered around Union Square, itself. A grassy plaza, with its southern side sloping downward to Geary Street, it covered a full square block, with clusters of three or four elegant palm trees anchoring each corner.

The towering Victory Monument, commemorating Admiral Dewey's victory at Manila, held the honored spot at the center of the plaza. The monument had been donated by the Spreckel family, of the Spreckel's Sugar Company. Pigeons had made the monument their home, to the distress of the Union Square merchants and visitors to the plaza.

I had read *The Maltese Falcon*, by Dasshiel Hammet, when I was in high school, and now gloried that I was walking in an area in which the story had been set. I looked forward, later, to exploring more, to find the places that were mentioned in the book, though I knew many had given way to the bulldozer and wrecking ball of progress. Some, however, were still much as they were in Hammett's day. For example, John's Grill on Ellis Street, and, of course, the Saint Francis Hotel, which Hammett called St. Mark's.

I had extra time, so I walked around the square, itself, and then explored some of the shop areas, housed in tall, brick buildings, many of them decades old. I hoped that this would be my milieu in the near future.

Walking to the east side of the plaza, I crossed Stockton Street onto Maiden Lane. The Chanel Company had donated the off-white metal gates which blocked off each end of the street from eleven to five each day, creating a pedestrian walkway. During those hours, restaurants set out tables, with blue and white umbrellas, along the street, creating outdoor dining areas.

All the shops were so exciting, including Chanel, Laura Ashley, and one of my favorites, Britex Fabrics, reputed to be the largest fabric store in the world. How delightful it was to stroll along, dreaming of being a part of all this.

I believe I passed the interview with flying colors. There were, however, four others that were being interviewed, so I would have to wait to see if I got a second interview.

I had parked my car in the underground parking garage of Union Square. This had been a pioneer project, the first park atop an underground parking garage. After leaving Devon's, I walked down the ramp, thinking of all the cars that had parked here in the past, some of them ancient models to us now.

When I reached my car and started to unlock my door, I became aware that I was not alone; Judson stood at my left, grinning as usual. "Hi, sugar, how did the interview go?" he asked, as if he were really interested.

I angrily yanked the door open and started to slide into the seat, but he grabbed my arm. "Come on, sugar, I want to take you to lunch." How had he found where I was? The only way would have been to wait somewhere along the road and follow me. I was amazed at the lengths to which he would go!

"I will not go to lunch with you, Judson! I'd throw up if I did! Now, leave me alone!" I jerked with all my might, pulling my arm loose, and quickly getting into the car. I slammed the door and pushed the lock button before he could react. For once, I had been quicker than he was.

Backing out of the parking space at full speed, I heard my tires squealing on the concrete surface. I fled the parking garage, dumping my ticket and money in the hands of a startled attendant, and, miraculously, catching an opening in traffic on Geary Street.

All the way home, I kept constant watch in the rear view mirror, but did not see a red Corvette. By the time I reached the safety of my home, I had regained some semblance of composure, but I wasted no time in telling Mom what had happened.

"This has got to stop, Rachelle. We've got to do something. I'm going to call Ernesto Martinez, the Sheriff's Deputy that I met last fall at the meeting that was held concerning juvenile crime." The Santa Clara Sheriff's Department provided police services for Saratoga on a contract basis. "He's the type of person who will really listen to what you have to say, and may be able to give you some advice."

ONCE AGAIN I FEAR

"I have to agree with you, Mom. I can't take this anymore, always worrying that Judson is going to show up wherever I go and make a scene. I'm scared of him, Mom!" There, I had said it. I couldn't deny it anymore.

Mom called Ernesto and he came out to the house to talk to us. I related all that had happened with Judson from the moment I met him until now. Ernesto listened attentively, occasionally asking a question, and making notes.

When I had finished, he looked me directly in the eye and said, "This is a terrible situation to find yourself in, but, Rachelle, unfortunately, there is little we can do, unless he actually attacks you, because we don't have a stalking law yet. Even as I say it, I shudder to think of that actual attack. The law is very weak in this instance; I'm so sorry. There are people working very hard to get a stalking law.

"I would suggest, however, that you get a restraining order against him. Then, keep a log of every contact he makes with you, with the time and details. Name any witnesses that can back you up. If he does flagrantly defy the order, he can be called in to account for it. I wouldn't depend on any punishment, however. Sometimes an RO will scare off a stalker—and that's what he's become—but many times, as I must warn you, it'll only anger him further. It can only be your choice. If you had called the police when you still had bruises, you might have been able to press charges."

My heart sank deeper with every word he spoke. What was the use? The cards were all in the hands of the victimizer and the victim had none. What was wrong with our system of law enforcement? I started to cry, helpless, hopeless tears. Ernesto reached to touch my arm, and my mother put her arm around me, drawing me close.

"We'll get the restraining order, Ernesto," Mom said determinedly. "Tell us what we have to do."

Chapter 17

With the new telephone number, I got no more calls from Judson. I could imagine that he was furious about that and frustrated that he no longer had that easy means of harassing me.

Mom and I had to go to the District Attorney's office in San Jose to take out the restraining order. It was a humiliating experience, baring my personal life to total strangers. However, the female assistant D. A. was very understanding, telling us she had gone through a similar experience ten years ago. In her case, the stalker had been killed by a hit-and-run driver, a rather ironic end to the man's pursuit of her.

After signing the papers, we were told Judson would be served within a week, hopefully in about three days. I could take no real comfort in that, because I knew Judson too well to think that would stop him.

A week later, Mom and I went out to the tennis courts at eight o'clock, before summer heat made it unbearable to play. I was feeling somewhat excited, because I had a second interview for the job in San Francisco the following day.

Mom and I had been discussing what I should wear and each speculating on what I might expect at this important interview.

"You will be just fine, honeybunch," Mom said. "Look, they called you for a second interview, so I would imagine that means they have narrowed it down to you and one other person. Come on, let's concentrate on playing, and forget about everything else. Okay?" She trotted across the green-painted court, her short, pleated skirt bobbing

ONCE AGAIN I FEAR

behind her. She looked so great in tennis clothes; her long, slender dancer's legs were tanned a golden hue and her trim body moved with total grace.

We had been playing for about a half hour, and had finished a set. We started to exchange ends of the court, when I noticed movement in some bushes outside the fence. It was only a tiny sway of the bush, but it brought me up short. "Did you see something over there, like something moving in the bushes?" I asked Mom, pointing in that direction.

There was a clump of woods to the north of the tennis courts, in which we sometimes saw deer or human trespassers. She watched for a moment and then assured me, "No, I don't see anything. Don't you imagine it was the wind or perhaps a small animal causing the bush to move?"

"Maybe, but I could have sworn I caught a glimpse of something blue moving over there. Oh, well, it might be some kid roaming around in the woods." Some inner sense told me that wasn't true, but I really wanted to believe it.

When we had finished the last set, with me narrowly beating my mother, we went laughing into the side door and down the hall to the kitchen. "Some lemonade would taste glorious right now," Mom said, opening the refrigerator.

We carried two tall, frosty glasses of lemonade to the game room and sat down on the leather sofa, sighing happily. Cleo jumped up on my lap and settled down for a snooze. "Tennis is not quite as easy for me as it used to be," Mom said, laughing.

"It must not be; you used to easily beat me, just a year ago. I never could win! Of course, it could be that I have just gotten better, Mom," I opined teasingly.

"Oh, sure, that must be it," she retorted. "I'll comfort myself in my old age with that idea. Oh, I did want to ask you; would you let me go to San Francisco with you tomorrow? Please. I would feel so much better if you did."

"Judson will have no idea that I'm coming up there tomorrow, Mom, so how could he cause me any problem? Besides, if I get the job, I've got to figure out how to handle my problem with him on a permanent basis. Perhaps the restraining order will take care of that."

77

As I voiced those words, I saw Mom's face go white and her eyes widen in shock. My back was to the hall door, and she was looking beyond me. I turned to see Judson Bard standing in the doorway, smiling with a malevolent glint in his eyes.

Mom and I both jumped to our feet, Cleo being hurled to the floor, and Mom reached for the phone on the end table. Judson leaped toward her, slapped her across the face, and shoved her down on the sofa. Her lemonade glass fell off the table, spraying its contents in a wide arc.

Cleo shot around behind the sofa, her tail fuzzed up in total terror. In one swift move, Judson had an iron grip on my arm and started dragging me toward the center of the room. I screamed involuntarily, the pain in my arm mixed with overwhelming fear. What was he going to do?

He brought his fist full force against my face, yelling in fury at me. "So you thought a little piece of paper would get rid of me, did you? Don't you believe it, you slut! You're going to be sorry you ever did me wrong, that you could not accept my love for you when it was offered!"

"Love!" I screamed, "You don't know what love is! You're insane, and I wish to God I had never laid eyes on you." Then, his fist hit me again, and I felt the room start to sway around me.

Mom rushed to her feet and ran toward us, beating on Judson's back. "Let go of her, Judson, let go of her!" she shouted. "Stop it!"

I glance down at Judson's fist, expecting to see it coming toward my face again. That's when I saw the knife! A slender blade, about eight inches long, curved and deadly sharp!

I hardly had time to react, but as the blade came toward my chest, I must have crouched a little, because it was driven in just below my collar bone.

In the past, I had heard it said that, when a person is stabbed, he or she feels little or no pain for a moment, the result of shock. Now I found that this was true. It felt something like a bee sting, only bigger. The room seemed to sway sickeningly, and I heard screaming, suddenly realizing it was coming from me, but echoed by my mother, still beating on Judson's back.

Then, to my shocked dismay, he let go of me and turned on my mother, grabbing her long hair in a tight grip and raising the knife above

ONCE AGAIN I FEAR

her. One long scream came rising out of my soul, but I stood frozen, unable to move. At last, the pain was sweeping through me in waves of agony, as blood gushed from my wound.

Judson's hand rose and swooped down, time after time, light glinting on the shiny blade, which was now dripping red. My mother's screams grew weaker and weaker, as blood flowed down the front of her white tennis dress and splattered on the floor and the nearby pool table. With the last bit of breath she could manage, Mom screamed, "Run, Rachelle, run!"

Finally, I could move, a burst of adrenaline propelling me toward the hall and to the front door. I don't know how I managed to get the door open, or where I hoped to go to elude this crazed killer. Somehow, I got the door open and ran out, hearing Judson's footsteps behind me. I didn't dare think about Mom; I could be of no help to her, anyway. Her wish had been for me to get away, so I would use every ounce of energy to effect that.

I was nearly blind with pain, my left arm totally numb and useless. Rushing down the steps to the cobblestone area, I, at that moment, saw Dad's silver-gray Lincoln turn into the drive. He jumped out almost before the car was stopped, and ran toward me, yelling at Judson, "You stop this minute, Judson, don't you touch her again!"

Judson's footsteps stopped behind me and then he sped around me to the right, heading for the road, his hands and clothes saturated with blood. I lost sight of him as he turned down the road, running as fast as I had ever seen him run.

Dad grabbed me in his arms, picked me up and carried me inside. I was weeping uncontrollably, crying in jumbled words, "Mom—blood—the knife—Mom!"

I could feel Dad trembling as he neared the door of the game room, following the red trail from the front door. I'm sure he knew he was going to face his worst fear in that room.

It couldn't have been worse. Mom lay sprawled on her back near the pool table, the light-beige carpet a virtual lake of crimson all around her. Her once-white dress was now completely red, deep gashes in the bodice, a dozen, at least.

Her long hair, fanning out in shiny rivulets around her head, was daubed with blood where her bloody hand had touched it. Her green eyes stared toward the ceiling.

Dad was weeping loudly, now, and kneeling beside her. "Annabel, Annabel, look at me. Oh, Annabel, I love you; don't die, please!"

He touched her face, and, for a moment, her eyes focused on him. She breathed a gurgling breath and whispered, "Stan, I love you so much. And, Rachelle, I love you. Find comfort in God, my dear ones."

For a moment she turned her eyes to something behind us, and smiled, a glow suffusing her blood-stained face. Then, her eyes closed. I was beside Dad on the floor, weeping with him, my one good arm clinging to him.

Almost simultaneously, we came out of the shocked trance, into which we had both sunk. Dad rose quickly and pulled me up. "We've got to call the Sheriff's office so they can catch that maniac!" he cried. "Then we've got to get you some help. How bad is it?"

"It's bad, but I'm sure I'll live," I answered, gulping back my tears. "There are towels in the dance studio. I can make it that far, while you make the call."

Chapter 18

The next hours are a blur of pain, anger, and grief. Mom was dead! Unbelievable! Mom, so full of life, so beautiful, so full of love and joy, was gone. Dad and I clung to each other, but found little comfort from the reality of the fact that the person we both loved beyond words was gone.

I was taken to Los Gatos Community Hospital, where a surgeon spent two hours repairing the damage that Judson's knife had done to my chest. He had missed my heart and lung, but it would be months before all the damage he had done would heal.

It seemed that Judson had scaled the fence around the tennis courts, an impossible feat for most people, and entered the house through the side door, which we had left unlocked.

After Dad's call to the Sheriff, Judson was caught by the state police within an hour, speeding up the Junipero Serra Freeway, near Woodside. He was still wearing the blood-soaked clothes, mute testimony to his guilt in murdering my mother and trying to murder me.

Five days later, I insisted on being allowed out of the hospital to attend my mother's funeral. My grief was deepened by not being able to be with Dad, helping him to make the arrangements.

It warmed my heart considerably when he told me that people from her church had taken over some of the endless errands that had to be run, and were helping Lorraine with work that had to be done around the house. Lorraine, too, was grief-stricken and welcomed the help these kind people gave.

After the Sheriff's investigation was completed, Dad called in a flooring company to remove the bloody carpet from the game room and replace it with new, matching carpet. The pool table was sent to the manufacturer to be refinished and new baize applied to the top. Some areas of the walls had not escaped the deluge of blood and had to be repainted.

When I returned home, pushed in a wheelchair, my left arm in a sling, the road out front was clogged with the media, vans from network stations, reporters with cameramen in tow, and newspaper people with still cameras. Dad had to order a van to move, so he could maneuver his car to our driveway. As he got out, he was besieged by people with microphones, which they stuck under his nose, jostling to get as close as possible.

Dad got my wheelchair out of the trunk and set it up, pushing people out of the way and repeating, over and over, "No comment, now. Excuse us, please." I don't know how he managed it, but he did succeed in lifting me into the chair and pushing his way through the mob to our front door.

Before opening the door, he turned and articulated, firmly, "I'm asking all of you to get off my property. I have nothing to say to you, and my daughter has suffered a great trauma. Please, be decent enough to leave us alone in our grief." Something in his voice must have made an impression, for, after a moment of staring at us, they all turned and moved out toward the road.

I knew they would still be around, though. This was a big story: The son of one of the wealthiest men in California had murdered the wife of the CEO of one of the Silicon Valley's biggest companies. As we went inside, we heard the sound of a helicopter circling overhead, no doubt sent by one of the tabloids.

Inside, the house looked clean and fresh, almost the same as it looked before that dreadful morning, but the smell of fresh paint and new carpet was unmistakable. As I looked through the game room door, reality was slammed back to me by the missing pool table.

As Dad wheeled me across the foyer, I looked up at him and asked a question that I had not asked yet. "Why did you come home that day? It was mid-morning, and you never are here at that time."

ONCE AGAIN I FEAR

Dad stopped pushing and came around to kneel in front of me. "I just felt a strong urge to come home. I can't explain it. I've never felt anything like that before. I walked out in the middle of an important meeting, and broke every speed limit getting here." His eyes filled with tears, and his strong chin quivered. "If only I had come a few minutes earlier."

I threw my free arm around him and leaned my face against his dark hair. "Daddy, don't think that way. You did what you could, and you definitely saved me. I wish you could have been here earlier, too, but, somehow, I feel this is all part of some greater plan. I can't imagine what, but I can't shake that feeling. Mom talked about God a lot and really believed in Him; I can't imagine He would not have some purpose in allowing this to happen to her."

The funeral the next day was held at Our Saviour Community Church, where Mom had found such peace—and a large group of friends. Again, we had to fight our way through the media frenzy at the door. Fortunately, police had been called to keep order and so that mourners could enter the church. Reporters were not allowed inside the church.

Dad and I sat on the front pew, holding hands, desperate for comfort. His sister, Veronica, sat on the other side of Dad. Mom's sister, Emily, had also flown out to be with us, and sat holding my other hand. Mom's parents had been dead for several years now. Some of Mom's cousins were there, too, but they, as well as Veronica, would have to leave immediately after the service. The cousins sat behind us, weeping quietly. Grandpa and Grandma Atherly had not been able to come because Grandpa had had a heart attack after hearing of Mom's death. He had loved her dearly.

There had been a viewing the night before, so the flower-decked casket was closed today. On top of it, sat an eleven by fourteen portrait of Mom, smiling the sweet smile that endeared her to everyone.

Sitting there, staring at her picture, questions boiled up inside of me. Why? Why Mom? I didn't believe she had ever purposely hurt anyone in her life. She had always been there for Dad and me, even when we were neglectful of her, busy with our own activities.

It tore at my heart that she had, finally, found happiness and deep contentment, but hadn't been allowed to enjoy it very long.

Guilt also nearly consumed me. I had brought Judson Bard into our lives; in that way, I was responsible for her death. If only, if only, if only! Tears streamed down my face and my heart felt it would break inside me.

Dad was crying too, and squeezing my hand as if he understood exactly what I was thinking.

The funeral began, with some of the most beautiful music I had ever heard. Was this what Mom listened to here every week? No wonder she loved coming. The voices of the choir seemed to swell and rise to the high ceiling, pouring back down over the people assembled here to pay their last respects to my beautiful mother.

After the choir had sung three songs, and a violinist and a flautist played two duets, Pastor Lanson Harrington stood and said, "Many of you may feel that we are overdoing it on the music today, but I assure you this is what Annabel Atherly would want. She loved music, and once said, you may think, prophetically, that when she died she wanted a music concert at her funeral, instead of a long, sad sermon and eulogies. That was Annabel; a heart and soul full of music, a tongue that spoke love and comfort, and a hope that rose higher than the sky. She's with Jesus now, singing and dancing with the angels, laughing with the people who have gone on before. There is great rejoicing in Heaven this day, I can assure you. The Psalmist sang these words: 'Precious in the sight of the Lord is the death of his saints.' Annabel was one of God's precious saints, and He has welcomed her as she entered Heaven to be with Him."

He sat down and a female quartet rose to sing a medley of lovely songs, their voices blending in intricate harmonies. My heart swelled inside me, and my tears dried. Dad and I had entered Mom's world. Her last words came back to my mind, "Find comfort in God." I knew that He was, indeed, comforting me. I glanced at Dad and saw a look of joy on his face which echoed what I felt in my heart.

Pastor Harrington's short sermon answered some of my questions. He told of Mom's love for the people at the church and also for those to whom the church ministered. She had gone to nursing homes, homeless shelters, women's shelters, the Crisis Pregnancy Center, and many other ministries of the church, doing anything that was needed to offer comfort, aid, and love to these people. One by one, he named people who

ONCE AGAIN I FEAR

had come to know the Lord through Mom's ministrations, people who had loved her as a mother, sister and friend, whatever need she filled in their lives.

"She was a true sister to my wife and me, loving us and caring for us when our daughter came so close to death. I don't know what we would have done without her. I am just one of so many who will mourn the passing of Annabel Atherly, but I, along with everyone in this church, will rejoice that she is in Heaven, filled with more happiness than we can even imagine. I can almost hear her saying, 'Don't you go around crying for me; there's too much to be happy about.' That's what I am going to endeavor to do; rejoice that my sister is with the God that she loved so much."

The reporters were again crowded around, when we arrived home from the cemetery. This time, we ignored them, saying absolutely nothing.

Dad and I were still in a state which we could not name—I saw an echo of my feelings in his face. On the one hand, our hearts were torn with grief, but, on the other, there was such a profound comfort that we were completely mystified as to what to say or do.

Lorraine had been to the funeral, too, and I saw something of the same ambivalence in her expression. As she served Dad, Aunt Emily, and me, a cold supper in the kitchen, she opened up the discussion about our feelings. "When that preacher was talking about Annabel being in Heaven, I thought I'd burst with happiness. Then, I thought, 'Lorraine, how can you be happy, when your heart is broken clear in two?' You know, I'm still going to cry my eyes out, sometimes, but I am happy, and I don't care who knows it. Annabel is in the best place possible."

Dad smiled at her and concurred, "I know what you are saying, Lorraine. I, honestly, never thought much beyond this life, you know, about Heaven. I never even thought much about God. Annabel had found something these last months, and I kept being envious of her serenity. I think I'm beginning, at least partially, to understand what she was trying to tell us about Jesus; He seems to be the only way to find happiness like that. Do you two think we could have what Annabel had?"

"I've been reading the Bible a lot lately and some books I got at the Christian Book Store. It still didn't come clear what they were trying to say

85

until today. Pastor Harrington said Jesus welcomes everybody to come to him. Actually, that's about what Mom said about Him, too. I've been too dense to comprehend this very simple truth. Yes, Dad, I know you, and Lorraine and I can have Jesus in our lives, too." I glanced at Lorraine and she was nodding.

Aunt Emily's expression told me that she, too, had been touched by what the pastor had said. I would learn later that she had taken home to Vermont a message that eventually would change her life and those of her family.

We sat quietly, each mulling over what we had heard and experienced today. I knew in my heart that today was the beginning of a new journey for us. There were still some things that I questioned, but I was on the right road, and I would soon learn what all God had for me, I was sure. By the expression on Dad's face, I knew he had also started his quest down that road.

Chapter 19

We had resigned ourselves to the constant media craze; it showed no signs of letting up. I could not believe the tenacity of these people, probing and speculating, digging for whatever they could use to make a story. One 'scum sheet' tracked down Lorraine's address and sent a reporter to ask her to give her exclusive story. Behind the scenes, he said. Lorraine is a lady, in the old-fashioned sense of the word, but what she yelled at him probably burned blisters on his ear drums. She huffed and puffed, totally incensed, and mumbling under her breath, for days.

We were to find in days to come, that there was no depths too low for some of the tabloids to sink. There was even a television tabloid story that hinted that the situation was a love triangle, featuring Judson, my mother and me. That made me physically sick, and hurt so much, that I screamed out loud when I happened to run across it by accident.

There were a few, though, who were kind and considerate of our feelings. We knew they had a job to do, and we tried to cooperate with the ones who were polite and asked only enough questions to keep their readers or listeners up to date on events.

The Bard family members were targeted by the media, also. One evening, on the six o'clock news, we saw reporters surrounding Mr. and Mrs. Bard as they came out of a theater.

Mr. Bard, big, broad-shouldered, with iron gray hair and an obvious paunch, gripped his much smaller wife's arm, practically dragging her to the limousine waiting by the curb. She seemed to be resisting his brute force, but, then, tucking her head meekly, followed him toward the limo.

Judson bore a remarkable resemblance to his mother, translated into his strong, masculine face. I could see nothing of Judson in his father's strong features, a high, broad forehead, aquiline nose, heavy eyebrows, and strong, square chin. The one similarity between father and son, though, was the look in the eyes, anger, overbearing strength, and something I felt was pure evil. In that few seconds, I knew, without doubt what the Bard home life had been like: Mr. Bard holding an iron fist, probably an abusive one, over his family, and his wife surrendering her own personality and vitality to this bully who ruled her very existence. Judson had learned the art of control and violence from his father, I was sure.

We knew we were in for a long haul, through the arraignment, the indictment, and the actual trial. The District Attorney, Michael Lamb, told us that Judson was already surrounded by a plethora of high-priced lawyers, his own personal "Dream Team". They had clamped a muzzle on him, so tight that it was impossible to get a word out of him. He assured us, though, that the evidence against Judson was so overwhelming that it would take God, himself, to get him off.

The indictment was handed down in record time and a trial date was set for the middle of December. Mr. Lamb warned us, however, that the defense team would, without doubt, ask to have that date moved further and further into the future. "I wouldn't be surprised if it isn't close to next summer before we bring Judson Bard to trial."

Inside, I seethed that someone, with endless monetary backing, could have so much power in the judicial system. We were far from poor, but, even if we were also wealthy beyond counting, we could never bring any pressure in the other direction, to bring Judson to justice without delay.

We were kept informed about how the D.A. team would present the case. We were called in for depositions, as were the arresting officer and witnesses who saw Judson speeding down the road near our house. The Corvette had been impounded, and Judson's clothes and the knife, which he had under the seat, were taken as evidence. Police found hairs from my mother and me on Judson's clothes, and also hair from Cleo, which had been on me and rubbed off on his clothes. He also had a tear in his blue chambray shirt, from climbing over the fence. Bits of fiber were recovered from the fence. His footprints had also been found in the woods beyond the tennis courts, and his bloody ones in the house. His fingerprints had been lifted from the back door and from the wall in the foyer. It was an open and shut case, according to the Mr. Lamb.

However, the absolute shock of our lives came on a day in mid August, when Mr., Lamb telephoned and informed us, "You're not going to believe this, but Judson Bard, the second, has managed somehow to get a judge to release his son on bail. At first, the ruling came down that Judson was a flight risk, so bail was denied. An appeal was made to another judge, and this judge set bail at one million dollars, hardly a figure to daunt the Bard family. Judson Bard, the third, walked out of jail about half an hour ago. Believe me, Miss Atherly; we fought this tooth and toe nail. We're all just flabbergasted!"

I had put the phone on speaker setting, so Dad heard it along with me. We both stood staring at each other. I felt my face go white, and my stomach sink to its depths. Dad managed to regain his voice first. "My daughter is in a lot of danger, now, don't you think?"

"We certainly do. I've contacted the Sheriff's department to send people out to protect you both. They should be there any minute."

"They're probably having trouble getting through all the reporters out front," I suggested.

"They've had experience with journalists of every ilk, so don't worry, they'll get to you."

The D.A. was correct. We heard sirens out front at that moment, and then the doorbell ringing. Outside, Ernesto Martinez stood with another deputy, and beyond them were three patrol cars, the reporters were shoved back into the road.

During the days following this earth shaking event, Dad and I huddled together behind locked doors, getting out only with Sheriff's escort. Even Lorraine was given protection as she came and went from our home. We all were enraged that we were being kept virtual prisoners because of the unfairness of one judge. How would he feel if the victims had been his wife and daughter? Would he like to have to be constantly guarded so that a maniac wouldn't be able to reach him? I hardly thought so.

The media continued its relentless siege. One reporter was routed out of the woods, where he apparently hoped to scale the tennis court fence, as Judson had done. The FAA had to take action against the tabloid with the helicopter. They had flown so low above the house that a chaise lounge had blown across the deck and smashed into the glass wall behind the living room. It was only due to super-strong glass that a minor disaster had been averted. I had seen them there before, so close that I could see the face of the photographer, holding a camera with a long lens. It occurred to me that, in some instances, he could have been in danger of being shot by people enraged by this invasion of privacy. After the FAA had been notified of the violations, the helicopter did not appear again.

Chapter 20

Gradually, the number of reporters outside our door diminished, though there were a few diehards that were presumably there for the duration.

Dad finally gathered the strength to go to work again, and I settled down for the business of healing, both physically and emotionally. Lorraine was such a blessing to me, caring for my physical needs, driving me to the doctor, physical therapy, or wherever else I needed to go, loving me in a grandmotherly way, and, sometimes, crying with me. She had been with us for such a long time, that she was part of the family.

The house seemed so much bigger than it had before our tragedy, so empty and hollow. Mom had filled each room with the light of her presence, the sound of her voice, the scent of her perfume. At times, I would catch a hint of Paris, the scent she wore, in the hall closet where her coats still hung, and in my room, where she had left a sweater lying on my window seat. I would be caught off guard, expecting to see her or hear her. Then my heart would twist into a pain too enormous to be born.

Dad had decided he couldn't bear to sleep in the bedroom he had shared with Mom. "I keep reaching to touch her on the other side of the bed," he told me. "She and I always opted for a queen-sized bed, over a king-sized one, because we wouldn't have always been in arm's reach of each other. Many times, I would wake up in the night and find her little hand lying against my back; she would just want to touch me. I did the same thing, just assuring myself that she was there. I can't do that now."

Dad and I were not alone in our suffering. Cleo had been traumatized by the horrible event that she had witnessed, and, for days, after I returned home, had sat behind the couch, coming out only on rare occasions to go to her litter box. I noticed that she ate little, and that she had grown thin.

I, finally, decided to close off the game room; entering that room was something that I could not bear. I asked Lorraine to extract Cleo from her hiding place and put her in my lap in the living room. My beautiful, gray cat was, at first, stiff and unresponsive, her light green eyes staring, wide and fixed, into space. She shook violently with every sudden noise, especially the sound of a helicopter overhead or a scream on television. She was, no doubt, reliving the horror she had endured. I sat holding her soft little body, stroking her short, thick, gray fur. I hoped that, perhaps, merely being removed from the scene of her trauma would help her to focus on me and the comfort I could give her.

Gradually, she began to respond to me, and, after a few days, she relaxed and slept, draped over my thighs, as she had done in the past. At night, she now came and curled her body close to mine and slept, unmoving until I awoke. One day, Lorraine reported that she had found Cleo's food dish empty, a sure sign that my beloved cat was recovering.

I spent my days reading, watching television and doing crossword puzzles. Lorraine wouldn't let me do any work, insisting that I relax either on the deck or in the living room. I would sometimes sit in the kitchen, watching Lorraine cook, drawing comfort from her presence. She would pat me gently, every time she passed me.

During this time, I also thought a lot about my relationship with God. I had made a first step, but I had a long way to go. I talked to Lorraine about it at times, and found she, too, was exploring what God had to offer her. Lorraine had started to attend Our Saviour Community, and was enjoying it a great deal. Dad and I hadn't made that move yet, but I knew it was only a matter of time.

I reread some of the books I had gotten in Palo Alto, this time absorbing things that I had missed the first time.

Pastor Harrington and several members of the church came often, offering to run errands, or to do anything that we needed done. We, actually, had things pretty well in hand, but I did enjoy their company when they stopped by.

Pastor Harrington sat with me one afternoon, talking again about the joy Mom had brought to the church. I found great comfort in all the stories he had to tell me about her.

He then noticed the books I had stacked on the table beside me. "Oh, you have some great choices in reading there. I've read all of them except *Abuse in the Name of Love*. I would imagine that one speaks a lot of wisdom to you."

"Yes, I got it shortly before all this happened, so I knew that there was a possibility of Judson's violence escalating. I had no idea, however, that my mother would be the one to die." Tears started to pour down my cheeks.

The Pastor handed me a tissue from a nearby box, and murmured, "We don't ever know the future, do we? It is a good thing that we don't, I think. Annabel's future was in God's hands, so nothing could happen to her unless God allowed it."

"But why did He allow it?" I asked between sobs.

"I'll tell you truthfully, I don't know. We may never know, Rachelle. Bad things do happen to good people and will as long as there's evil in the world. Sometimes God intervenes and prevents harm to His people, but, other times, he lets events take their course. When that happens, God will turn events to accomplish His own purpose."

"That's what I told Dad! I don't know why, but I felt that was true. I still question, though. What do you think might be the purpose, Pastor Harrington?"

"As I said, I don't know, but I can venture a couple of guesses. Perhaps, there are people who would not have come to the Lord, if Annabel had lived, but now will do so. Perhaps, too, there are people who will think more deeply about the terrible heartache that violence brings into people's lives. There may be other possibilities."

I sat quietly for a moment, staring out the glass toward the sloped lawn beyond the deck and on to the free-form swimming pool, its surrounding area paved with cobblestone. A brilliant red cardinal swooped down from a tree and lit on the redwood banister of the deck and sat, surveying his milieu. Apparently, satisfied with what he had observed, he flew away into the trees to the south. "I'm new at these spiritual things, so I suppose I can only try to trust God that He is doing the right thing. It is so hard, though, to give up someone you love so much." My tears would not stop flowing.

Tears were in the Pastor's eyes also as he said gently, "I know, Rachelle; my father died when I was ten years old, and I thought I wanted to die, too. I was so mad at God for a year that I refused to pray, and went to church only because my mother insisted. It gradually sank in on me that God is a lot smarter than I am, and He has a right to do whatever He feels fits into his plan.

"There's a scripture in Isaiah, chapter forty, verse thirteen, which asks the question: 'Who hath directed the Spirit of the Lord, or being his counselor hath taught him?' I don't think God minds that we question, if we do it with the willingness to listen to His answers, but, ultimately, we have no right to try to tell God what to do. Does that make sense to you?"

"I think so. It is a difficult concept to accept, but I'm sure people who do are less apt to grumble about events that befall them."

"True," he agreed. Then he smiled and asked, "Would you like for me to pray with you?"

I remembered the man in the book store who had asked me that, and, suddenly, my heart yearned for someone to talk to God about me.

The prayer that the pastor prayed was simple, but from the heart. I found myself joining in silently and sincerely. When he had finished, he asked me another question: "Have you accepted Jesus as your Saviour and Lord, Rachelle?"

"I have come to believe that He is the way. I'm not really sure how to make that final step, though. My mother did, and she talked to me about it. It sounds so simple, but I can't seem to grasp exactly what I'm to do." There was a plea in my voice.

"Everyone tries to make it so difficult, when it's the easiest thing in the world. Just ask him to come into your heart and take over you life. If you do, and mean it, He's promised that He'll do just that."

I bowed my head, then, and prayed, "Jesus, come into my heart. Take over my life from now on. I've made a mess of things, so I need you to guide me from now on."

ONCE AGAIN I FEAR

I didn't hear any thunder claps or see any bright light around me, or get any wave of feeling, but, at that moment, I knew that I belonged to Jesus. It was a quiet, profound knowing.

Pastor Harrington squeezed my hand and smiled broadly. I found myself returning his smile, even though tears still ran down my cheeks.

When Dad came home, I told him of Pastor Harrington's visit. He was thoughtful for a moment and then admitted, "I'm about ready to make that decision myself, Rachelle. There's a lot I don't fully understand, yet, but I've been reading Annabel's Bible to learn more. Perhaps you'll pray for me that my mind will be fully opened."

"I will, Daddy, I promise. And I know you'll find what you need to know soon."

Chapter 21

I continued to heal rapidly throughout the month of August and into September. My surgeon had referred me to a physical therapist, because of muscle and nerve damage in my shoulder which still affected the use of my left arm. The sessions with the therapist were painful, but productive, resulting in continued improvement in the strength and mobility of the arm.

My emotional state was another matter. There were days when I would abruptly burst into inconsolable weeping, unable to control the storm of tears, before I had cried until I was totally drained. Other days, I was able to feel almost happy, even laughing with Lorraine or Dad over some funny story one of them told. I was assured by many of my visitors that this was normal, the roller coaster a grieving person must ride until the pain gradually subsided. I knew Dad was riding it, too.

Stephanie Kulin flew down to see me shortly before her wedding. She was terribly disappointed that I would not be able to be her Maid of Honor, but assured me that she would be thinking of me all day during the festivities. She borrowed a large portrait of me, which she said would be displayed on her wedding dinner table, in front of an empty chair with a place set for me. "I want people to know you are there in my heart," she told me, hugging me tightly.

We cried together for a few moments, and, then, she held me at arms' length and smiled. "You are going to get through this, Rachelle; you are one of the strongest people I know. Also, maybe I will someday get past

96

the old 'what if' syndrome—what if I had never introduced you to Judson?"

"You really had nothing to do with my actually meeting him, Steph. You invited me to the track meet, but Judson came over to us without your invitation."

"I know, but I had heard some little things about him before that, just hints, you understand. Perhaps I should have warned you to be careful right from the first."

"Steph, the way I was so totally smitten by Judson from the minute I saw him, your warning would have landed on deaf ears, I can assure you. Now, darling friend, you are going to stop beating yourself up over something that was not your fault in any way. I know you; you would never do anything to hurt or endanger me—not now and, certainly, not then. Please say you will stop this nonsense!"

"I'll try, but it will take time."

"This may seem strange to you, Steph, but could we pray together about it? I'm finding that prayer is the only thing that really helps when I'm blue."

Stephanie's eyes widened. "That's exactly what Colleen McConnell told me. Yes, I would like to pray with you."

We held hands and I prayed the way I had learned to talk to my Father in Heaven, just the way I would talk to my father on earth. I asked Him to lift the burden of guilt that Stephanie and I both had and to give us peace in our hearts.

Stephanie smiled warmly at me and I returned her smile. "I am learning a lot about my spiritual side lately, Rachelle. Rick and I have been attending a great church up in Denver, and we have decided to have our wedding there. Perhaps we are all on our way to something better in our lives because of what has happened."

"Yes, I have always had this feeling that there is a purpose in all this pain. A new spiritual life for all of us may be that purpose."

Stephanie's visit had boosted my spirits a great deal. The visit was followed by phone calls and letters, keeping me up to date on everything that was happening in her life. I got several cards, signed by her and Rick, during their honeymoon to Cabo San Lucas; they were blissfully happy.

My heart was filled with joy for them, but, at the same time, I felt a certain sadness when I thought that I might never experience the love that Stephanie had.

The D.A. continued to call us frequently, explaining what was being done to prepare for the trial. He had been correct in predicting that Judson's legal team would request a postponement of the trial until June. They claimed they needed that much time, at least, to formulate his defense. I couldn't imagine what they could possibly present that would even remotely constitute a valid defense.

Mr. Lamb told me to be patient, that this was the usual chain of events in a high profile case, in which a large law team was working together on a case. Each lawyer had to have his own part in the case, and, usually, there developed among them a struggle to be the "top dog", with the most media coverage. These were enormous egos, walking around in Armani suits, and carrying Gucci brief cases.

I had just about relaxed into an acceptance that the wheels of justice did turn slowly, but surely. However, my hard-won tranquility was shattered the day in early October when Mr. Lamb, himself, rang our doorbell. He had called my father's office and been told that he had gone home early, so he had driven directly to our house.

Dad answered the door, and brought the burly, medium-height man, with nearly bald head and wire-rimmed glasses, back to the living room where we had been sitting, waiting for one of Lorraine's delicious casseroles to heat in the oven.

"I felt I couldn't talk to you about this on the phone, Mr. Atherly, and Miss Atherly," he said, nodding to each of us in turn. "Can we all sit down while we talk?"

Dad motioned toward an arm chair covered in rose damask, and the large-bodied D.A. sat, looking dreadfully out of place in the delicate chair. He crossed his ankles—crossing his legs was probably impossible—and tried to smooth the fabric of his rumpled, beige suit jacket.

Without preamble, Mr. Lamb came to the point. "Judson Bard has skipped." He watched our faces, to see how we would accept such a bombshell. I quickly looked toward Dad, and met his horrified eyes. I knew my face reflected his look of consternation.

"How could this have happened?" Dad managed to ask, his voice rising with each word.

"When your father is one of the richest men in the country? It's easy. Remember the old man owns a fleet of freight liners, so, maybe, sonny can be tucked away in a corner of a hold and nobody's the wiser. We can just bet that is exactly what happened.

"Preston Schillinger, who heads up his legal team, came to see me about an hour ago to inform me that they couldn't find their client. They are all as stunned as we are. Hey, this will mean they won't be able to keep billing the old man for hundreds of hours of legal time. The goose who was laying all those golden eggs has flown the coop, to mix metaphors."

Mr. Lamb's moon face, red and perspiring, was a mask of total frustration and anger. From where I sat, I could see a vein pulsing in his fleshy throat. I sat silent, my insides knotted with a renewed terror and my thoughts reeling. Had Judson really skipped the country, or could it be he was lurking around, awaiting a chance once more to get at me?

Mr. Lamb must have read my thoughts. "We are pretty sure he isn't anywhere around here, Miss Atherly. His lawyers tell me that he has not been seen by anybody, since ten days ago. They have investigators working on finding him, and, so far, nothing. Of course, my own investigators, and those of the SFPD, are out in full force, questioning everyone who might have furnished him with fake papers, sneaked him on a ship, or anything that would aid his escape. Of course, false papers are easy to come by, and then, we can't get a word out of anybody, because everybody suddenly has a case of lock jaw. I'm sure somebody pocketed a big wad of moola to help Bard get the passport, visa, you name it, declaring that he is Joe Blow, from Kokomo, or whatever. Money buys silence."

I liked this big man with the street-smart way of expressing himself. He was a bit rough around the edges, but I knew that he had earned a Phi Beta Kappa Key at Duke University, and had graduated second in his class from Yale Law School. He had chosen to pass up offers from big law firm, in order to be a public servant. The Assistant DA who had filed our restraining order against Judson had shown great pride in reciting her boss's accomplishments.

"So, what happens now?" I asked, the hopelessness of the turn of events pouring in on me.

"All we can do is keep looking, in the off chance that Bard is still around here someplace, which, as I say, I very much doubt. My people are already contacting foreign law enforcement agencies to enlist their help in looking for him. We can be quite sure that he left the country from San Francisco. If it was me, I would go to Tahiti or Australia, but, then, let's face it, our boy isn't me. He might go to Antarctica, for all I know. My bet is, though, he will head for someplace warm until spring, because Europe gets mighty cold in the wintertime."

Dad got up and paced around the room, rubbing his chin thoughtfully.

"If he is picked up in some other country, how hard is it going to be to get him extradited?" he asked

Lamb shifted his considerable weight in the rose-colored chair, producing an ominous creak. "It depends on the country. The U. S. doesn't have an extradition treaty with some countries; that poses a problem. Another hang-up can be with a country that doesn't have the death penalty. They might refuse to turn him over to us because his trial here could result in a death sentence. We'll have to play it by ear when the time comes. Our State Department would probably get involved, if we ran into a snag. Let's just hope he's caught in a country that has an extradition treaty with us and also has the death penalty for first degree murder."

Chapter 22

That day was the beginning of my six years of seeking justice, but finding only frustration. Dad and I both, right from the beginning, had a foreboding that Judson would not be caught for many, many years, if ever. We wondered, also, how many other young women, in the meantime, would be introduced to his kind of "love".

For the next few months, while my therapy continued, I still felt that I wanted to hole up in the house, hiding from the world. I harbored so many fears, fears of men, fears of my own vulnerability. Thank God, though, there were people who had other ideas. The College and Career group from Our Saviour made me their project, coming over and gently forcing me into a car, and taking me on outings. I gradually began to enjoy going with them; they were people who loved God, and passed God's love to others. It didn't matter that I, since the funeral, had not gone to church, though my father had now begun to attend regularly. They knew I had suffered a great deal and wanted to bring me out of the shell I had built around myself. And I was Annabel's daughter.

There was a trip to Big Basin, where we walked among redwoods, so tall it was difficult to see the tops. Then we all went to Felton, where we rode the rustic railway through the wooded hillsides, and walked through Henry Cowell Redwoods, another redwood wonderland. Of course, there was a seafood dinner on the wharf at Santa Cruz, and, on a Saturday in December, we toured the Winchester House in San Jose. I had been through it before, but I would never lose my fascination for that monstrously-contorted, one hundred and sixty room Victorian mansion, with opulent beauty and priceless Tiffany windows. Its countless additions, some with seemingly no plan in mind, were like a jigsaw puzzle put together wrong. A staircase leading to the ceiling, secret passages, and architectural crooks and turns, denoted a tormented mind behind their inception. This was the mind of Sara Winchester, heiress to the Winchester Rifle fortune.

In early January, it snowed several inches up on the summit. A group of the young people loaded me into someone's Jeep Cherokee and took me, along with sleds and snowboards, to play in the snow up on Skyline Boulevard. I had to admit it was the most fun I had had in years.

It was through these godly people, that I began to emerge from the darkness that had clouded my life. It was a rather watery sun that shined through, but I grasped the promise of a future. Finally, I consented to attend church with my new friends, and, thus, my real healing began.

By spring, I felt that I must pick up the pieces of my life. I had a college degree and, once, I had had plans for a career. The department store position, that had been available in July, was now beyond my reach, or so I thought.

However, I was pleasantly shocked when, in May, the general manager of the store called me. "Rachelle, this is Robert Bainbridge at Devon's Department Store. I met you when you were here for an interview last July."

"Oh, yes, Mr. Bainbridge, I remember you quite well," I told him, my voice betraying my surprise at hearing his voice.

"We here at Devon's were puzzled when you didn't come for your second interview, but, then, we learned of the tragedy that befell your family. We're all so sorry for what happened. Perhaps I should have called you sooner, but I didn't want to intrude on your grief. Today, though, I decided to make the call to see what your plans are for the future." He seemed to be working around something he had in mind.

"As a matter of fact, I've been thinking the last couple of days that I need to get on with my life. You probably know that Judson Bard skipped, so there seems to be no chance of a trial in the foreseeable future."

"Yes, I've been following the whole thing, Rachelle. Everyone I know is just stunned by what has happened. A lot of people that I know are

ONCE AGAIN I FEAR

acquainted with the Bard family, and some can understand how he could have skipped."

"It's hard to believe any human being can do such things to other human beings and, then, run away from the consequences. Most of us would never hurt anyone, so it's hard to understand anyone who would purposely inflict the kind of pain my mother and I endured," I said.

"Again, I'm so sorry, Rachelle, to the depths of my heart. However, I do want to try to brighten your day if I can. The position of associate buyer is again open. The person we hired, well, just didn't work out. You were actually our first choice, so we would be delighted if you would again consider working for us. Everyone here was greatly impressed with you." I could hear a smile in Mr. Bainbridge's voice.

I started to laugh, a very happy, relieved laugh. I would not have to pound the pavement to find a job after all. "Oh, Mr. Bainbridge, that is just wonderful. It's like an answer to prayer."

"The answer to our prayers, I assure you. Could you come up tomorrow at, say, ten o'clock, so we can discuss the details? "

"Yes, I can. My shoulder is about ninety percent healed now, so I can drive again. I must tell you I'm so excited about finally getting started with my career, that I can't put it into words."

"That's what we like, enthusiasm. We'll be delighted to have you on our staff, Rachelle, believe me. So, I'll see you tomorrow at ten. We'll plan lunch with Barbara Crestwell, the head buyer. She, too, hoped that you would accept the position."

When I hung up, I was so happy that I hugged myself and danced around the room. Lorraine walked in just then, and she grinned broadly. "Rachelle, I haven't seen you dance for months; something wonderful must have happened."

"It did, Lorraine." I told her about Mr. Bainbridge's call and she, too, shared my joy.

My time with Mr. Bainbridge and Barbara had gone well, to all our satisfaction. Though my move to San Francisco was now set, I knew that it would be an emotional wrench for my father and me. I hated leaving him alone in this big house, his grief still so raw. However, he urged me

103

to go on with my life, expressing great pleasure that I would have the job I wanted.

"I've been thinking, baby," he told me, "that maybe I should sell this house. It holds so many painful memories for us, and, besides, it's so big. What do I need with six bedrooms? I know an agent at Coldwell Banker Real Estate; perhaps she could find me a smaller house somewhere, one that would better fulfill the needs of one person."

"I think that might be best," I told him, trying to hide the sorrow in my voice. "You could have a couple of extra bedrooms for when company comes, like me, for instance." I smiled at him.

"You'll never be company, baby. Whatever house I get will have a bedroom for you, and you will be welcome anytime. In fact, I will insist you spend as much time as possible in it."

I hugged him tight, thinking that, now, it was just Dad and me, alone in the world. Mom's parents were dead, and Dad's lived in New York State. Grandpa and Grandma Atherly traveled a lot, spending a lot of time in London where they had lived at one time, when Grandpa was employed in the American embassy there. Veronica was Dad's only sibling, and she lived in Minnesota. Mom had the one sister, Emily, who lived in Vermont. We had only occasional visits from any of them and rarely went to their homes. It seemed sad, but that was the way of modern life.

In the last months, Dad and I had formed a relationship that was so warm and precious to us both, that it was difficult for me to believe that he had once been the "Invisible Man". It would be so hard to leave him.

"You know I haven't touched your mother's things," Dad said slowly, "and it will tear my heart out to give them away or store them. I want you to go through them with me and take what you want, and then I'll try to decide what to do with the rest."

"There are some of her things I would love to keep, things that remind me of her so strongly. There are very few of her clothes that I can wear, but I think Aunt Emily is exactly the same size as Mom. I don't think she has a lot of worldly goods, so she would probably be glad to have Mom's clothes." My heart was torn to be talking about these things, but I knew it had to be done.

ONCE AGAIN I FEAR

"You're right; Emily doesn't have a lot, but I think she is very happy with her life. Emily is a lovely person, so I would be pleased to have her wear your mother's things."

"I start my job in two weeks, Dad, so maybe we could both look around a bit for a house. Maybe you'll have the luck I did in finding my apartment so soon. Barbara Crestwell is amazed that I was able to find an apartment so quickly. It's in a beautiful building on Clay Street, right near the cable car line and bus line, both of which will take me right to the store, except for days when I will have to have my car at work. However, it was a great to know that I could get some relief, at least part of the time, from having to drive to work in that traffic, even for such a short distance."

I spent the next week packing my things for my move to the city. Dad told me to pick anything in the house that I wanted to take to furnish my apartment; he wouldn't need all the furnishings in a smaller house, anyway. I decided to leave my bedroom furniture; it would be put into "my room" in Dad's new house. I chose, instead, a lovely white-washed oak dresser and armoire from one of the other bedrooms. A glass-topped bedside table, a round table with an elegant, blue silk skirt, and a heavy brass headboard, which would be perfect in my apartment, came from a second bedroom. These were pieces that I had admired since I was a child.

In the far south end of the first floor, there was an entertainment room, with a big-screened television, a retractable movie screen, state of the art stereo system, a wet bar, and, at one end, a small white-washed oak dining table and six chairs, upholstered in blue brocade. The dining suite would fit perfectly into my small dining room. There was also a white sofa and two blue upholstered chairs. Absolutely perfect.

It was something like prowling through a huge furniture store, with interior designer floor displays. I was free to pick and choose what I wanted. By the end of the week, I had picked everything that I would need to furnish my first home.

The movers came at the first of the following week; Dad had arranged to be home that day to help me supervise the loading. He then came with me to the apartment to help me to arrange everything to my liking.

105

Dad and I were dreading the separation ahead of us, but, that day, we had so much fun, that we ended up laughing and sharing a lot of things that we had never talked about before. I wondered, that day, why we couldn't have had times like this during my growing up years. I could only be thankful that we finally had a relationship with each other that was worth more than anything in the world to both of us.

Chapter 23

I quickly settled into my new life in San Francisco and my job at Devon's, the trend-setting department store in the Union Square area. I was, at last, a part of the huge, sprawling city-within-a-city, a Mecca for shoppers and tourists. The job was more satisfying than I had ever imagined it would be, testing my business and creative skills to the limit.

Devon's standards were every bit as demanding as those at Stanford. These standards resulted in Devon's being the most successful upscale department store in the Bay area. Customers were treated like royalty, their every whim taken seriously, with the aim to do everything within the power of the Devon organization to satisfy that whim.

I spent hours, at times, calling all across the country to find a particular item that a customer wanted, sometimes having to order it from another country. A Devon customer could definitely have exceptionally fine, totally unique merchandise.

It was exhilarating to get up every morning, dress in my most becoming clothes, and join the hustle and bustle of this exciting city. On days that I took a cable car, I found that grabbing a good seat took a skill at which I soon became fairly adept. Even so, I sometimes ended up sitting in a corner seat with people crammed so tightly in front of me, that I thanked God I wasn't claustrophobic. The competition for seats came with the territory and I loved it, as well as the sound of the wheels on the rails and the clang of the bell, warning pedestrians and cars to get out of the way.

One of my first priorities in the city was to find a church. Pastor Harrington had recommended Word of Life Church, which was only two blocks from my apartment. The first time I attended a service, I felt almost as if Our Saviour Community had been transplanted into San Francisco. There was the same Spirit and the same friendliness from the people. I was immediately welcomed into the College and Career group, my very good friends from day-one.

At the store, I found quite a few compatible people, ones who shared some of my interests, music, the ballet, books and physical fitness. I joined the Star Fitness Center, within walking distance of the store, and went there often after work. At the Center, I also met a few people to whom I could relate. None of these people, though, could compare with the people at church, because, there, we shared more than activities and intellectual pursuits; we shared a divine bond that couldn't be matched.

Right from the first, I realized that I could not feel much attraction for men, even the godly young men in my church. Though I yearned for such a relationship, inside my heart was a frozen place, one that Judson Bard had created by his terrorizing of me.

I prayed that God would take away the fear. Surely, I had no need to be concerned about these young men that were part of my life now. Still, I could not overcome the panic that gripped me when a man began to show signs of being attracted to me. I did accept a few dates, but the men who took me out soon felt my reluctance to be involved in a deeper relationship. I hated feeling this way, knowing I probably hurt at least two of my friends, but I couldn't rid myself of the fear, or release it to my Lord.

The years passed, and I continued with the routine of my life, the store, my church, my fitness regimen.

I also spent as much time as I could in Saratoga with Dad. He finally sold the house and moved into another one in the same general area. The new house was considerably smaller, but no less elegant, just right for Dad living alone, and my frequent visits.

The first time I went to the new house, I found all my things, neatly packed and sitting among my furniture that I had had since I was a child. "I decided to let you put away your own things; you know better where you want everything," Dad told me.

ONCE AGAIN I FEAR

Dad had grown a tremendous amount in his faith since Mom died. His brilliant mind absorbed the Bible at a remarkable rate. He had collected an extensive Christian library, study books, biographies, fiction, and books on varied subjects such as science, psychology, medicine, archeology, and many, many more. We had some wonderful discussions about Bible doctrine as well as a wide range of other subjects, and I found that he was teaching me spiritual truths that I had never grasped. Those sharing times were so very precious to me. It totally amazed me that my Dad had changed so much and come so far.

I never did confide in Dad about my fear of getting involved with men. With God's help, he was learning to cope with his life without Mom; I did not want to burden him with my worries. Someday, I hoped, I would be able to overcome this and, perhaps, find a relationship like Mom and Dad had had in the last months of Mom's life.

Though my life was reasonably happy, I sometimes still had nightmares; cold, dark dreams, in which a knife flashed, and I heard screaming, with blood soaking my clothes. I would wake chilled, but sweating, my heart pounding. Shadows in my room were menacing, dark entities, threatening my peace, my very life.

Then I realized that six whole years had passed, and I was still in the same pattern of existence in which I had been those first months in San Francisco. The only real difference was that a year ago, Barbara Crestwell had been transferred to Devon's New York store, and I had been moved into the position of head buyer. My career dream had come true.

I still was involved in my church, including teaching aerobics classes on occasion in the church family center. However, I still could not get seriously involved with a man, even a Christian one. There was always the fear that I could not trust him, that he would become violent and controlling. Another experience of that kind was something I would not be able to handle.

Many of my church friends, who had been single when I met them, were now married, leaving me with the nagging feeling of being left behind. However, new people had come into the group, and the ones who were now couples, remained my friends.

I had acquired some other friends that I valued. My secretary, Trish Willingham, who had been with me for my year as head buyer, was an intelligent, efficient young woman. Barbara's secretary had retired at the time that Barbara had left for New York, and I had been fortunate to find Trish through an agency. At twenty three, she seemed content with her position, not aiming toward a lifetime career. She confided that she hoped to be married by the time she was thirty, at which time, her home would be her career. I admired her for having that goal. It would be wonderful to feel that way myself. Trish definitely had no fear of men; that was obvious.

Trish and I went to lunch once in a while, usually at one of the restaurants in Maiden Lane, and, occasionally, attended a concert or movie together. I usually took her as my guest, because I knew she couldn't afford the restaurant tabs or the tickets. She protested my paying, but I assured her that I enjoyed her company. She was easy to talk to and had a marvelous sense of humor.

In recent months, though, I had, at odd moments, caught a glimpse of sadness in her expression that I had not noticed before. I wondered about the cause of it, but felt she would tell me about it if she wanted me to know. In like manner, I don't believe she knew what had happened to me, and I never brought up the subject.

Another delightful person whom I considered a friend was Drucilla Warren, the area representative for DuBois Cosmetic Company. She was a perfect model for her products: clear, smooth skin, enormous dark eyes, and thick auburn hair, which she wore in a long, layered cut. Her figure was perfectly proportioned, and she carried herself with an elegance that made everything she wore look as if it came from a Paris showroom.

Drucilla was divorced and not looking for another relationship in the foreseeable future. "I don't know if I ever want to try marriage again," she told me. "My ex did about everything in the book to hurt me, and I don't wish to go through that again."

"But not all men are like that," I found myself saying to her. I, then, stopped and thought, you're one to talk, Rachelle Atherly; not all men are like Judson Bard, either, you can be sure.

Drucilla and I were two wounded people. I found myself confiding in her, telling her all about Judson, and my mother's death. She cried with me and then squeezed my hand. "You and I have a lot to overcome, don't

ONCE AGAIN I FEAR

we? Let's promise right now that we won't feed on each other's pain; that can only make our recovery longer and more difficult. Let's vow that we will not hash it over again, just try to uplift each other."

"That's a promise, Dru," I told her. And we never did. She became a joy to be with, the person who helped me most in facing my fears and moving along with my life.

I had walked through the men's department one day, about six months ago, when I noticed a new employee. His badge proclaimed that his name was Mark Bussell, a sales associate. I introduced myself and wished him well in his job. He was a friendly person, very outgoing, but not overly so, self-assured, but not arrogant. He stood about six feet two, slender, but well-muscled, with dark hair, cut fashionably short, slightly tip-tilted, olive green eyes, and a wide smile. His nose was straight and his jaw line firm.

I learned that Mark and I were the same age, almost twenty nine. A native of Sacramento, he had started college at UC-Davis, studying accounting, but had gotten bored after two years. He quit and went on a jaunt across country, working only when he ran out of money. He had then stayed in Chicago for two years, saving every penny he could. Afterward, he took off for Europe, hitchhiking around the continent for two years. "I got the best education I could have, doing that," he told me. "However, I couldn't be a vagabond forever, so decided I better come home and finish my formal education." He was now enrolled at San Francisco State, and had changed his major to European history, with the aim of becoming a teacher on the college level.

I liked Mark immediately. He had a relaxed attitude about life, but didn't seem aimless. He showed me his grade report once, proud of his 3.6 GPA.

Though we became good friends, because of my position in the store, Mark didn't ask me out. It was a rule that managers did not date employees of lesser rank. He and I did, however, occasionally eat lunch together in the store restaurant. I thoroughly enjoyed talking to him and hearing of all the adventures he had had both in the U.S. and abroad.

My apartment had become more and more like a home to me. I had, over my six years residence, decorated the apartment to suit my own tastes, painting all the walls a cool white, replacing the dull window

111

treatments with matching white drapes, and recarpeting, also in white. Then I added the smaller touches that gave the apartment personality, all in cheerful, bright colors, blue, turquoise, rose, sage green, yellow, and orchid.

I had also added the presence of my cat, Tache, about a year ago. A home was not a home without a cat, I had always believed. I had not brought Cleo from Saratoga; she was an old cat, and I felt she should stay with familiar surroundings. When Dad had moved, Cleo had adapted well, sleeping in her usual spot on my bed. Then, last November, she had developed a tumor in her mouth. Dad and Lorraine had taken her to the vet, who had advised that she be put to sleep. She was, by then, past seventeen years old, very aged for a cat.

I had grieved deeply for Cleo, but decided that I would be soothed if I had a new cat to love. Tache had provided that comfort, giving me the unquestioning love that only a pet can give.

Within my apartment walls, I could retreat to my books and music, inviting into my sanctuary only those whom I trusted and loved. I gave occasional small dinner parties, mostly for my church friends. On another occasion, I asked Mark, Trish, Drucilla, Damon Ledyard, my trainer at the Fitness Center, and Greg Phillips, my associate buyer at Devon's, to come for dinner, which I served as a buffet. They were all genial, articulate people with a diversity of interests.

One thing, to which I introduced them, was the world of Christian music. None of them had heard much of that genre, and found that they very much enjoyed Sandi Patti, Amy Grant, Point of Grace, Twyla Paris, Michael W. Smith, Steve Green, Carman, and others. They were amazed at the variety and quality of these singers and musicians. It was my way of opening the door to show them something about my faith.

Then came that last day of November, when I walked back to my apartment from the cable car stop. As I walked along, I thought of Thanksgiving, which Dad had shared with me. We had gone out for dinner to the Compass Rose Room in the Westin St. Francis at Union Square. He had stayed overnight and we had gone to the Macy's tree lighting at the square the next day. It was so exciting to share something of my life with him.

ONCE AGAIN I FEAR

I had left my office at six o'clock, tired from having been there since eight that morning. I looked forward to a quiet evening with some good music and Tache on my lap.

That was when I had seen the dark, menace from my past, Judson Bard. Now, as I stood here in my apartment, holding Tache close to my heart, I felt I had been plunged off a cliff into icy water, which chilled me and threatened to cover my head. A smothering fear gripped me, paralyzing me so that I could not move.

"Dear Jesus, I prayed, help me!" That was all that I could manage to say, but it was enough. To my great amazement, I felt a comforting hand on my shoulder. It was real, and from it flowed a deep peace that could only have come from God.

The tears that had stained my cheeks were now dried, and I could move about my home. I knew that, no matter what terror awaited me, I was not alone.

Chapter 24

I prepared a chef's salad for my dinner, and sat slowly eating while my mind raced. What should I do about Judson? Should I call the police or the D. A.'s office in San Jose?

Michael Lamb had died eighteen months ago from a heart attack. I could still picture the big, heavy man, his face red, perspiration beading his lip and forehead. It was obvious, then, that he could be in danger of just such an attack.

Mr. Lamb had been my crusader. He had worked all those years, trying to make his foreign counterparts grasp the appalling nature of Judson's crime and the danger he posed to other young women. His pleas apparently fell on either deaf, or apathetic, ears; Judson had been allowed to roam free and, now, return to haunt my life.

The assistant D. A., Laura Maxwell, who had filed my restraining order against Judson, was now the District Attorney. I decided to call her first thing in the morning for advice on what I should do.

Another question was: Should I call Dad? Would he be able to help me in any way, or would he just be worried unnecessarily? The best thing, I decided, was to talk to Laura first.

With those decisions made, I sat with my Bible, trying to find something that would give me guidance. A verse that struck me forcefully was Psalms 27:1: "The Lord is my light and my salvation; whom shall I fear? The Lord is the strength of my life; of whom shall I be afraid?" David had been trailed relentlessly by his enemies; the verse gave the secret of his strength during that fearful time. I clung to the scripture and, again, felt the warm loving hand on my shoulder.

I called Laura Maxwell's office the next morning, but was told she was on a business trip and would not return until the end of next week. I didn't want to talk to someone I didn't know, so left my number for her to call me a week from Monday.

At noon, I took the elevator down to the second floor from my third-floor office. The restaurant was to the left of the elevator, past the Infants and Toddlers Department. As I waked through the door, I was greeted by Tess, the hostess. A few feet ahead of me, Mark Bussell stood talking to Greg Phillips. They spotted me and Mark grinned, showing his perfect white teeth. "Hi, Rachelle, come join us. They're cleaning off a table over by the window."

"Sure, why not? I dislike eating alone," I smiled at both of the young men. "I guess I'm set for a table," I told Tess and then went to where Greg and Mark stood.

When we had been served our lunch, and I was enjoying my chicken salad sandwich, I noticed Greg observing me intently. "Oh, sorry to stare at you, Rachelle," he said when I caught his eye. "It's just that you look a little worried. Anything we can help you with?"

"Oh, it's nothing much," I answered vaguely. "I was just thinking about the fact that I saw someone last night that I hadn't seen in a long time. I had thought maybe he was dead."

Greg and Mark were both staring at me now. "That would be a jolt," Mark grimaced. "Was it someone you knew well?"

"Yes, quite well. Anyway, it isn't anything for you two to be concerned about; it was just strange, that's all." I quickly changed the subject, asking Mark how well the new Ralph Lauren line of men's clothing was moving. It was a sure way to get Mark and Greg both distracted; the men's department was the special interest of both of them.

In mid afternoon, Trish, my secretary, came into my office with a computer printout. A tall, willowy brunette with brown eyes, she was attractive, though not a real beauty. She leaned over my desk, her shoulder-length bob falling forward over her cheek. "I thought you would need to take care of these before you leave for the New York showings next week. Mr. Devon, the third, will have a cow if he doesn't have your summary of this data on his desk in New York by Friday, and that's three days away."

"Trish, what would I do without you? I'm glad you have a good idea of what pressures the powers-that-be put on me. Both Mr. Bainbridge and our Mr. Devon are extremely demanding. They are both, however, very nice men, underneath all that strictly-business exterior. I've come to respect Mr. Devon greatly, knowing he's working hard to carry on the traditions that his grandfather established for Devon's. All the while, he has managed keep the stores state-of-the-art. Some stores don't have local buyers, just New York people who choose for all their stores. Mr. Devon prefers to have buyers in each store, people who know their own particular markets. I'm really thankful that he has given me total leeway in choosing the merchandise that we sell here, just expecting me to be able to sell what I choose, to put it pure and simple."

Trish smiled. "Rachelle, you have such exquisite taste, and you have chosen an associate buyer with similar taste, so that I see very little on the heavily marked-down racks. I'm always shocked when I walk into some stores at the end of a season and see rack upon rack of the most ghastly merchandise, stuff that they couldn't give away. Who chooses to put that garbage in the stores?"

"That's always been a real puzzle to me, too. And, it isn't just the lower-cost stores, either. This was something I vowed would never happen here at Devon's. I want our sales to be true sales, with first-class merchandise, only with a marked-down price. We do the sales to give our regular customers a special break on prices, and, also, to allow some who ordinarily would not be able to afford our prices to be able to buy things here. You know that Devon's has always had what is termed 'snob appeal', and that's okay to boost the bottom line. But I think about all those people out there who can't afford to have the clothes and other things that the A-List people buy here. I feel a real thrill in seeing some of those middle class or blue collar people in our store, being able to buy a 'snob appeal' item or two. They are just as important as the elite of San Francisco. Also, think about it: Someday they may have a better financial situation and be able to shop here all the time."

ONCE AGAIN I FEAR

"I really admire your compassion for people, Rachelle. You're right about these people. Actually, I'm one of them; I couldn't afford Devon's clothes, except for the sales and my discount. Even with all that, I have to make a lot of my own clothes and watch my budget carefully, considering the cost of living in this town."

I caught a strained look around Trish's eyes and wondered if money might not be a bigger problem than she let on. Devon's paid her above the average salary for a secretary, but I had noticed she brought a sack lunch most days, and some of her clothes were far from being new or were clothes she had sewn herself. She had told me she did her own hair, including cutting and perming it. It was a blessing to her that she seemed to wield a skillful hand in that department, and in sewing.

"You always look great, Trish. I'm proud to introduce you as my secretary. Actually, with your height and figure, you could wear a potato sack and make it look good."

Momentarily, the strained look dissolved into a smile that crinkled her lovely brown eyes. "Maybe I'll try wearing a potato sack to work someday to test your theory. What do you think Mr. Devon would think of that?"

"Oh, probably have a real hissy fit, I would say," I responded, laughing at the picture of such a breach of Devon's dress code.

"Rachelle, could I leave about a half hour early today? I have a really pressing situation that I need to take care of." Her face wore an imploring look.

"Of course, Trish; with all the time you put in on this job, you deserve a little time off, more than half an hour, in my opinion." I saw a look of relief cross her face.

"Thanks, I'll confirm the New York hotel reservations and the flight before I leave; don't want any slip-ups, do we?"

As she left the office, I sat thoughtfully considering what I had seen in Trish's expression. Something definitely was bothering her, but I would have to wait until she was willing to tell me of her own accord.

Chapter 25

On Thursday, when I left the store at six o'clock, I walked down Geary Street to the Star Fitness Center, where I worked out as many times a week as I could. Fog swirled in gauzy wisps, as a cold, wet wind blew from the west, the forerunner of the storm that was forecast for later tonight. My coat suddenly felt too thin, the cold biting into my skin and chilling me. A sudden gust took my breath.

As I lowered my head seeking whatever protection that might offer, I glanced over my left shoulder. My heart raced and a deeper chill swept over me as I saw a gray-trench coated figure striding a few feet behind me. Judson!

I quickened my steps and quickly reached the door of the center. As I reached for the door handle, another hand gripped mine.

Turning, I looked into those cold, gray-blue eyes that, at one time, had warmed my heart. Now, all I felt was the deepest fear that I had known since that terrible day when my mother had died. My throat froze and I could say nothing, only stare at Judson.

"Well, well, look who I've been fortunate to run into. My little Chelle, and as beautiful as ever." There was a terrifying smile on his face; I would expect to see that smile on the face of a lion as it pounced on prey. Determined, cold, arrogant.

"Let go of me, Judson," I managed finally to say. "How dare you come near me after what you've done?"

ONCE AGAIN I FEAR

"Oh, come on, sugar. Don't be like that. You know everything I've ever done was because I love you. We're back together now, and we're going to start making up for all the time we've lost. I saw you that day by your apartment, but I decided to wait awhile to approach you. You needed time to get used to the idea that the love of your life was back. Say you're happy to see me Rachelle; you know you are."

I hated him at that moment, with a blind, unrelenting hatred. How could he stand there smiling and talking as if nothing had really happened? He had murdered my mother and nearly murdered me.

"What do you plan, Judson, to finish the job of murdering me? Am I supposed to give you that chance? Get away from me before I start screaming to the top of my lungs." I'm not sure how much of what I said came across with the strength that I intended. I was scared out of my wits.

Judson let go of my hand and took a step back. "I'll be seeing you, Rachelle. You can count on that. I love you, and I won't ever let you get away from me. Do you understand?" The smile was gone, and there was a promise in his voice that indicated to me exactly what he meant.

I noticed, at that moment, that my trainer, Damon Ledyard, had come into the lobby of the fitness center. I believe Judson had seen him, and Damon had seen me standing outside. He seemed to catch the look of fear on my face and came to the door, pushing it open. "Oh, there you are, Rachelle. You were a little late, so I came to see if you were out here."

I rushed inside, and stood sobbing uncontrollably as Damon placed an arm around my shoulders. "Who was that guy, Rachelle? I didn't get a good look at him, but you act like you're terrified of him."

I gulped back my tears and leaned weakly against Damon. "That man killed my mother six years ago," I told him. "He almost killed me, and now he's back. I don't know what he wants, but I'm really afraid he plans, eventually, to finish what he failed to do six years ago."

"Rachelle," Damon gasped, "you never told me any of this. Why in the world is that guy out on the street?"

"He skipped bail and fled to Europe. I had thought he might be dead until Monday night, when I saw him near my apartment. What am I going to do? I can't live in terror of him all the time and still function."

"First thing, we're going to call the police and report him. You've got to have protection."

I was still shaking when we sat down in Damon's office. Central Precinct had sent out two patrol cars, obviously hearing the urgency in Damon's voice. Sergeant Win Keffler, the elder of the two police officers who had arrived, held a clipboard on his knee and clicked a ballpoint pen, ready to write. He asked for details about me, my address, my age, where I worked. "Now, Miss Atherly, tell us what happened. You were accosted by someone outside the Star Fitness Center door, is that correct?"

Sergeant Keffler gave the appearance of being bored with the whole proceedings. His heavy-featured face, with a dark shadow of beard, short-clipped dark hair, small black eyes, and thick black brows, showed no sign of sympathy for my obvious terror.

"Yes, I was almost to the door when I noticed someone behind me, a man I recognized immediately. Damon explained on the phone, it's Judson Edward Bard, the third, a man to whom I was once engaged. He killed my mother six years ago and stabbed me. I'm sure you can find records of his arrest and subsequent bail jumping."

"Yeah, the dispatcher told us Judson Bard was the suspect in this incident," he confirmed, peering at me with his little dark eyes, so much like jet beads. "That's not the son of Judson Bard, who owns the freight liners, is it?"

"Yes," I answered. "His parents live in Sausalito. He fled to Europe after he jumped bail, and was seen there many times over many years. I haven't heard anything about him in a couple of years, so I thought he might be dead. Then, I saw him just recently near my apartment."

"Are you sure it was Judson Bard? It was dark out there tonight." My heart sank as I heard skepticism in his voice. It also flashed through my mind that the Bard name carried a lot of clout in this town.

"I'm positive. I knew Judson very well, so I couldn't possibly be mistaken. Besides, he talked to me. What more do you need in the way of identification?" My voice rose as anger threatened to overwhelm me.

"Judson Bard, eh? Come on, Miss Atherly, the Bards are fine, upstanding citizens in the Bay area. Are you sure this guy is one of the San Francisco Bards?"

ONCE AGAIN I FEAR

I was outraged! Judson's arrest had been in all the papers, and his disappearance had also been widely covered. Sergeant Keffler was certainly old enough to have been around at the time.

Before I could voice my anger, I glanced over at the younger officer. He had introduced himself as Officer Lucas Dayton and now was sitting in a chair behind the sergeant. It was obvious that he had been studying me, for he now returned my look with clear, blue-green eyes. He didn't seem to be intimidated by Keffler's superior rank, because he immediately spoke up. "Sarg, why don't I go run this guy through the computer and see what we've got on him? That might save us a lot of time here."

Officer Dayton was on his feet before Keffler had a chance to answer. I noticed a look of annoyance flicker across the older man's face as he answered, "Okay, Dayton, go ahead. We'll see how this story checks out."

When the younger officer had left the room, after giving me a look of support, Sergeant Keffler turned back to me. "Okay, let's say the guy you saw was Judson Bard; tell me the rest of what happened."

I swallowed hard, and glanced over at Damon, sitting behind his desk. His face showed the fury that I was feeling. "I hadn't been aware anyone was behind me until I got to the door. I really don't think he was there before that; it's like he was hidden somewhere nearby, waiting for me, and stepped out behind me. There are deep doorways all along the street where someone could stand unobserved. Anyway, he was there all of a sudden, and it was too late for me to run inside before he caught up. He grabbed my hand as I started to open the door."

"What did he say to you?"

I recounted the conversation between Judson Bard and myself, trying to impress on the police officer the underlying threats in what Judson had said to me.

"So he didn't actually threaten you, correct?"

I felt quick tears stinging my eyes, gripped by the total hopelessness of trying to get this cold man, so lacking in compassion, to grasp what had really happened. "His tone of voice was definitely threatening. When he stated that I would never get away from him, what else would you call that but a threat?" My voice was shaking as much as my body.

"Well, it sounded like he was glad to see you, Miss Atherly, and that he loves you. I suppose a lot of young men like to pursue beautiful young ladies."

Damon could stand no more. He jumped to his feet, his eyes blazing. "Now you look here, Sergeant, Judson Bard murdered Rachelle's mother and tried to murder her; how can you sit there so blasé, about his grabbing her on the street? He could have had a knife and stabbed her right in front of our door. I think he's playing some kind of sick game with Rachelle, and, apparently, you're making a joke of it!"

"Okay, okay, Mr. Ledyard, we'll look into it and see if we can bring Mr. Bard in and talk to him."

At that moment, Lucas Dayton appeared in the doorway. "Sarg, Miss Atherly is telling you the truth. Judson Bard was arrested for murdering her mother and the attempted murder of Miss Atherly. When he was arrested, he was covered with blood, which proved to be that of Miss Atherly and her mother. He also had the bloody knife under the seat of his car. This would appear to be one bad boy, Sarg."

The Sergeant's face changed immediately to a business-like expression, but I, momentarily, had caught a stunned look in his eyes. The evidence was on record that I was telling the truth; why was it so hard for him to admit that? "Okay, Miss Atherly. I have a few more questions to ask you, and, then, we'll see if we can round up Mr. Bard."

"Good luck on trying to do that, Sergeant," I told him. "Judson Bard has eluded the authorities for a long time, so I doubt you'll find him walking down the street or at his parents' home. He's an evil man, with all the money he could possible need behind him. I know him, Sergeant; he's going to be hard to find and he's going to be after me until he decides to kill me." Damon came over and put his arm around me as I started to cry again.

"We'll make this case a priority, won't we, Sarg?" Officer Dayton asked, meeting my eyes again.

"Yeah, sure. A bail jumper in a capital case goes to the top of the list, once he's spotted."

"Don't you think Rachelle should have some protection, Sergeant?" Damon asked.

ONCE AGAIN I FEAR

"Well, we're spread pretty thin, Mr. Ledyard. Can't provide protection for everyone, you know. I'd suggest Miss Atherly leave town for a while." The sergeant was not going to be much help to me, I could tell that now.

"I can't leave my job, just like that!" I gasped, trying to keep from screaming at the complacent man before me. "I'm going to New York next week, but I can't stay away indefinitely. Judson isn't going to give up; he told me that. This could go on for weeks or even months."

Lucas Dayton continued to observe me, and a tiny sympathetic smile tilted the corners of his mouth upward. I could see in his blue-green eyes the compassion that I needed. He ran his hands through his short brown hair and said, "Miss Atherly, I'm sure I could cruise by your place while I'm on duty tonight; your apartment is on our beat. We could have the guys who come on the graveyard do the same thing. My four days off start tomorrow and I would be happy to come escort you to work, if you would like me to." I gathered that Officer Dayton was very anxious for me to take him up on the offer.

There was a slightly boyish eagerness about Lucas Dayton. Looking at him, a rush of hope swept through me. If I had one person with the police department who fully perceived the danger that stalked me, perhaps I would be protected. I then remembered the warm hand on my shoulder and knew that I had other protection on which I could depend.

"You don't have to do that, Officer Dayton, but I certainly would feel safer with an escort. Thank you for volunteering to do that. I would also appreciate some extra police presence in my neighborhood." I smiled, a watery smile, at the young officer, hoping that he saw the gratitude in my face.

Damon took a deep breath and let it out, an indication that he shared my feeling of relief. "Thanks, Officer Dayton, that will make me feel better about Rachelle's safety, I can tell you. Oh, and I'll take her home now and see her safely into her building." He turned to me. "I'll do everything I can to help keep you safe, Rachelle."

I turned a grateful smile on him and felt comforted by the presence of this big body-builder, with a neck like a tree trunk and biceps like soccer balls under his skin. I knew that he was tough, and Judson wouldn't stand a chance against him.

Chapter 26

I lay in bed that night, staring at the dark ceiling, trying to sort through my feelings and impressions. Would the police, and, specifically, Lucas Dayton, be able to protect me?

Could I continue to live with this numbing fear, continue to carry on my life as I had done the last six years? It was unbelievable that one man should have the power to disrupt the course of my life, causing me constantly to look over my shoulder. The menace of Judson Bard was always lurking, a dark shadow that threatened to overwhelm me at any moment.

Could I somehow elude that hovering threat? My building was fairly secure, a security guard on duty in the foyer at all times. No one was allowed in the building without a key or permission from a tenant, giving clearance for admission past the front door. But, nevertheless, once I was outside the front door, I was fair game for Judson. He could attack me at any time, be waiting for me in any doorway.

Waiting! The word exploded inside my head. I sat up and started to shake again, as a dreadful thought hit me. Judson had been waiting for me by the fitness center, perhaps in a doorway nearby. He had known I was coming there. But how? Few people knew that I went to the center regularly.

Could he have been following me for some time, to learn my schedule? No, following at a distance didn't seem to be Judson's style. He had tended

124

ONCE AGAIN I FEAR

to be obvious in his dealings with me, usually accosting me face to face. Even that day outside my apartment, he had made no effort to hide himself.

How then did he know where I would be? The thought which I had difficulty accepting was that someone had told him where I would be. But who? It would have to be someone I knew well, who knew that I was going to Star this evening?

And, now that I thought of it, how did Judson know where I lived? No one at my church would tell anyone that without my permission; I would stake my life on that. Gruesome choice of words, I thought. But who else? The people with whom I worked were the only other people who would know my address and my schedule.

I could not perceive any one of them doing such a thing. Besides, who among my co-workers knew Judson Bard? It was all so farfetched that I desperately tried to dismiss the suspicion from my mind.

I lay back down and willed myself to clear my mind and relax. There was no way I could face the days to come without adequate sleep. The kind, handsome face of Lucas Dayton kept coming into my memory. There was something so sweet about him, and so much strength; he was a person on whom one could depend. With a prayer in my heart, I finally drifted off and slept soundly.

True to his word, Lucas Dayton arrived at my apartment at seven-thirty the following morning. His hair was still damp from his morning shower, but his eyes were bright and smiling.

"Thanks so much for doing this, Officer Dayton; you don't know how much I appreciate it," I told him, as I ushered him into my apartment.

"Hey, you can drop the Officer Dayton bit; I'm off duty," he announced, a teasing smile on his face. "The name is Lucas, a name I share with my grandfather."

"Lucas, it is, and no more Miss Atherly either, just Rachelle. Come on into the kitchen and have some coffee and a bagel. I was just getting ready to eat." I didn't wait for him to accept my invitation, just went on into my kitchen and began preparing the food.

Lucas sat at the breakfast bar, looking quite at home. "This is really nice," he said, looking around the cheerful room. "You have a real knack for interior decorating. Everything is bright and tasteful, but, at the same time, very comfortable. I really like it."

"Why, thank you, Lucas, that's very sweet of you. That's exactly the effect I tried to create here. Oh, do you take cream or sugar?" I looked at him questioningly.

"No, I drink it black, thanks. That toasted bagel looks wonderful; I guess I'm hungrier than I thought. And blackberry preserves, great. I love it."

I filled my cup and brought my plate around the breakfast bar, seating myself next to Lucas. He immediately started eating with gusto. He was such a comforting presence, that the knot in my stomach gradually relaxed and disappeared.

I found myself studying the man at my side. Again, I was struck by the aura of strength that surrounded Lucas Dayton. He was probably six feet one, very handsome, with a straight, but strong, nose; dark, straight brows; slightly rounded cheeks; and a firm chin with a hint of a cleft. His mouth was generous and always on the verge of a smile, which crinkled the corners of his eyes. And those thick, dark eyelashes! Most women would give a fortune for eyelashes like that. All this, wrapped in boyish sweetness, definitely was an attractive package.

At that moment, Tache decided to inspect our guest, sniffing his pants leg, and then turning her amber eyes upward to appraise the person who wore the pants. She apparently liked what she smelled and saw, because she then rubbed her face vigorously against his leg.

"This is Tache, Lucas. Her name rhymes with 'cash' and it's French for 'Spot'."

Lucas chuckled. "That's a very clever name for a tortoise shell cat, I must say."

"She's putting her scent on you." I told him. "You've passed her inspection, and she's welcoming you into our home. She doesn't do that with everyone, believe me."

"I'm flattered, beyond words," Lucas averred, his mouth full of bagel. He swallowed and continued. "My mom had a tortoise shell cat like that, when I was a kid. I always think they look as if someone has splattered orange and yellow paint in the face and on the body of a black cat. Tache

ONCE AGAIN I FEAR

looks as if an orange drop ran down the side of her nose. Mom's cat had similar markings and was a really good cat. Never did any no-nos on the floor or scratched the furniture."

"Sounds like Tache," I said. "She's a great cat. There's only one problem with her. I read somewhere that one should choose a pet to color-coordinate with one's decor; I struck out there. It's a constant battle to keep black, orange and other assorted-colored cat hair off my white sofa and carpet." I then found myself telling him all about Cleo, sharing my grief at her death.

"I know all about that, Rachelle. I had a dog when I was a kid. We got him when I was five, and he was still around when I was in my junior year of high school. Then, one day, Dad backed out of the driveway, not knowing that Rowdy had gotten out of the back yard. He ran over him. It just tore Dad up! I was at school, and he really dreaded telling me. It hurt. I still remember how I felt."

He set his coffee cup down and swiveled his stool around to face me. "You and I are a couple of softies, aren't we?" he asked, smiling at me.

"Sure looks that way. It would be awful to be unable to grieve for a pet, wouldn't it? There are people I know that say they hate dogs and cats; I can't imagine it."

Lucas sat quietly for a moment and then said, "Rachelle, it would grieve me deeply if anything happened to you. I'll do whatever it takes, whatever's in my power, to see that Judson Bard doesn't get to you. That's a promise."

Tears came to my eyes, and my heart contracted. "I'm so scared, Lucas, I can't tell you how scared. The only thing that keeps me from going into hysterics is the knowledge that God is watching out for me. Terrible things do happen to His children, but nothing can happen that He doesn't allow."

A glow suffused Lucas' face. "It's wonderful to hear that you share my faith in the Lord. God certainly will watch out for you, better than I ever can. He's kept His hand on me since I've been on the force, delivering me from certain death several times."

"I know the Lord will be there with me, even if Judson does hurt me; I'm glad I know that now. I've come to know the Lord only since my

Mother's death, Lucas. I was learning about Him before, because Mom had asked Him into her own life, but it took me a while to get it through my head how easy it is to know to Him." It felt so good to talk about my faith with a friend who obviously understood.

"I know about that, believe me. A friend invited me to church about five years ago, just after I got out of college, but it took me a year to catch on to what my friend and the preacher were trying to tell me. I had just finished the police academy when I finally made my decision for Christ. I'm so glad I've had Him with me the whole time I've been in uniform."

In the next hour, as Lucas and I sat there, I found myself sharing with him a lot about my life and my dreams. I also told him, in detail, what had happened that terrible day when my mother had died. It amazed me that, for the first time, I had told the story without crying.

Lucas sat quietly until I finished and then took my hand, gently stroking it with his thumb. "I'm so sorry, Rachelle," he murmured softly. "You have been through so much that now you deserve to have some peace of mind. Perhaps we can catch Judson Bard and give you that peace. One thing, you can be so thankful that you know where your mother is, a much better place than this old world."

"Oh, yes, that's been such a comfort to me. I think, somehow, she knows that Dad and I are in the Kingdom now and will see her someday."

"I'm sure, when the angels started singing about your conversion, your mother joined in," Lucas pointed out.

"What a lovely thought. Yes, I believe that. Thanks for saying it, Lucas." I closed my eyes and formed a picture in my mind of my mother singing with the angels, and probably dancing, too. How beautiful!

I sat quietly, as Lucas continued to hold my hand. Again the peace of God flowed over me.

Chapter 27

Lucas not only took me to the store, but parked his car and walked me all the way to my office. I think we were both reluctant to end our time together. Lucas Dayton was a remarkably sweet, insightful man.

At the door of my office, he stopped and read the name plate on the door, "'Rachelle Atherly, Head Buyer'. Hey, I'm impressed, Miss Rachelle Atherly. You've done very well for yourself—you must be a mighty smart girl."

"Or, maybe, a mighty blessed girl," I countered, meaning it with all my heart. Looking into Lucas' eyes, I didn't mean it only in regard to my job, either.

"That too, I'm sure," Lucas agreed. "Hey, let's continue this conversation after you get off work today. Just tell me the time, and I'll be here to pick you up, if that's all right with you."

"I'd like that," I told him. "I'll probably be here until about six-thirty, since I'm coming in late today."

"Okay, I'll be right here at that time," he promised. "Maybe we could have some dinner."

"I'd like that, too." I saw the warmth in his blue-green eyes and my heart did a sort of somersault, taking my breath away. What was happening to me? I hadn't felt this way in more than six years—had believed I might never feel this utter giddiness again. I had met Lucas Dayton just the evening before; how could I become so taken with him

129

this soon? It was clear to me that our shared faith figured into the equation much more than I ever would have imagined.

Trish looked up as I opened the door, her eyes immediately going to Lucas as he turned to leave. As I walked into the office, she grinned and asked, "Who's the hunk? Wow, he's gorgeous!"

"He's a friend. His name is Lucas Dayton." I didn't want to go into any details about who Lucas was.

"Umm, I'd like to meet someone like him," Trish gushed. My secretary probably had come to realize that any dates I had were few and far between, though I had never really discussed it with her. She kept my business calendar, but knew little about my personal schedule.

Or did she? I suddenly wondered, trying hard to remember what I had told her about my activities after work, the ones, of course, that did not include her. Yes, she did know that I went to Star Fitness Center regularly. I had been expecting the confirmation of a meeting some months ago and had asked her to call me at the center and leave a message.

A little at a time, it sank in that Trish did, indeed, know quite a few things about my personal life, bits and pieces dropped into normal conversation over the last year.

Come on, I thought, it's ridiculous that Trish would know Judson and give him information on me. But she had been acting rather strangely lately. Oh, no, that couldn't have anything to do with my situation. With that, I shoved the whole idea aside as totally ridiculous.

I smiled at Trish and started asking for information I needed to get my day under way. Since this was Friday, I had to get everything cleared so that I could go to New York without worrying about business back here in San Francisco.

Trish and I worked together all morning, putting everything in order, making any needed phone calls, and writing memos that needed to be sent to various departments.

By twelve o'clock, I felt we had everything pretty much under control, so I told Trish to go to lunch and take an extra half hour, if she wished. "Thanks, I can use it. I have some business of my own to take care of. See you at a one-thirty." With that, she grabbed her purse and went out the door.

ONCE AGAIN I FEAR

When Trish had mentioned business, I had, again, seen a flicker of worry pass over her face. What could be troubling her? Once more, unwanted, the thought crept in that she might be meeting Judson to tell him of my plans. No, no, I would not believe that!

I had a few last minute things to take care of before going to New York, calling the alterations department to see if my new suit was ready, checking to see if the pet sitter I had hired for Tache had my schedule, calling a jewelry repair shop to see if they had finished replacing the clasp on my gold chain, and confirming my hair appointment tomorrow afternoon. Two years ago, I had finally, reluctantly, decided to have my waist-length hair cut to a more fashionable, more manageable, length. It now hung below my shoulders, layered softly, and with blonde highlights woven into it. This style required trips to the salon every six weeks to keep it looking its best.

Everything was as it should be: The suit would be sent to my office immediately, the pet sitter was delighted to be caring for my "darling little Tache", my chain was ready and was on its way to me as I spoke, and my hairdresser was expecting me. I was relieved to know that these small parts of my life were going exceedingly smoothly.

At one o'clock, I went down to the restaurant to have lunch. The bagel I had had for breakfast was long gone, and my stomach was starting to growl in a very unladylike fashion.

The lunchtime crowd had diminished a little at this time of day, but I saw several people I knew, including Greg Phillips. He saw me and motioned me over to his table. That suited me, because I wasn't in the mood for any solitary contemplation.

Greg was dressed in his usual crisply-tailored suit, today navy blue, with a white shirt, and sporting a colorful silk tie in a contemporary design of red, navy and gray. Greg was a very handsome man, and wore his clothes with great style. He was perhaps a shade under six feet tall, trim of figure, straight, almost in a military manner. His dark ash blond hair was cut short, except on top where it swept back in a soft wave. His eyes were a smoky gray, flecked with amber, and his bone structure was that of a male model, finely molded, but strong. His nose was slightly aquiline, his lips somewhat thin, but, when he smiled, his straight, white teeth flashed and his face lit up.

I knew Greg was twenty-three and a native of San Francisco. He had graduated from the University of Nevada Las Vegas a year ago, where he had a decent, but not extraordinary, GPA. I had had some reservations about hiring Greg, sensing that there might be something of the frivolous about him. But I had wanted to hire a man, and since there were no women applicants that showed any promise at all, I chose to hire him. I needed a male perspective, especially in the men's and the boy's departments. Greg's style of dress, and his perfect manners, gave me the feeling that he had the taste, as well as the fashion and social insight to handle the job.

Never for a moment, had I been sorry that I had hired Greg. On the job, he had proven himself to be anything but frivolous; my first impressions had probably arisen from his fun-loving nature, I thought. There was, however, no one in the store more dedicated to his job, or more efficient, than Greg Phillips. I had come to depend on him, knowing I could trust his judgment and his work ethic. I was glad he was going to New York with me; his input would be most welcome as I made my choices for the spring season.

We had attended some earlier showings this fall. Now, we would round out our spring lines from the fashion houses that would be showing next week, two of which were new this season. Word had leaked out that one of the designers was going to be the next Dior, an exciting young talent with a bottomless well of ideas. I was very excited about seeing what all the fuss was about.

When I was seated across from Greg, I asked him, "Are you all set for our trip to The Big Apple?"

"Everything is a-okay. I'm really looking forward to seeing the Bradford Ederly line. Let's hope it lives up to all the hype and speculation in the trade papers." Greg scanned his menu as the server came to hand me one.

It took only a minute for me to decide. "I'll have the French onion soup and the turkey croissant sandwich, with iced tea," I told the server. Greg ordered a cheeseburger, fries, and a Coke.

When the server had gone, I continued, where we had left off. "Mr. Ederly certainly has received more than his share of publicity, hasn't he?

ONCE AGAIN I FEAR

Let's just make a guess where all the leaks about his fabulous line have come from."

Greg laughed and nodded vigorously. "My thought exactly. I don't think we'd need more than one guess, correct? It's a good ploy, though, don't you think? Get everyone excited about you, before you put one model on the runway."

"Oh, yes, I can't think of a better way to get all the buyers there to see what he has to offer. Actually, though, it makes me wonder if Suzie Lopez's showing might not be the one to anticipate. No one seems to have a clue as to what she is going to show; not one word has leaked out. I'd say the air of mystery about her might be a positive indication as to her offerings. They could be totally spectacular." Our drinks were set before us, and I tore open a packet of Sweet 'n Low to sweeten my tea.

Greg ripped the paper off his straw and poked it into the heavily-iced Coke, taking a deep drink before responding. "You could be right, Rachelle. Mr. Ederly could be all smoke and no fire. I really hope, though, that both of them are enormously talented and have produced some fashions, for both men and women, that are really new, but in excellent taste. I wouldn't buy anything that is so far out that there is danger that only a minute segment of our customers will buy them. I think the Devon customer knows that all our clothes are things they can wear for at least a few seasons without their going out of style. I think they quickly learn they can't expect to find all the latest, outrageous fads here; they can always find that junk in little shops in Union Square or elsewhere."

"You and I think a lot alike, Greg," I told him and he grinned, seemingly very pleased that I thought so.

Our meals arrived and we concentrated on eating. He seemed to be as hungry as I was.

When we were about halfway through, Greg glanced across at me and asked, "Have you seen any more of that person you had thought was dead?"

I was taken aback somewhat by the question, having almost forgotten that I had mentioned it to anyone. "Yes, I saw him last night. He seems to want to make himself a problem, but I think I have some help in dealing

133

with it." I was being purposely vague, since I didn't particularly want to have anyone else in on this situation.

Greg seemed to grasp that I wasn't going to go into any detail. He did add, though, "Well, I hope he didn't cause you any problem at the fitness center."

My head jerked up in alarm. Why would he mention the fitness center? How did he know I had gone to Star last night? "What makes you say that, Greg?" I asked, cautiously.

"Oh, you said you saw him last night, and I knew you were going to the center. Trish told me once that you go every Thursday night."

Alarm continued to spread through me as I realized that still another person knew something of my schedule. "How did she happen to tell you that?" I tried to keep my voice even

"I stopped into your office last week to see you. It was late, and you had already left. Trish was just leaving. She said you had left to go to the fitness center. I hope you aren't upset that she told me; it didn't seem to be of any real importance at the time. She just commented that it was your regular routine to go there every Thursday and work with a trainer."

"No, I'm not really upset, Greg. I can understand how Trish might think nothing of telling you, since you are my assistant. Don't worry about it, really. Trish isn't in any trouble with me."

I was a little concerned, though, that Trish might have told someone else, the wrong person. How could I know for sure that she hadn't? I would have to instruct her, gently, not to disclose any of my plans to anyone, not now, when it could mean my life.

Drucilla Warren called me that afternoon, wishing me a pleasant trip, and wishing she could go with me. I shared her thinking; Dru would make a great traveling companion.

"How about having dinner with me tonight, Chelle; I'm rather at loose ends, and your company would be welcome," A slight, almost imperceptible, melancholy had entered Dru's usually chipper voice.

"Oh, Dru, I'm sorry, I have a date." My heart flip-flopped when I said the word "date", picturing Lucas' smiling face.

"A date! Um, who's the guy?" Dru was always very straightforward.

ONCE AGAIN I FEAR

"A guy I just met. His name is Lucas Dayton. Very nice, too." Again, I didn't want to elaborate, even to Dru, with whom I had shared so much.

"I'm suspecting that the fair Rachelle doesn't want to talk too much about her Prince Charming, for fear of jinxing everything." Dru laughed a low, throaty laugh.

I hated being so evasive with her, but I felt I must wait until I knew how the situation with Judson shaped up before talking with anyone about anything or any person connected with it. Every move I made and every word I spoke from here on out was critical to my safety.

I managed to say, "Something like that, Dru; you know how it is. Don't worry, I'll tell you all about him if anything momentous transpires. Greg and I are flying to New York on Sunday, so the rest of the weekend will be spent on last-minute details of the trip. One of those details is trying to make Tache understand that I'll be back soon."

"Tache is a smart girl, Chelle," Dru interjected. "She'll pout and make you feel guilty, when, all the while, she's looking forward to seeing that pet sitter who spoils her rotten every time you go on a business trip."

I had to laugh at Dru's assessment of my pet. She could be right. "You've probably got Tache pegged for what she really is. I can't believe it, my own cat deceiving me. Oh, well, if she enjoys the game, I'll let her. Now, tell me what you're doing this weekend."

"Well," Dru answered, slowly, and somewhat mysteriously, "I'm invited to a party, a big party, Saturday night. It's going to be at the Mark Hopkins, black tie—you know, posh to the max. I have a gorgeous, green-sequin dress that's positively stunning, and I'm being escorted by my own Prince Charming. Actually, he's an old friend from college, nothing romantic. Come to think of it, I wouldn't really mind if it were romantic; he's kinda grown on me over the years, and I know I could trust him."

Dru, again with a touch of sadness, laughed. "Oh, don't mind me. Remember, I said I didn't think I would ever want to marry again. It's just that I do get a bit tired of the Dru, solo, routine, and the scramble to find an escort when an occasion seems to require one. It occurs to me sometimes that it would be rather nice to have a permanent date."

"I understand; the thought has occurred to me, too, now and then. I guess I haven't found anyone whom I would like to have as a steady-for-life guy. Who knows what the future holds for us, Dru, who is just around the corner?" Again, I thought of Lucas' blue-green eyes and wonderful smile. Was Lucas to figure into my future? At that thought, I again felt the quiver of fear that I had always felt when getting too close to a man. Would I be able to get completely past that fear with Lucas?

Chapter 28

Lucas was waiting for me in the executive reception room when I emerged from my office at a little past six-thirty. He quickly put aside a magazine and rose, pleasure shining on his face. He was wearing gray slacks, a cranberry-colored sport shirt, and a gray suede jacket, looking so handsome that my heart, again, did a somersault.

"Sorry I'm a few minutes later than I said I would be, Lucas," I told him, knowing my own face must be lit like a Christmas tree.

"No problem, Rachelle. This is a very comfortable place to wait, even for a few minutes. All set to leave?" He reached to take my plastic-covered suit that I was carrying and slung it over his shoulder.

"Yes, but I must tell you that I have to go out through the employee exit. It's a hard and fast rule. As you see, we women have to carry these clear plastic purses, too, all to avoid employee theft, which can be a huge problem. If I expect my employees to follow these rules, I'll follow them also."

I watched as an amused grin spread over his face. "You're talking to an expert on theft, and all the means to carry it out. I applaud Devon's for taking all these precautions, and you for thinking you're not above the rules."

We took the elevator to the first floor, walking back through the men's department toward the employee exit. Mark Bussell stood behind the cash register desk, talking on the phone. He looked up as we passed and smiled. I noted that he gave Lucas a careful look, as if analyzing him in

137

some way. Could Mark be jealous? That's silly, I thought, and shook myself away from such an idea.

Near the employee exit, we met Greg, also about to leave the store, talking to the security guard. There was clear speculation in his eyes, as I introduced him to Lucas, again referring to him as a friend. Greg extended his hand and smiled. "Glad to meet you, Lucas." Then, he added something which was a bit out of character for Greg. "You take good care of this lady; she's one of the good ones." Why did he say something like that to a man that he had just met? I had given him no hint that Lucas was anything more than a casual friend.

"I certainly intend to do just that, Greg. I'm glad she has friends who know her worth." He stated it in a rather teasing voice, but I felt he was entirely serious.

Lucas and I emerged from the store, walking around from where the employee entrance was tucked away at the side of the building. We walked across Geary, skirted the corner of the Union Square, the vast plaza lovely under street lights, and descended to the parking garage. As we walked toward Lucas' car, which was perhaps forty feet from the entrance, I caught a glimpse, out of the corner of my eye, of a dark green Toyota pulling out of a parking space which we had just passed. I wouldn't have noticed, except that the driver was wearing a hat, pulled down over his forehead, and large, aviator-style sunglasses, covering much of the upper part of the face. I could not have sworn whether it was a man or a woman, but it was obvious the driver was watching Lucas and me intently. The car moved slowly, as Lucas and I continued down the drive toward the front of Lucas' car. Then, the car shot forward, screeching its tires, and headed straight toward us. Lucas grabbed my arm and ran between two cars, dragging me with him. The green Toyota sped past us and continued at high speed, circling the end of the parking lane, and out the entrance.

Lucas stood staring after the car which had come so close to hitting us, shaking his head in amazement. "Dear God in Heaven, I would swear that driver did that on purpose! He could have killed or maimed both of us. Why would someone do a crazy thing like that?"

ONCE AGAIN I FEAR

My heart was pounding so hard that I could hardly speak, but my mind was rapidly forming an answer to Lucas' question. Who else but Judson Bard would want to run us down? Judson. It always came back to Judson

I was on the verge of helpless, angry tears, but I endeavored to control myself. "I can think of one reason, Lucas; someone is trying to kill me. There's only one person who would want to do that—Judson Bard. I couldn't see the driver's face very well, but I'd be willing to bet anything I own that that's exactly who it was."

Lucas put his arm around me and held me close to him for a moment without saying anything. When he finally spoke, it was softly, but with firmness. "You're probably right. From what you've told me, Judson is eaten up with vengeance and will do anything to hurt you. The other thing is that he'll do the same to any man he sees you with. I've probably just been added to his hit list."

He held me away from him and looked me squarely in the eyes. "Don't you worry about that, though, Rachelle; I can take care of myself. And look at it this way, if he starts targeting both of us that will double our chances of getting him. He's going to make a mistake, eventually, and his reign of terror is going to end. You and I have to be on guard every minute and try to outsmart him."

"That makes sense. If you're right, and he comes after both of us, it may spread his efforts in two directions, so that he is more apt to foul up in some way." I sounded more confident than I felt.

"You've got the idea."

Lucas kept his arm around me, as we made our way to his parking space. We got into the car, after he had hung my suit on a hook in the back. Then, he picked up the microphone of the police radio that was installed in his car, and called in to his precinct.

"Lucas Dayton here; let me speak to Sgt. Keffler."

A female voice, surrounded by minor static and background noise, responded, "Hey, Lucas, I wasn't expecting to hear from you on your day off. Keffler is filling out some reports, but I think he's about to sign the last one. Could you hang on a minute?"

"Okay, Bonny, thanks."

There was a pause of about two minutes and then Keffler's somewhat gruff voice came on the line. "Hi, Dayton; what's up?"

Lucas was immediately the cop, the professional. "I'm with Rachelle Atherly, in the parking garage below Union Square, where she works. Someone just tried to run us down. We couldn't get a good look at the driver because he or she was wearing a hat, pulled down low, and aviator sunglasses. However, we both had the definite impression it was a man. He was driving a ninety-eight Toyota Corolla, dark green, with a Triple A sticker on the back bumper." Lucas then gave the license plate number. "There was a City College of San Francisco parking sticker in the rear right window."

"Were either of you hurt?" Keffler asked.

"No, just shook up. We had to move mighty fast to avoid being hit."

"Could have been some college kid feeling his oats, thinking it was funny to make two people run." I heard the same edge in Keffler's voice that had been there last night.

"Feeling his oats, my eye," Lucas gritted, his voice rising, "This was deliberate. He seemed to be waiting in a parking space here and pulled out, just as we got past him. He would definitely have hit us if we hadn't been quick on our feet."

"Okay, okay, Lucas, so it was deliberate. Now, who would want to do that to you?" I could not believe Keffler's attitude. What was his problem?

"Me?" Lucas asked. "Granted there are a few crooks out there who hate my guts, but this was at Miss Atherly's place of business, so it's reasonable to assume she was the target, don't you think?"

"Well, I'll send a unit over there and take a report. In the meantime, we'll run the plate through to see who owns the car."

"Why not run it through right now, Sergeant? It might be interesting what we find out." Lucas was obviously as puzzled by Keffler's attitude as I was.

"Sure thing; just a minute."

We waited what seemed like a half hour, but, in reality, was only about three minutes. Then Keffler's voice returned to the radio. "Okay, the Toyota Corolla is registered to Tony Bianci; address 221 Rankin St.,

That's up in the North Beach area, off Union. The car was reported stolen this afternoon from the City College parking lot. That leaves the identity of the driver a mystery, doesn't it?"

"It isn't a mystery to me, Sergeant. There's only one person who wants to harm Miss Atherly, and that's Judson Bard, the third. I doubt he has a car of his own since he is wanted, and I don't think he would use his papa's to try to run us down, do you?"

"I really don't think you can make any such assumptions, Dayton. Let's be professional about this and not let emotions get in the way. I saw how you were looking at Miss Atherly last night."

"Sergeant, it seems to me that I'm not the one being unprofessional here. We have an attempted double homicide on our hands, me being one of the intended victims, simply by being here at the time, and you're telling me not to be emotional. Come on, Sarg, think about it. Judson Bard is the only person who could possibly be trying to kill Rachelle Atherly!" Lucas was breathing heavily with the anger that he obviously felt.

"I have a car on the way, Dayton. I've already sent an APB for the Toyota, so we should find out something soon. You have a nice night, and don't worry about Miss Atherly."

Lucas clicked the radio off and sat taking deep breaths for a few seconds. I sat beside him, still shaking with the horror of what had just happened. He turned to me and sighed deeply, taking my hand, holding it tightly.

"I can't imagine what has gotten into Keffler," he said, finally. "This is so unlike him. Before this, I would have said he was the best officer on the force. He seems determined not to look into this case."

"Does he know Judson Bard?" I asked.

"I can't imagine that he does. People like the Bards don't usually hobnob with lowly people like cops. I can't think of any connection Keffler could have with the Bards. You heard him, though, last night and just now; he's reluctant to pursue this."

We sat in silence for a long time, his hand still holding mine, firmly, but warmly. I kept mulling over everything that I had heard from Keffler, and I knew Lucas was doing the same thing. Why didn't Keffler want to believe that Judson Bard was after me, particularly, in sight of the fact that he had already been indicted for murdering my mother and trying to murder me? It didn't make sense. Could it be he was just a naturally skeptical person? No, that didn't fit with what Lucas had said about him.

"How long has he been on the force, Lucas?" I finally asked.

"About twenty-five years. I would stake my life on the fact that he is completely dedicated to his job, completely clean."

"What do you know about him personally?"

"Well, not much, really. I've known him casually for most of my four years on the force, but he's not one to talk about himself and his personal life much, just a word here and there. He said once that he had had a tough childhood, growing up in a section of Oakland in which a boy learned to fight, or he was dead."

Lucas rubbed his left hand around the steering wheel, seeming to gather his thoughts. "One thing that always struck me as being strange was his attitude toward drunks; he hates them. Once, he and I both came to an apartment on a domestic disturbance call and found a drunken husband pounding away on his wife, his kids cowering in the corner. Keffler's face hardened and he grabbed the husband, literally throwing him across the room. He roared something like, 'I've seen enough of this in my lifetime; don't want to see any more.' I got the impression he was talking from personal experience."

"Anything else? Something that would perhaps explain his behavior now?" My terror was subsiding, leaving my mind racing, trying to put the pieces of this puzzle together.

"I really can't. Like I say, I've always thought he was the best officer I had ever worked with. I felt that anyone could have a particular area of disgust for human behavior, and his was drunks."

A patrol car pulled into the space next to Lucas' car and two young officers stepped out into the orangey light of the parking garage. Lucas gave my hand a final squeeze, and we also got out.

"Hey, Dayton, heard you had a little problem here," the slender, sandy-haired driver, Officer Dale Bently, said.

"I wouldn't call attempted homicide 'little'," Lucas answered without a hint of irritation in his voice.

ONCE AGAIN I FEAR

The other officer, a bulky, Hispanic young man, with a pleasant face, cleared his throat. "Keffler made it sound like some sort of prank had been played on you." He turned to me. "I'm Officer Amador Mendez. You're Rachelle Atherly, is that right?"

"Yes, and I think I was the main target. A former boyfriend of mine is after me and has made threats against my life. He killed my mother six years ago and almost ended my own life. He skipped to Europe when he was put on bail before coming to trial. I've seen him twice before tonight, and he tried to grab me one of those times."

"Oh, this puts a different light on things," Officer Bently acknowledged. "I take it he isn't the Tony Bianci who owns the Toyota, correct?"

"No, he's Judson Bard, the third," I answered, seeing Bently and Mendez's eyes widen.

Mendez whistled through his teeth and let out a big breath. "Bard, huh?" he interposed. "Wow, we're talking mucho money and power here. Where did you meet him?"

"While we were at Stanford. I met him through a mutual friend."

"So you dated him. Was it serious?" Bently asked.

"We were engaged, until he became violent. I ended the relationship, or thought I had done so. Judson was determined it wasn't over. That's when he came to my house in Saratoga and killed my mother. I was badly hurt and would have been dead if my father hadn't arrived. Judson was caught with blood all over him and the knife under his car seat. His parents got him out on bail, after he was indicted, and he skipped." I had told the story many times, but it was always a gut-wrenching experience.

"I think I remember something about that case," Mendez put in. "I was in my senior year of high school when it happened. All my friends talked about it, wondering how a guy could do something like that. I had forgotten that it was a member of the Bard family involved."

"What amazes me," Bently interjected, "is that he was able to get out on bail! Maybe the Bards have even more clout than I realized.

"That seems to be the case," I concurred, a note of bitterness in my voice.

"Okay," Bently said. "Give me all the details, Lucas, and we'll see what we can do. I still can't believe that Keffler made such light of this."

Lucas recounted the entire episode, clearly and with regard to minute detail. I was astonished that he had noticed such small details. To me, the whole occurrence had been a total blur. All I had seen was a quick glimpse of the driver and was aware that the car was dark green.

Chapter 29

The patrol car had gone and we were again seated in Lucas' car. "We can only wait to see if they find anything," Lucas said. "They're going to page me if they get any leads. Now, let's go get something to eat and talk this thing over. Maybe we can think of some way to catch the dastardly villain." He said the last with a remarkably good imitation of an old movie hero; I realized he was trying to lighten my mood.

We ate in a small Italian restaurant on Mason Street. We sat at a table in the rear where faces were hardly discernible in the dim lighting. Candlelight flickered and soft voices around us blended with the music of mandolins and guitars. The fragrance of garlic, herbs, and burning candles was a pleasant scent in the air.

We ordered iced tea and pored over the huge glossy menus. The drinks arrived after only a few minutes. On the center of the table, the server also placed a basket of foccaccia bread, an herb quick-bread, topped with sun-dried tomatoes and Parmesan. He poured olive oil from a cruet into small bowls for dipping our bread. I ordered chicken Marsala and Caesar salad. Lucas also ordered the Caesar salad with shrimp fradiavolo, large shrimp sautéed in olive oil, garlic, and herbs, served on a bed of linguini with marinara sauce, and garnished with clams and mussels.

Sipping our tea in the dim, charming atmosphere, I let myself relax, feeling at peace in the presence of the man across the table from me. "I come here often," Lucas said. I was again aware of his direct observation of me. "There isn't a place in town that has better Italian food, not even in North Beach. I've never been disappointed in any dish I've sampled. The service, too, is excellent."

"This bread is wonderful," I said, munching on the hot, herby bread, dripping with olive oil.

"Just wait until you taste the salad. Um, um! It's very cold and crisp, and they leave off those disgusting anchovies. Then comes the entrees! To die for!" We smiled at each other and then burst into laughter, because of his ironic choice of words.

"Never mind, Lucas, you don't have to watch everything you say for fear of my reaction. I really do have a good sense of humor."

The food lived up to Lucas' word. The salads were huge, but, before I knew it, mine was gone. The chicken Marsala was topped with a tangy sauce and mushrooms. The pasta accompaniment was mostaccioli in a mixture of chopped tomato, garlic, and green pepper. The vegetable dish was tender Italian squashes sautéed in oil, garlic and herbs. Nothing had ever tasted so good.

Finally, as we were finishing the last of our food, Lucas brought the conversation around to the serious subject of Judson Bard and his attempts to kill me. "How do you think Judson seems to know where you are so often?" he asked, voicing the conclusion that I had reluctantly accepted.

"I think someone is telling him where I am and what I'm doing," I answered. "It's very painful to think that someone I know is allied with him in his plot to hurt me. But it's the only thing that makes sense. Lucas, who could be doing this to me? Who?" Again, I felt tears threatening.

"Let's go over everyone who is close to you and could know about your movements. Start naming them, and we'll try to come to some conclusion as to who could be best suited to the job of spy."

Spy! I hated the thought of that idea. It sounded more like a government mole, playing both sides of the game. Who did I know that was capable of being so sneaky and, also, so clever that I would not comprehend what she or he was doing?

"Well, I guess we start with my secretary, Trish Willingham. Oh, Lucas, how I hate this! I love Trish like a little sister. She's wonderful, always there to help me when I need her. She's been with me a year! This

ONCE AGAIN I FEAR

trouble with Judson has just started. Okay, okay, we'll talk about Trish. She's twenty-three and single. She lives here in San Francisco on Post Street, in what I gather is a tiny, studio apartment with a kitchenette window overlooking an air shaft. She doesn't seem to have any boyfriends. In fact, I never hear her mention any friends. I take her to a concert or play occasionally, paying for the tickets myself, because I'm sure she can't afford them. I pay her well, quite a bit more than the average secretary gets, but she seems to be short of money all the time. She often drops little things along that line into our conversations."

"So, she could be open to a payoff for giving Judson information about you, couldn't she?" It sounded more like a statement than a question.

"Oh, Lucas, yes, maybe she could, but I can't imagine it. Besides, she's still struggling financially—no sign yet of any payoff, as you put it. Wouldn't she suddenly have extra money? I haven't seen any indication of that." I rubbed my forehead and closed my eyes, trying to picture such a scenario.

"Well, it could be that he's promised her money when the deed is done. Okay, let's consider anyone else that could be in a position to divulge the information that Judson would need." He looked questioningly at me.

"It would be someone who knows where I live and that I go to Star Fitness Center on Thursday nights; we know that much. That includes Trish, the store general manager, Robert Bainbridge, Greg Phillips, my friend, Drucilla Warren, and, oh, probably Mark Bussell. I can't remember if I have ever told him that I go to Star. As to their knowing where my apartment is, I had all of them, except Mr. Bainbridge, over for dinner one night, along with my trainer, Damon Ledyard. You met Damon last night. Lots of people at church know where I live and that I go to Star, but I refuse to even consider that any of them would pass that information to anyone. They all know about Judson and have been supportive of me to the ultimate degree."

"Have you perhaps dated someone whom you subsequently dropped?" Lucas kept his voice even, the voice of a police officer interrogating a witness.

147

"I've dated a few young men at church, but I made it clear right from the beginning that it wasn't going to be serious. I think a couple of them were, shall we say, disappointed. But, Lucas, both of them, since then, have married, and very happily. The others are either dating someone else, married, or still good friends of mine. They've all done everything they can to be helpful and kind to me. This is a very deeply spiritual group of people, committed to God and to every other person in the group. I trust them implicitly."

"Let's say, then, that we can scratch all these people. We, now, have to consider all the other people you know. What about Robert Bainbridge? He's your boss, correct?"

"Yes, technically, but he is a lamb, really! He knew about my mother's death, and the circumstances surrounding it, when he hired me. He has been so supportive of me. I'm very blessed to be working with someone like him. He allows me almost total freedom in making choices for the store; that's not true in every company, so I've been told. Mr. Bainbridge has been married for thirty five years and has three grown children. I think there are numerous grandchildren. He's devoted to Devon's, but his family comes first. He's a good man. In fact, I think he teaches a men's Bible study somewhere. I don't know all the details about his life, because he isn't much to talk about himself. Let's leave him out of the list of possible suspects, okay?"

"I think I have to agree with you. He doesn't seem like someone who would get involved in something like this shoddy business. Okay, what about Mark Bussell? He's about your age, isn't he? And I caught a strange look in his eye when we passed him in the men's department tonight. Tell me about him."

"He is about the same age I am and a native of Sacramento. He started college at UC-Davis, studying accounting, but dropped out to travel. He spent a couple of years in Chicago, and then bummed around Europe for a few years. Then, he decided to come back and enroll at San Francisco State. He's been at Devon's for a little over six months now. I like Mark a lot. He's a very good employee, very well-liked by everyone, and has become a good friend of mine."

"Has he ever shown any romantic interest in you?"

ONCE AGAIN I FEAR

"He couldn't, Lucas. It's company policy that he and I couldn't date, since I am in management. He has never shown any inclination toward any relationship other than friendship where I'm concerned. We do have lunch together in the store restaurant occasionally, but it's always when we both happen to be there at the same time. We've never planned to meet there or anything like that. He's always very polite, very casual and just—nice. There's no other word for it."

"Let's skip over Mark, then, for the time being. Who else?"

I took a deep breath and let it out slowly. "There's Dru Warren, of course. I've been more open with her than anyone else, confiding a lot of things, including the original trouble with Judson. The others know nothing about him. Dru is thirty, divorced, and works for Chantal DuBois Cosmetics as an area rep."

"Just what does an area rep do?" Lucas asked.

"She's over all the other sales people at DuBois' regional offices, coordinating all sales campaigns. She arranges seminars for sales associates who sell DuBois products in department stores, day-long affairs where they learn of all the latest products and application techniques. The associates love it. They also love Dru, just as I do. She's wonderful, so full of life. Each year, the DuBois Company has a regional sales competition for the month of August. After the month, all sales are tallied, and the sales associate team who has the highest total, each receives dinners for two at one of the area's priciest restaurants. It's quite an honor for the associate teams. We've had two Devon's teams win it in the last three years."

I knew I was getting a little off the track, but Lucas waited patiently for me to get back to Dru herself. "As I said, Dru and I are very good friends. She comes to my apartment often and I go to hers, which is down in the Marina area. We have dinner out at least once a month, and sometimes attend other functions together. Some of those functions have to do with business, and some are just for fun, performances at American Conservatory Theater, trips to the de Young and Legion of Honor Museums, the Midsummer Mozart Festival, movies, a picnic at Stow Lake in Golden Gate Park, that kind of thing."

"Have you ever worked out at Star together?"

"Only once. Dru works out at the DuBois Spa, which is designed for society women who have a world of time and money to spend. Dru, as a management employee, has access to the spa at any time. It's a state-of-the-art facility, with all the amenities that wealthy ladies expect, and everything in the spa done in shades of pink. It was a real come-down for Dru to work out at Star." I had to laugh when I remembered Dru's reaction, which she carefully tried to hide, to the rather plain, but adequate Star Fitness Center.

"The truth is, though, that Dru knows almost everything there is to know about you, right?"

"Almost. I haven't told her about seeing Judson again, though. It just seems better not to discuss it with anyone who doesn't have to know. I'm really scared, Lucas, and I think the less people who know, the better. Don't you agree?"

Lucas was thoughtful for a moment and then agreed, "You're probably right. I can't think of anything that could be gained by telling everyone around you. Also, the person who's responsible could feel a bit more confident, realizing that no one around you knows what is happening. It might make him or her more apt to slip up. Do continue to keep things quiet for the time being."

"Oh, I did tell a of couple people that I'd seen someone that I had thought might be dead. That was after I saw Judson near my apartment. They had sensed that I was worried about something. Let's see, I think it was just Greg and Mark. I tried to pass it off as nothing important. Greg did bring it up at lunch today, though, asking me if I had seen the guy again? I just shrugged it off and changed the subject. I wondered at the time why he asked me about it. I can only hope that Greg is just concerned about me, as a friend would be."

"Yes, let's hope so. Tell me about Greg," Lucas prompted.

"Well, Greg is the person I depend on most, uh, along with Trish, of course. He's young, full of fun, handsome, as you probably noted. There doesn't seem to be any conceit in him, though. It's as if he just takes his looks for granted—no big deal. I would imagine he has girls after him all the time; I know there are some sales associates that get positively breathless when Greg is around. He doesn't date anyone in the store,

ONCE AGAIN I FEAR

though, and has said he thought that doing so would be a very bad idea. Co-worker dating can get pretty messy, when the relationship breaks up. He grew up here in the city; I think his parents live in Pacific Heights."

"So, they aren't exactly poverty cases?" Lucas asked.

"I would say not. Greg has a lot of class; it's obvious he's been exposed to, shall we say, the finer things of life." I smiled, remembering Greg's flawless style of dressing and his excellent manners.

Lucas continued to probe. "He also would have met a lot of people in the social scene here in this area, true?"

"I suppose so. He and I have talked some about his family and his growing up years, but not in deep detail. I know he has a few friends that live in Pacific Heights, but he lives in an apartment on, oh, I'm drawing a blank on the street name. I definitely don't know if his family knows the Bards. They well may, that's for sure. Again, as in the case of the other people I know, I can't imagine that Greg would be in on this."

"Let's move on, then; is there anyone else you can think of?" Lucas asked.

"I've become acquainted with, I think, four people who come to Star regularly. I don't think, however, that I've told any of them much about myself. I think they know I'm a buyer at Devon's, but not much else. We mostly talk about abs and triceps, things like that." Lucas laughed and sipped the last of his iced tea.

"And, of course, there's Damon," I continued. "He's about twenty-six, I think. He earned a physical education degree at Northern Arizona University in Flagstaff and moved here because he knows the owner of Star, John Page. He's buying into the business, now. Damon is very good at his job; he's fully certified by the American College of Sports Medicine. He also went up to the University of Colorado and took a summer course with a professor who specializes in training personal trainers. Besides all that, he's a really nice person, and doesn't come on to the clientele. I've been going to Star for the entire six years I've been here, and Damon has been there four of those years. His family, mom, dad, two sisters, and a brother, live back in Flagstaff; they own a restaurant, I think. He speaks very highly of them. He has a girlfriend, Theresa, a young woman who teaches at the City College. I've never met her and don't even know her last name."

Our server came to refill our tea glasses and asked if we wished dessert. We ordered spumoni, having no room for anything heavier.

"So, you and Damon are friends and have never been anything else? Right?" Lucas asked. It was a professional query, but I suspected he had a personal interest in my answer.

"That's it. I trust Damon. Actually, I have to trust him, since I depend on him so much for my physical training. I was in good shape when I started at Star, from all my years of ballet, but Damon has taught me a lot about exercising for muscle development—actually, muscle definition. That's all I can say about him."

The server set our spumoni in front of us along with spoons, which obviously had been kept in the refrigerator.

"So you have studied ballet?" There was admiration in his voice.

"Lots of years of ballet," I answered.

"I would like to see you dance sometime," Lucas said, obviously meaning it.

"Maybe that can be arranged. I use an aerobics room in Star sometimes, and practice my ballet. I paid to have a barré installed there, just for my use. I'm sure you could come with me sometime."

"I'm looking forward to it," Lucas said. "I'll bet you're very good."

"I'm pretty good, but not nearly as good as my mom was. She had a chance to audition with the San Francisco Ballet, but turned it down to marry my dad." I felt tears threatening to well up.

Gulping a deep breath, I continued. "I suspect she hoped I would fulfill her dream of becoming a ballerina, but I just wasn't quite of that quality. I really don't believe I was a disappointment to her, though. In fact, she was my biggest supporter in my career pursuit. I wish you could have met her, Lucas. She was the most beautiful woman I've ever known, both physically and in her spirit. Love just oozed out of her every pore; at least that was my mental image of her. I learned, after her death, how much she had done for so many people, things I never even dreamed. She was wonderful."

At that moment, our eyes met across the candlelit table, and I felt a flow of warmth between us. We sat in silence, no words needed.

ONCE AGAIN I FEAR

As we were finishing the last of the ice cream, Lucas' pager let out a low, unintrusive beep. "I'll bet that's Bently. I'll go out in the foyer and call him on my cell phone. Be back in a jiff."

He was gone only about five minutes before he slipped back into his chair opposite me. "They found the Toyota, abandoned about three blocks from Union Square. It's being towed back to headquarters, where the forensic team will go over every inch of it.

Let's hope Bard got careless and left some clue in it."

Chapter 30

It was getting a bit late, and I had a busy day ahead of me on Saturday, so Lucas drove me directly home. At the door of my apartment building, he handed me my plastic-covered suit, which I slung over my left shoulder.

Before I took my key out of my purse, Lucas took my right hand in both his large, strong ones. "I've certainly enjoyed this evening, Rachelle. It would be wonderful to have another just like it, but without our having to discuss all this distressing business you're going through."

I sighed and concurred, "That would improve things a lot. But I did enjoy it, too, Lucas, really. Thanks for taking me to that wonderful restaurant; I didn't realize it was there."

"I'm off until Tuesday, so I'll be free tomorrow, but I take it you'll be busy all day getting ready for your trip," Lucas said. "Would it be okay if I give you a call in the morning, if you are going to be here? I suppose I just want to assure myself that you're safe. Besides, I like talking to you."

"Ditto to that. Do call; I'll be looking forward to it. You could come over tomorrow evening and I'll fix us some dinner here. Would you like that?"

"Does San Francisco have cable cars?" Lucas asked with a grin. "Just tell me the time."

"I'll have my packing done in the morning, and I'll be back from my hair appointment about a quarter to five. So, come over about five-thirty. That way we'll have plenty of time to talk."

ONCE AGAIN I FEAR

"That sounds mighty fine to me, beautiful lady." Lucas smiled at me, a slow, warm smile and then raised my hand up to his lips.

No man had ever kissed my hand before. It was, somehow, a very intimate kiss. I felt warmth flooding through me, and something strange happening to my knees, a pleasant weakness. I knew in that moment that I was in love with Lucas Dayton, with a love that I had never known before. Nothing like the wild madness with Judson, or the shy, self-conscious emotion that I had felt for others. Those past sensations faded into nothingness compared to this.

I wanted, more than anything, to go into Lucas' arms and have him hold me close, but I knew that the magic of this moment would be broken if I did. We stood there on the sidewalk, with space between us, but it seemed that we were melding into each other, as close as any two people can be. Somehow, I knew, without doubt, that Lucas was feeling the same thing. He looked into my eyes and smiled again, holding my hand close to his heart.

How long we stood like that I don't know, perhaps only seconds, but it was an eternity full of promise. Finally, he lowered his hands, still holding my hand, and murmured, "Rachelle, I'm so overjoyed that I met you. I believe tonight is only the beginning of something wonderful. Don't forget, I'll call you in the morning." He squeezed my hand and, reluctantly, I thought, let go of it.

I retrieved my key and inserted it into the lock, hardly aware of my own movements, my hand shaking. "Until tomorrow morning, then," I said, and opened the door. When I had stepped inside, Lucas turned and walked to his car, looking back over his shoulder to wave at me as I stood in the doorway.

I lay in bed that night, my heart feeling as if it would burst. Lucas! Lucas! I found myself saying his name aloud, savoring it on my tongue. It had never entered into my fondest dreams that love could be this delicious, this overwhelming. For the first time in many days, the dark shadows could not find their way into my room. I breathed deeply, a freshness, an excitement filling my being. The frozen core of my soul had melted, the exquisite oil of gladness flowed where the coldness had been. I was not afraid to love Lucas Dayton. I'm in love! I'm in love! I wanted to sing it to the top of my lungs!

155

With great difficulty, I finally fell asleep. My dreams were filled with the images of laughing, blue-green eyes and warm, strong hands. At last, in the dream, he was reaching his arms to me, and I was running into them. Suddenly, I woke with a start, expecting to see him standing in my room.

Sunlight streamed through filmy white curtains, and painted shining, geometric patterns on my bed. It was as if the world were saying to me, "Wake up, I want to share your joy."

To my surprise, I saw by my bedside clock that it was eight o'clock. I jumped out of bed, upsetting Tache, who slept at the foot, and started toward the shower. Then the phone rang.

When I picked it up, the voice that made my heart sing, said, "Good morning, beautiful lady. I hope this isn't too early; I couldn't wait a minute longer."

"No, not at all." I tried to keep my voice from betraying too much of the emotions that he aroused in me. "I'm just getting going here, but talking to you will be the best way to do that." I found, to my consternation, that I was giggling. When had I last done that?

"Did you have a good night's sleep?" Lucas asked. I suspected he was fishing to see if I had been thinking about him. That idea pleased me beyond belief.

"I did—slept like the proverbial log. My dreams were very pleasant, though." I laughed, my giggles now under control.

"And did a certain police officer invade those dreams?" Lucas asked.

"Oh, he was the main character in the whole scenario," I answered. "Very lovely dreams, I must say." This was what he wanted to hear, I was sure.

"In my case, I hardly slept. My thoughts were whirling around, constantly drifting from here, on Pine Street, over to Clay Street and up the elevator to the third floor. A beautiful lady with warm brown eyes and blonde-streaked hair was opening the door for me. Perhaps I was rehearsing for five-thirty this evening. Beautiful lady, that seems like an eternity from now."

"Now, you're tempting me to ask you over for breakfast, Lucas. I can't do that, of course, with all the things I have to do—much as I'd like to. I'm sure you can find something to do until then, right?"

ONCE AGAIN I FEAR

"You're right; I can find something really intellectually stimulating to do, such as cleaning my apartment. Hey, I may even take an exciting trip to the super market." He was laughing, his laughter echoing the joy that was in my heart.

"Now," he continued, "I had better hang up and let you get started with your packing. I'll see you promptly at five-thirty, so tell your hairdresser not to take any extra time, okay?"

"I promise. And, Lucas, don't expect anything too elaborate for dinner. It'll be something thrown together, without a lot of planning and preparation."

"Oh, don't worry; I'll probably not even taste it, anyway. I'll be concentrating on my dinner companion. Bye now, beautiful lady, until five-thirty."

"Until five-thirty," I replied.

I laid the phone in its cradle and stood with my arms wrapped around myself, breathing deeply of the seemingly perfumed air of my room. The whole world was scented with roses and warm spices. Imagine, love has a scent, I marveled out loud.

The day moved past amazingly fast. I had thought the hours would drag. Before I could even think, I had all my bags packed, the house prepared for my absence, and I was sitting in the chair at my hairdresser.

My hair had been shampooed and trimmed and the weaving process begun. The process was a slow one, each strand, which would be lightened, daubed with the lightening mixture and wrapped in foil. Afterwards, I would be put under a hot dryer to speed the lightening process. I always had to laugh at the sight that met my eyes in the mirror. My head looking like something from a science fiction movie, flat, foil tendrils sticking out in every direction. My hairdresser, Shamika Jones, was a genius when it came to getting just the right shade, not too light and not too dark, to compliment my light brown color. The finished product made my hair appear to have been exposed to the sun for weeks.

While I sat under her ministrations, she eyed me closely. We had become good friends and she knew me quite well. I think she immediately sensed my joyful mood today. Her black eyes were full of questions.

157

"You're in love." Shamika stated flatly. "I know all the signs, and you have 'em all, girlfriend."

A smile was wreathing her walnut-hued face, an extra sparkle in her eyes.

"I can't hide a thing from you, Shamika," I exclaimed, laughing. "Oh, yes, I'm in love, wonderfully, completely."

"Wow, it's about time, girl. I've wondered for years why a beautiful, nice lady like you wasn't hitched. Who's the guy?"

"His name is Lucas Dayton, and he's a police officer. He's wonderful!"

"Lucas Dayton, huh? Hey, I know Officer Dayton. He came here to the salon a couple times when we had some vandalism. He's a real cool guy, very polite and nice. Gorgeous, too! Officer Dayton? That's awesome!"

"It is, Shamika. I haven't told him I love him yet, and he hasn't said he loves me either, but I'm sure, very sure, that he does. I dreamed of him all last night. We're having dinner together again tonight, this time at my apartment."

"And dessert?" she asked a twinkle in her eyes.

I knew what she meant, and it startled me. I had not had any such thoughts about my relationship with Lucas. "No, Shamika, no 'dessert', as you call it. Lucas and I are both Christians and we wouldn't do that before marriage, I assure you."

Shamika grinned. "I'm sorry, girl; I should have known that's how you'd feel. It must be nice to have that kind of feeling about sex. I guess I got started on the wrong foot in that department, and it's hard to change my thinking and actions. I've wished many times that I could go back to my first experience and say a flat out no. Maybe my life would be different now. I've had so many men, that sex doesn't even mean much anymore."

There was a definite sadness in my friend's voice. "Shamika, God can take your life and make it all new again, if you ask Jesus into your life. That's a promise in the Bible. At that point, it would be as if you were a virgin again. And, from then on, the Lord would help you to remain a 'virgin'. I've talked to girls, and guys, for that matter, who have made that decision and never turned back."

ONCE AGAIN I FEAR

"My mama took me to church all the time when I was a kid. Of course, when I reached my teens, I fought tooth and toenail to keep from going. Now, listening to you talk, I can remember being told something about being a new creature. Could I really be a new creature?" I felt she wanted very much for me to reassure her that it was true.

"Shamika, God cannot lie. When He promises something, He means it, period! I learned in my own life how easy it is to come to Jesus. All you have to do is tell Him that is what you want. He'll forgive anything and everything you have ever done and set you on a new track." I wanted very much to see the sadness gone from those lovely dark eyes.

"Would you pray for me, Rachelle?" There were tears starting to glisten in her eyes.

"I would be delighted to pray with you, right here and now." We were in a private booth, so no prying eyes were staring at us as we linked hands and prayed together.

"Thank, you, Rachelle," Shamika said. "I feel great, like a big weight just lifted off me. I think this sex thing is what has bothered me most in my life, and hearing from you that there was a solution was just what I needed to hear. I'm going to call Mama and tell her that I'll be going to church with her tomorrow." She laughed a merry little laugh.

Suddenly, I looked in the mirror and saw my science-fiction image staring back at me and burst into laughter, in which Shamika joined. Oh, God is good, I thought.

Chapter 31

My doorbell rang promptly at five-thirty, and Lucas stood there in the hall, a bouquet of pink tea roses in his hand, his coat over his arm. I ushered him in and accepted the roses. "This is so sweet of you, Lucas. You couldn't have known that I adore tea roses!"

"I knew it in my heart," he said teasingly, as he laid his coat on a chair. "I'm so glad to see you, beautiful lady. I couldn't have made it through the evening without seeing you."

I set the roses on a table in the foyer and turned toward Lucas. Without hesitation, we were in each other's arms, clinging, our hearts beating against each other. Then, his kiss was on my lips and my heart melted, leaving me shaking with delight. It was a warm, sweet kiss, gentle, but full of emotion. This was not a hard, demanding kiss like those that I had experienced with Judson. Instead, it was a caress of love, but also respect, asking nothing but what was given at the moment.

He held me tightly, breathing deeply against my ear and saying my name softly. I loved the way he smelled, a faint hint of soap mixed with the indescribably wondrous scent of his skin. I clung to him, feeling the strength of his body, knowing it was right that my arms should be around him. It was as if I had come home, to a place where I belonged and had always belonged.

"I love you, Rachelle," he whispered, kissing me again, longer this time.

When I could catch my breath, I said, "Oh, Lucas, I love you, too. My heart is so full right now that I can hardly speak."

ONCE AGAIN I FEAR

His eyes mirrored my feelings; his words confirmed them. "I've never felt like this before, Rachelle, never. I feel you are the one God has had for me all these years. That's why I could never get too serious about anyone before; you were out there waiting for me." His lips touched mine again, a light, gentle touch.

"I feel as if I've walked into a whole new world," I breathed happily, "one that I could only dream of before. I was just thinking that I feel, here in your arms, that I've come home. It's a delicious sensation." I laughed with pure joy.

"That's remarkable; I was thinking an almost identical thought. We belong together, Rachelle. I knew it the minute I saw you at Star, so scared, so vulnerable, and needing someone to help you. There was this big twang on my heart strings, if you know what I mean. I wanted, in the worst way, to walk over to you and hold you in my arms and tell you that I would be there for you. It really shook me up. All I could think of was you, from that moment one." He looked at me, his eyes traveling over each of my features, a smile on his lips.

"After I went to bed that night," I told him, "I thought of you, over and over, remembering how compassionate you had been and how willing to listen to me. I also remembered your blue-green eyes and your smile. Maybe God was trying to tell me, then, that you were the one I had waited for. But it was last night, outside the apartment door, that I knew, for sure, that I loved you, and sensed that you felt the same way. I do love you, Lucas."

He kissed me once more, a kiss that told me that everything he had said was true. I returned the kiss with all my heart.

We finally pulled apart, and Lucas was the first to speak, his voice a little shaky. "Well, I think we should find out what the lady chef has prepared for us, don't you?"

"Oh, indeed," I managed to say, "I suspect it's her gourmet hamburgers and cole slaw, from the deli, of course." I led the way to the kitchen and motioned toward a bar stool. "Sit down and the lady chef will serve you, sir."

As we ate, we found ourselves laughing constantly, everything joyful and funny. Tache sat at our feet, watching us curiously. We couldn't keep our eyes off each other. A few times, we paused to share light kisses, kisses tasting of mustard and ketchup, but delightful, anyway.

After clearing the dishes and starting the dishwasher, I led the way into the living room. We sat close together on the sofa, holding hands, his arm around me, while the piano music of Byron Janus, playing Chopin, streamed from my stereo. Tache curled up on a chair and was soon fast asleep. I wanted this time to go on forever.

"Rachelle," Lucas said slowly, "we're going to get you through this terrible time, and, then, we'll talk about our future. Our relationship has happened very fast, but I feel it's God's plan. We both know we are together permanently, don't we?"

"Oh, yes, Lucas. It has, certainly, been breathtakingly fast, but I couldn't imagine life without you, now." Again, my heart felt incredibly full.

"Okay, that will hold us together for now, baby. Let's get past this troublesome time, and, then, we'll talk about where we go from there. I'm probably going to be impatient, but we'll have to let God show us His time for everything. For now, let's try to keep our mind focused on finding a solution to this mystery and making sure that Judson Bard is out of your life forever. I have more reason than ever, now, to want this thing cleared up. It breaks my heart to see you so frightened of that man, and it also scares me to death to think that he could hurt you. I'm going to keep after Keffler and everybody else on the force to catch him and bring him to justice." He leaned his cheek against my hair, sitting quietly holding me.

Suddenly, he turned to me and, with a serious look on his face, said, "I think right now is the best time to tell you something and say it straight out. I will never try to get you into bed before we are married." The statement startled me, but the mention of marriage gave me a deep, lovely thrill. He was saying that he knew we would eventually marry. I certainly agreed with that.

He continued. "I want you to know that I'm still a virgin. That may be hard to believe, but, though I'm probably the only twenty-seven-year-old, male virgin in San Francisco, it's true. There's a story behind it. I was a late bloomer, where girls were concerned. I didn't have my first date until my senior year in high school, and that was nothing serious. I was always too busy with sports and working after school, that kind of thing. Also, I think it was because I had so many great women and girls around me, my mom, my very special sister, my grandmother, my aunts, that I didn't really feel any need of any kind of relationship with girls at that time. My dad was my pal, and he was a truly fantastic role model for me, teaching me respect for all women.

"The thing, though, that really made the difference happened in my freshman year of college. I was pursuing my Administration of Justice degree at Sacramento State. That semester, I was assigned a research paper in a sociology class. We had several topics from which to choose, but I chose to delve into the difference in attitude toward sex between men and women. I read everything I could find in the library, books and papers written by psychiatrists, psychologists, religious leaders, you name it.

"I must admit, I had started to lean toward the usual guy thing in college, see how many conquests I could make. I had not, however, carried out the plan to start on that course. To my surprise, in my research, I learned some things that really set me back on my heels. I learned, bottom line, that, most men, though there are many exceptions, think of sex as selfish gratification, but women connect it with love. They want to be loved, and even the promiscuous ones want the same thing. Many of them will get entangled in the social sex thing, and then can't seem to find their way out. Men also, definitely, do that. They lose sight of the real meaning of the relationship."

I remembered what Shamika had said to me that day and knew that Lucas was telling the truth.

"Well, after all that research, I decided I didn't want to use women for my own pleasure. I thought about all the women that I loved, and felt I couldn't let them down by hurting other young women. I vowed, then, that I would remain celibate until I could give my whole heart to a girl, when I made love to her. When I came to Christ, I knew that I had simply done what God wanted people to do. At that time, I added the vow that, even when I loved a girl, I would ask nothing of her before marriage. My relationship with Jesus was added incentive to remain pure, no matter how difficult it was at times, and how much razzing I got from other guys.

You can't even imagine what I've gone through with the guys on the force!"

He grinned at me and continued. "One thing that made me know that it could be done was hearing a Christian NBA star saying he, by choice, was still a virgin in his early thirties. I wrote him a letter thanking him for being so open about his commitment."

I was so surprised and pleased at this revelation, that I could hardly find words to express myself. "Lucas, I'm a virgin, too. It always seemed that there was some force holding me away from the wrong kinds of experiences with men. Judson pressured me constantly, but I never gave in. I've thanked God a thousand times, since, that I didn't. Like you, when I came to know the Lord, I knew that purity was His plan for me. A thought has nagged at me, though, that it would be doubtful I would find a man who was a virgin also, particularly at my age. This makes me love you even more, Lucas, I mean that." I leaned over and kissed him, my lips telling him what I was feeling.

As, with a sigh of happiness, I nestled my head against his shoulder, his beeper suddenly sounded, startling us out of our blissful cloud. We jerked apart, and he pressed the button on his beeper. "It's Bently. I told him to call me anytime, if he learned anything of importance. He's calling me from Central."

He reached for the phone on the white-washed end table, dialing a number rapidly. "Dale, hi, it's Lucas."

He sat listening for a full minute, nodding, his face becoming concerned. "Nothing else, then?" he finally asked. "Okay, so the prints definitely match Bard's. Well, we'll have to wait for the rest of the report. Thanks for calling me. I'm not sure what this all means, but let's hope we find out. Okay, take care, good buddy, and let me know if anything else comes up. I'm off duty until Tuesday, but keep me posted. Bye now."

He turned to me, frowning deeply. "They found Bard's prints all over the car. It's almost as if he doesn't care if we know it was him behind the wheel. The other thing they found may not make you too happy." He observed my face for a moment before continuing. "There was a card in the floorboard, with Judson Bard's thumb print on it. It was from the Star Fitness Center, and had Damon Ledyard's name imprinted on it."

ONCE AGAIN I FEAR

I sucked in my breath, shock reverberating through me. "Oh, no, not Damon, not Damon. He couldn't be the one! Lucas, no!"

"Let's not jump to any conclusions, baby. I know it looks bad for Damon, but we have to keep an open mind. There may be some logical explanation for the card. I know, I know, I sound more confident of that than I really feel. Darlin', you may have to face the fact that Bard's accomplice is someone you care for and trust implicitly. It could be Damon, as easily as it could be anyone else. I'm like you, though, I have a really difficult time accepting that, after seeing his concern for you Thursday night."

He ran a finger along my cheek, stopping to touch my chin. "Rachelle, when we find out who is behind this, I'm going to have to do a lot of praying, asking God to give me the strength not to beat him to a pulp. And, if it's a woman, I'll want very much to wring her neck. For every reason I can think of, we need to pray with all our hearts for God's help, guidance, and peace of mind. You need to get a lot of people praying for you, to provide a cover over you against the danger you're in. I remember a scripture in Acts, in which Paul was in great danger. The Lord told him to go ahead and speak His word. Then He told him, 'For I am with thee, and no man shall set on thee to hurt thee; for I have much people in this city.' Rachelle, God has much people in San Francisco, also. The other thing is we need to pray for the person who is abetting Bard, that he or she will feel pangs of conscience. God can move behind the scenes of this thing. Why don't we pray right now that the truth will come out and that Judson Bard will be brought to justice?"

I nodded and reached for Lucas' hands. We agreed then together about every detail of the situation. Lucas ended his prayer by asking God to wrap me in His protective arms and keep me safe. He also prayed that God would bless our relationship and make it what would be pleasing in His sight. I silently said 'amen' to that one. I knew, with the powerful attraction between us, how difficult it was going to be for us to remain true to our resolve. With God, all things are possible, I thought.

As I got into bed that night, I felt wide-awake, savoring memories of every detail of the evening, from Lucas' arrival, to our last kiss at the door. Lucas loves me, I thought, over and over again. I had known it, really, before he told me, but just hearing him put it into words was more precious than anything I had ever experienced. Someday, I thought, I will be Rachelle Dayton, Mrs. Lucas Dayton. Such a glorious thought.

Suddenly, I wanted to share it with Dad. He would still be up, I knew, so I dialed the number, a big smile on my face.

He answered with a note of alarm in his voice; few people would call at eleven p. m.

"Dad, it's Rachelle; I just had to call you!" I heard the giggles start again, but I didn't care; this was Dad. "I've got the most wonderful news to tell you."

"Have they caught Bard?" he asked hopefully. I had called him after my second encounter with Judson, at Star.

"Oh, I wish I could tell you that, but this is even better, I think. I've found someone who is incredibly wonderful, and I am head over heels in love." My words were a song in my heart.

"Rachelle, that is what I have wanted for you for so long. I don't like to think of you alone. Tell me all about it, baby." I could tell he was very happy to hear my news.

"His name is Lucas Dayton, and he is a San Francisco police officer. Remember when I told you about the police officers who came to Star, after Judson grabbed me on the street? Well, Lucas was one of them. He immediately realized the depth of my fears and took it upon himself to protect me. He told me he knew immediately that I was the one for him. Isn't that awesome, Dad?"

"Honey, you're talking to someone who knows all about that. The minute I laid eyes on Annabel, I knew she was mine. Just like that." He was laughing, enjoying our sharing.

"Let me tell you," he continued. "As you know, we met at a party, right? Well, when I first saw Annabel, she was standing perhaps twenty feet away from me. She was so beautiful! My heart about jumped out of my mouth, I swear it. I went toward her, as if a rope were pulling me, until I was standing next to her. Someone I knew was there, too, and introduced us. At that moment, I wondered how I could go about asking her, that very night, to marry me, without her thinking I was a raving lunatic. When she turned those beautiful green eyes on me, I saw a startled

ONCE AGAIN I FEAR

look, as if she felt the exact thing I did. When we shook hands, both our hands were trembling. The handshake turned into hand-holding. Very soon, we left the party together—fortunately I had come alone and she with a group. I told her I loved her about an hour later."

"She felt the same way about you, too, Dad; she told me that many times. She said when she looked at you she felt she was drowning in those wonderful brown eyes of yours. She told you she loved you that night, too, didn't she?"

"You bet she did, and that made me feel ten feet tall."

I knew he was telling me this so I would know he understood how love could happen without warning.

"Oh, Dad," I said, "I kept thinking about Lucas all that evening, after I met him, remembering his smile and how his eyes sparkle with blue-green lights. He came to take me to work the next morning and had breakfast with me. We talked and talked—it was so great! Then he picked me up after work and took me to the most wonderful Italian restaurant." I purposely left out the attempt on our lives. Dad didn't need to know that, now.

"Do you know when I knew I loved him? This may sound really old-fashioned, but Lucas kissed my hand at the apartment house door. At that moment, I loved him with so much love, that I could hardly stand it. I could see he felt the same way. He called me this morning first thing and I had to confess to him that I had dreamed of him all night. He said he had thought of me most of the night. Isn't that fantastic?"

I caught my breath deeply; emotion was threatening to overcome my ability to talk. "Then, Dad, he came over this evening. He brought me pink tea roses, my favorite. Then, we looked at each other, and, without even saying anything, we were holding each other and kissing, saying everything we felt. I thought my heart would explode inside me with pure joy. Oh, Dad, I love him so much! I have never been so happy in my life, even with this cloud hanging over me. I feel, now, that everything is going to be okay; it has to be. Oh, I forgot the most wonderful thing of all; Lucas is a Christian, a real, committed Christian. Our shared faith is the thing that convinces us that this was God's plan for our lives.

"I know this is extremely fast, but please believe me, it is the real thing. I feel so totally right with Lucas. We prayed together tonight before he left."

"Baby, I am overwhelmed. As I said, I have prayed for this to happen to you. Now that it has, my joy is totally full. One thing that bothers me, though, is thinking what Bard might do, when he learns you are involved with someone else. Baby, be careful, please." There was a heart-rending plea in his voice.

"I promise, Dad. Lucas is taking me to the airport in the morning, and I should be safe in New York. After I return, Lucas has promised to enlist the help of his fellow officers to provide me the protection I need. Pray for me, Dad; that is the best protection I can have. I have felt God's hand on me, literally, and I know nothing can happen to me without His knowing."

"I'll ask the people at Our Savior to pray for you, too. My own prayers have been bombarding Heaven for six years."

"That's all I need to hear. I love you, Dad. As soon as I get back, I'm going to make plans to bring Lucas down to Saratoga. You'll love him."

"I'm sure I will, baby. I will pray for God's blessing on him, too."

I lay in bed thinking not only of Lucas, but also of my Dad. The two men that I loved most in the world. Dad had always been the man in my life, but, now, he was very willingly stepping back and letting Lucas have that number one place. Dad and Lucas would be friends, I knew it. Perhaps Lucas would, in a way, be the son that Dad had never had. I certainly hoped so.

The one thing that marred my happiness was the news that Damon's card had been found in the Toyota. There was a possible explanation for that which I didn't even want to contemplate. Surely, though, Damon's cards were in lots of cars in San Francisco. Perhaps Tony Bianci had, at some time, come into the gym. And, also, Judson could have simply picked it up in the car. I wanted to believe that, so I felt some comfort.

Sleep crept into my body, softly, pleasantly. Then, I was startled by the phone ringing. Could it be Lucas?

Picking it up, I said a quick "Hello".

"Hi, sugar, all ready for dreamland?"

Horror literally shook me. Judson! How had he gotten my number? It was unlisted, and very few people had it. I couldn't say a word, just sat shaking. "Oh, sugar, you're surprised, aren't you? I wanted to let you know I'm thinking of you. Your boyfriend's gone and you're all alone. Why don't you let me come up and keep you company in that big bed. We'll watch the sun rise through those sheer, white curtains. Of course, your cat will have to find somewhere else to sleep."

I nearly choked, the horror too great to bear. He knew all about my room and my cat. How? How?

I could take no more and slammed the phone down. I was weeping uncontrollably now, and buried my face in my pillow. I felt so vulnerable. Had he been in my apartment? If so, how? And could he get in again? I had a dead bolt and a chain on my door, but would that stop him? Oh, God, help me, help me.

A warm hand again was laid on my shoulder, and the horror subsided. I was surrounded by prayer, Lucas' and my Dad's. Nothing could hurt me.

The phone rang again. I picked it up and slammed it down again. Then I laid the receiver on the table. I didn't like to do that, for fear someone else might try to reach me, but I couldn't bear to hear that nightmarish voice again.

I lay back on my pillow and Tache came to lie close to me. I stroked her soft fur, and she purred contentedly. Praying to my Lord, I willed myself to relax, imagining Lucas' arms around me, and that warm, invisible hand on my shoulder. Peace seeped into me, a bit at a time, and soon I slept.

Chapter 32

The next morning, I woke early, a little after six. I had set the alarm for six-thirty, so, on waking, I reached to shut it off, and put the phone back on its cradle. For a few minutes, I lay, gathering my thoughts. I tried to keep the fear of Judson Bard's intrusion into my safe little world from returning in full force.

Who was doing this to me, telling Judson such personal things about me? I was reasonably sure that he had not been in my apartment, so it had to be someone who had been here. That took in a lot of people, Damon, included. But it also included Dru, Mark, Greg, Trish, and, of course, numerous people from my church.

Who, among all those people, had been in my bedroom and knew Tache slept on my bed? I searched through my memories, trying to think of anyone who had had the chance to go into my bedroom. Of course, almost everyone took a trip to the guest bathroom during the evenings when I had had dinners here. It would be easy for any one of them to detour into the rest of the apartment, the two bedrooms and my own bathroom. What else had Judson been told about my home?

Tache moved from my feet up to where my hand lay, pushing her head into my palm. She loved having her head rubbed. I obliged her, the touch of her warm fur comforting.

My mind, then, turned to Lucas. My Lucas. He had said we would be together permanently, the thing I wanted most in all the world. We belonged to each other, and would for the rest of our lives. I closed my eyes and thanked God for this great gift that had been given to me so suddenly, so unexpectedly. Even Judson Bard and his accomplice could not take away my joy at finding such a precious love.

Lucas arrived about twenty minutes after seven. When he kissed me warmly, I could smell the scent of his soap and shampoo. No expensive men's cologne for Lucas, just fresh cleanness. I was struck by all the differences in Lucas, compared to Judson, so many little things, but things that meant so much to me: His gentleness, his concern for my wishes, his down-to-earth qualities, the purity of him. Yes, purity, as I knew now.

He held me for a few minutes, gently stroking my hair and kissing my face, my nose, my chin, my lips. I had never felt so loved, so secure.

It was with difficulty that we finally let go of each other, and went to the kitchen to share coffee and toast.

When we were finishing, Lucas took a final drink of his coffee and set the cup down. "I can hardly bear thinking of your going away for six days. I am going to miss you more than you know."

"I do know, my darling," I assured him. "I wish I didn't have to go, but it is essential that I round out our spring offerings. I'll be thinking of you every minute, I promise you. I'll call you every morning, say about eight. Oh, but that would be about five a.m. here. Would that be too early for you?"

"That would be fine. I'll make sure I'm right by the phone," Lucas promised.

"At least we'll be able to hear each other's voices; that should be some comfort to us. Oh, Lucas, I do love you. I think I have had to grow a bigger heart to hold all the love I have for you." Again, the giggles were threatening. I had to remind myself that I was twenty-nine, not sixteen.

Lucas leaned over and kissed me softly. "Baby, I never had any idea that I could love anyone as much as I do you. And, do you know, I don't think we would feel this much for each other if the Lord wasn't behind it. He is the one who has placed this love in out hearts. Does that sound like some kind of fantasy?"

"No," I answered emphatically. "I think this has God's anointing on it; is that theologically correct? The other night, in front of the apartment, I had the sensation that you and I were melding into each other, not physically, of course, but spiritually. That has to be of God."

A look of wonder was on Lucas' face. "That's exactly what I felt at that moment. You knew it, didn't you? I believe the Lord has something special for us, perhaps something he wants us to do together for Him. That is one of the things we will have to find out as we yield to His will for our lives. In the meantime, I, personally, am just going to enjoy to the fullest being with you and loving you. Also I want to tell you, I will spend a lot of time delighting in the fact that you love me. That is miraculous, in my estimation." I could swear he was on the verge of giggles, too. I wasn't sure, though, that men giggled. Whatever it was, it was a happy sound.

"Lucas, please be careful" I cautioned, suddenly serious. "Judson will be after you, probably more so, since he will know I'm out of town. There will be so many opportunities for him to take aim at you, since you are out on the streets so much. I'll bet he has followed you, to see where you live. I can also be sure that he knows you're with the police. I just have this fear, that even your gun won't be protection enough. Just promise me you'll be alert every minute." It was a plea from my heart.

"I promise. As I told you, I'm off duty until Tuesday, and I'll be watchful everywhere I go. When I go back, I'll talk to Keffler about the possibility that I may become a target; let's hope he takes it seriously. Also, Bently and Mendez are already aware of that possibility. Perhaps we're wrong, though; it may have been simply that I was there, when he tried to run you down. Again, prayer will be the best protection." He touched my face, caressing my cheek.

I then, reluctantly, told him about Judson's call the night before.

Lucas slammed his fist on the breakfast bar. "This is incredible! Someone has given him your unlisted number and a description of your bedroom. First thing, when you get back, you will get your phone number changed. I can get an order of emergency to force the phone company to do it immediately, if that is necessary. Let me know if they want you to wait even one day. And give the new number to no one, no one." He stopped and grinned. "Except me, of course, and your father."

He returned to his serious expression. "Don't give it even to Trish, baby, I mean it. Give Trish the number of the security desk downstairs, and tell her that is an emergency number only. I think some people around you are going to have to be made aware that you are in danger; I

ONCE AGAIN I FEAR

can see no other choice. Another thing, get the phone company to put a block on Caller ID on your phone. We want to close off all means of your number falling into the wrong hands."

He got up and paced back and forth in the kitchen area. "We've got to find a way to narrow down who could be behind this thing. Right now Damon seems to be the prime suspect, but it is purely circumstantial. Let's find out how his card got into Bianci's car, to see if there is a logical explanation. I'm going to go have a talk with him."

"Lots of people probably have his card, Lucas," I offered. "It could be just a coincidence that Tony Bianci had one. And Judson was in the car. Perhaps he saw the card and it surprised him, to see a Star card there. He would naturally have picked it up. His accomplice, of course, knows that Damon is my trainer, which leads to the assumption that Judson also knows. So seeing his name on the card must have shaken him up."

"You make a good case for that scenario, darlin'," Lucas confessed, stopping his pacing for a moment. "You could be right, you know. It would be a real coincidence, though, you have to admit."

"Well, at least, this week, you won't have to worry about me, Lucas. I'll be safely stowed away in The Big Apple." I reached across the breakfast bar and took Lucas' hand. "Come back over here and sit with me. You're going to wear the soles off your sneakers."

Lucas grinned and came to sit by me, still holding my hand. "I get so angry when I think that there are two people out there plotting to harm you, Rachelle. It's almost more than I can stand. I'd really like to lock you in a safe room somewhere, with guards at the door, until we get that maniac and his buddy. While you're gone, I'm going to get together with a few other people on the force and see if we can't figure some strategy to catch Bard. It has to come to an end! You and I can't constantly be waiting for him to attack us. I want so much to start planning our future, but I don't want a dark shadow hanging over those plans."

"When I get back, Lucas, I'm going to have a talk with my pastor, Tom Lane. We're fighting a spiritual battle, I'm sure; perhaps Tom can give me some guidance from God's word about how to do that. If you had seen Judson that hideous day, you would have seen something satanic in his eyes. Pure evil! I saw it again that night outside Star. I don't know how to fight that kind of spiritual warfare." I shuddered with my memories.

Lucas stood and drew me into his arms, holding me close. "My darling, I just ache inside when I think what you have seen and suffered. I'm sure you are right, that it was a satanic force driving Judson Bard. It's hard to imagine that that much malevolence could be in a human being, without its coming from Satan. That's a good idea to seek guidance. Perhaps I'll talk to my pastor, Doug West, too. He's been in the ministry probably forty years, so I imagine he's seen it all. The Lord is going to show us a way, Rachelle, I'm sure of it. Now, before you leave, let's pray together; prayer is our best weapon."

We knelt together, our arms around each other, and prayed to the Lord that we both loved and trusted. Once more, I felt the warm hand on my shoulder, telling me of God's presence in my life.

My flight was scheduled to leave at nine-forty-five, so we had to leave about eight fifteen, to get me there an hour before flight time. San Francisco International Airport isn't actually in San Francisco, but fourteen miles south of the city, almost all the way to Burlingame. The traffic on Highway 101, on an early Sunday morning, was relatively light, not the mad rush of weekday mornings. Lucas drove smoothly and with a skill that came from years behind the wheel of a patrol car. I watched his profile, memorizing every detail to hold in my heart for the six days I would be gone. A literal pain squeezed my heart when I thought of saying good-bye to him.

He sensed my observation of him and turned to smile at me. "I'm going to miss you, baby. I really wish I had a picture of you, so I could look at it while you're gone."

"I can fix that, love," I said. I took out my wallet and extracted a picture of me with my father, taken about six months ago. We had decided to have the pictures taken so that each of us could be reminded of our closeness even when apart. "I hope you won't mind also looking at my father; it's the only picture of me that I have with me. I'll get you one of me when I get back, I promise. I'll want this one back, then, of course."

Lucas took the picture and studied it, one eye on the road. "Beautiful, just beautiful; and you're not bad, either." We both laughed heartily. "I'm teasing, baby. You are so beautiful I'm surprised the camera could record it. I see a little resemblance to your father, but not a lot."

"I look more like my mother," I said. "However, I do have my father's brown eyes and a few touches, here and there, of him. I like that, looking like both my parents."

"I look like both my parents, too," Lucas said. "I have my mother's eye color, but she has light auburn hair, almost a strawberry blonde. I have Dad's brown hair and definitely his chin. The rest is just a blend of both of them, with a few assorted ancestors thrown in."

"It's a fantastic blend," I told him, "and I love it."

Lucas laid the picture on the console and reached for my hand. "I'm going to hang onto you until the last minute when you walk toward the plane. When you get back, I may not want to let go of you even for a minute." He turned and winked at me.

"If that were possible, I would go for it in a big way. We are going to have to do some real planning to have time together, you know, with your working nights, and having irregular days off, and my working rather strange hours, sometimes, during the day. Well, we'll have to work on it."

"Actually, with my schedule with three or four-day weekends, it might not be too hard. I always have the long weekends, but the days are rotated through the weeks. Oh, I haven't told you something. My rank now is Patrolman Q-four, the highest level as patrolman, but I should be getting my promotion to inspector before long. In other cities that would be 'detective'. We're like zee French—Inspector Cleuseau, remembair?" He kept a totally straight face.

I rolled my eyes. Should I encourage him? Oh, of course I should! I had to laugh.

He continued, smiling now, "I've taken the test and passed very high, thank the Lord. That puts my name near the top of the list, so I'm just waiting for an opening. I really look for it to happen any day. Keffler is about to get his lieutenant rank, something that should have happened years ago. I think Keffler prefers working the streets and also likes the night shift. Refused to go on days recently when an opening came up. He wouldn't take the lieutenant test until just recently. Amazingly enough, he scored number one of all the ones taking it. When he moves up, one of our inspectors will move up to sergeant. It's a chain reaction thing."

"Speaking of Keffler," I said, "please try to find out why he's acting so strangely about my case. It's almost like he took an instant dislike to me, or something."

"I assure you that isn't true," Lucas asserted. "In fact, he told me that night after we came to Star, that he admired your courage. He said a lot of women would have been in hysterics, and not worth anything as a witness. He even observed that you were a 'looker'. Now, coming from Keffler, that's the ultimate compliment. No, he has some other reason for being reluctant, but, for the life of me, I can't figure it out. I'm going to keep trying, though."

I suggested that Lucas just let me off at the front of the airport and drive on home, without having to go park in the parking garage, but he wouldn't hear of it. He did let me off in front, and saw me safely accompanied by a skycap, with the promise that he would meet me at the ticket counter in a few minutes.

Greg was already in line when I got to the counter area. He came back to the end of the line where I stood, carrying his large suitcase and a carry-on bag. "I might as well wait with you, Rachelle;" he commented, "we'll be sitting together, anyway."

He surveyed my casual outfit, slacks, made of light-weight winter-white wool and a cashmere sweater to match, topped with a coat in the same shade. I wore taupe-colored flats with crepe soles. "You look as good in slacks as you do in a business suit," he complimented me, grinning.

"Thanks, Greg. I never would wear a suit and heels on a plane; casual clothes and flat shoes are safer in case of an emergency. I also wear clothes in natural fibers which don't melt in case of fire. I'm not at all paranoid, honestly, just cautious."

"I never thought of that. I guess I'm safe, though, all natural from the skin out." I liked the way he laughed, a youthful exuberance bursting forth. There was no way I could imagine that he was abetting Judson's pursuit of me.

Lucas trotted across the wide area beyond the ticket counter and stopped at my side. Greg looked startled. "Greg, you remember Lucas," I said.

ONCE AGAIN I FEAR

"Oh, sure. Hi, Lucas. Come to see our beautiful Rachelle off to New York, eh?"

"Coming to cry when she leaves," Lucas announced, with a grin. He put his arm around me and pulled me close to his side. "Now, it's my turn to tell you to take good care of her, Greg. You and I both know what a special lady she is."

Again, Greg looked startled, but nodded. "Hey, you bet, my pleasure. I think we have rooms booked right across the hall from each other, so I'll be on the lookout that no bad guys get her." He seemed to be teasing, but I had a sudden sense that he was serious. But why?

After checking our bags and getting our boarding passes, Greg and I, with Lucas holding my hand, walked the seemingly endless distance to the gate from which we were to board. We still had a few minutes until flight time. Lucas and I sat in chairs in the waiting area, and Greg, seeming to sense we wished to be alone, walked over to the window to watch planes landing and taking off.

"I get the feeling Greg is concerned about you, baby," Lucas said. "Do you have any idea why?"

"Not the foggiest. I'm as puzzled as you are. Do you think he knows something? And, if he's Judson's confederate, why would he show such concern for me? It doesn't make sense. If he isn't working with Judson, how would he have any conception that I'm in danger? Do you think I should question him?"

"Use your own judgment, just take it really easy. We don't want to scare anyone off. Perhaps if you just keep him talking, he'll open up and tell you what's on his mind, if he doesn't have anything really terrible to hide. I'm trying to remember that everyone is innocent until proven guilty. He may just be a nice kid that thinks all women need protection." Lucas laughed lightly, probably to take my mind off being worried.

I clung to Lucas' hand, dreading when I would have to let go of it and board the plane. His eyes hadn't left my face for an instant, his love for me shining brightly there. Suddenly, he let go of my hand and said, "Oh, I just remembered, I have a picture of me, if you want it."

"Does San Francisco have cable cars?" I asked laughing. "Of course, you dope, I want it."

177

He took from his wallet a picture of himself in his dark blue uniform, with the patch, depicting the city seal, on the shoulder and his seven-point star gleaming on his chest. His shoulders were straight, his blue-green eyes staring, somewhat mischievously, into the camera. That wonderful smile that I loved now smiled at me from the picture. "Oh, Lucas, it's just like you. I love it. I'll have it with me every minute I'm in New York. By the way what is the Latin inscription on the patch?"

"It means 'Gold in peace, iron in war.' Rather interesting, don't you think?"

"Sounds very San Franciscoish," I answered.

After I had put the picture in my purse, Lucas grabbed my hand again. At that moment, my flight was called and we stood, Lucas picking up my carry-on bag. It was a few minutes before the first-class passengers were called, and all that time, Lucas hung onto me, his arm now around me. When the call came, I took my bag, and he wrapped his arms around me, kissing me soundly right there in front of all the passengers. When I looked around, a bright-eyed little old lady caught my eye and smiled. Leave it to little old ladies to appreciate romance.

Greg sidled up to me and shook hands with Lucas. "We'll be seeing you Saturday night; I'm sure you will be here to pick up your lady."

Lucas grinned. "You can bet on it." He leaned over and gave me a short, gentle kiss and then stepped back. My heart constricted, and I fought not to cry. That would be silly; I was only going to be gone six days. When I got to the door and handed over my boarding pass, I turned and waved to Lucas one last time. Taking back our passes, Greg and I walked down the long jet sleeve to the plane.

Chapter 33

We landed at New York's La Guardia Airport in a driving rain, the runway totally invisible to me. I breathed a prayer for the pilot, as he landed the aircraft, so many lives in his hands. Other than a slight bump as the plane hit the tarmac, the landing was smooth.

After picking up our bags, Greg and I followed a skycap, pushing our luggage on a cart, to the main entrance. Outside, I stood hunched against the wind, trying to hold onto my shoulder bag and, at the same time, shield my face from the freezing rain. It was only two or three minutes before the limo, sent by Devon's New York, pulled to the curb, the driver swiftly jumping out to stow our luggage. He had to fight the cold, rain-sodden wind that whipped around him, threatening to blow away his neat chauffeur's cap.

I had never really gotten used to the royal treatment of having a limo waiting for me; Devon's always provided the service for all their people attending any store-related functions in the city. Greg, however, seemed to take it in stride. When we were seated in the spacious interior, I asked him, "You're accustomed to limo service, aren't you?"

He grinned and answered, "Yeah, I guess so. Anyway, my parents always had a limo to chauffeur us around. I remember I went to a public school in first and second grades. Mom insisted the limo take me and pick me up."

"That must have been nice," I remarked.

"Actually, it was pretty embarrassing. I was the only kid in school who arrived that way. I begged my mom to let me ride the school bus like the rest of the kids, but she wouldn't hear of it. No son of hers was going to go to school like the 'commoners'. Oh, she didn't say anything that derisive—Mom's really pretty nice—but I saw something near to that in her expression. I'm surprised she even let me go to a public school for those two years. I knew I was going to have to grin and bear it, in spite of all the joshing I got from the other kids. I suppose some were envious, I don't know. Well, in third grade, mom enrolled me in a private school, where my limo had to wait in line for all the other limos to unload their passengers. One good thing about being sent away to a boarding school, in my sophomore year of high school—no limo. Yeah, I'm too, too used to limos!" He shook his head, seeming to see the humor in his life story.

I knew this might be a chance to get him to open up to me. Here in this Italian leather-lined compartment, lit by lamps on each side, and shut away from the storm whirling around us outside. "You have a brother, don't you?" I asked, as casually as possible.

"A younger brother and, also, an older sister. My sister, Eileen, is five years older than I am. She went away to college when I was in eighth grade, and she wasn't really around much after that. Always off on a jaunt to Europe or spending time with friends in Malibu, that kind of thing. Then she got married right after college and went with her new husband to Japan. He works with a company that has offices over there. They were there two years and then went to Paris. That's where they are now."

"And your younger brother?"

"Trey is two years younger than I am. He's in his senior year at the Air Force Academy. Mom was pretty unhappy, when he told her he had applied for admission to the academy. She wanted him to go into the family business."

"Which is what?" I asked, trying to show only casual interest.

"Dad is the 'P' in P and R Investments Incorporated. That's Phillips and Rostow, with offices in ten major cities."

"What about you, Greg? Didn't they want you to go into the business, too?" I was genuinely curious about this.

ONCE AGAIN I FEAR

"I suppose so, but I had made it clear, when I was a kid, that I had no intention of doing that. Mom finally just shrugged and turned her attention to Trey. Thank God. I am not the least interested in stocks, bonds, annuities, and all that stuff, except in my personal finances."

I observed him closely as I said, "You did get a business degree. So how did you decide to go into buying?"

Greg fiddled with the leather piping on his armrest for a moment and then grinned at me. "I saw the ad in the paper and said to myself, 'That sounds interesting; maybe I'll try that.' Are you shocked that I would admit that to you?"

I had to laugh in spite of myself. I had been right to think of Greg as being a bit frivolous a year ago. "Oh, I'm shocked to the marrow," I told him. "Well, after working at Devon's for almost a year, what do you think?"

"It surprised me, Rachelle; I really liked it from the beginning. Now, I'm looking forward to being head buyer in one of Devon's stores, someday. I know I have a lot to learn, but I'm sure, now, that I can do it. What do you think?" He sincerely wanted to know.

"I have no doubt in the world that you can, Greg. I'm very pleased with your work, and your work ethic. You have a great deal of good taste to bring to the job, and your looks and charm certainly don't hurt."

Now, Greg blushed. I had been right, also, in feeling that Greg placed no great value on his looks. I wanted to relieve his embarrassment. "Greg, I'm not just flattering you. I'm simply stating a fact. You are, indeed, a good-looking, charming young man, and you also are very nice. I mean that. I think you also have a lot of common sense. Your decision not to date co-workers is one example. I could have told you that, but you came to that conclusion on your own; that's good common sense. I predict you will go far in this business."

"That means more to me than I can tell you, Rachelle, particularly coming from you. I think I admire you more than anyone I know. It was a lucky day when I was hired at Devon's."

We sat quietly for a while, watching the wet city streets outside our windows. The city was decked out for Christmas, but the colorful lights shone only a watery, dim light through the rain of this December night.

Because of the darkness and the rain, I could tell little of where we were at any given minute, but knew I could trust the driver, since Devon hired only the best.

Finally, I looked over at Greg and saw that he was watching me now. "May I ask you a personal question?" I asked him.

"Sure, anything."

"Do you have a girlfriend? Okay, I know that is a little personal, but I can't help being curious."

Greg laughed and answered, "I've been seeing someone for a few weeks. Her name is Penny. I'm not sure it's anything serious, yet. She's really cool, very funny, and smart as anything. She's a student at San Francisco State, studying, get this, biochemistry. I met her through some friends. One minute I think I'm in love with her, and, the next, I'm just not sure."

"Don't push things, Greg. When it's right, you'll know it." Lucas' face flashed into my mind, and my heart did its familiar somersault.

"You sound as if that comes from experience," Greg observed, a question in his eyes.

"Yes," I told him, "that's from experience."

"Lucas Dayton?" Greg asked. He then hastily added, "Now I'm the one who is getting personal."

"It's okay. Yes, I love Lucas Dayton, beyond my wildest imaginings. It's like a miracle has happened for us, a gift from God himself." I knew my face was reflecting the joy that was in my heart.

"That's funny you should say that about God. Penny talks like that. She said real love comes from God, and is a gift. She scares me sometimes talking about God. It's as if she's best friends with Him, or something. I feel sort of left out of the equation. Know what I mean?"

"I think so. I believe your Penny does consider God her best friend. I do too, Greg. He's with me every minute and I can depend on him completely. Sending me the love of my life was one thing with which I should have trusted Him, but I didn't know that until it happened. Lucas feels the same way about God, so it's something we can talk about and share."

ONCE AGAIN I FEAR

Greg was getting uncomfortable with the direction of our conversation; he obviously wasn't ready to hear more. I silently breathed a prayer for him and changed the subject. "Since you've lived in San Francisco all your life, you know a lot of people there, don't you?"

"Some I wish I didn't know. My family was very much into the society thing, parties, balls, good works, you name it. I hated some of those affairs that I had an obligation to attend, like cotillions, debutante balls, etcetera. Yuck! Then there were the parties they dragged me to. Worst of all, I hated some of the stuffed shirts that attended. All the talk about money, houses, cars, trips around the world! I, very early on, felt acutely revolted by the pomposity of those people. I wondered, sometimes, if they really cared about each other. It was if the gatherings were simply for the sake of bragging to each other about how much they had. I really wanted no part of that." He leaned his head forward and rubbed his forehead.

"I saw some of that, too, Greg. In Saratoga, my home town, and in San Jose, there were all those Silicon Valley millionaires, mostly self-made, so it was there. I never was impressed with it. Actually, I'm sure my parents weren't, either. My dad, particularly, was proud of what he had accomplished and acquired, but I never heard him brag about it. Mom couldn't have cared less. I think she would have been happy being June Cleaver." I had to laugh, picturing my mom in June Cleaver's kitchen.

"Do your parents still live in Saratoga?" Greg asked.

"My dad does. My mom died six years ago." Again, it hurt to say it to anyone.

Greg frowned. "I'm so sorry, Rachelle. I didn't know that. That must have been tough." He paused and glanced at me and then looked away. "I started to ask some questions, but I'm not sure what questions you would want to answer."

I decided to tell him something of my mother's death, to see what his reaction would be. "Someone killed my mother, Greg. He tried to kill me, also, but I escaped. It was more horrible than I can tell you."

Greg sat up straight and stared at me. "Rachelle, I had no idea. Was it someone you knew?"

183

"It was a man I had been dating; I had broken up with him. He didn't want to let go of me."

Greg's eyes were wide with horror. "Is that why Lucas Dayton is so protective of you?"

I nodded, still shaken by once more telling something of my story.

"But, if the man was caught, surely he's in prison."

"No, he got out on bail and skipped. Just like that. I'm sure he had help from his family." I turned to look out at the streets, now recognizing that we were close to the hotel.

A light seemed to dawn in Greg's mind. "Is that the person you saw recently, the one you thought might be dead?"

I sighed and nodded. "It was him, all right."

"Have you seen him again?"

I didn't know if, perhaps, I was telling Greg too much, but I saw no real harm in it, even if he were the one helping Judson. If he were, he probably knew all this already. He was some terrific actor, if he did already know, I thought.

"I have," I told him, not elaborating. "Lucas is taking every precaution he can to protect me."

"As a police officer, he has some means of protecting you, but not every minute." Greg watched me intently.

I felt a shock wash through me. "You know he's a police officer?"

"Yes. I was at a club one night, there in Union Square, and there was a disturbance. Someone called the police; Lucas Dayton was one of the officers who arrived on the scene. I really admired the way he handled it, kept his cool and settled everything down. Didn't even arrest anyone, just sent a couple guys home with sober drivers."

"So that's why you looked at Lucas so oddly when you first met him? And why you told him to look out for me? I wondered."

"I knew you had been worried about something ever since you mentioned seeing that guy. Of course, now, I know why. Then, when I saw you with Officer Dayton, I wondered if he was really your bodyguard, or something."

"A self-appointed bodyguard, I suppose," I confirmed, smiling at the young man across from me. Greg's recent actions were beginning to

ONCE AGAIN I FEAR

come clear to me. "You've been worried about me, haven't you?" I asked him.

Greg blushed a little and nodded. "I would be so crushed if anything happened to you, Rachelle. I consider you a terrific friend. I didn't know what was bothering you, but I felt it concerned that mysterious guy you had seen. It makes me feel so much better, knowing that Lucas Dayton is looking out for you."

"Lucas has been having his fellow officers help him watch out for me. I also have the Lord to watch me every minute, day or night."

As we pulled up in front of the hotel, I was filled with relief. I could scratch Greg off the suspect list; I knew now he had nothing but concern for me.

The week in New York was a whirl of activity. We buyers were wined and dined, royally, by the fashion houses showing their wares that week. I had to pace myself to make sure that I didn't end up worn out and totally frazzled. I made sure that I was in bed before midnight, even if I had to leave a party early. Also, I never drank anything but non-alcoholic beverages, so I kept a much clearer head than many of my fellow buyers.

Greg hovered around me, true to his promise to Lucas, walking me to my door each night, and waiting until I had closed and bolted it. I had the feeling he was sleeping across the hall with one eye open, and definitely both ears open. He didn't, however, show any fatigue from his constant vigil, always ready to go to the next event.

True to my word, I called Lucas each morning as soon as I was out of bed. His voice and words of love kept me going for the twenty-four hours until my next call.

On Tuesday morning, he had news for me. "Bently has been trying to reach Tony Bianci, but it seems the young man is out of town this week. I suppose his finals were over and he just took off for a little r and r. I really wanted to talk to him and see what he had to say. His car is sitting in the impound lot, waiting for him. Damon is also out of town for a few days, so no one has been able to question him. In the meantime, my darling, every officer in San Francisco is watching closely, with the hope someone will see Bard. Starting tonight, that will include me. We have a great bunch

185

of guys here, and I know they sense that I have more than professional interest in you."

"You didn't tell anyone?" I asked, pretending to sound hurt.

"Well, Win Keffler can wait to hear the news, at least until we find out what his problem is. I did tell Dale Bently and Amador Mendez that I had fallen head-over-heels for you. I don't think they were really surprised. I asked them not to talk about it to anyone else for a while, since you were at the center of an investigation. They saw the sense in that, but I think they are extremely pleased that the virgin cop has finally fallen in love." He laughed heartily.

I think I might have blushed if he had been with me, but, now, I laughed, too. "Lucas, you are so funny. Not many guys would see the humor in being teased about their chastity. But, then, as you pointed out, not many guys are chaste." Lucas really laughed at that. I felt a wave of happiness that Lucas and I had gotten close enough to talk so easily, about so personal a matter. I knew, too, that it was personal to both of us.

"Is Greg still watching over you?" Lucas asked.

"Like a mother hen. As I told you yesterday, I'm convinced that he has nothing to do with Judson Bard. In fact, I'm going to question him further and see if he knows the Bard family. He might be able to provide some insight, who knows?

"Rachelle, be careful, really. I think you're probably right about Greg, but you still have to be careful with everybody." There was deep concern in Lucas' voice.

"I promise I will. Any questioning will be done on 'little cat's feet', if you know what I mean."

"I trust your intelligence, baby, I really do. It's just that you are so warm-hearted, and probably don't see the bad in some people, when perhaps you should."

"I plead guilty to that, Lucas. I hate thinking anyone is capable of being evil. But, also, darling, I have seen the worst evil that can be in a human, so, now, I can accept the fact that it is a reality. Greg, though, is so transparent. It's as if I can look into his soul. Does that make sense? If you could have seen his face, his eyes, in the limo, I think you would agree with me. He really cares about me. Lucas, I rather suspect that if he and I were

ONCE AGAIN I FEAR

in different circumstances, and he wasn't so much younger than I am, he could have some pretty intense feelings for me. Honestly, I don't think he does now, but I think it would be possible under those circumstances."

"Perhaps I have to trust your feminine intuition on that, Rachelle. That may well be possible; therefore, he would never want to hurt you. Oh, by the way, I don't think it's so hard to imagine a guy falling in love with someone who is a wee bit older, do you?"

"Now, Lucas," I responded, laughing again. "Because I'm a year and a half older than you, I'll constantly have to remind you to respect your elders. So there."

"So that's the way it is, huh? Oh, well, I'll just have to make sure I never mention our ages again, won't I?"

"You may, anytime you wish, my darling," I answered. "I don't think, even if you had been six years younger, like Greg, it would have mattered in the least. I lost my heart to you, not your age."

We talked for a few minutes more and then I had to ring off to prepare for the day. Before hanging up, we prayed together as we had the day before. I replaced the receiver and picked up the picture of my handsome police officer, and kissed it. "I love you, Lucas Dayton," I informed the photograph. "It will be so wonderful when I'm your wife."

For the first time, I turned the picture over. On the back, in very feminine handwriting, were the words: "Lucas, this picture is for the girl you will love. Carry it with you, because you never know when you will meet her." It was signed, "Mom." I stood staring at the words. Did Lucas remember that they were written there? He hadn't mentioned them to me, when he gave me the picture. I would have to ask him. For now, I stood marveling at the sentiment expressed by the other woman in my Lucas' life. She would not be the kind of woman to hang onto her son. I was very anxious to meet this remarkable lady.

On Wednesday, the Bradford Ederly line was scheduled to be shown. That morning, Greg had gone out shopping for Big Apple gifts to take home to family members and his girlfriend, Penny. The rain of Sunday evening had turned to snow in the early hours of Monday, and had continued to fall intermittently. Greg, like most native Californians, relished the idea of getting outside to enjoy the winter scene.

At noon, he and I met in the ballroom where a luncheon was being served to all those who had tickets to the fashion show. We found our place cards and sat at the round table, covered in gray linen, with burgundy napkins folded into impossible shapes. Someday, I thought, I want someone to show me how they fold those things.

Greg, as usual, was dressed to perfection. His gray suit was perfectly accented with a blue shirt and a tie in darker blue, gray, and a muted magenta. His ash blonde hair lay in perfect waves above his forehead. What a handsome man, I thought. I hoped that Penny would be right for him, and would have a spiritual influence on him. It seemed to me, sitting there observing Greg, that he had become almost the younger brother that I had never had. Please, God, I prayed, let me be positive, beyond any doubt, that he has nothing to do with this Judson business.

He must have felt my eyes on him, because he turned and grinned. "This is a better place than the rooms where we saw the other shows. Nothing but the biggest and the best for Bradford Ederly. I've seen some enormous ballrooms before, but this has got to be the mother of them all. Wow! The Forty-Niners and the Jets could have a game in here, with plenty of room for the cheerleaders, and a heap of spectators. Let's see, over there, where that lady in red is standing would be the fifty yard line."

I followed his eyes and saw the lady in red, and, just beyond her, stood my friend, Barbara Crestwell. "Oh, there's Barbara. She'll be sitting with us. It's always so good to see her."

Barbara walked toward our table, stopping to greet people along the way. Barbara was a tall woman, near to six feet, probably twenty pounds overweight, but well-proportioned, and wore a perpetual smile. Her silver hair was cut in a perky short style that suited her ebullient personality perfectly.

When she finally arrived at our table, Greg and I stood, and I hugged her, feeling myself engulfed in long, strong arms. "Rachelle, I am so happy to see you again. I miss a lot about San Francisco, but I think I miss you most of all. Hey, I sound like Dorothy in The Wizard of Oz. Greg, how's it goin', kid?"

I saw Greg flinch, but then he grinned good-naturedly. He had met Barbara before and knew her motherly attitude toward younger people in the business. "Everything is going just great, Barbara," Greg answered. "You're looking good; that aqua wool looks stunning on you."

Barbara actually blushed. In spite of her breezy, devil-may-care nature, she also was susceptible to flattery, just the same as most women. "Oh, I like this boy, Rachelle," she announced and slapped Greg on the shoulder. "Come on, let's sit; they're about to serve the food. It's Lobster Newburg, guaranteed to add two inches to your hips."

We sat down, with me between Greg and Barbara. I loved Barbara. She had been my mentor at Devon's, but also my very dear friend. I loved her personality, her concern that everyone around her should feel comfortable. It seemed to me that she always talked in italics, and at mach-one speed, but she also took time to listen to what others had to say. Right now, she was listening closely to something Greg was saying, looking him directly in the eye, and smiling warmly.

My mind started to wander, back to San Francisco, back to Lucas. I loved these New York trips, but, now, I would have given up every minute of it to be back in Lucas' arms.

I didn't realize, for a few seconds, that Barbara was speaking to me. "Earth to Rachelle, earth to Rachelle." Barbara poked me, laughing merrily. "Rachelle, dear, you are a thousand miles away. Something very important must be on your mind."

"Oh, I'm sorry, Barb, really. My mind had wandered, but you had the distance wrong, more like three thousand miles."

I sighed, and Greg interjected, "I think, Barbara, that Rachelle's mind is with a certain police officer in San Francisco."

"Oh, is that right, kiddo?" she asked me. "Pray tell us who this police officer is." She winked slyly at me.

"His name is Lucas Dayton, and I'm hopelessly in love. He's the most wonderful thing that has ever happened to me. And to think, I met him just last week." I knew my eyes were shining.

"Ah, I had a feeling there was something different about you the minute I saw you. So you're in love, eh? And I take it this Lucas is in love, too?" A question was in her eye, one to which she already knew the answer.

"Absolutely, positively; isn't it awesome?"

"Well, this guy works fast, I must say. Are you engaged?"

"Oh, Barbara, it wasn't Lucas that worked fast. It was God, himself. Lucas and I feel that God meant us for each other. No, we're not really engaged, not yet, officially, anyway. We will be, though, you can count on it. We want to be together for always, I do know that for sure. Really, he's everything I ever wanted in a man, everything."

"This makes me so happy for you, my dear. You know I love you like a daughter, and I promise I'll be there for the wedding, whenever or wherever it happens. I absolutely must have an invitation." Barbara reached over and hugged me again.

"That is a promise. I doubt very much it will be too far in the future. We're going to talk about it when some other things are cleared up."

Barbara looked at me quizzically, and a light seemed to burst in her mind. "Are you having some problems with that guy that killed your mom? Is he back?"

I knew Barbara had been fully aware of my past right from the beginning, but it was a shock to hear someone ask, right out, about it.

"Yes, he's back, and he's after me. I'm really scared, but I feel better, now that I have Lucas looking out for me."

"You know I'd like to catch that guy myself and do some things to him that I couldn't mention here," Barbara said, with her usual fervor. "I'm so pleased you have a cop that loves you so much and wants to take care of you."

Our salads were being served, so we turned the conversation to something lighter. I didn't want anyone's day spoiled by my problems.

At two o'clock, the fashion show started. Greg and I glanced at each other, the excitement of anticipation a palpable thing between us. However, we were in for a big let-down. All the hype about the Ederly showing had been just what we had feared, all smoke and no fire, leaving just a bitter taste of disappointment.

The collection was obviously created with very young people in mind. Skirts were incredibly short and tight, blouses see-through, and dresses unbelievably décolleté, with their skirts hanging in oddly uneven lines. The men's line was equally as bizarre, with suits, trousers, and shirts cut in a strange angular fashion, and shown in colors that were jarring to the senses. I wondered if the models were ashamed to be seen in these clothes.

Again, Greg and I looked at each other, this time in astonishment. We both mouthed the one word, "Dior?" I thought Dior would throw tomatoes at this collection. I also knew, though, that some of the trendy, small shops would probably carry some of these monstrosities, or copies of them.

When the last model had strutted his or her stuff, the designer, Bradford Ederly, and all the models grouped themselves on stage for pictures and accolades. I felt the applause was more polite than appreciative. However, Ederly, obviously with a colossal ego, beamed at the audience and into the cameras.

Lights came up and people started leaving, some of them gratefully, I thought. "Let's go get something to drink," Greg suggested, as he, Barbara, and I left the ballroom. None of us was saying anything right now, waiting until our minds had digested the fiasco we had just seen.

In the hotel coffee shop, we sat shaking our heads, not knowing exactly what to say to describe our feelings. Finally, Barbara screamed, "Dior! Dior! What a slam on that sacred name! Who ever thought of likening Bradford Ederly to the great one?"

"I suspect it was Ederly, himself," I answered. "I think he is the only one who has the enormous nerve to say that and, of course, he considered it a big joke on everyone."

"Perhaps it was for shock value," Greg suggested. "Maybe, by saying he was the next Dior, people would expect clothes that were classically beautiful, and would be shocked by his collection. If that was his aim, it certainly worked, but with a negative impact, in my opinion."

"You could be right," Barbara agreed. "I'll guarantee you this, not a stitch of his collection will ever be hanging on a Devon's rack."

Greg and I both said an emphatic, "Amen".

Thursday morning, Lucas informed me that Tony Bianci and Damon were still among the missing. "The people at Star said Damon had some sort of emergency and would be gone all week. I didn't press it, but it makes me wonder if there is a connection, since both of them are gone. We'll just have to wait and see."

When I asked about him, personally, Lucas seemed a bit evasive in some of his answers. I became suspicious that something had happened. "Okay, Lucas, out with it; something has happened that you don't want to tell me. What is it?"

"I didn't want to tell you until you got back, baby, but I might as well since you have sensed something is wrong. Someone fired a shot at me last night."

Fear washed over me in waves. It was worse than being afraid for me. "How did it happen?" I managed to say, though I was shaking as though I had a chill.

"There was a call to what was reported as a domestic disturbance in an apartment house. Keffler and I both arrived on the scene. We got out of the car, and the shot zinged over my head. Must have come from an upper window in one of the buildings. There are hundreds of windows from which it could have come, so we could do nothing but call back-up to start canvassing the area. I knew it would be hopeless, and it was."

"And the domestic disturbance? There wasn't one, was there, Lucas?" I wanted to cry, but held it back.

"No. There wasn't even an apartment with the number given to us. As you can guess, it was a ploy to get us out there."

"Oh, Lucas this is what I feared. There is no way you can protect yourself from something like that. Can't they pull you off the street until they find Judson?" I was crying now, unable to stop the tears.

"There's no proof that it was Judson Bard. This could just have been some kook shooting at whichever officer answered the call. And, as I said, there's no proof that Bard was after me when he tried to run you over. When there is a definite indication that I am his target, I will be pulled off the street immediately and transferred to SID—that's Special Investigation Division. Until then, I think we are going to have to trust the Lord to keep me safe, and pray that Bard makes a mistake. I've never wanted to catch anyone as much as I do him." I could hear the anxiety in his voice, but also the undercurrent of strength that I had always admired.

I felt myself near to hysterics. My mother had died because of Judson Bard, would Lucas also have to die at his hands? I prayed silently, as I said,

"You're right about having to trust the Lord. It's really hard for me to do that, when you're in danger."

We were silent for a few seconds and, then, to change the subject, I said, "Lucas, I have something to ask you. I read what was on the back of your picture; did you remember what was written there?"

"Baby, I remembered every word of it. It seems prophetic, don't you think, particularly since that picture was made only three months ago? Mom prays for me a lot, so maybe God whispers things to her about me. I wanted you to find it, yourself, and know what an extraordinary mom I have. I think it also confirms how I feel about you, the girl I do love with all my heart." He then laughed. "I also hoped you would know that I wasn't being egotistical, carrying a picture of myself around."

"I'm so anxious to meet the lady who wrote such an exceptional note to her son. I can imagine, now, where you got your compassion and concern for people." My tears were now drying on my cheeks.

"She is quite a lady. I went to see her Sunday afternoon and told her all about you, and she said I must bring you to see her as soon as you get back."

"And I told my father that I wanted to arrange to bring you down to meet him. He's very happy that I've found someone that I love so very much. I'm counting the minutes until I get back."

"I'm counting those minutes too, baby. Do you know that I'm still amazed the way I feel about you? I didn't know I was capable of loving someone this much."

"Me, too. Isn't it wonderful?"

We stayed on the line for a few minutes more. I told him briefly about seeing Barbara and about the Ederly show. Finally, I rang off, telling him that I hoped I would have a better reaction to the Suzie Lopez show this afternoon.

The Suzie Lopez show was, indeed, a pleasant surprise. I had sat waiting for it to begin, still shaking inside with fear for Lucas. But when Suzie moved onto the stage, I felt the fear subside and a stir of excitement take its place.

Suzie was a small, classically pretty young woman, with dark hair, pulled into a chignon, and warm brown eyes in a bright animated face. She had nothing of the aura of egotism that Ederly had shown, but, rather, a quiet self-confidence. She made a brief announcement before the show started and then moved behind the curtain, as the first model appeared.

After a few models had come down the runway, I reached over and squeezed Greg's hand for a second. My message was clear, this was a collection to sit up and take notice of.

The collection was varied in line and fabric, but each item was in the most exquisite taste. Her suits were crisply cut of fabrics that held the line perfectly as the models moved. There were two suits which would have been just right for an evening at the opera or a wedding, softly tailored of embroidered silk. Some of her dresses and evening wear bore the distinct flavor of her Hispanic lineage. Some skirts were tiered, or ruffled, in the most delicate multicolored fabric imaginable. The colors were either muted or pastel so as not to be gaudy, and the skirts draped softly, flouncing slightly with the movement of the models.

The models were another surprise. Not one of them had the emaciated look that was so popular with some designers. They were all slender, certainly, but had a healthy glow, bright eyes and smiles. There was none of the revolting heroin-chic or vacant faces and messy hair I had seen so often. They also did not walk with the exaggerated wiggle that had become the vogue in the last decades. Instead, the girls walked with a smooth glide, with just a hint of natural hip movement.

I did not recognize any of the models; there was not one of the current super models. I wondered if Suzie recruited and trained her own models. If so, she had done a magnificent job. Few fashion houses would have had the nerve to try that.

At the conclusion of the show, Suzie and her models appeared together, with Suzie making tiny bows to each of the girls, and motioning for them to receive applause. It was clear, though, that the audience wished their applause to be directed to this remarkable young lady who, with a velvet hand, had just shaken some hard-set fashion attitudes.

When we were out of the ballroom, Greg, Barbara and I, again, went for something to drink. Today, though, the conversation was entirely different from that of the day before. We could not say enough to describe our enthusiasm for the Lopez collection. We agreed that Devon's would be creating a new department devoted to Suzie Lopez.

There was a party that evening, hosted by Devon's, a formal affair for all the attendees of the Ederly and Lopez showings. It was a tradition for Devon's to extend this welcome to buyers and management people from all over the world.

I knew I had to go, though I had little interest. My mind was still on Lucas and the danger he might, this very evening, be facing. Before going downstairs, I spent some time with my Bible and in prayer; that was my only source of comfort. As I finished my prayer, the now familiar warm hand was touching my shoulder.

Greg escorted me downstairs, looking dashing in a black dinner jacket. I wore a blue, spaghetti-strapped sheath gown, embroidered with tiny beads in various shades of blue. My hair was pulled up into a mass of curls and held with clips encrusted with matching beads.

Greg's expression showed his appreciation of the way I looked. "Wow! And double wow!" he exclaimed. "You look smashing, Miss Atherly!"

I took his extended arm and we walked to the elevator. "You are certainly good for a girl's ego, Greg. You look pretty spiffy yourself. I'll bet we'll knock 'em dead when we arrive." I was only teasing, of course, knowing there would be hundreds of equally spiffy people in the ballroom.

Barbara Crestwell met us just inside the door, dressed in lavender chiffon, accented with exquisite beading. It complemented her pink and white skin and merry blue eyes. She gushed over Greg and me, hugging us with enthusiasm, and leading us to a table in front of the head table. "I have to sit at the head table, kids, but I wanted you two right where I could see you all evening. There's no one I would rather look at."

With that she flitted off, waving at people, and blowing kisses, in all directions. Greg and I glanced at each other and burst out laughing.

The warm hand on my shoulder remained there throughout the entire evening. I treasured the comfort, but wondered if it signified that Lucas was again in danger, and that I must not worry. I kept up a constant silent prayer throughout the evening, having some difficulty conversing with people around me. No one seemed to notice, perhaps because they were too wrapped up in themselves.

Greg did, however, casting a questioning glance my way from time to time. Once, he reached over and held my hand for a minute, a gesture that said he was with me in whatever was concerning me. He had an exceptional sensitivity to the moods of those around him. I thanked God that I had this young friend to keep me company.

I awoke on Friday morning, still tired, a logy feeling holding me down like a heavy weight. I lay thinking of the party last night. It had lasted until well past midnight, the music and voices beating incessantly on my ears. Eventually, my hearing now dulled, I became unable to respond with anything more than superficial enthusiasm. How I wanted to leave, but knew I must not.

Greg seemed to enjoy the evening, dancing with first one pretty girl and then another. I had seen at least a dozen pairs of feminine eyes watching him constantly throughout the evening. Dancing was the last thing I wanted to do, so after the formalities were over, Barbara and I ended up circulating among the crowd, greeting people in the name of Devon's.

It was obvious that she, too, was beginning to sag with fatigue and boredom; even her bubbly personality couldn't keep bubbling indefinitely. It was with utter relief when the orchestra played their last number and started placing instruments into cases.

I snagged Greg away from still another pretty girl, and said, "Okay, chum, it's time you went beddy-bye. I'll be knocking on your door bright and early, since we have meetings in the morning." Greg complied good-naturedly and said good-night to a disappointed young lady. She probably had hoped he would suggest further activities.

I saw Barbara trundling off toward the exit and blew a kiss in her direction.

I had had a hard time going to sleep, my nerves strained tight like guitar strings. Every small sound plunked them painfully. Finally, around two am, I had drifted off, but woke at eight, dreading having to get out of my bed.

ONCE AGAIN I FEAR

The meeting at Devon's was scheduled for eleven o'clock, giving everyone time to sleep in from the night before. I wished, profoundly, that I could have slept a little longer, too. However, I did want to call Lucas around nine o'clock. I had told him I would call a little later today.

Unable to go back to sleep, I arose and went to the bathroom for a long, hot bath. I had my prayer time while I luxuriated in the fragrant water, my still-taut nerves relaxing and my spirit connecting with my Heavenly Father.

At nine, when I called Lucas, his voice sounded rather muffled. "What's wrong?" I asked, my heart pounding.

"I had a small accident, if you could call it that. A full-sized, Ford pickup truck smashed into me in an intersection, obviously on purpose. The driver then backed away quickly and took off. He hit me broad-side, just behind my seat. If he had hit dead on, I wouldn't be talking to you. As it was, even with the air bag, I got my head twisted sharply, pulling my jaw out of whack. Really weird, really painful, but not life-threatening. Should be okay by the time you get back."

"Lucas, did you find the truck that hit you?"

"Another unit had to come take over, since I had to go to the hospital and be checked over. The truck was discovered about six blocks away, abandoned. A stolen vehicle, as you've probably already guessed. Bard's fingerprints all over it. Of course, no one saw hide or hair of Bard; he just seemed to vanish. Oh, baby, please don't worry. I've been yanked off the street and transferred to SID. I will still be involved, as much as possible, in the investigation, but not out on the street. So it would seem, I'm his target. A massive effort is being waged to bring an end to Bard's little reign of terror. We'll find him, I promise you. With God's help, we will."

"Lucas, I can hardly bear it until I get home. I want to be with you. But I can't tell you how relieved I am that you won't be out on the street. One thing, though, don't forget he could be after you when you aren't on duty, so please be careful." I was fighting tears, knowing that Lucas didn't want me to worry too much about him. How could I help it, though, when he had had two narrow escapes?

"Rachelle, my pastor, Doug West, is coming over in a few minutes to pray with me. He's bringing the associate pastor, the college and career director, and the youth director. We are going to storm the gates of Heaven for your safety and mine. Judson Bard and all the demons of Hell are not going to be able to withstand these prayers." His voice was full of faith, and my heart responded to it. God would protect us. He had already kept Lucas from certain death twice.

We prayed fervently together and reassured each other with words of love. The warm hand, my comforter, touched my shoulder, melting the fear in my heart.

Chapter 34

Greg and I arrived at San Francisco International Airport at about six-thirty Saturday evening. Lucas was standing fidgeting in the waiting room, anxiously watching every passenger that came through the door. I could see him when there were a half dozen people still ahead of me. Then, he finally saw me, his face lighting up.

I ran to him and flung myself into his arms, where, for six days, I had yearned to be. My carry-on dropped with a thud, as my arms went around him. His lips were so warm and so sweet as he kissed me over and over, oblivious to those around us.

Finally, we just stood, holding each other and not saying a word. Then, out of the corner of my eye, I saw Greg standing to one side, grinning. "Lucas," I murmured, "I think people are staring."

"Let 'em stare," he said, squeezing me against him.

"Really, we had better get going, darling. People are lining up for the next flight, and I fear we are a bit in the way."

Reluctantly, he loosened his hold on me and picked up my carry-on. He kept one arm tightly around me. Then, he noticed Greg a few feet away. "Oh, hi, Greg; didn't see you. Too busy with my girl." His face bore a mischievous expression, the boyish quality that I had seen the first night I had met him.

"Oh, don't mind me, Lucas," Greg said. "That was better than a schmaltzy movie any day. Love must be nice."

"Take my word for it," Lucas confirmed, grinning.

When we returned to my apartment, Lucas stowed my luggage in my bedroom while I held Tache and listened to her purring happily, because I had returned. I set Tache down as Lucas hung our coats in the foyer closet. Then, he again pulled me into his arms. "I can't keep my hands off you, babe. Dear God, how I have missed you. I know I don't ever want you away from me again. Rachelle, I know we have talked in terms of the future and our being a permanent thing. I know, too, that we are going to have to wait about firm plans, waiting for God's time. But I do want, very much, to ask you the big, important question. Will you marry me?"

"Lucas, I'd marry you right this minute, if it were possible. Yes, yes, I'll marry you."

He kissed me warmly and held me close. Then, he let go of me and reached into his pocket. "I bought this yesterday, just on the off-chance you might say yes."

He held out a small black-velvet ring box and opened it. Inside was the most beautiful ring that I had ever seen. It was not a huge stone—I would not have wanted that—perhaps a half carat, in a marquise cut. On each side of the center stone, smaller stones, in carved settings, added a delicate beauty to the ring. Just right to suit my taste. As he placed it on my finger, the light caught the facets, glittering and beautiful.

"Oh, I love it! It is so beautiful!" I said, holding it to the light, so that it sparkled. "Lucas, you couldn't have picked anything I would like better. It means so much to me, because you mean the world to me."

When he had finished kissing me, he sighed, "Well, that's it, babe, we're officially engaged. I know we can't make definite plans for our wedding right now, with this Bard thing hanging over us, but we will soon, and I, for one, don't want a long engagement. See, I warned you I was going to be impatient."

"I don't want a long engagement, either," I told him, breathlessly. "As I said, this minute would suit me fine. By the way, it's becoming a habit for us to smooch here in the foyer. Let's go sit down in the living room."

We sat close together, holding hands, and just looking at each other. It was that simple; we loved the sight of each other. Finally, Lucas broke the silence. "I'm really glad I had this day off, so I could come pick you up.

ONCE AGAIN I FEAR

God seems to have arranged things for us, even with my rotating schedule," Lucas said.

"I don't quite understand how this rotation works; explain it to me." I had been wondering about it, and wanting to know how we could plan our time together.

"Well, we work ten-hour days. We're on a six-week cycle: Three rotations of four days on, four days off, each successive rotation moving up a day of the week. Then, there are three rotations of five days on, three days off in the same manner. For instance, last week started my four and four rotations. I worked four days and then had Friday, Saturday, Sunday, and Monday off. I worked Tuesday, Wednesday, Thursday, and Friday, and had Saturday through Tuesday off. It goes on from there. It seems a little odd for people on regular schedules, but it works quite well, giving us long work periods, but also plenty of time off to unwind and retain our sanity."

"And you, for one, are quite sane, I can tell," I teased him. "So what are your hours on the second shift?"

"I work from four til two. Some guys work from five until three. I don't really mind it. I do hope you can adjust to my crazy hours, though." He looked at me questioningly.

"If it goes with your territory, darling, I will adjust, no question. Now, there's another thing to talk about, Devon's Christmas party. We're having it a week from tomorrow night—not to my liking to have it on a Sunday night, but we couldn't get the party scheduled any other night. It's going to be a Hornblower Yacht Dining Cruise. We did that three years ago, and it was fabulous. Will you go with me? I figure you have the night off."

"Absolutely; I wouldn't want you to go alone or with someone else, you know." Lucas was teasing again.

"Oh, most definitely, we couldn't have that. The party is semi-formal, so you don't have to wear a tux—a suit will be fine. I'll be wearing something eveningish, but not too elaborate. It should be fun. It's really neat, cruising around the bay, looking back on the city with all its lights, and the wind blowing our hair."

"I'll be looking forward to it. I've taken a daytime cruise on the Red and White Fleet a few times, but never a cruise at night."

He reached over and stroked Tache, who was lying next to me, and she revved up her motor again, stretching around to push her head into his hand. "She's a fool for having her head rubbed," I told Lucas. He rubbed Tache's head, while she purred louder and louder.

"Oh, hey, babe, are you going to put up a Christmas tree?" Lucas asked. I'd like to, but my apartment is so small, I couldn't squeeze a twig in. As my Grandpa Dayton used to say, 'it's so small; you couldn't cuss a cat without getting hair in your mouth.'"

"Lucas, that's terrible!" I couldn't help laughing. "Did your grandpa really say that?"

"Honey, he has a million of those little, homely sayings. I've forgotten most of them, but, now and then, one just seems to pop into my mind when it's apropos."

"I have a small fake tree that I usually put up," I told him. "It isn't bad, and it's much safer than a real one. I've heard of too many families being burned out because of Christmas trees."

"Why don't you get it out, and I'll come over Monday night and help you put it up and decorate it. I want a really Christmasy Christmas this year. Sharing it with you will make it better than usual."

"That would be such fun. I'll do it. And will you go to church with me tomorrow? I promise I won't try to take you away from yours, but I'd love to introduce you to Tom Lane and all my friends at church." I feigned a really pleading expression.

"I will, if you promise to go with me next Sunday. I have a pastor and friends who will love meeting you." He kissed the tip of my nose, and waited for my answer.

"That sounds fair. I would really like to meet your friends. I want to know everyone who is part of your life."

"You realize we're going to have to decide where we're going to church after we're married, don't you?" he asked.

"I suppose you're right. Do you think that's one of the things we're going to have to have the Lord show us?" I tilted my head and looked at him questioningly.

"I'm sure He can settle it much better that we can. And now, sweet lady, I have another question. Will you go to meet my family tomorrow afternoon? Mom is dying to meet you. I have to warn you, there may be a houseful of relatives, parents, siblings, aunts, cousins, etcetera. I'm sure everyone in the family has heard all about you from Mom."

"After reading what your mom wrote on your picture, I have wanted so much to meet her. As for the rest of the family, that would be wonderful. After all, they are going to be my family, too, before long. Then, my darling, I want you to go to Saratoga with me. How about the day after the Christmas party? I'll take the day off, since I have been working some terribly long hours the last few weeks."

"I'd like that very much, baby. Your father sounds like a great guy."

We settled back for a long evening of just talking and listening to music. Tache curled up close to me, purred for awhile, and then fell asleep. My heart was full of thanksgiving to God for the happiness He had brought me. How could anything dark and sinister be in our wonderful world? I had no way of knowing how many times in the near future I would remember asking myself that question.

The next day was a whirl of our meeting people and being warmly welcomed into each other's circle of love. My pastor and church friends couldn't have been more welcoming, although Lucas was carefully observed by a lot of the young men who probably had wondered if I would ever be deeply interested in a man. I think a lot of people were happily shocked when they saw the diamond on my finger. I didn't care what anyone thought, I was deliriously happy. Tom Lane kissed my cheek and hugged me tight. He then pronounced a blessing on Lucas and me.

At Lucas' family home, the welcome for me was almost overwhelming. There were, indeed, a lot of relatives there—come especially to meet me, I believed. They were so welcoming, hugging, kissing, and patting me, telling Lucas how beautiful they thought I was.

His sister, Elise, who I knew was thirty, was there with her husband, Don, and their two sons. His younger brother, Joel, age twenty-five, came with his wife, Margie, and their baby daughter. The youngest Dayton son, Steve, who was twenty-one and a senior at San Francisco State, hadn't been able to make it.

There were three aunts and two of their husbands, as well as Lucas' grandma Dayton, and grandpa Dayton—the other Lucas—who proved himself the wit that Lucas had described. And, of course, his parents, Frank and Belinda.

Lucas' mom was the best of all. She held me in her arms and told me how happy she was that Lucas had finally fallen in love. She also told me that she thought I was absolutely perfect for him. Could Lucas have been right that God whispered things to Belinda Dayton? I thought I was perfect for him, too.

Lucas stood beaming at everyone and making sure that no one missed seeing my ring. I wanted to cry for joy, feeling that all these people had an amazing capacity for love. No wonder Lucas had become the remarkable man that he was.

Chapter 35

Lucas arrived at seven-thirty the next morning, all ready to drive me to work. "You don't have to keep doing this, Lucas," I assured him. "You know you aren't used to getting up so early, except, of course, for those phone calls from New York. Honestly, I feel quite safe, walking down to the cable car line or driving my car."

"I can sleep later, if I so choose. I plan to be with you as much as I can until this is all over. I'll be here every morning, even if I have worked the night before. I couldn't bear it, if something happened to you, and I thought I might have prevented it. I know it won't be long, so don't worry about me. I promise I'll get a total eight hours of sleep; will that make you happy?"

I saw tears starting to glisten in his eyes, so I didn't push it further. "I see I am up against a brick wall, my love. Okay, if it makes you feel better and, if you keep your promise about the sleep, I'll give in. But don't you expect that I'll be this big a push-over every time we argue." I grinned at him and tip-toed up to kiss him.

"Oh, I'm sure you can be pretty stubborn, when you think you're right." He hugged me tight and nuzzled my ear. "You know, one of my aunts said that every couple should have at least one good fight before they get married. She thinks they should learn how each one reacts to anger, and how they go about making up. I really don't think you and I are going to be engaged long enough to have even one good fight."

"I don't think we need to; we'll figure everything out as it happens."

I pulled a little away from him and chuckled. "I just remembered something my mom told me once. She said, when she and dad got mad, Dad would say, 'Let's stop this and go get an ice cream cone.' She said their first year Dad put on ten pounds, from eating so much ice cream. Let's make a promise, when we start getting angry with each other, that we'll go get an ice cream cone." I was half teasing, but hoped he would agree. He did.

There was quite a stir at Devon's that day when I showed my ring to everyone. Trish, Greg, and Mark gathered in the executive reception room to congratulate me. Trish grabbed me and hugged me, squeezing the breath out of me. "You're going to marry that hunk? Wow! Girl, you are one lucky chick. One thing sure, you two will have beautiful children."

Children! I hadn't even thought that far. Now, I thought, oh, yes, I will want Lucas' children, and I knew, with his big, warm family, that he would want them, too.

Greg hugged me, too, and smirked. "Why am I not surprised, Rachelle? After that scene at the airport Saturday, I'd be surprised if you weren't engaged. This is awesome, and I'm so happy for you. Tell Lucas what a lucky man I think he is."

Mark Bussell congratulated me with a bear hug, and said he would like to meet Lucas. "Lucas is getting a real treasure, tell him that for me," he said, grinning at me.

Robert Bainbridge came out of his office when he heard all the giggling, kissed my cheek, and offered his best wishes, also. "I've always hoped you would find someone who would love you, like you deserve, my dear. Life has a lot of making up to do, where you're concerned." I believed the others around me didn't know the full meaning of Robert's words, except, maybe Greg.

My eyes suddenly filled with tears, and I hastily wiped them away. "That's so sweet of you, Robert," I told him. "Lucas has already made up for everything, I assure you." I then smiled through my tears.

Laura Maxwell called me at nine o'clock. "Hi, Rachelle, I hear you've got problems with the bad boy again."

"How did you know? That's why I wanted to talk to you." I was shaken that she knew about Judson being back.

ONCE AGAIN I FEAR

"Oh, when I got back Friday, I got a call from, the SFPD—Sergeant Win Keffler. They had the computer records of your mother's murder and of Judson's flight to avoid prosecution. I also hear one of their patrolmen is being targeted by that bozo."

"Unfortunately, he was with me when Judson tried to run me down one night. Any man who had been with me would have become a target, I'm afraid. However, I'm sure he's seen Lucas Dayton with me more than once. That's another thing I wanted to tell you about; Lucas and I are engaged. How I wish this Judson thing was over! It's like the guillotine hanging over our necks. We can't plan anything until Judson is safely out of our lives. Can you imagine if we had a wedding and he showed up? I wouldn't put it past him. Laura, he knows everything I do and everywhere I go. He even called my apartment and talked about things inside my bedroom, just as if he had been there."

"So, it would seem, someone is feeding him information. Got any idea who?"

"Lucas and I have been over and over it, but I can't imagine anyone I know being that mean! My trainer's card was found in the stolen car he drove to try to run me down. But, Laura, there could be a couple of reasons why it would be there. Damon is a perfect gentleman, and has been a really good friend to me."

"Rachelle, getting back to your engagement; I couldn't be happier for you. You deserve some happiness. In the meantime, before your wedding, we have got to figure out how to outsmart his guy, and get him out of your life. Believe me, we here in Santa Clara County are bearing down on this case in earnest, in cooperation with the SFPD. It certainly makes me feel better to know you have that police officer is in your life, on a personal basis. He could save your life, you know?"

"Or lose his," I countered, a lump in my throat that felt like a golf ball.

"We're not even going to entertain such thoughts. I understand Lucas Dayton is safely in SID, now, and not on the streets."

"That's true, but I feel if Judson Bard wants to get at him, that isn't going to assure his safety. Lucas and I pray a lot for God's protection, and, honestly, I feel that we will both survive this."

"Let's continue to pray that that is true, Rachelle," Laura said.

I called Dru after I hung up, telling her my terrific news. She gushed her joy and begged to be invited to the wedding, whenever that occurred. I promised her an invitation.

"And how was your swanky party last week?" I asked.

"Marvelous, simply marvelous. Everyone that is anyone was there. If I told you everybody, it would be like a Who's Who list of San Francisco society. I had such fun. And my friend who escorted me couldn't have been sweeter or more laughs. Honestly, Chelle, I think I may just fall in love with him. At least, I'll think about it."

"You do that, Dru," I said sarcastically. I didn't believe a word of it.

After saying good-bye to my friend, I glanced over at a section of newspaper that lay on a table beyond my desk. It was the "San Francisco Life" section of a San Francisco paper, dated a week ago Sunday. Perhaps Trish had placed it there while I was gone.

A picture on the front page caught my eye. It showed a group of people at a party with the caption, "Gala Bash at The Mark Hopkins". I walked over and picked it up, staring at the picture. In full color, Dru smiled back at me, standing with five other people, the arm of a handsome man draped around her shoulders. This was why Trish had placed the paper for me to see.

A name under the picture sent shock waves through me. The smiling, dark-haired young woman next to Dru was identified as Gwynneth Bard Reynolds. Judson's sister! Did Dru know Gwynneth? I had told her about Judson Bard; why hadn't she mentioned that she knew Gwynneth?

I tried to shake suspicions from my mind. Perhaps Dru didn't know her, but had simply been included in a picture with her. I wanted to call Lucas, but he had promised me that he would go home and sleep. I would see him tonight; I would show him the picture then. Maybe he could help me decide how to approach Dru with what I knew." I leaned my head into my hands and prayed a heart-felt prayer that God would help us find the truth.

That evening, I showed Lucas the picture of Dru and Gwynneth Bard Reynolds together. He seemed perplexed by what he was seeing. "Your friend, Dru, seems totally at ease with Gwynneth Reynolds, doesn't she? Like old friends. I think we're going to have to question her, to get at the truth. She could hold the key to all this mess."

ONCE AGAIN I FEAR

"Why, Lucas? Why must it be one of my friends doing this? It's so painful even to consider that Dru could do such a thing. Okay, I know, I have to consider everyone, and Dru definitely knows a lot about me. I know she knows what my bedroom looks like; she's been in there several times, when I wanted to show her a dress I had bought, or something like that. She and Tache are great friends, so she could definitely tell someone that Tache sleeps on my bed. Oh, God, please, please, not Dru!"

"Honey, just forget it for tonight. Let's decorate your tree—our tree— and, try to think happy thoughts. Think how much I love you, and how much you love me." He pulled me close to him, and just held me quietly for a few minutes.

I did feel better when he talked like that, and held me close. "Okay, I'll think only of you, and concentrate on hanging all my ornaments on the tree.

"That's better, baby; let's get started." He squeezed me once more and then let go of me. Funny, he and my father both called me "baby", but it sounded totally different coming from each of them.

When we had the tree up and decorated, Lucas ordered a pizza to be sent, and we set about fixing iced soft drinks and setting out napkins and plates. I really felt happy by now, thanks to Lucas' presence.

It usually took only a half hour for Pizza to arrive, but when forty minutes had passed, there was still no sign of it. I had called the security desk to have the deliveryman admitted. Now, I called again to see if he had gotten there yet.

The guard said, "No, not yet, Miss Atherly. Oh, wait a minute, he's here now. He'll be up in a minute."

A few minutes later, my doorbell rang, and Lucas went to answer it. The deliveryman held out the pizza, and told Lucas the amount due. As Lucas reached for his wallet, I suddenly caught the eye of the deliveryman, beneath the pizza company cap—cold blue-gray eyes, full of hatred.

"Lucas!" I screamed. "Its Judson! Shut the door!"

I was too late with the warning; Judson had his foot in the door, and his free hand holding onto it. The pizza dropped to the floor as Lucas lunged at Judson, knocking him to the floor in the hall. Tache, who had been standing nearby, scooted down the hall toward my bedroom.

209

Lucas was bigger, more well-developed, than Judson, but, as I remembered, Judson was fast. He leaped to his feet and swung a fist at Lucas, missing as Lucas ducked. Lucas grabbed for Judson's shirt front, but Judson sidestepped the attempt.

I then saw that Judson had a knife in his hand, and my blood ran cold, remembering another time when his hand had held a bloody knife. I screamed, as my body turned to ice. Lucas crouched a little, as if he were ready to spring. The knife swooped toward Lucas' chest, but his arm came up at the same time, knocking it out of Judson's hand. The knife went skittering across the floor and hit the wall. Judson, apparently thinking better of a hand-to-hand battle with a bigger, much stronger opponent, ran down the hall.

Lucas ran after him, as I stood watching, tears of terror streaming down my face. Judson disappeared through the door to the stairs, followed a short time later by Lucas.

I went back inside and called the security guard, gasping out what had happened. He sounded totally shocked, when I told him who the 'deliveryman' really was. "Miss Atherly, I'll call the police immediately and go to help Mr. Dayton."

I then ran down the hall and opened the stair door. Neither Lucas nor Judson was in sight. Slowly, I descended the stairs, praying every second for Lucas. Oh, God, he had to be okay.

When I reached the second floor level, I heard a door slam below, on the first-floor level, then the sound of running feet on the stairs. The African-American security guard came into view, his dark eyes wide with fear; probably fear that he would be deemed the cause of someone being hurt or killed.

"Did you see them?" I screamed.

"No, I don't know where they went. Maybe they went onto the second floor. I'll go see." He passed me on the stairs and ran through the second floor door. I followed, my heart bursting with fear.

In the hallway, I didn't see anyone at first. Then, Lucas came slowly up the hallway, anger suffusing his face, his fists clenched at his sides. "He got away!" He said when he saw me. "I can't figure, for the life of me, where he went. I was only starting down the stairs, when he had already

ONCE AGAIN I FEAR

reached the second floor door, and disappeared through it. When I got through the door, he had totally disappeared. When the officers get here, I want a search of this building. I would swear someone let him into one of the rooms on this floor. Where, I don't know." He looked so dejected, that I ran to put my arms around him.

The police came and knocked on every door on the second floor, and then on the other floors, for good measure. A quick search of each apartment was made. Nothing. No one had seen a man in a pizza delivery uniform, or at least admitted to it.

Lucas must have been feeling the same frustration that surged through me. Judson had managed to get inside my building!

The real pizza deliveryman was found unconscious in an alley behind the building. After an ambulance had taken him away, Lucas returned to my apartment and stood shaking his head. "I can't believe the nerve of that guy! Also, I can't believe how he managed to disappear. It's almost like he isn't human. I've never seen anyone move so fast."

"Lucas, Judson was the eight-hundred meter Pac-Ten Champion his senior year at Stanford. He is incredibly fast."

I shut the door, stepping over the place where the pizza box had fallen. Sauce had flung out of the box onto the white tile, like splatters of blood. The police had taken the box as evidence; for all any of us knew, it could be poisoned, Judson's attempt to cover all bases.

I went into the kitchen and leaned on a counter, my head in my hands. I was still shaking so hard, that my teeth were chattering. Lucas came up behind me and wrapped his arms around my waist, leaning his head against me. I could feel his body shaking, too.

"What am I going to do, Lucas? He found a way into my only haven of safety. When will he do it again? I'm so scared, that I can't even think straight right now."

Lucas turned me around and looked directly at me. "We can't give up, honey. God is still with us. Think about it, Bard didn't succeed in his effort to hurt either you or me. He won't succeed ever, I'm sure of it."

"With my head, I know you're right, but I'm human enough to still be scared. But how did he know we were ordering pizza? He seems to know everything else about me, but that seems impossible to me."

"I would bet it was simply opportunistic. He was, most likely, watching your apartment house, probably knowing I was inside, and saw the pizza man arrive. It was simply his way of getting past the guard. He must have crowed for joy when he saw your name on the pizza ticket." What Lucas said made sense.

I closed my eyes and sighed deeply, actual pain in my chest. "I'm still shaking; can't you feel it? Just hold me, Lucas."

He enfolded me warmly in his strong arms, whispering words of endearment and comfort. Then, he started to pray, softly, but sincerely, asking God to take away my fear and give me assurance. The warm hand was soon there, as I knew it would be.

When he released me, he said, "Baby, we need to eat something. Maybe just some soup, if you have any."

"I do," I said pulling gently away and going toward the pantry.

Soon the hearty soup was heating in the microwave and we had gained some control over our emotions.

As I poured ice water into glasses, Lucas dumped out the soft drinks that I had originally poured for us, the ice in them now melted. As he set the empty glasses on the counter, he said, "You're not staying here alone tonight; I'm staying with you. Please don't argue with me, either, or we may have our first fight." He then grinned, his familiar mischievous grin.

"I wouldn't think of it," I said, managing to smile, too. "Dad said the bed in the spare room is quite comfortable. Actually, I will love having you nearby; things going bump in the night would be pretty scary, if I were here alone."

"Okay, that's settled, and the wave is screaming at us. Let's eat. I'm suddenly hungry."

Lucas did spend the night and, next morning, got his first glimpse of me wrapped in a terry cloth robe, without a smidgen of makeup, and my hair wet from the shower. He ambled into the kitchen as I set the coffee carafe under the drip basket, and stood looking at me with a grin. "Hey, babe, you're beautiful, even without the war paint." He came over and kissed me, running his fingers through my wet hair.

I had to laugh. "Now, you know what you're really getting, sweet thing. At least you didn't scream."

ONCE AGAIN I FEAR

"Hey, don't insult the woman I love. Honestly, Rachelle, you look wonderful, all fresh-faced and smelling like flowers. Besides, you don't wear all that much makeup, anyway."

"Dru has taught me how to wear makeup, so that it seems I'm not wearing makeup. Know what I mean? It's a real art. And, Lucas, you're going to have to stop saying such complimentary things, or else I'm going to start believing you. Then I'll be so conceited you won't be able to stand me." I faked a scowl.

"Never, my lovely, never. I promise you, I'm going to tell you how beautiful you are every day of our lives. You'd better learn to live with it—and with me."

"That will be my pleasure, particularly the last part. Lucas, I love you; I love everything about you." I twined my arms around his neck and drew his head down for another kiss.

We were startled apart by the sound of my doorbell. "Who in the world can that be?" Lucas asked.

"I have no idea. Is it possible Judson got back in the building?" My heart was racing, my hands starting to sweat.

"That's hard to imagine. Stay here and I'll look through the viewer."

At the door, he turned toward me, his expression questioning. "It's an elderly lady, very short and silver-haired."

"The short part sounds like Mrs. Riley, down on the second floor. Let her in; I'm sure it's okay."

Lucas opened the door, as I walked into the foyer. Mrs. Riley looked at me, in my bathrobe, and then at Lucas. I think she was putting two and two together—and getting five. "I'm sorry to bother you, Rachelle," she said, timidly, "but there's something I have to tell you—and your young man."

"Come in, then, Mrs. Riley." I motioned toward the living room.

"Oh, no, I can't stay but a minute. I just have to tell you what happened last night, when that awful young man burst into my apartment."

I know my mouth dropped open, and I saw Lucas' eyes widen. "Tell us," Lucas prompted, with the tone of voice that young men use for grandmother-types.

"Well, I had just opened my door to go down the hall to visit Mrs. Walters, when I heard running footsteps and saw this young man coming, like the wind, toward me. Never saw anyone run so fast in my life. He grabbed me and shoved me back into my apartment and shut the door, his arm around my throat. He snarled at me, like a dog. Worst sound I've ever heard. Then, he told me he would break my neck, if I made a sound.

"He dragged me over to the glass doors that lead out to my balcony and again snarled at me, that, if I told anyone he had been there, he would come back and get me. I was so scared! I have a bad heart, and I was afraid I was going to have a heart attack. Anyway, he let himself out onto the balcony and climbed over the railing, hanging by his hands for a minute and then dropping to the ground. He was tall and had long arms, so I don't think he had too far to drop. I was too scared to tell anyone. But this morning, I thought, I'm old and don't have long anyway, so I'm not going to help that horrid man get away with whatever he'd done to you two."

She exhaled one big gush of breath and then said, "There, I feel better." She smiled at Lucas. "I was told you are a policeman, and thought you had to know. Now, what should I do?"

I got the distinct impression that Mrs. Riley was, by now, enjoying this, feeling very important.

"You certainly did the right thing, Mrs. Riley," Lucas reassured her. "We had no idea where the man had gone. You've solved that for us. Keep your doors bolted and I doubt the man will come after you." He patted her on her tiny shoulder, as she turned to go. "Stay around home today, and I'll have an officer come and take your statement. Thank you very much; you've been very helpful."

Mrs. Riley beamed, looking as if she had grown a couple of inches, and strutted off toward the elevator, waving over her shoulder.

When Lucas had closed the door, he breathed a sigh of relief. "Well, now we know how the vanishing man managed to do it.

In my office that morning, I tried to call Dru, to see if I could feel her out about the picture in the paper. However, I was told by her secretary that she was at a seminar in Los Angeles and wouldn't be back until next Monday. It seemed everybody we wanted to question had suddenly disappeared.

ONCE AGAIN I FEAR

I, at first, wondered why she had not called to tell me of her trip, but decided it was probably because she knew I was well occupied with my own life now. Poor Dru, she would feel really left out of my life from now on. I brought myself up straight. Poor Dru, indeed, if she were the one helping Judson Bard terrorize me.

At that moment, I felt more confused than I ever had in my life. It was as if my world had been put into a blender and, now, nothing of the former things was discernible as whole, real and solid. The only sanity in my life was Lucas, and I hung onto thoughts of him with all my strength.

Lucas spent Tuesday night in my apartment, also.

On Wednesday morning, a funny incident occurred. I was dressed for work, and, as usual, Lucas was up, ready to take me. The doorbell rang, and it was, again, Mrs. Riley.

She apologized profusely, seeing I was ready for work. She asked Lucas how the investigation was going, and he admitted that not a lot of headway had been made.

"I was just checking," Mrs. Riley explained. "Don't forget, if there's any more I can do, let me know."

I noticed that she, again, seemed a bit embarrassed by what she considered an inappropriate situation between Lucas and me. She was a nice old lady, who had grown up in a different time, and was not at ease with the moral laxness of many of today's young people.

A sudden idea hit me; I would relieve her mind where we were concerned. I noticed that a finger on her right hand was bandaged, and that blood was seeping through the gauze. I took her hand and said, "You've cut your finger, Mrs. Riley, and you need a fresh bandage. Come on, I'll put a fresh one on."

She didn't have to be coaxed; she probably liked the attention I was giving her. I led her down the hall past my guest room where Lucas had slept. In plain view was his unmade bed but it was obvious that only one person had slept in it. One pillow bore the indentation where his head had lain, but the covers had not been pulled completely off the other pillow.

I knew she took a good look as we passed. I then led her into my more spacious room, and, again, my bed showed no sign of more than one

215

occupant. One pillow was mussed, and indented; the other was plump and unwrinkled.

I could have bandaged her finger in the hall bathroom, but chose to take her to my bathroom. While I applied the bandage, she asked, "Your young man is protecting you, isn't he?" She had a twinkle in her eyes.

"Yes, he is. And, Mrs. Riley, he is a very honorable man."

"Oh, yes, I'm sure of that. He's a very nice young man." I could see that she was relieved, knowing Lucas and I weren't doing shocking things in my apartment.

Lucas persuaded a patrolwoman friend of his, who was on day shifts, to spend the next four nights with me. Each morning, though, he was there to drive me to work. He insisted I take a taxi home each evening.

He kept me up to date on the investigation, although, as yet, there was little to report. Judson Bard, as usual, had vanished from sight, with the police unable to find anyone who had seen him. The whole SFPD was baffled by lack of leads.

The only piece of information they had gleaned was finding that the knife had been purchased at a local pawn shop. The clerk remembered, distinctly, selling it to a tall young man with cold blue-gray eyes. He had frightened her so much, that she was reluctant to sell him the knife. She couldn't, however, think of any reason to refuse. She had not seen the man before, and had not seen him since. Police had combed the immediate area, showing a picture of Judson Bard, with no one remembering seeing him.

My nerves were on edge, and I jumped at ever sound or movement out of the corner of my eye. Footsteps, approaching me from the rear, would send me into a momentary panic.

Once, I was standing by a bulletin board in the employee lounge, waiting for Trish to go with me to lunch. As I rather absently read some of the varied notices, a hand touched my shoulder. I gave a small shriek, before I could stop myself. Turning, I saw it was Mark Bussell. He was quite taken aback by my reaction, and I hastily apologized. "I'm sorry, Mark, my nerves are just on the raw edge these days."

ONCE AGAIN I FEAR

"I'm really sorry I scared you. Hey, I thought you were bubbling over with *joie de vivre*, with your engagement and all. Anything you could talk to old buddy Mark about?" He grinned at me and tilted his head to one side.

I suddenly felt a little silly, and smiled back at him. "No, my friend, just some problems I'm having with someone. Not Lucas, I'll tell you, before you ask. Where he is concerned, I'm full of joy. Thanks for offering to listen to my problems, though; I appreciate it."

"Anytime, Rachelle, and I mean it. I think a lot of you, I hope you know that."

"I do, and the feeling is mutual. You have become a very good friend." I laid my hand on his arm for a second and then smiled over his shoulder at Trish, who had emerged from the ladies room.

Thanks to Pacific Bell's prompt service of my request for a new phone number, I received no more calls from Judson. I had had to tell Trish a little of what was happening; simply saying that someone was stalking me. Because she needed to be able to reach me at odd times, sometimes, I gave her the security desk number, which she solemnly wrote down.

She frowned and said, "This has to be just awful for you, Rachelle. Gosh, if it happened to me, I would probably die of heart failure. Some guys are really creeps." I wondered what she would think, if I had told her more than just superficial details. I also wondered if she could possibly already know all this, coming straight from Judson.

Judson made no other attempts on either Lucas or me all that week, and I was tempted to be lulled into complacency. Lucas was the one to bring me up short each time I suggested maybe Judson had given up. He told me on Thursday morning, "No way is he going to give up. We've had to deal with others like him; they don't give up until the victim is dead— or *they* are. I don't mean to scare you any more than you already are, but that's the facts. I've dealt with stalking cases with other women."

"I know that, Lucas, but I try to push it aside so I won't be scared. I'm like David in the Bible. He was pursued, and he trusted God, but sometimes he was quaking in his boots. He may even have tried to tell himself his pursuers had given up. I think the fifty-fifth Psalm is his cry to

God because he was terrified. I remember, particularly, the ninth verse, in which he cries, 'Destroy, O Lord, and divide their tongues; for I have seen violence and strife in the city.' Am I right, or am I wrong?"

Lucas gave a slight laugh. "You're right, I have to admit. David was very human and ran the whole gamut of emotions, when he was hiding away in a cave or running for his life. I know all about the violence and strife in this city, and you are pursued by one particular person out to do violence. Maybe God gave us the psalms to show us that we are just like everyone else who has been on this earth for centuries, millennia. Just don't forget, David had a happy ending, as did Job. You'll have your happy ending, baby, and I'm going to be there to share it with you."

He smiled and added, "I'll keep reminding you that you have more protection than I or the whole force can give you."

Friday morning, about eleven o'clock, Laura Maxwell called me to assure me that they were still working on my case. "Sometimes when a victim doesn't hear anything from us, she may think that we have forgotten her case. I, most assuredly, can tell you that's not true in this instance. Hardly a minute goes by that I don't think of you and, many times a day, I consult with my people to see what is being done. We have investigators out, and our computers are humming, trying to find out anything possible to help you. Win Keffler has people working day and night on his end, too, I promise you. Win is a great person and tops in his profession."

"You speak as if you know him personally," I said, a big question in my mind.

"Oh, I've known Win Keffler all my life. We came from the same neighborhood in Oakland, and he was best buds with my uncle Tim, who was only eight years older than I. Win was at our house a lot, and I thought he was the coolest guy in Oakland.

"Once, when I was seven, and he was about fifteen, he came over with Tim. He had a horrible shiner and some other bruises, as well as a limp. Being a seven-year-old, I had no qualms about asking him, point-blank about his injuries. He told me he got into a fight. Well, later, I heard some

ONCE AGAIN I FEAR

of the adults talking, and gathered from their conversation that Win's father had beaten the crud out of him. I went into my bedroom and cried.

"One time, he held me on his lap and told me, 'Laura, if anyone ever tries to hurt you, you tell them Uncle Win will take care of it for you.' I took it to heart. When I was about nine and he was a senior in high school, some teenagers decided my lunch money belonged in their pockets. I told Win. He asked for a description and the location where they accosted me. He said, 'Yeah, I know those guys. I'll take care of it.' From then on, those guys just stared at me and slunk off. Win's a good guy."

"Laura, something has been bothering Lucas and me about Keffler. He acted, at first, as if he were reluctant to pursue this case. He still hum-haws around about it. Lucas is baffled by his attitude. And, yet, you say he's actively pursuing the case. What is the problem?"

"Don't you worry, Rachelle; Win will keep pursuing the case. The problem may be because of his son." She paused.

"His son? What's his son got to do with it?" I asked, incredulously.

"You don't know? His son, Ben, works for the Bard Company. Win wanted, more than anything, that his son should have everything that his own alcoholic father denied him. He sacrificed a lot to get that boy through college and through his MBA, although I thought Ben was an arrogant little twerp. When he was hired at Bard, Win was ecstatic. And Ben, surprisingly enough, is doing very well there, moving up the ladder in record time. I think Win may have some real fears that if old Jud Bard's son is apprehended and sent to jail, and the Keffler name is associated with the apprehension, he just might take it out on Ben. Old Jud is a mean old so-and-so and could, conceivably, do just that."

After Laura and I hung up, I sat thinking about what she had told me. It explained so many things that had puzzled both Lucas and me. It relieved my mind a lot, knowing that Win Keffler wasn't the cold man that I had taken him to be. A lot of people were scared, it seemed to me.

Chapter 36

On Sunday, I went to church with Lucas, and met Doug West and all Lucas' other friends. They were just as great as Lucas had said. Of course, I got the usual close observations, especially by some young women, who, I thought, at some point, probably had had designs on Lucas, themselves. I felt no rancor in their stares, just curiosity. They were all cordial, and admired my ring.

Doug West took us aside and prayed over us, asking God's blessing and protection. "You're fighting a spiritual battle here," he counseled us. "I can feel it as a tangible thing. We must keep you two bathed in prayer until this is all over."

"But how do you fight it?" I yearned for an answer.

"Plead the blood of Jesus, for one thing; demons can't stand against that. I will have our prayer groups here pray specifically in that manner. Concentrated prayer forms a boundary beyond which demonic powers cannot go. The other weapon we have is the Word. Jesus used that weapon, as did his disciples. Also, remember what James said in the fourth chapter: 'Submit yourselves therefore to God. Resist the devil, and he will flee from you.' I have always thought the word 'submit' means to give one's self over to the care of another. I think that fits in this scripture. Give yourselves over to the care of God, resist the devil with prayer and the Word, and God will fight your battle for you, forcing demonic powers to flee."

ONCE AGAIN I FEAR

"I get the feeling that you have had experience with that concept," Lucas said.

"On many occasions," Doug replied, shaking his head. "When we started this work here, satanic forces came at us from all sides, in many forms. First it was the city zoning people, then certain people who didn't want this kind of message preached in this city, speaking up against us. We had stood firm on moral issues, which infuriated a lot of people. Finally, it was in the form of physical attacks. I was viciously beaten and stabbed outside the church once, in broad daylight, by three men. I got in a few good licks, but I feared for a while that I was done for.

"Then, I saw the man in the purple sweat suit. He jogged right up to those three men and pointed his finger at them, telling them to get out of there. They started shaking, and ran, as if their lives depended on it. The man picked me up off the pavement and escorted me inside the church, where I called for help. When the paramedics arrived, the man was nowhere to be found. Amazingly, although my wounds were extensive, I healed in record time. I'm sure you know who I think the man in the purple sweat suit was." He smiled, raising his eyes to Heaven.

"I have no doubt about that one, Doug," Lucas said. "That boosts my faith, to think there may be a man in a purple sweat suit hanging around Rachelle." He squeezed my hand and smiled down at me.

When Lucas had picked me up for church, he had brought his clothes, for the party that night, with him. He had no intention of leaving me alone, even for a few minutes, that day.

After we finished talking to Doug, we went to a nearby restaurant for lunch. There, we saw several of his friends from church, who invited us to sit with them. I really enjoyed these congenial people, finding them very easy to talk to. Lucas seemed pleased that I fitted in with his long-time friends, and so was I; they would be my friends, from now on, too.

When we arrived at my apartment, Lucas said that he felt he needed to take a nap, since he had gotten only about six hours of sleep the night before. It sounded like a good idea to me, too, so that is how we spent the afternoon—him in the guestroom, and me in my room, curled up with Tache.

The party would start at six-thirty, so, at a little after four, I went into the guestroom, where Lucas lay sleeping. He was curled on his left side, his hand under his cheek. My heart swelled with love for him. I would see him this way many times, from now on, I knew.

I knelt by the bed and kissed him gently. He muttered in his sleep, and then, beginning to waken, pulled me into his arms, holding me tight. We stayed that way for a minute or two, and then I whispered, "Time to get up, sleepy head; our yacht awaits."

Now fully awake, he kissed me gently, and moved to get up. "If I must, I must. One thing for sure, beautiful lady, I'll never get tired of being wakened that way. Much better than an alarm clock."

When we both stood up, he again pulled me against him and kissed me lovingly.

At about a quarter after six, we arrived at Pier 33, where the ghostly-white California Hornblower stood ready to receive her passengers for the evening. The stars and stripes flapped from the stern, and, at the prow, the blue Hornblower ensign fluttered in the wind.

Lucas, wearing a dark gray suit, with a faint teal thread woven through it, and a teal blue tie, looked so handsome that I had a hard time looking at anything else. However, the charm of the waterfront, as usual, eventually drew my attention, bringing with it a sense of adventure. We were embarking on a voyage together. No matter that it was only three hours long; it was our first trip, and an exciting one.

After Lucas had parked the car in the parking lot, at the end of the pier, we walked, hand in hand toward the magnificent yacht. I had purposely chosen to wear two-inch heel, rather than the dressier three-inch ones, because I knew I would be walking a lot tonight.

Wind whipped at me, cutting through my faux-fur jacket, and wrapped strands of hair around my face, sticking them to my lipstick. It was a continual effort to uncover my eyes so I could see. I had not worn an elaborate hairdo, knowing what would happen here. At least a few strokes of a brush would put my simple do back in order.

When we reached the pier, I turned and looked back toward the city. Lights dotted the hills above us, and Coit Tower, on Telegraph Hill, reached gracefully into the night sky some distance beyond. I sighed with exquisite pleasure.

We walked down the pier, and mounted the short ramp leading into the port side of the yacht. I was kept busy greeting people and introducing Lucas, as we walked up the ramp, and made our way to the top level. It was always fun to sit up high, to get the maximum view the yacht afforded.

Everyone around us was in a festive mood, with lots of laughter and chatter swirling around the room. The whole yacht was decorated with Christmas greenery, and red bows. A brightly ornamented Christmas tree sat on the second level, where some of the guests would dine, dance, and drink at the bar. Another welcomed us at the top of the stairway to the uppermost deck. I saw Robert Bainbridge, his wife, and Trish Willingham at a table near a window so Lucas and I joined them. I introduced Lucas to my co-workers, and saw looks of approval from all three of them. After Lucas helped me remove my jacket, we sat down at the table, which was covered with a white cloth, with red napkins folded in intricate shapes and standing in long-stemmed wine glasses

We wondered who our other three dinner companions would be, but we didn't have long to wait. Greg Phillips soon arrived with a striking little redhead, introducing her as Penny Logan. I liked her immediately, sensing both humor and intelligence in her blue eyes.

Then, Mark Bussell ambled over to the table, stag, I noted, with a mixed drink in his hand, the ice clinking as he walked. He sat in the vacant chair between Trish and me. "I'm so glad you two beautiful women saved this chair for me," Mark said, grinning at both Trish and me. "Now, Rachelle, I want to meet this impossibly wonderful man you've been raving about." He was in a mischievous mood, and I wondered how many drinks he had already had.

It struck me, then, how little of my co-workers' lives I really knew. For instance, I knew nothing, really, about how much of a drinker Mark was. I had seen him at company dinners and meetings, where drinks were served, but I had paid little attention to his drinking habits.

Trish, I knew a little better, and Greg, of course. But, even with them, there were areas of their lives that were hidden from me. Could it be that they, too, wondered about my life? It was a fact that I had at least one big secret that I had kept from them. Greg, now, of course, knew something of my past, but there were details that I had not felt he needed to know.

Even after talking to Greg at great lengths in New York, I still felt there were things about which he chose not to talk.

And what about Trish? Yes, we had spent quite a few lunches and evenings together, but there was always a hint of mystery about the girl. I remembered the looks of sadness and worry I had seen on her face, and, also, the unexplained 'business' meetings to which she had gone. She had been very vague about them, and I had not probed.

Suddenly, like a spark of light before my eyes, I realized that Trish no longer looked anxious, nor had she for a few days now. Also, she was wearing a new outfit, a red velvet dress, which I knew came from Devon's, and cost much more than the things Trish usually wore. Now, it sank into my consciousness, that she had been wearing a perky new suit on Friday, also a Devon's high-end item. I had been so full of my own worries, that I had not really grasped that fact.

I watched Trish, now, as she conversed with Mark, bright, bubbly, teasing, even flirting a little. A new Trish. She had overcome something that had been worrying her for months, and had come into some money, from somewhere, I was sure of it. I made a mental note to set her down and make her tell me what was going on, if she were willing to tell me, that is.

I could detect that Lucas was closely observing these people, while maintaining a friendly demeanor. He was a trained observer; they would never perceive that they were under his professional microscope. He engaged in some sports talk with Greg and Robert Bainbridge, and asked Mrs. Bainbridge about her children and grandchildren.

Lucas told Penny that he had heard she was studying biochemistry, asking her how her studies were progressing, and what she planned for the future. She seemed pleasantly surprised that he knew so much about her, telling him her schooling was going very well, and that she had plans to work in a creation research lab.

Lucas urged her to tell him more.

ONCE AGAIN I FEAR

Penny's voice was filled with enthusiasm as she said, "Scientists there are finding that scientific discoveries of the late 20th century increasingly point to the reality of an intelligent design in the universe and challenge the scientific paradigm surrounding Darwinian evolution," she said.

She looked around the table, seeing a couple of baffled looks, but continued, "Research by biochemists point to some type of intelligent design underlying cellular systems, systems so complex they could not have been created by a series of gradual changes necessary for Darwinian evolution to take place. I want, very much, to be vitally involved in this kind of research. I think it's God's plan for my life."

Even though I did not understand all of what Penny said, I did grasp that, in simple words, she was preparing to devote her life proving that God created the universe. The fire of wonder in her eyes was testimony to her commitment and devotion to her chosen field.

"I think that's fascinating," Lucas said. "I've read quite a few articles in secular science magazines that have some theories that I find impossible to swallow. And this gradual change theory is probably the hardest. Of course, I accept that there has been evolution within species; people have gotten bigger, for instance. But to gradually change from one species to another is unbelievable to me."

Penny's eyes sparkled. "Charles Darwin, himself, stated that his theory would absolutely break down if any complex organism could be cited which could not possibly have been formed by numerous, successive slight modifications. Scientists are finding just that, in cellular systems." She looked around and then said, "Oh, I'm sorry. I get so wound up when I start talking about all this, that I forget there are people who aren't the least interested in science."

"My dear," Robert Bainbridge said, smiling, "I wish there were more young people in the scientific field who had your enthusiasm for doing research to back up God's word. The Bible will always be proven true, you can count on it."

Penny's eyes were shining, and even Greg was beaming. He knew that the "Big Boss" had warmed to Penny. I saw him observing her with new respect.

The conversation took many interesting turns, as the eight people around the table shared with one another. Trish asked Mark about his days in Chicago, since she said she had relatives there. He told several amusing anecdotes, mostly about his poverty, while he saved his money to go to Europe. Robert then told of some similar incidences in his own younger life. Mrs. Bainbridge was quieter than the rest of us, talking only when prompted, but sat smiling and, obviously, enjoying the talk around the table.

We all ordered drinks to precede the dinner, everyone ordering a non-alcoholic drink, except Mark and Greg. Greg and Penny ordered grilled prawns with Red Onion Confit, topped with Citrus Salsa, as an appetizer. The rest of us decided not to order any appetizers. Afterwards, the white-coated waiters brought delicious tossed salads, with the house vinaigrette. Assorted rolls and butter, in napkin-lined baskets were placed in easy-to-reach places on the table.

Trish and Mark, by this time, were definitely flirting with each other, in a way that I had never seen between them. I caught Greg glance disapprovingly across the table, trying, it would seem, to send a message to Mark about the problems possible with co-worker involvement. Mark didn't pick up the message, I could see. Could he possibly be interested in Trish? I doubted it; it was a game, fed by alcohol. I said a silent prayer that Trish would be wise in this situation.

The Bainbridges were served baked orange roughy, with a coconut curry cream sauce. The rest of us had chosen filet mignon, with a tangy sauce, tiny new potatoes, roasted with butter, and a vegetable medley. After everyone had been served, the talk quieted. The flirting between Mark and Trish subsided in favor of eating. It was a relief, for the moment, not to feel that little worry about my friend.

Dessert was a heavenly cheese cake, topped with strawberries—probably flown in from Mexico—filling me to the point I felt I would burst. Sighing contentedly, I turned to Lucas and asked if he would like to go for a stroll out on the deck. He rose and held my chair as I got up. "Now we're going to see the lights that I enjoy so much," I said to our dinner companions.

ONCE AGAIN I FEAR

"Maybe Mona and I will do that after we finish our coffee," Robert said, smiling at his petite wife.

Trish and Mark had gone down to a lower level to dance. Greg and Penny had gone to have their pictures done by the photographer hired for the occasion. The rest of us would eventually do the same. I very much wanted a picture made with Lucas. Our first together.

Out on the deck, the wind, oddly enough, was calmer than it had been on the pier. I did not wear my jacket, taking the chance that I would not be too uncomfortable. I was wearing a long-sleeved, burgundy velveteen top, over burgundy, wool crepe palazzo pants. The outfit offered some warmth, and Lucas' arm around me offered more, two kinds of warmth.

As we strolled along the deck, on the port side of the yacht, we looked first at the city, spread in glittering splendor over the hills—usually said to be seven hills; others swore there were forty-three. I wondered where, among all those lights, Judson Bard crouched in his shadowy lair, waiting to emerge to torment me. I shivered and drew near to Lucas.

We could see, over the prow, the majestic Golden Gate Bridge, soaring high into the mist above the bay. To starboard, would be the lights of Alcatraz, once the scene of misery and despair, now a mere curiosity. After going under the Golden Gate, we would swing around and, then head toward the Bay Bridge, that double-decked link to Oakland, Walnut Creek and the other cities in the east bay area.

I sighed deeply, gulping in salty sea air, and listening to the braying and sloshing of a ship heading out to sea. Could it be one of the Bard liners? Lucas and I stood still, surveying our world, gloriously happy being here together. He pulled me into his arms and held me close, saying nothing, but, in his silence, saying everything I wanted to hear.

A waiter walked quickly toward the prow end of the deck. He did not look our way, apparently intent on carrying out some duty to which he had been assigned. A red scarf fluttered at his throat as he disappeared from our view, through a door.

Mark and Trish then came out onto the deck, through the same door, holding hands and laughing. Trish's hair blew in the breeze, a dark fluttering cloud about her head.

They stopped about fifteen feet from us, but did not seem to notice that we were there. Trish seemed oblivious to anything but the handsome young man by her side. Then, they were close, their arms around each other, and kissing eagerly. Trish, Trish, I thought, what are you getting yourself into? I had to turn away, unable to bear seeing what I felt was the beginning of pain for Trish Willingham.

"Let's go inside," Lucas suggested, sensing my discomfort.

We walked to the room set aside for photographs, and found, to our pleasant surprise, that there was no line of people waiting. The Bainbridges came out, holding hands and grinning at each other. When they saw us, Mona said, "Oh that was fun. Robert and I haven't had our picture made together for quite a while. This should be a real souvenir."

Robert nodded and led his wife out into the upper level dining area.

The photographer was skillful at bringing fun into the photography session, having Lucas and me saying silly things to each other to make us laugh. He saw the sparkle on my left hand, and rightly guessed that we were newly engaged. He posed us in a close embrace, my left hand carefully arranged on Lucas' right arm.

When we left the room, I again saw the waiter that had walked near us on the deck. As before, I did not see his face, but recognized the red scarf that he had tied around his neck, inside the collar of his white jacket. Unlike the other waiters, he didn't carry a tray or towel, just rapidly walked from one place to another, outside the regular serving areas. I dismissed him from my mind and concentrated on the man by my side. How glad I was to have him with me. These Christmas parties were, sometimes, affairs that I just tolerated.

As we came back into the dining area, I suddenly heard a familiar, trilling laugh. I turned in the direction from which it came and saw Dru Warren, with the handsome man in the newspaper picture, walking down the stairs to the lower level. I knew she was usually invited to Devon's Christmas parties, but I had not known she would be back from LA in time to attend this one. I supposed that she had been on the lower level most of the evening, so I would not have seen her. I was again seized by fear of what I might learn about my friend, but determined to talk to her as soon as possible. Lucas, also, wished to have some time with her.

228

ONCE AGAIN I FEAR

The evening wore on, with dancing and drinking going on downstairs. Various events livened the evening, such as door-prize drawings, and gifts given to certain employees who had contributed something special to Devon's. Greg was one of these employees, mainly because I had nominated him.

Some gag gifts were given, as good-natured ribbing of some employees. They were accepted in good grace, and with a lot of laughter. These were good people.

Once more, I saw Dru and her friend, in the crowd, but she had her back to me, and was too far away for me to call to her. Something seemed out of kilter about the whole thing.

Chapter 37

As nine-thirty drew near, and the yacht was heading back to the pier, people started donning coats, picking up gifts, and gathering in groups, ready to leave. I knew that many of these groups would go to other locations for further partying.

Before Lucas and I got to the ramp, Dru and her friend had already stepped down to the pier and were heading to a limousine parked nearby, supplied by DuBois, no doubt.

Trish and Mark were standing over against the rail, still holding hands, but no longer laughing. Mark appeared very drunk, and Trish seemed a bit squiffy, herself. They seemed in no hurry to leave the yacht.

Greg and Penny stood talking to Robert and Mona, with the older couple obviously enjoying the company of the young couple. I thought, "Greg, are you really all you seem to be?' I longed to be sure. For a while, in New York, I had been sure, but it kept occurring to me that I had missed something in his story about his growing up years, but what? Something kept niggling at my mind, but I couldn't quite latch onto it. Would he tell me, if I really pressed him? In my dangerous situation, I felt it might be advisable to do just that.

Then, a thought occurred to me. "He had said he had been sent away to boarding school in his sophomore year of high school. Why then? Usually, the son of a wealthy family would be enrolled in boarding school long before high school even started. It was highly unusual to wait until the sophomore year. He had not even said if it was the beginning of the

ONCE AGAIN I FEAR

year or during the year. Could something have happened to cause him to be, in essence, banished to the school, perhaps for his own good? And what kind of school? I had noted that his carriage was that of someone trained in the military. Could it have been a military school?

I realized I had been deep in thought when Lucas shook me slightly and enquired, "Rachelle, where have you been? Not here with me for the last few minutes, I'm sure." His tone was not accusatory, but somewhat concerned.

"Oh, darling, I was just thinking about Greg. There are still things about him I don't understand. We'll talk about it when we get home."

"I'm wondering about your friend, Dru. You pointed her out to me—attractive woman, your Dru. What seems strange to me is that she never looked for you, her very close friend, probably knowing you must be here. Could she be avoiding you?" A perplexed look clouded his face.

"That's it, Lucas. I knew there was something not quite right; she didn't try to find me. I would have looked all over for her, if I had known she was here. When I first saw her there on the stairs, I felt a vague discomfort that kept me from catching up with her. It was almost as of she knew I was watching her, and deliberately kept her eyes averted. But why? I can't figure all this out, Lucas."

"Don't worry about it right now, baby; we'll go over everything together tonight, and see if we can come up with any explanations."

At that point, I glanced down the ramp, and saw the waiter, with the red scarf around his neck, descending to the pier. When he reached the bottom of the ramp, he walked quickly down the pier, looking straight ahead, as if he were in a hurry. Strange, I would have thought all personnel on the yacht would have been engaged in cleaning up.

When Lucas and I finally reached the pier, we strolled along, in no hurry, enjoying the night sounds of the harbor: the creaking of sailing ships, the sloshing and slurping of water against the pier, voices and laughter, the call of a tern, somewhere nearby. The smell of salt and wet wood assailed our nostrils.

Above the sounds of the night, I suddenly heard a woman shrieking, "Look out, he's got a gun!" Then, many running feet, as people reacted to the woman's warning. More screams and shrieks joined the cacophony, chilling me to the marrow.

231

Lucas' hold on my arm tightened, as we reached land, drawing me behind him. Then I saw him—the waiter with the red scarf. He stood perhaps twenty feet from us, the ugly metal of the gun barrel glinting in light from overhead lamps. His face was clear now, twisted with hatred, his eyes, colorless in this light, squinted in concentration. Wind whipped his shoulder-length hair across his face.

I knew him then, his long, trim body standing slightly leaned forward, his arms extended with the weapon, pointed straight at me. Judson!

A scream rose in my throat, and I felt Lucas tense, ready for action. He had recognized our enemy, too.

The parking lot was now more than half empty, and most of the people who had been around us had run away. But a few stood nearby, waiting to see what would happen, some probably in concern, but some driven by morbid curiosity. Would they see blood shed, here by the shore?

Waves of terror swept over me, paralyzing me. We had no place to go, nothing behind which we could hide. "Lucas," I whispered, "what are we going to do?"

I knew Lucas was scared, too, but he was also a professional, who had faced this kind of danger before. "You're making a big mistake, Bard," he called to Judson, in a level, unemotional voice. "You will never get away with shooting us here, before all these witnesses. Yes, you, Judson Edward Bard, the third, who have killed before, and won't give up on trying to kill again. Everyone here now knows who you are, and what you are. You'll be hunted down until you're caught and brought to justice."

Judson was staring at us, his eyes steady and hard, but I could see what Lucas was doing; giving the people around us information that could make them valuable witnesses, in case Judson carried out what was obviously the threat to kill us. He was also taking Judson off balance mentally, making him feel less in control of the situation. He was no longer hiding behind a disguise; he, too, was vulnerable, in a sense.

Lucas kept me behind him and slowly edged toward Judson. "You're going to have to kill me to get to Rachelle; you know that don't you?" he asked calmly.

"I'll kill you both, Dayton," Judson sneered. "You're not going to have Rachelle, not ever. If I can't have her, you won't either. You can die with

ONCE AGAIN I FEAR

her, if you want to." The hardness in his voice sent waves of terror through me. He meant what he said.

"Do you know what kind of manhunt ensues when someone kills a police officer? You'll never have a moment's peace, always wondering who is behind you, who is watching you."

Out of the corner of my eye, I saw Robert Bainbridge, standing by a parked car, his body posed somewhat like a prize fighter, ready to engage in battle. Oh, God, I thought, don't let Robert try to intervene. I couldn't bear to have him killed to protect me.

Lucas noticed Robert, too, as well as two young men, who worked in the shipping department of Devon's, standing about ten feet from Judson's right side. Then, a man that I didn't know, dressed in jeans and a blue windbreaker, moved up slowly behind Judson, his footsteps silent, his strength apparent in his body movements. Essentially, Judson was surrounded, although he was not aware of it.

With the cold, bitter taste of fear in my mouth, I started to pray, silently at first, and then aloud. "Father, we're submitted to your care. Send your angels to protect us and the people around us."

"Father, I agree with Rachelle in that request," Lucas professed to our Heavenly Father. "You are able to send the enemy fleeing. Take away his strength and put up a defense against him."

The gun, in Judson's hand was beginning to shake, our Heavenly Father obviously answering our request. Suddenly, the man behind Judson leaped forward and shoved Judson to the ground. He then stepped on Judson's hand. When Judson had let go of the gun, the man kicked it out of his hand, sending it skidding a few feet away from him.

With his characteristic quickness, Judson was on his feet in seconds, and took off running westward on The Embarcadero. The wide walk along The Embarcadero was a popular place for joggers, even at night, so Judson would simply become one of them, I thought. His fleetness carried him out of sight in seconds. The young men from Devon's attempted to catch up with him, but soon gave up in defeat.

Lucas and I stood holding each other, as people now appeared out of the shadows to gather around us. "Wow! That guy is a nut case!" someone said, echoing what I had said to Judson six years ago at Stanford.

233

I raised my head from Lucas' shoulder and looked around at the people standing in groups in the parking area. The man who had knocked Judson down was nowhere to be seen.

"The police have been called," someone else said. "They should be here in a minute." As if on cue, sirens blasted the night, and the roar of speeding cars sounded on The Embarcadero.

Three quarters of an hour later, Lucas and I stood under a stream of light cast by one of the lights that were attached along the sides of the buildings around the parking lot. Win Keffler and three other officers that I did not know—but Lucas obviously did—stood with us. Keffler had arrived after the others, probably having been notified that this concerned his case against Judson.

"Nasty, nasty, nasty," Keffler muttered under his breath. Then, in a normal voice, he told me, "Miss Atherly, that guy is determined to get you, I would say. Well, we'll bear down on trying to find him. We have the gun, and we have witnesses who saw him. He, now, is in danger of being recognized by a lot of people, if he sticks his head out of hiding. Someone said they saw him run down The Embarcadero, cross over onto Beach Street, a half mile down, and around the Pier Thirty Nine Garage. We have men on foot looking for him in that vicinity. It's my bet, that he had a car waiting somewhere around there, but one never knows."

I watched Keffler's face as he talked, seeing the little black eyes, now full of what I felt was seething anger at Judson Bard. This was not a face lacking in emotion, as I had thought; he would follow through on his promise to me.

"Sergeant Keffler, I know about your son," I stated bluntly. I had already told Lucas what Laura had told me. I watched Keffler's face, gauging his reaction. It came instantly, a mixture of surprise, shame, and, yes, guilt.

"Judson Bard's father could take revenge on Ben, if you apprehend his son," I continued. "We'll pray that won't happen. Besides, you may not be the one to apprehend him; there are a lot of people out after him. I want you to know, I understand what you are going through with this, and I assure you that I know you will do the right thing, no matter what."

ONCE AGAIN I FEAR

Keffler tucked his head, and rubbed his forehead with a big, strong hand. He stood that way for several seconds, until I feared he was crying. Then he looked me squarely in the eye and promised, "My son's position with the Bard Company has ceased to have any effect on how I handle this. I ask your forgiveness for my letting it influence my thinking, even for those few days. It won't happen again."

"There's nothing to forgive, Sergeant," I said, laying a hand on his sleeve. "You're Lucas' friend; I hope you'll be mine." I would tell him about Laura Maxwell at a later date.

The big, heavy face broke into a grin as he patted me on the shoulder. "I think we already are friends, Miss—oh, may I call you Rachelle?"

"You may, if I may call you Win," I answered, smiling at him.

"I'd like that, Rachelle. Dear God, I feel better. I've hated myself these last days, feeling I'd betrayed my profession, and you. I should have known better than to let my personal life interfere with my judgement."

A paramedic team had arrived with the police; their vehicle now stood near to where Lucas and I had spoken with Keffler. Lucas had walked a few feet away to talk to another officer, and Keffler disappeared around the emergency vehicle. I stood alone, feeling at peace, knowing, beyond doubt, now, that God had his hand on my life and on Lucas', also.

Voices carried in the sharp sea air, and I became aware of Keffler's voice coming from the other side of the emergency vehicle. "Oh, hi, there, Greg; how're ya doing, boy? Good to see you."

Greg's voice also reached me. "Sergeant! Good to see you, too. Oh, Penny, I want you to meet Sergeant Keffler, an old buddy. And, Sergeant, Penny is a good friend of mine." A murmur of exchanged greetings followed.

"Sergeant Keffler is the one that helped me get myself back on the right track, after that trouble I got into when I was fifteen." A pause. "I've told Penny all about it, Sergeant."

"You've come a long way, Greg; I'm proud of you. A lot of kids would have gone right on getting into trouble and ending up where we don't even like to think about." Keffler's voice held traces of sadness, perhaps from memories of countless kids he had known.

"I was very angry when you suggested to mom that she send me to that military academy in Missouri, but, now I know it was the best thing that ever happened to me. It got me off drugs, and away from that crowd I had started hanging with. The academy taught me self-respect and respect for other people. I, also, think getting arrested for shoplifting, to support my habit, was the best thing that ever happened to me."

It was a shock to hear Greg so calmly talking about what must have been a terrible time in his life.

"Greg, what you did, and what you might have kept doing, could have ruined your life. I'm proud that you went ahead and finished school and went to college. I talk to your mom once in a while, and she's one proud lady, too. I'm just glad that your record was a juvenile one, and is now past history. You got the chance to start over, as if the past never happened."

Greg's voice was slightly hoarse, as if with unshed tears, as he responded. "Like being born again, huh? I think something like that is what you've been trying to tell me, Penny. Maybe I'll listen a little more carefully from now on."

So that was what Greg had been unable to tell me. Tears gathered in my eyes and spilled down my cheeks. "Oh, Lord," I prayed, "thank you for what you are doing in Greg's life. Bring him all the way to the truth."

Lucas moved back to my side and noticed my tears. "It's over for now, baby, don't cry." He put his arm around me and drew me close to him.

"Oh, Lucas, God is so good." I told him what I had just heard, and added, "I think Greg is definitely on his way to a relationship with our heavenly Father.

Chapter 38

In my apartment that night, Lucas and I sat on the sofa, the songs of Sandi Patti soothing and uplifting us from the stereo. My heart no longer raced, and my hands were no longer sweaty. I could only vaguely remember the chill in my body as I stood by the pier, facing the gun that could have taken my life. My mind now felt clear, my heart at peace; I was ready to sort through the puzzles that existed in my life.

"Do you think the man in the purple sweat suit was wearing jeans and a blue windbreaker tonight?" Lucas asked, rubbing his hand along the side of my neck.

I gasped. "Oh, Lucas, I didn't even think about that. Isn't that what the Bible means when it speaks of 'angels unaware'? Probably, many times, we don't recognize those heavenly beings."

"He rescued us, you know," Lucas averred. "Bard's hand was shaking, but, from my experience, I know that is when a lot of gun-toters shoot. It's desperation, probably. I have no doubt Judson would have fired the gun in another five seconds."

"You read him a lot differently than I did," I acknowledge. "I could have sworn he was ready to drop the gun, and maybe even give himself up. A lot I know. I'm so glad you were there."

"So am I, baby; so am I."

"I can't wait to see Dad tomorrow and introduce you to him." I felt my face light up, as I smiled with happy anticipation.

"I used to dread meeting a girl's father. I mean it. But, you know, I'm really looking forward to meeting the man who is going to be my father-in-law. From what you've told me about him, he has to be a great man. Well, he'd have to be, to have a daughter like you." He leaned over and kissed me lightly.

"I plan to tell Dad everything that has happened to us, Lucas. I've kept him in the dark about some of it, not wanting him to worry. Your being there should give him some feeling that I'm being protected."

"Yes, I agree that your dad should know everything. After all, he is praying for you, and he needs to know how to pray specifically."

"Uh, huh, that's true. Now, we've got to go over all the things that have happened and see if we can make some sense of them."

We talked until one a.m., but could come to no definite conclusions about where the people I knew fitted into the horror that was hanging over my life.

We drove to Saratoga early next morning, taking Highway 280, the Junipero Serra Expressway. We definitely did not want to be on the Bayshore Freeway at rush hour.

The expressway cut through green mountains, lush from early winter rains, and dotted with luxury homes, and ornamented with small, upscale towns. It was such a beautiful drive, that I relaxed and enjoyed it to the fullest.

"I don't come down this way often," Lucas remarked. "I had forgotten how beautiful it is. I suppose a police officer in a city can forget that there is anything but traffic, crime, and too much dirt, both on streets and on lives. It's good to see God's fresh, clean creation."

"I always feel the same way when I drive this road. Now, I have an added pleasure; I know the two men I love best in the entire world are going to meet today. I can hardly wait."

When we reached the road to my father's house, Lucas was obviously astonished at the luxury of this neighborhood. When we pulled into the driveway of Dad's house, however, I think he was relieved to find it was not one of the sprawling mansions that we had passed.

ONCE AGAIN I FEAR

Dad heard our car and met us at the door, ushering us inside. "Dad, I want you to meet Lucas; Lucas, my father."

They shook hands and grinned at each other. "I am very pleased to meet you, Mr. Atherly," Lucas beamed. "Hey, you're not ten feet tall; I could have sworn you were, from what your daughter has been telling me."

Dad laughed good-naturedly and countered, "And I expected to see Prince Charming on a white horse. And, Lucas, you can call me Stan, no formalities here."

Dad hugged me and kissed me on the cheek, then placed an arm around each of us, leading us to the living room.

Lorraine came running out of the kitchen, wiping her brow on her apron and crooning, "Rachelle, Rachelle darling, you're home! Let me have a hug!" She wrapped me in her warm, plump arms and patted me, as if I were a child. "Sweetie, I'm so glad to see you."

"Lorraine, I'm always happy to see you. I really love you, you know?"

"You bet I know it. And I love you, as if you were my own granddaughter, which you practically are." Lorraine grinned and kissed me soundly on the cheek.

"Now, Lorraine, I want you to meet someone very special. This is Lucas. I want you and Dad both to know that I'm going to marry him as soon as possible." Lucas smiled with pleasure and nodded. "And, Lucas," I added, "Lorraine is my surrogate grandmother, even though she's not really old enough to be my grandmother. I don't know how I would have survived without her."

"Oh, I've waited a long time for this, Lucas. I mean, I've wanted my little sweetheart to meet a good man and find some happiness." She went over and hugged Lucas, vigorously patting him, too. I could not keep from laughing.

"Welcome to the family, Lucas," I said, still laughing.

Lorraine served us a late breakfast and then left us alone, while she went to clean Dad's room and bath. Lucas, Dad and I ate in companionable silence for a while. Then, Dad asked Lucas some questions about his job and his family, seemingly liking what he heard. It

239

was as I had suspected it would be: these two wonderful men liked each other instantly.

When we had finished, we then went into the living room to continue our conversation. Before long, I got around to telling Dad everything that had happened in recent days, the good and the bad. I saw joy on my father's face when I told him how happy I was, and he asked to see my ring.

"Lucas, I believe you're the one I prayed would come into Rachelle's life. I prayed the Lord would send a Christian man, who would love her even more than I do, if that were possible. I think God answered my prayer."

Then, when I related all the attempts that had been made on our lives, tears spilled from Dad's eyes, and he wiped them with the back of his hand. "Oh, Rachelle, I'm so sorry you're having to endure this. I've asked God when it's ever going to stop. He's spoken to me, in His still, small voice, telling me that you're in His hands, hands that are much bigger than mine. Now, tell me, Lucas, what is being done to catch this monster?"

Lucas told him all about the massive search, the canvassing of neighborhoods where Judson might possibly be, the contacting of every officer's "snitch", questioning everyone who had known Judson at any time, and the numerous times his family had been questioned. "Old Jud Bard about blew a gasket the second time he was brought in and questioned. According to him, his son's still in Europe and he hasn't heard from him in years. We all know he's lying—but just try proving that he's aware his son's in town. He refused to accept that the son's fingerprints had been found at the scenes, and that Rachelle had positively identified him.

"We're convinced, as is the D.A.'s office in San Jose, that old Jud was getting money to sonny boy in Europe, probably through a Swiss bank account, otherwise, Judson wouldn't have been able to survive over there. He was seen in some pretty fancy places. Jud won't admit a thing, and there's no way to trace money funneled through Switzerland. I promise you, when we catch the son, and, if we are able to prove his daddy's participation in all this, old Jud's going to have the book thrown at him." I saw Lucas' jaw clench.

ONCE AGAIN I FEAR

Dad sat listening intently to Lucas and, then turned to me. "Rachelle, I'm going home with you, until this is over. And don't you argue with me." Sounds like Lucas, I thought. "I wanted to come up for Christmas, anyway, and that's just a few days away. I'm going to take a leave of absence from the company. There's nothing really pressing right now, and I have some excellent people under me, trained to handle everything, about as well as I do. I'm fifty-five now, and I'm planning to take an early retirement when I'm fifty-eight, so I'm preparing to turn over the reins."

He stopped and broke into a grin. "After all," he continued, "I'll want to have plenty of time to spend with my grandchildren. I'm even thinking of taking a flat up there, maybe in the Marina area. I'd love having a view of the bay from my front window."

Lucas smiled at me and then at Dad. "Hey, it sounds like you have it all planned. You know, I think that's a wonderful idea, Stan; our children will love having Granddaddy around a lot."

He squeezed my hand and then said, seriously, "Stan, I would love to have you come and help me watch over Rachelle. I get so scared sometime—that I'll not be nearby, at some point, and that creep will get to her. Having you there all the time will relieve my mind a lot."

"Good, that settles it. Now, hang on, and I'll go make some phone calls and pack some things." He got up and left the room, his footsteps then sounding on the stairs.

I turned to Lucas. "Lucas, what did I do to deserve you two? You both make me feel so safe, in spite of the danger."

"Baby, your dad and I would both lay our lives down for you, you know that. You deserve any good that comes your way, I can assure you."

We got up and strolled out to the back patio, overlooking a wooded area, which climbed up the side of the mountain. A sparrow flitted from where it had been perched on the barbecue grill and flew to a nearby oak tree, joining another sparrow, perhaps its mate. The air was clear and cool, a slight wind blowing against our faces and rustling the trees.

Darkness and danger seemed far away, as we stood holding hands and talking in subdued voices. I believed God's angels were hovering around us.

We left Saratoga at seven o'clock that evening, hoping the rush-hour traffic had, by that time, subsided. Dad didn't take his car, knowing he could use mine most of the time, and thus avoiding the problem of a place to park. He sat in the back seat of Lucas' Taurus and kept a steady flow of conversation going. There was never a lack of things about which to talk with my father. I silently thanked God for the blessing of having these two men in my life.

Lucas told us he was going to continue staying in my apartment, when he had the night off, and Dad agreed to that. I had an extra room in my apartment, where I kept my computer and sewing machine. There was also a fold-out sofa in there, which would make a decent bed for Lucas.

How could darkness ever creep into these rooms, when so much love was being brought into them?

Chapter 39

When I entered my office on Tuesday, Trish was sitting at her desk in the outer office, typing on the keyboard of her computer. She turned to greet me, but I noticed she had difficulty meeting my eyes.

"Hi, Trish, how did everything go yesterday?" I asked her.

She glanced up briefly, and, then, tucked her head. "No problems at all. Barbara Crestwell called, but said it wasn't anything earth-shaking, so you can call her back today. Some memos are on your desk, and some paperwork from Suzie Lopez is also there."

Then, as if gathering courage, she stood up and, with a catch in her voice, said, "Rachelle, that was such a horrible thing that happened to you Sunday night! Was that the guy who has been stalking you?"

"Yes," I said, taking a deep breath. "I suppose I might as well tell you more about it. I was engaged to him in college, but broke it up when he became violent. He wouldn't accept the breakup and stalked me even then. After I graduated, he came to my home and tried to stab me to death. My mother intervened and he killed her. I was badly wounded."

Trish gasped, a horrified expression suffusing her face.

I continued, "He was caught and indicted, but his rich parents got him out on bail. He fled to Europe, obviously with help from someone. His name is Judson Bard, and his father owns the Bard Oceanlines."

"Bard! Yes, I've heard about them; filthy rich!" Trish's eyes grew big and round. "They can probably buy their way out of anything. So, now,

243

he's back and trying to finish killing you. Oh, Rachelle, that is so awful! I'm so sorry!" Now tears filled her eyes.

"Trish, the Lord has been with Lucas and me through several attacks already, and Judson has not succeeded. He's after Lucas, too, because I'm involved with him. We're trusting the Lord to continue to protect us, and to help the police to catch Judson."

Trish sat back down, idly tapping a pen on the edge of her desk. She seemed extremely subdued, for such an ebullient person.

I stood looking at Trish for a few seconds, thinking of all the questions I had about my secretary. It was hard to decide how to approach her with what I had planned to say—and ask. With a prayer in my heart, I finally said, "Trish, come into my office. We need to talk, in the worst way."

I went in and sat in a chair in a conversation area in the corner. "Shut the door, and sit down, Trish." I made it a mild order.

When Trish was seated, fidgeting nervously in her chair, I opened the conversation. "Now, Trish, I want you to tell me what's been going on with you. Also perhaps I may be butting into your personal life, but I want to talk to you about Mark Bussell."

Trish's eyes widened. "Oh, Rachelle, I'm so embarrassed about how I acted at the party. I don't know what got into me. I could blame it all on the fact that I'd had a few, but, that doesn't excuse it. It was fun being with Mark, and having him notice me, but I had no real illusions that he was truly interested in me. He was very drunk, too, so he really came on to me. I had never seen Mark act like that; he's usually so in control of himself."

I kept quiet, but gazed steadily at her. She folded and unfolded the material of her teal challis skirt, and then continued. "Mark had come to the party with one of the other guys, so I offered him a ride home in my car. We were standing on the pier together, when that awful thing happened to you and Lucas."

She looked steadily at me for a few seconds and then continued. "When we were on our way, Mark asked if he could come up to my apartment. It was plain what he had in mind, and I was tempted—Mark is a really good-looking guy. Fun, too. But, Rachelle, I started thinking what you have said so many times about getting involved with co-workers. Then, I pictured telling you that I'd gone to bed with Mark. It

ONCE AGAIN I FEAR

horrified me. I, also, know how you feel about premarital sex, and I know you're right. I just couldn't do it. I drove Mark straight home. He was so out of it, I wonder if anything really would have happened if he had come to my apartment; he probably would have just zonked out." At this point she gave a little chuckle.

"I'm very proud of you, Trish. You were very wise. If something should develop between you and Mark, it shouldn't start in bed. That gets things all confused."

We sat silently for a few seconds, and, then, I broached the touchier subject. "Now, Trish, I want to know what has been going on with you the last few months. Maybe I don't have a right to know, but we are friends, aren't we? I know I'm your supervisor here, and I'm not using that position to force you to tell me. I just think you've been going through something heavy, but, now, seem to have come out on top of whatever it is. I'm not blind, Trish; I see that you've lost that worried look you've had for so long, and I, also, have noticed the smashing clothes you've been wearing the last few days. Ready to tell me?"

Trish had been looking intently at her hands in her lap, but, now, raised her eyes to meet my gaze. "It's a long story, Rachelle; I wanted to tell you so bad, but I was afraid to tell you everything, for fear you would think less of me."

"Don't worry about that, just tell me."

"I have a son, Rachelle. He's eighteen months old and the most beautiful little boy in the world. When I was on my job at Bowman Technologies in Walnut Creek, my boss, Geoff Bowman, was a very attractive man, and I guess he thought he was God's gift to women. Unfortunately, I was very naive, thinking he was really interested in me. The old bells, from that situation, rang Sunday night with Mark.

"Anyway, Geoff asked me out, and, like a fool, I accepted. We went out a few times, to a concert, to dinner, that kind of thing. He was the perfect gentleman at first. Then, he started getting a little more intense when he kissed me, his hands roaming around a little. One night, I made the mistake of allowing him to come up to my apartment. He wanted more than just kissing, and, again like a fool, I gave in. He declared that he loved me, told me he would always love me. I believed him. I didn't know he had told that to half a dozen other girls in the company.

245

"Well, the affair went on for six month—I'm surprised it lasted that long. However, I found out much later that he'd also been seeing other girls at the same time, telling them the same thing.

"Then, two years ago last September, I found out I was pregnant. I was horrified, but, then, I figured Geoff would marry me, and everything would be just ducky. Boy, was I wrong! He raged at me, 'How could you let this happen?' as if he had nothing to do with it. He insisted I get an abortion, at his expense, of course. I refused. He stormed about the office, throwing things and calling me all kinds of names. Rachelle, I can't tell you what that did to me."

"I can imagine, Trish; you must have felt very betrayed."

"That was one of the many emotions I felt at that moment. I really had thought I was in love with him. I was so hurt, that all I could do was cry. That infuriated him more. He called me a stupid b——and told me to get out of his office. Which I did."

"Then what happened?" I prompted.

"I sat at my desk and cried for a long time. Fortunately, there was a door on my small outer office, sort of like it is here. Then, he came out of his office and sat in a chair next to my desk and said, 'Since you refuse to have an abortion, I guess we better make some arrangements for the birth. I'm sure you can find someone to adopt the kid.' At that point, I felt nothing but anger. How dare he speak so nonchalantly about our baby, as if it was a thing! The tears dried up immediately. I told him, yes, we had to make arrangements for the birth, but also for the raising of the child. I said I intended to keep it.

"He was furious, I knew, but saw that I could be very stubborn. He said, 'Okay, make arrangements and I'll pay for it. I'll arrange for your confinement and for health insurance for it, after it's born.' He couldn't even bring himself to call it a baby! He told me that he would pay all my expenses with an obstetrician and the hospital, and then give me a small stipend after 'it' came. The one condition he specified was that I never tell anyone who the father was, or else all financial support would stop. I was really dumb, not knowing that the baby and I had legal rights. I just agreed to what he said.

ONCE AGAIN I FEAR

"He told me I had to leave the company, and the story after would be that I had gotten a better job. I moved back to live with my mother in Concord. She didn't mind since she was a widow, and she wanted to help me and her grandchild.

"Well, my son was born a year ago June first. I named him Derek Austin Willingham—such a big name for such a little boy. He was so beautiful, that I fell in love with him immediately. Actually, in a way, I loved him, before he was born. He looks a lot like Geoff—as I said, Geoff is very attractive. He has blonde hair and big blue eyes, and the sweetest little smile."

Trish's face glowed. I could see she loved her baby intensely.

"I worked for an agency, doing temp, most of my pregnancy and as soon as I was able, after he was born. Then, the agency told me about this job, and I thought, why not? I needed a change, since everyone in Concord knew about my troubles, though not who Derek's father was. I was thrilled to death when I got the job. Mom agreed to keep Derek in Concord, and I would come home to spend every weekend with him. I didn't like leaving him, but I felt I just had to do something to rearrange my life.

"Geoff kept his bargain to that point. Then, I saw in the paper that he had married this really rich society girl; her daddy had a ton of money, and she was the heir to her late mother's fortune. Geoff was rich, by my standards, but her family's fortune made his look like poverty. With his marriage, Geoff, apparently, got scared his wife would find out he was taking care of a baby that he had sired.

"About eight months ago, Derek got really sick, and was in the hospital for a few days. I was frantic, but was sure his hospital and medical bills would be paid. Again, I was wrong. When I got notices from the insurance company that Derek was no longer insured, I faced about twenty thousand dollars in bills. Geoff had dropped his health insurance, without telling me, even though I had told no one he was Derek's father, except Mom. I had even had 'father unknown' put on his birth certificate. I was staggered. My pleas to the hospital and doctors fell on deaf ears; I owed the money, and that was it. I made too much money to get Medi-Cal for him, and putting him on my insurance wouldn't pay past bills. Neither

Mom nor I had that much money. So I have been having to pay huge payments on the bills since then.

"I hadn't gotten any money from Geoff for a while, either. I tried to call him, but he refused to speak to me. I can't believe how dumb I was, and how long it took me to listen to a friend's advice and seek legal counsel.

"With the help of a good lawyer, I filed for support for my child, and payment of his medical bills. I also demanded that Geoff set aside a fund to cover the cost of Derek's medical insurance and expenses. In addition, I asked that he establish a college fund for him, and pay my legal expenses. Geoff hit the roof. He phoned me and called me every name in the book. His society wife was furious with him, for not telling her, and, also, for not taking responsibility for his child.

"In court, he denied that he was Derek's father, so the judge ordered DNA tests. Those take months, so I was on pins and needles, until they came back. They showed that it was a ninety-nine-point-seven percent chance that Geoff was the father, enough for the courts. Last week, he made his final court appearance. I didn't have to be there, just my attorney. The judge ordered Geoff to pay all the medical bills, establish the insurance fund and a college fund, and also to pay me twenty-five hundred dollars a month in child support, as well as my legal expenses. The judge really laid into him for his irresponsibility, both in fathering a child out of wedlock, and, also, for feeling little responsibility for him. He ordered that I would have full custody, with visitation by Geoff, only if I allowed it. Needless to say, Geoff isn't interested in seeing Derek, which pleases me.

"The judge ordered that Geoff immediately send me a month's support, plus a check for full payment for all the months he hasn't paid in the past. Quite a tidy little sum. I'm afraid I went a bit wild, buying some really nice clothes for Derek and me. Doggone it, I've worn homemade clothes and brought sack lunches for a long time, while Geoff went around in Armani suits and ate at pricey restaurants. I felt I deserved a few nice things. Now, I think I've got it out of my system, so I'll be a little more conservative from now on." She laughed a merry little laugh.

ONCE AGAIN I FEAR

"I think you have a right to spend some of that money on yourself, Trish. Your homemade clothes were very stylish and well-made, but I'm very happy to see you are able to have some designer clothes, for a change. Good for you."

"Now, for the rest of the story," Trish said, her eyes now sparkling. "I wanted to get out of that awful apartment I've been living in. Also, Mom's tired of keeping up that house she has, and would like to live in a condo. I want her and Derek with me. So—she's going to sell her house, which is all paid for, and, together, we're going to buy a condo, big enough for the three of us here in the city. Mom loves San Francisco—she lived here when she was a kid.

"She already has an interested buyer for her house. She's stunned how much the house has appreciated, over the thirty-five thousand they paid for it thirty years ago. Now, it's worth more than three hundred thousand! Dad was a building contractor, so he kept the house really up-to-date, until he died four years ago. The neighborhood has also been kept up just wonderfully. She'll take her one-time, over fifty-five, capital gains write-off, so she'll have the entire amount, less real estate fees, to put in on something else. My older brother, Shane, is in real estate and is handling the sale through his broker. He told Mom he would forego his share of the fees—his gift to her. I'm insisting that she invest part of the money. Anyway, I've seen one condo here that could be the very thing. I have to take Mom to see it, first, however. Oh, Rachelle, I'm so excited that all these awful months are over, and I can finally start to live."

"And I think your dream of being married by the time you're thirty, may come true," I predicted. "With that pretty smile back, it may happen sooner than that. I'm sure there's some terrific guy out there, who would love to have a wife and a little son, all in one package."

I got up and pulled Trish to her feet. "Another thing, Trish, I assure you, you could have told me about your son; I would not have thought less of you. It seems to me you have grown up a lot, since you were that naive girl who got herself into trouble. Your little Derek is as precious as any child born within a marriage. I'm sure you're a wonderful mother to him. I can't wait to see him."

Trish was beaming, as I put my arms around her and hugged her tight. "If you need time off to go see that condo, just let me know. In fact, I'd love to go with you, if you don't mind."

"Would you? It's not too far from where you live. Maybe Mom can come over Thursday afternoon. Derek has to go for a checkup today, and Mom has a women's group meeting tomorrow."

"Thursday would be fine. Of course, you know my calendar better than I do. Christmas Eve will be a wonderful time to make happy plans. We'll have lunch and then meet your mother over there. Okay?"

"Perfect. I'll tell her to be there about two o'clock. Her name is Gloria, by the way. Oh, I have to get to work. I have a lot of computer work to do. Thanks, Rachelle, for being so understanding. I think I was very wrong in not trusting you to understand all this time, but I'm so relieved that I've finally told you."

I decided to call Dru, to see if I could find out what was going on with her. She was in a meeting, I was told. Would Dru call me back? From her actions Sunday night, I doubted it. I would call again, later.

I went down to the restaurant at about one o'clock, and found Mark just arriving, too. "Hi, Rachelle, want to keep me company at lunch?" he asked, grinning, but a little wary about meeting my eyes. I knew he was remembering his getting so sloshed at the party Sunday night.

"Sure thing," I assented. "There's a table over by the window. Tess, can we sit over there?" She nodded and we made our way through the tables.

When we had ordered, Mark frowned and said, "That scene at the pier Sunday night will haunt me for the rest of my life. I was scared spitless that you and Lucas would be shot. Did you know that guy?"

"I knew him in college." I again gave a brief outline of what had transpired with Judson and me.

Mark seemed stunned by what I told him, especially the death of my mother. "So he killed your mother, when he hardly knew her, right? It's hard to believe that someone could be that lacking in feeling."

"I've thought for a long time that it is a demonic force in Judson. It's hard to imagine that that kind of evil can come from a man. Anyway, Mark; let's not talk about that anymore. Lucas and I are trusting God to take care of us. There have been several attempts already, and all have failed, through intervention from God."

"Intervention from God," Mark murmured. He then continued, "That guy who pushed Judson down—he was a little odd. I know I was soused, so my vision probably wasn't too good, but I could swear that he was, well, sort of transparent. And there was a kind of diffused light around him. I was totally amazed. I didn't see where he came from—he was just there, all of a sudden. Then, after he kicked the gun away, I didn't see where he went."

My heart suddenly felt very light; Mark had seen God's work without knowing it. A bubble of joy arose inside me. Everything was going to work out for Lucas and me.

Mark was silent, then, pushing a fork around on the table. I looked directly at him and asked, "Is there anything you want to say to me?" Now, I was trying to keep from laughing—he looked so uncomfortable.

He grinned wryly, and met my eyes. "Yeah, I have to apologize for getting blotto at the party. I haven't done that for probably three years. Man, what a jerk I was, to do that at a company party. And then to start pawing Trish, right in front of God and everybody." He tucked his head and rapped his forehead with his fist.

"You were pretty bad, Mark," I said, fighting to control a fit of laughter. "But I didn't notice Trish fighting you off. So, what are your intentions toward my secretary?" I adopted the tone of a father questioning a young man.

"Rachelle, honestly, I didn't have any. She was, shall we say, handy. I just started coming on to her. I'm lucky I had someone else driving me home; I would probably have had a DUI if I had driven myself." He exhaled in a rush of breath. "I'll tell you the truth, I had the worst headache all day yesterday that I've ever had in my life. It was agony getting out of bed; my mouth tasted like dirty sox. Yuck!" He shivered and grimaced.

"Well, you look your old perky self today. But you didn't answer my question about Trish."

"That's a thing that has me puzzled. As I say, I had no intentions, when I started flirting with her. Then, I really enjoyed her company—and kissing her. She's very sweet and intelligent. She told me some stuff about her past that surprised me, but made me see what an exceptional girl she is."

"You mean about Derek?" I asked, knowing that, if she hadn't told him about her child, he wouldn't know who Derek was.

"Yes, and about her fight to get his father to accept his responsibilities for him. I even promised her I would go with her to see Derek this Sunday. I'd really like to see him; I like little kids. And, Rachelle, she refused to let me come up to her apartment, knowing full well what I had in mind. Not many girls refuse these days, sad to say. When she said a flat no to me, I suddenly had tremendous respect for her. It showed she had learned from past mistakes and had no intention of repeating them. Now, I find myself thinking about her a lot, and trying to think of ways to be where I'll see her. I got off at five yesterday, but hung around to 'just happen' to walk out when she did, so I could walk her to the bus stop. Funny, I don't even know if she's interested in me. She did remind me that we were going to Concord Sunday, but I, for some reason, couldn't get up the nerve to ask her out. Do you think I should?"

"Don't get me in the middle of this," I countered. "You have to decide that for yourself—you know, decide if you like her enough to want to start something. I've always been very negative about co-workers dating each other, but it would seem you and Trish have already made a step in that direction, so it's a bit late to think of that."

I sat looking fixedly at him for a second, then added, "Mark, be sure you aren't going to hurt Trish. She's been through a lot already. I care for both of you too much to want to see an emotional disaster, where you two are concerned. Search your heart, before you decide. Hey, maybe the trip to Concord will solidify your feelings, in one direction or another. I don't know how Trish feels, but I do know she is wary, so take things slowly."

"I don't want to hurt anyone, Rachelle," Mark said. "It would just tear me up to hurt someone."

"If you really mean that, then follow your heart." I smiled at Mark, and he smiled back at me.

My own personal guess was that Trish was definitely interested. I would never, however, tell Mark that. It was something he would have to find out on his own. It was a certainty that Trish would not allow herself to fall too hard, until she was sure Mark was serious.

Chapter 40

That night, Lucas, Dad and I spent the evening together. I loved having Dad there; it seemed so natural. We were a family already.

Lucas waited until after dinner, when we were seated in the living room, to give us some news. "One of our guys found a matchbook near the Pier Thirty Nine Garage. It was from a bar in North Beach. There was a fingerprint on it, but it was smudged. There were a few features that matched Bard's prints, but it's not enough to make a definite identification. We are, however, going on the supposition that it's his print, and are going to bear down on that area, to try to find where he's staying. There are a lot of apartment buildings there, over several blocks. Bard's picture is being shown all around and everybody possible is being questioned. One informant says he would swear he's seen him in the area."

"It sounds to me as if a lot of effort is being expended on this investigation," Dad interjected.

"That's the truth," Lucas responded. "There are a lot of different reasons members of the squad want to find this guy. Some, I know, are sickened by the way money seems to buy freedom from justice. There may even be those who know Judson Bard, and would love to see him in prison. Of course, there are the others who are chivalrous ones, who like coming to the rescue of a damsel in distress." He grinned at me.

Lucas continued, "Then, last of all, there's the knowledge that he has tried to kill one of their own. I believe they think, 'It could have been me'.

Any law enforcement group takes such an attack personally. They'll get him; I guarantee it, no matter what emotions motivate them."

Wednesday morning, Lucas called me at my office to tell me he had been given the news that the investigation had been narrowed to a single block. Several people had reported seeing Judson in that area. There were three large apartment buildings on the block, so they still had some closing in to do.

When Lucas had hung up, I leaned my head over my desk and prayed for all those people out there working to free me of the darkness in my life.

Lucas, as usual, picked me up after work, and drove me home. When we arrived, Dad told me that a letter had come for me that day. I picked it up off the breakfast bar, and looked at it curiously. It was addressed in printing, rather than in cursive. How strange.

I opened the letter, feeling a sense of foreboding. Inside, was a single sheet, again bearing printed words. "Don't think you're going to get away, B———," it said. "You and your boyfriend are as good as dead. Don't ever think you can outsmart me."

The letter was unsigned, but I didn't need to see a signature. I started to shake, tears spilling down my face.

Lucas took the letter and read it, handing it to Dad. Then, he put his arms around me and held me close. I could feel he was shaking, too, whether for fear or anger, I couldn't tell.

"That dirty so-and-so," Dad said through clenched teeth. He slammed the letter down on the breakfast bar and, then, reached out to lay his hand on my shoulder.

"We aren't going to let him carry out that threat, Rachelle, I promise you. God is with us, and He won't let that evil man hurt you." There was the sound of tears in his voice, without doubt because of his memories of the day Mom died.

I pulled away from Lucas and put my arms around Dad. We held each other and cried for a few minutes, while Lucas stood with bowed head, probably praying.

ONCE AGAIN I FEAR

Then, I felt the warm hand on my shoulder, in the exact spot where Dad had laid his hand. Dad and God: a great combination. A peace flooded into the room, and took away the fear.

Chapter 41

On Thursday morning, I still had not heard from Dru. I decided to wait until after Christmas to try calling her again.

Trish was lighthearted, full of happiness, because of her plans for the future, which were coming together so rapidly. Her mother, Gloria, had sold her house, and the deal would be through in about thirty days. She was excited about the prospect of moving to the city with Trish and Derek.

No one was in the mood to work, everyone in the Holiday spirit. The store would close at six today, but was filled this morning with last minute shoppers. Probably, there would be people who would scoot in at five before six.

There was a pile of gifts on my desk, including a large box from Robert Bainbridge. Another, obviously a jeweler's box, bore a card from Greg, a rather long, flat box was from Mark, and a cube-shaped box with a huge, red ribbon was from Trish. There were other gifts, from people that had become my friends in the store, and some from vendors and fashion houses. I felt extremely blessed.

I opened a cabinet in the corner and took out the gifts I had yet to deliver. One, a book from a Christian book store, for Robert, and a lovely, soft, blue, wool-crepe dress for Trish. I usually did not buy such an expensive gift for her, but, this year, I wanted very much to do it, in celebration of her new life. I had a leather day-planner for Greg. I bought an attaché case for Mark, to use for his college classes, because he had

ONCE AGAIN I FEAR

once complained about constantly losing papers. A messenger service would be here in a few minutes, to deliver the gift to his apartment. I did not want to give it to him in front of other employees, who might think it strange that I had bought for only one sales associate. The messenger would also take my gifts to my apartment. The company had given Christmas bonuses to all the employees, and a wide array of sweets was available in the employee lounge.

Christmas carols rang out from the music system in the store, and Santa's bells rang in the Toy department. I didn't want to stay in my office today. After putting Mark's gift and my large collection of treasures into the hands of the messenger, and delivering my other gifts, I took the elevator down to walk through various departments, wishing people a Merry Christmas and asking about their plans.

In the toy department, a long line of children waited to make last-minute requests of the jolly, bearded Santa. I knew he was John Farley, a man who usually worked here as a janitor. However, he bore such a resemblance to Santa, except for the beard, of course, that, each year, Devon's relieved him of janitorial duties, so that he could don a beard and hold children on his knee. He delighted in his holiday role, and winked at me as I passed by.

When I returned to my office, Trish was on the phone. She motioned that it was for me, and then returned to admiring her new dress. I went to sit at my desk and picked up the receiver. It was Lucas. "Hey, beautiful lady, good news! Our guys have discovered the exact apartment in which our bad boy is living. They called me to be in on the apprehension, because they know this is personal with me. A SWAT team is being brought in and should be ready to start closing in around noon. Pray hard, baby; this could be it."

When I hung up the receiver, I sat at my desk, shaking. It was not terror this time, but anticipation that my ordeal might soon be over. I prayed fervently that God would direct these men who were fighting so hard for Lucas and me.

At noon, Trish and I closed up the office. Trish carried her many gifts to her car in the underground garage, and then we went to lunch at the Cafe Akimbo on Maiden Lane. We were in such a cheerful mood that we giggled much more than was appropriate for two sophisticated young ladies. My own heart was very light, knowing that Judson would soon be in custody.

Trish had driven her ancient Datsun today; a vehicle that I was sure would soon be replaced. We gaily drove down Geary and continued on to Jones Street, at which point, Trish turned the car north, climbing up the steeply inclined street toward Nob Hill. "I was so excited about this today, that I had to tell everyone," Trish enthused. "I guess everybody thinks I'm wacko getting so wound up about seeing a condo. Greg hinted as much, and Mark just rolled his eyes. They both said this was a nice neighborhood, and hoped it worked out for me."

A momentary fear washed through me. A lot of people knew I was out, without protection. I had promised Lucas that I would always take a taxi home, when he couldn't come pick me up. But, today didn't count, did it? After all, the police were closing in on Judson, and I was in a car unknown to Judson, with a friend who would be a witness.

Witness? There had been multiple witnesses at the pier. Had I been foolish to come out this way? Oh, come on, Rachelle, I thought, Judson, at this moment, is being taken into custody. I relaxed and pushed aside my feeling of uneasiness.

On Sacramento Street, Trish turned left at Grace Cathedral, a replica of Notre Dame in Paris. A short distance west, she pulled up in front of a Mediterranean-style condominium, pale terra cotta-colored stucco, with a red tile roof. Ornate frescos made an elegant border between the first and second floors, giving it a further old-world ambiance, but with a fresh, nearly-new look.

Gloria was waiting in front of the building, trying to keep a tiny, towheaded toddler from running into the street. Trish parked her car, and we both got out. As I stepped onto the curb, I caught a glimpse of movement beyond where Gloria stood. Then, from behind a parked van, the figure of my nightmare stepped onto the sidewalk. Judson stood smirking at me, a threatening gleam in his eyes. My heart sank to my feet.

Trish seemed confused when I drew back. She saw Judson, then, and I believe comprehended the threat in his demeanor. My heart started to pound, as I saw that he, again, held a knife in his hand. "Oh, God, no," I

ONCE AGAIN I FEAR

breathed, "don't let me die like this. Forgive me for being foolish and disregarding Lucas' instructions to me. Please help me, please."

"This is it, sugar," Judson sneered. "Your boyfriend isn't here to protect you. You got my letter, didn't you? I meant what I said." He was slowly advancing toward me.

Gloria grabbed Derek and held him to her, her face white. Trish stood frozen, but I could hear her gulping air, trying to keep from screaming.

It was highly unlikely I could outrun Judson, but that was all I could do now. Fighting him off, when he had that long, shiny knife was an impossibility that I didn't want to attempt. At that moment, I had a picture in my mind of Word of Life Church, less than two blocks away. The doors would be unlocked today, Christmas Eve, because people were always invited to come in all afternoon to pray, before the evening service. Making it to the church was all I could think to do.

Fortunately, I had worn a pants suit and low, comfortable shoes today. With a spurt of energy, born of fear, I started running down Sacramento and turned north on Leavenworth. I could hear Judson's footsteps gaining on me. Trish screamed, a long, mournful sound, full of sheer terror. I could hear her mother wailing, like someone lost in agony.

I glanced over my shoulder to gauge where Judson was, and, at that moment, I saw a sight that startled and filled me with hope. Near the sidewalk, stood a man with a heavy walking cane in his hand. As Judson passed him, the man stuck the cane into his path. Judson got his legs entangled with the cane and went sprawling on the cement. He landed hard on his knees, a string of profanity pouring out of his mouth, followed by loud groans of pain.

He had been badly hurt, for certain, but he got to his feet and, again, started after me. His injuries had slowed him down, I could tell, because there was an uneven sound to his footfalls, as if he were limping badly. I took heart as I raced onto Clay Street, where the church stood, a fortress it seemed to me in my panic.

The front door was, indeed, unlocked, and I fled inside. I tried to lock the door, but my hands were shaking so badly I couldn't move the heavy bolt.

Where could I go? I didn't want to endanger anyone else, but I needed help. One woman sat in a pew near the front, and I could hear children's voices in a room off to the right of me, rehearsing a carol for their part of the program tonight. I knew Tom Lane would be here somewhere, too, but where? If I screamed, the children might come into the sanctuary, and I didn't want that.

"God, help me," I prayed out loud, as I headed toward the front of the church. I heard the faint sounds of footfalls on the front steps of the church, which I thought might be Judson's, so I dropped to the floor, and crawled under a pew on the right. I didn't have time to make it to the right side of the platform, where a door led to Tom's office. I crawled to the far end of the pew and lay hunched in the dimness.

My heart lurched as I heard the big, heavy doors being flung open. Then, Judson's voice bellowed out, "Rachelle, you can't hide. You're not getting away from me again. Rachelle!"

I started to cry quietly, tears of terror and of remorse at my folly. Obviously, someone had told Judson where I was going, and he had been waiting for me. Who? Who! "Oh, Father, please help me."

Then I remembered what Doug West had said about fighting demonic forces. Plead the blood of Jesus, he had said. I did that now, from my heart, whispering it under my breath. I knew I had been redeemed from the power of Satan through the blood of Jesus, and now, that same blood was my covering from satanic powers.

Ragged, uneven footsteps were proceeding down the aisle. I heard the woman up front scream, and then she began to echo my prayer in a loud voice, "I plead the blood of Jesus, I plead the blood of Jesus!"

I thought of Jesus' words in Matthew, "If two of you shall agree on earth as touching any thing that they shall ask, it shall be done for them of my Father which is in heaven." I was agreeing with the woman who was pleading Jesus' blood.

I realized, then, that she was moving toward Judson, and now stood at the end of the pew where I crouched. I couldn't let her endanger herself for me. Pulling myself out from under the pew, I ran toward the Tom's office door. Judson shouted a profanity and took off after me, between the pews and down the side aisle, moving amazingly fast once more.

ONCE AGAIN I FEAR

He caught up with me, near the piano, which sat at the right side of the platform. I felt sharp pain, as he grabbed my hair and twisted it in his hand. A shriek rose from my throat, mixed with a prayer.

I fell as he suddenly let go, and he was over me, the knife above my chest.

Then, I heard another voice, from the rear, "Judson, don't do this! Please! I've done everything you asked, but I didn't know you were going to kill her! You told me you just wanted to scare her. I wouldn't have helped you, if I'd known you were going to do this." It was a voice I knew well, but which was now filled with fear. The pain of realization shot through me, burning the inside of me raw.

The voice was coming closer, now, though I couldn't see around Judson to place the source. "Judson, I don't care what happens to me now; you can do what you want to. Tell everybody what I did, I don't care. I don't want you to kill her! I couldn't bear that!"

The sound of children's voices, this time laughing and talking, grew louder, as if someone had opened a door. Then, the frantic voice of an adult, shushed the children, before the door was closed.

Judson again grabbed my hair and pulled me to my feet, as he turned to look behind him. "I wouldn't have had to do this, if she had listened to reason!" he screamed. "If she had come back to me, as I wanted her to, I wouldn't have had to do this. And don't play so innocent with me; you knew I'd kill her if she didn't listen to reason." I could sense the demonic forces in Judson Bard, and my body shrank away from him in horror.

Judson again raised the knife. My flesh quivering with dreadful anticipation, I prayed for God's help. Then, I caught a glimpse of Tom Lane standing near his open office door. He must have seen the pleading in my eyes. "Demons of Hell, I take authority over you; you will not hurt Rachelle. Stand back, in the name of Jesus!" His voice was strong and forceful.

Judson hesitated and then glared at Tom, who continued to stand in authority over the evil that was in the man who held me. Suddenly, I felt a profound peace, one that could only come from God. "Thank you, Jesus," I whispered.

The doors at the rear were flung open, and, over Judson's shoulder, I saw Lucas standing, with light shining behind him. "Let go of her, Bard," he yelled at the top of his lungs, walking quickly down the aisle.

Mark Bussell now sat in a pew near the right side of the church, moaning and pleading with Judson. Then my father was in the doorway and running around the right side of the church.

Tom gave a final roar of his powerful voice, rebuking Satan. The woman stood in the aisle, asking for God's angels to intervene.

Suddenly, Judson let go of me, and I fell backward onto the carpet. He lowered his hand holding the knife, and, with eyes wide with fright, gazed at the rear of the church. He then put his arms up over his eyes and screamed in terror.

Lucas rushed forward and grabbed him, wrestling him to the floor. Mark ran toward us and pulled the knife out of Judson's hand. He stood looking at it, as if it were a snake that would bite him.

I heard running feet, and looked to see three uniformed officers rushing down the aisle. They handcuffed Judson, and dragged him outside, his eyes still bulging with horror.

Lucas pulled me to my feet and enfolded me in his strong arms. "It's over, baby, it's over. You're safe. Baby, baby, I love you so much. I would have died, if anything had happened to you." We were both crying, tears of relief, and knowledge of what might have happened. Tom Lane came toward us and continued to pray, now thanking God for His power. Dad came and put his arms around Lucas and me together.

Mark had now retreated to a pew, where he sat, shaking and still holding the knife. Then, I saw Trish moving down the side aisle toward him. She sat down beside him and put her arms around him. He leaned toward her, crying, great shuddering sobs. She crooned to him, as a mother would to a child.

"I don't know how you got here, Lucas, but I have never been so happy to see anyone in my life." I said through my tears.

"When the SWAT team found that he had managed to escape the apartment, I tried to call you, to tell you. The switchboard operator said you weren't in your office. I, then, asked to speak to Robert Bainbridge. My blood ran cold, when he told me you had gone with Trish to look at a condo. Luckily, Trish had told Robert where the condo was, and he gave me the address. Then, I gave your dad a quick call, to tell him where you were going, since I knew it was close to your apartment. He said he was on his way.

"Then I called in to have some units sent out. I just knew Bard would be there waiting for you. When I got to the condo, Trish was standing outside in hysterics. She told me you were headed this way, and had mentioned your church was nearby. I knew that's where you were headed. I could say I got here just in time, but I think the Lord had his forces here ahead of me. Did you see that look on Bard's face; I'm sure he saw what God wanted him to see."

"Oh, Lucas, I'm so relieved, but I'm also weeping inside to know that my friend, Mark, betrayed me. I don't know why, either. He said something about Judson telling something he did. He didn't want this to happen, I'm sure of it. Oh, dear Lord, I hope charges aren't brought against him; he's suffering unbelievable agony right now."

I pulled away from Lucas and walked toward Mark, as Lucas said softly, "My Rachelle, always the soft heart."

I sat sideways in the pew in front of Mark and Trish, and leaned toward them. "Mark, please tell me why. There has to be a reason."

He raised tortured eyes to me, profound pleading on his face. "Rachelle, I didn't want this to happen, believe me. I knew he was going to be at the pier Sunday night; I got drunk because I was so scared. When I saw him with the gun, I thought he was going to kill you, but, later, he assured me that he had just tried to scare you. I wanted to believe him, but I had terrible doubts. Then, today, when I knew you were coming here, I knew he would demand that I tell him, and he did just that. I believed he would have told if I hadn't told him. He could have made what I did sound worse than it was, I knew that. I thought I might go to prison for a long time. I couldn't stand that."

He gulped, and took a deep breath. "After you and Trish had left, I couldn't stand it. I drove up to the condo as fast as I could. Trish was there and screamed that you were headed down to Clay street, where your church was. I was terrified I was too late. Then, when I got inside here, I knew there was nothing I could really do, and I wanted to die."

"Mark, what was he holding over your head to get you to cooperate with him?" My voice demanded an answer.

"I met him in Monaco, in Monte Carlo, to be exact. We struck up a friendship, of sorts, although he always was in control. Then, he took me to a casino, where we started to gamble. Soon, all my money was gone, and I panicked. By then, though, I had begun to think if I just tried the wheel or the card table one more time, I would regain my money. I borrowed a large sum from Judson—someone was sending him lots of money—and started gambling again. It didn't take long to lose that. I felt totally hopeless, and considered suicide.

"Judson, however, told me he knew a way to get my money back. He said he had done it a lot, and it always worked. He had somehow found out where all the surveillance cameras were in the casino and knew how to hide his hands from them. He always wore this hat, like Indiana Jones wore. He would sidle up to a player who was drunk, or start playing next to one. He would then hold his hat in front of the man's stack of chips, as if he were examining the band of the hat. Behind it, he would slide a stack of chips either into the hat, or into his own stacks, if he were playing beside the man. He did it so slickly, that no one seemed to catch on. The player would be so drunk he probably didn't even miss one stack of chips. Therefore, no ruckus was ever raised about them.

"Well, he taught me how to do it, and told me I had to get his money back that way. I learned quickly, and soon had his money recouped. But that wasn't the end of it. He didn't need the money; it was a game to him, partly to keep me in line. He then told me that I had committed crimes, and he would report it, if I didn't continue to get him money that way. He also had a couple of other little tricks he used to get money.. One thing, he had played up to one of the casino employees, and I think she helped him with some of it.

"When he came back to the U. S., about seven months ago, I came with him, still low on funds, and dependent on him. Meanwhile, his father had seen your picture in the paper, when you were promoted to head buyer at Devon's. He mentioned it to Judson, in one of their phone conversations. Judson told me that I was to get a job here, and make friends with you, so I could know what you were doing, and tell him. I

ONCE AGAIN I FEAR

didn't want to do it, but he assured me he was just furious with you for dumping him, and he wanted to teach you a lesson."

My heart started to go out to Mark, the lost soul at the mercy of that demonic force.

"He told me that he had been accused of killing your mother, but that was ridiculous—he hardly knew your mother. Why would he kill her? He said he had been set up by someone you had once dated, and who wanted him out of the way. When you told me about your mother's death Tuesday, I knew you were telling me the truth, and I knew, for sure, he meant to kill you. He called me at the store this morning, and asked me what you were going to be doing this afternoon. He again threatened to turn me in to the Monte Carlo authorities, promising I would spend twenty years in jail. How could I be so dumb? I doubt he could even do that."

"So do I, Mark. I doubt there are even any records of a crime or crimes being committed. The money was probably never missed, and the victims are unknown. He had to have a hold over you, and he succeeded. Mark, you have a heavy burden to carry, but I doubt you'll be prosecuted for that. You may, however, have to answer for abetting Judson's attempts on Lucas and me."

His eyes met mine, full of resignation and hopelessness. "I don't care anymore, Rachelle. I've come to care a great deal about you; you're a good person. I deserve whatever happens to me."

"One thing, Mark, you tried your best to stop Judson today—you probably saved my life—and you did take the knife away from him. Look, you still have it in your hands. I don't think you're even aware of it. That may go in your favor. And, Mark, I'll speak for you, if you go to court."

Amazement washed over his features. "After what I've done to you? Why? I can't imagine you could ever forgive me."

"Mark, God will forgive you, if you ask. And I have already forgiven you. We've been friends, and I want us to remain friends. As far as I'm concerned, what happened here today was that you were worried about me, and came to help me. You helped subdue the person who intended to kill me. Judson probably won't implicate you, because he would have to confess to guilt in all this, in order to do that. He would have to say he had planned the whole thing, with your help. I doubt he'll try to say *you* planned the whole thing; that wouldn't wash, because you didn't have a motive.

I reached over and took the knife from him, handing it to Lucas, who now stood beside us. Then, I reached and took Mark's hand. "I meant it when I said God would forgive you, Mark. All you have to do is ask. Why don't we pray now, and then you'll see what I mean."

Tom Lane joined us, with his hand on Lucas' shoulder. Trish took Mark's other hand and said, "I want to ask God's forgiveness for a lot of things, too, Mark. Let's pray with Rachelle."

Mark nodded, and I reached for Lucas' hand, too. Tom, Lucas, and I prayed with the two people in the pew. Mark spoke aloud, asking forgiveness for his terrible sins. I prayed that he would ask Jesus to take over his life, and he and Trish both asked Jesus to do just that.

When Lucas had said a hearty 'amen', Mark looked at me with shining eyes. "Thank you, Rachelle, and I thank God, too. A weight has been lifted from me, one that was too heavy to bear. I feel everything will work out okay, now. If I have to go to prison, that will be okay, too."

"I'll stand by you too, Mark," Trish said, squeezing his hand. He smiled at her and held his eyes on her face, as if in growing recognition that she was precious to him. I knew, then, that this was only the beginning for Trish and Mark. They would also have God with them. I got up, still holding Lucas' hand. When I had given Tom a quick hug, we walked out of the church, leaving Trish and Mark with Tom's wise counsel.

Chapter 42

Christmas morning dawned clear and bright. Lucas had worked last night, so would come over later, after having slept. I had threatened him with bodily harm, if he came any earlier than eleven o'clock.

Dad got up ahead of me and made coffee and scrambled eggs. "These won't be as good as Lorraine's," he assured me, grinning happily.

I walked over to him and we held each other, relishing the freedom from anxiety, a new thing to us. "I'm so glad you were here, Dad," I said. "You can't know what it meant to me to see you appear in the church doorway, right after Lucas arrived. My two men, there to rescue me. However, I think the Lord was in the process of rescuing me, before either of you got there. God's angels were certainly there, I have no doubt. That sweet lady, who prayed there in the church, asked for the angels and they came. I have to find out who she is and thank her."

"Baby, when I thought that you might meet the same fate your mother did, I couldn't bear it. I think I ran from your apartment to the church in a faster time than I could have done it when I was eighteen. Dear God, I was terrified! When I saw you, still alive, I was overjoyed, even though I knew the danger was still there. I prayed harder than I ever have in my life. Then about half-way down the aisle, I was overwhelmed with a sense of peace that God was there. I wasn't scared anymore, and started praising God."

"I had the same feeling of peace, too, Dad. I knew we were surrounded by angels, and that the demonic forces didn't stand a chance."

We were just finishing the clean-up after breakfast, when my buzzer from the security guard downstairs sounded. "What in the world?" I said under my breath, as I went to the foyer and pressed the button.

"A lady to see you, Miss Atherly. Says her name is Dru Warren," the guard intoned into his speaker.

Dru? What was she doing here?

"Okay, send her on up. Thanks." I pressed the button again and waited by the door.

I opened the door to Dru a few minutes later. She stood in the hall, dressed all in red, and wearing a sprig of holly on her coat. "May I come in, Rachelle," she asked, as if unsure what my answer would be.

"Dru, you can always come in. I'm really glad to see you." I was, particularly since I knew she had had nothing to do with Judson's pursuit of me.

As I closed the door behind Dru, she handed me a large, heavy package, gaily wrapped in bright paper and ribbon. I had had a present delivered to her, a soft, lemon-yellow cashmere sweater. I took the gift, setting it on a table, and hugged her tightly, smelling the scent of one of DuBois Cosmetics' most expensive perfumes. "Thank you, Dru, that's sweet of you."

"And thank you for that gorgeous sweater," she said, returning my hug. She then pulled away from me. "I need to talk to you and explain something. I don't want anything to come between us, you know. Rachelle, I've considered you one of my best friends for a long time; I hope you believe that."

"I do Dru, and I feel the same about you. There are some things about which I'm confused, though." I looked her squarely in the eye.

At that moment, Dad walked into the foyer, probably to check on me. The habit was ingrained. "Oh, Dad, I want you to meet my friend, Dru Warren. She's come to bring some Christmas cheer. Dru, my dad, Stan Atherly."

Dru stuck out her well-manicured hand and took Dad's hand. "I'm very happy to meet Rachelle's dad, at last. We've always seemed to just miss meeting each other." She beamed a glittering smile at him.

ONCE AGAIN I FEAR

"It was my loss, not getting to meet such a beautiful lady, Dru," Dad replied. "Rachelle has talked a lot about you—all glowing, I might add."

"Now that you two have met at last, Dru and I have some girl talk to get out of the way. Excuse us, Dad, and come on into the living room, Dru."

Dru removed her coat and laid it on a chair. When we were seated, I looked at her questioningly.

"Well, Rachelle, I knew you saw that picture of me at the party, being really chummy with Gwynneth Reynolds. Gwynneth Bard Reynolds." She emphasized the name "Bard". "I promise you, Chelle, that I had no idea Gwynneth was a Bard, until that night. I met her in the DuBois Spa, where she comes to be pampered once a week. She and I hit it off immediately, sort of like you and I did. We always found something to talk and laugh about. She's really very nice, Chelle—actually, as nice as you are, and that's saying a whole bunch. She had never mentioned her maiden name, probably because she wanted to be accepted as just Gwynneth, and not a stinking-rich Bard. Know what I mean?"

I nodded, but kept still.

"Well, she talked a little about her family, but never mentioned any names. Said her father was a businessman, and her mother, well, was mother. She mentioned having a brother, but, again, never mentioned his name. It was all just in passing, you understand? She did say once, that her dad was an old devil, and her brother was following in his footsteps. She said something about feeling terribly sorry for her mother. I took it she didn't have too much to do with her family.

"Before the party, I had met her husband once—he's a doll, too. He's from a wealthy family too, but has been very successful on his own in the financial realm. He's a young executive with P and R Investments." I couldn't keep from smiling at that news.

"What's funny, Chelle," Dru questioned.

"Mr. P's son works for me. You know Greg Phillips, I'm sure."

"Greg, huh? Oh, that's very interesting." She elongated the word 'very'. "Well, anyway, when Gwynneth and I were chatting at the party, she said, 'Uh, oh, here comes Daddy dearest.' A very large man, with cold, hard, gray-blue eyes came up to us and Gwynneth introduced him as her father, Judson Bard, Jud, for short. I felt as if a bomb had landed on me, dead center. Everything you had told me came flooding back, and I mentally fitted it all in with what Gwynneth had told me of her father and brother. It wasn't a pretty picture. Somehow, I managed to mumble something coherent to the great man, but was extremely glad when he melted back into the crowd.

"That picture had already been made, but I thought of it all evening. I hoped you wouldn't see it. Then, that Monday after you had come back and had called me, I dropped into Devon's for just a brief time, no time to see you. I happened to run into Trish, running an errand for you in the cosmetic department. She told me she had seen the picture while you were gone, and had left the paper in your office for you to see, when you got back, which was that day. She said I looked beautiful, and that was some hunk draped all over me. Your Trish is a sweetheart, but, at that moment, I wanted to kill her. Oh, excuse the terminology.

"I prayed the paper would self-destruct, or something, but knew it wouldn't. Well, I had to leave the next day for that seminar, so I missed your call. On the yacht, I admit I avoided you, because I didn't want to talk to you, until I had explained, and I didn't think I would get a chance to do that, in that mob. I felt rotten. I'm sorry, Chelle, I mean it."

"I did wonder, Dru. Maybe I should have trusted you more, but, at that time, I knew someone was helping Judson torment me. You were, of necessity, on the suspect list; you knew a lot about me. That picture simply put you squarely on top of the list."

"And I didn't know all that was going on with Judson, either," Dru pointed out.

"I know that now, Dru, but, at the time, I had to consider everyone. My life depended on not trusting anyone too much."

"Okay, I understand. Now, I'll tell you the rest. When you called again, on Tuesday, DuBois was having a real crisis, and I was in meetings all that day and the next. It was pretty hairy, but we got things straightened out. I completely forgot about your call."

She sighed deeply and then continued. "I took yesterday off, and spent it with my friend from college. Oh, his name is George Bishop. Well, I

ONCE AGAIN I FEAR

have to admit I didn't think of you even once all day yesterday, or all evening." She grinned mischievously. "I found that I couldn't think of anything but George. Yeah, imagine that! Rachelle, I've broken my vow and fallen in love. He was right there under my nose all the time, and I didn't grasp that he was the best thing in my life. He's such a good friend, and has proven his loyalty to me for years. Now, we just realize that we are in love. He's as surprised as I am. We're going to get married right away; we don't want to wait a day more than necessary. New Year's Day is the wedding, in the little chapel of my family's church. You're going to be my maid of honor. Say you will, please!"

"Oh, Dru, I'll be so happy to be your maid of honor. I am so happy for you."

"There's one other thing that is so special about George and me," Dru continued happily. "We know each other so well, have seen each other through some tough times, and always been there for each other. But, Chelle, we've never gone to bed together. Now, we've agreed we won't until we're married. That way, everything will be fresh and new. Our wedding day will start our new life, in every way."

"That's the way it's going to be for Lucas and me, too," I said, pleased that at least one person understood my delight in this situation. One thing, I knew, though, Dru and George would not know the exclusiveness that Lucas and I would, at being each other's first lover.

"And, Dru, I'm happier than you can know that you weren't the one who was doing this awful thing to me."

Dru's face took on a solemn look, as she reached for my hand. "I read the papers this morning, Chelle. That was so horrible! And in a church, yet! I think Somebody was looking out for you."

"Maybe I'll tell you all about that, sometime, Dru. You know, I think about another girl, who recently fell from a six-story window here in town. At first, it was thought to be suicide, but, then, her friends were questioned closely. She had been visiting friends in Santa Cruz that weekend. They said she had told them that she was being stalked by someone, here in the city, and she was really afraid.

"Well, she went out that window on Monday. All her friends said she would never have committed suicide. So, go figure! Dru, that girl could have been me, except for the fact that I had so much protection, not only from Lucas and the police department, but, also, from my heavenly Father.

"I believe that last part, that's for sure," Dru said. "Thank God, we have a stalking law here in California, now! Now, let's think about happy things. I want to look at your ring. I'm sure I'll have one in a few days."

"Yes, right now, I just want to think about all the good things in my life. While I'm at it, I'll think about the good things in your life too." I sighed, a long, contented sigh.

Chapter 43

After Dru left, I opened her gift to me. Inside, was a complete set of DuBois cosmetics, in my favorite colors, along with some new shades that I had not tried, but Dru would know suited me. There were also fancy little brushes, applicators, combs, delicate little sponges, bath items, luxurious hair-care products, and a bottle of my favorite eau de toilette spray. How thoughtful of Dru. She must have guessed that many of my cosmetics were nearly gone or ready to be thrown out, because of age. And my bottle of scent was sucking fumes in the bottom. A thrill of feminine pleasure swept over me; it would be glorious to dip into all these new cosmetics.

Lucas arrived a few minutes after eleven, looking rested and full of Christmas joy. Gone were the lines of worry around his blue-green eyes. He noticed the mistletoe hanging over my head in the foyer, and took full advantage of it. Not that we needed mistletoe.

Dad allowed us some time to get our kissing out of the way, staying in the kitchen to finish the relish tray for our dinner. This was the first time Lucas and I had stood here, holding each other, without the darkness hovering around us. Now, only the brilliant light of God's blessings filled the room.

We finally went into the kitchen, where glasses of iced soda sat waiting for us. After we clinked our glasses together, Lucas announced, "This is the beginning of a wonderful life, for all of us. God has blessed us and, also, has great happiness ahead for us." I knew Lucas was right—it was a new beginning for Dad also. Closure in Mom's death had finally come.

Dad reached out and clinked his glass with ours, and we all took long contented drinks.

"You two go sit in the living room, and I'll watch everything here." Dad was being diplomatic, I could tell.

"No, Dad, I want you with us, while we talk over a few things. I have some things to tell both of you." I motioned for Dad to follow us into the living room.

When we were seated, Tache came in and made the rounds, to get head-rubbing from each of us. Getting her fill of that, she curled up on her favorite chair and fell asleep.

I, then, told Dad and Lucas what Dru had told me about her acquaintance with Gwynneth Reynolds. "What a misunderstanding! I wish she had phoned me or written me a note or something, so I wouldn't have had all those doubts about her. I adore Dru, and I'm ecstatic that she didn't have anything to do with what Judson did to me."

"So am I," Dad concurred. "Dru is a lovely young woman."

"There's something else; Dad you know about this," I added. "It's about Damon. I called Star yesterday, after I got home, to see if classes were being held. Since I wasn't going last night, I didn't want Damon to be expecting me. By this time, of course, I knew he didn't have anything to do with my problems. Anyway, when I called, the receptionist had gone home, and Damon was by the phone. He answered my call.

"He told me he was about ready to go home, too, because there would be no classes last night. Then, I asked him when he had gotten back from his trip. He told me that he had gone to Flagstaff, because his father was ill, and had gotten back Wednesday. Then, he said, 'Tonight I'm going with Theresa to spend Christmas Eve with her family. There'll probably be thirty Biancis there.'

"I almost fell off my chair, at the mention of that name. I asked if Theresa's name was Bianci. He said, yes. I asked if she had a relative named Tony. He said that was her cousin, who was a student at City College, where Theresa teaches. He then said, 'Tony had a bad time recently. Someone stole his Toyota, just before he was scheduled to leave

ONCE AGAIN I FEAR

for semester break. Fortunately, one of the guys he was going with was able to take his car instead. He got his car back, when he returned, but the thief banged it up some. He was really burned!' He also said he had brought Tony, as his guest, to work out at Star a few times. Lucas, it was just as I suspected, except I didn't know Tony was related to Damon's girlfriend. I am so happy to know that Damon was innocent, too."

"So am I, baby," Lucas said, "I liked Damon immediately. It was very difficult to believe he would try to hurt you." He hugged me close to him.

"The only sad thing is Mark's involvement. It is so unbelievable. In his mind, he had blown, way out of proportion, Judson's power to mess up his life. It's almost like a cobra mesmerizing its victim. Too bad he had to get mixed up in that mess in Monaco, but I really can't see how he could be charged with anything over there, since I doubt any crime was reported." I looked at Lucas for confirmation.

"You're probably right. He'll just have to bear the guilt of it on his conscience. It's still hard to see how those guys could pull those tricks off, with all the tight security in casinos. Either Judson was a real slight-of-hand artist, or the employee that he had sweet-talked must have been a big help."

"I think I remember his saying that he had had a magician show him some of his tricks. He used to demonstrate some amazing ones. Maybe that's how he managed it." I shrugged.

"Whatever went on in Monte Carlo, Mark has to answer to some charges here. However, you were right in saying that his actions in the church, most likely, are going to carry weight in his favor in court. He certainly was remorseful, that was obvious. Judges almost always take that into account. They're both being arraigned tomorrow, so we'll see what happens after that. What probably will happen is that Mark will cut a deal, giving his testimony against Judson, in exchange for immunity from prosecution. After all, Judson is the one the courts really want. That would serve Bard right, for using Mark like that.

"One thing that really pleases me is that, when Judson's apartment was searched, there was all kinds of evidence, including a statement from a Swiss bank that proved his father had been helping him. I'm sure prosecutors are busy, putting together a case to present to the grand jury."

Lucas frowned, and then chuckled. "Remember when I said I would want to beat the culprit to a pulp? Well, strangely enough, I don't want to do that to Mark at all. I feel sorry for the guy. Also, his commitment to the Lord yesterday, makes a totally different situation. I think we can just let the Lord take care of Mark, don't you?"

"Absolutely," I agreed. "I've always thought a lot of Mark, and that hasn't changed. I'm really hoping he doesn't have to go to prison, and that he and Trish can be there for each other. They both need someone. And I am hoping that Robert Bainbridge will agree with me to keep Mark on at Devon's"

"I honestly doubt that Mark will spend any time behind bars," Lucas said. "I've seen similar cases, and that's how it usually comes out. My hunch is that he won't be charged with anything"

Dad had sat listening and, seemingly, mulling something over in his mind. "I will never forget the look on Judson's face there in the church. He saw something that scared the bejeebers out of him. What do you two think it was?"

"Well, we've taken this as a spiritual battle, and asked for God to help us fight it. I believe he saw the warriors of Heaven, with their swords drawn. Can you imagine having perhaps hundreds of brightly-clad warriors, maybe ten feet tall, and with fiery swords pointing right at you? Wouldn't you be quaking in your boots?" Lucas laughed at the thought.

"And maybe it's possible he saw those warriors fighting the demons that had been controlling him for so long. If he did, and he knew those demons were seeking to keep controlling him, that would be scary, too," I said thoughtfully. "Anyway, we won't know, unless Judson tells what he saw. He's got a lot to answer for, and it's almost tempting to pity him."

"I do pity anyone who gets himself into that kind of condition, so far from God." Dad shook his head, sorrowfully.

"Lucas, I'm really sorry that I didn't keep following your instructions to stay off the streets, until Judson was in custody," I confessed. "I honestly thought it would be okay to go with Trish yesterday. But, very quickly, I learned that it had been a foolish decision on my part."

"On the surface, yes, darlin', but just look what happened. Judson had fled the apartment, and may not have come back. If so, we would have

ONCE AGAIN I FEAR

had to start from scratch to find him again. Without knowing it, you really smoked him out of hiding, even though you risked your life. Maybe it was God's plan to bring an end to this thing." Lucas squeezed my hand, and his face showed that he was not just trying to make me feel better. He meant what he said.

"You may be right. Anyway, that thought makes me feel better." I did feel a relief from guilt, thinking of it that way.

"There's another thing, Lucas, which gave me the most wonderful shivers ever. The man with the cane. I swear he wasn't there when I passed that spot right ahead of Judson. Then, I looked back, and there he was, tripping Judson to save me. Maybe he was the man in the purple sweat suit or the jeans and windbreaker."

"I've come to believe God has had many angels around you, baby. I praise Him every minute for that." He looked at me with love and wonder.

Lucas suddenly took his arm from around me, and clapped his hands once together. "Okay, now, we've drawn all the conclusions we can in this whole affair, but, now, let's start making some plans for us. Stan, I want you in on this, and I'm sure Rachelle does, too." He grinned at me, and I nodded.

"I've been praying a lot about what God wants us to do. You'll remember I said I wanted us to do things in God's time. Well, when I called Doug West this morning, we were just chatting and he said, 'You and Rachelle have no need to wait to be together. The Lord showed me that there is nothing hindering your union.' Let me tell you, I nearly whooped for joy. I had been feeling the same thing, and this was confirmation that I wasn't just entertaining wishful thinking. What about you, beautiful lady?"

"Last night, I prayed for a long time before I went to bed. I kept hearing a voice, very quiet, that said, 'I'm with you and Lucas; I have already blessed your coming together.' It was so strong inside me, that I knew that it was from the Lord. Now, what you and Doug have said confirms my feelings." I leaned my head against Lucas' shoulder and breathed the sweet smell of him. "As I've said before, I'd marry you this minute, if I could. But, perhaps Valentine's Day might be a perfect time.

I should have time by then, to get my dress—I've had my eye on one in the bridal department at Devon's—plan for the bridesmaids, and invite all our friends. Oh, and I have your ring already picked out in Devon's fine jewelry department. We'll have it at Word of Life, but Doug will come help Tom with the ceremony. We'll have a reception in the family center of the church. I know the ladies from the church will want to prepare the refreshments. One of them makes gorgeous wedding cakes. What do you think, my love?"

"Absolutely perfect," Lucas said. "Now, my job is to plan the honeymoon, I think. I've got time-off coming, so I'll take it then, and we'll go to Hawaii for a week. I'll go to a travel agent Monday to arrange everything."

"May I make a proposition, here," Dad interrupted. "If you can get two weeks off, why don't you plan for that? And let me give you the trip as my wedding present to the two of you. I think one of the happiest times Annabel and I had was the time that we spent two weeks at the Kea Lani Resort on Maui—just fabulous. A friend of mine is the general manager at the Kea Lani, and he would love supervising the arrangements for my daughter's honeymoon there. I don't want to take anything away from you, Lucas, but, please, let me do it, in memory of Annabel, shall we say."

Dad's eyes held a gentle pleading, which touched my heart. I turned to Lucas and saw my emotion mirrored in his face. "That is so kind of you, Stan. How can I refuse? Thank you. And I do have two weeks vacation time coming."

Lucas then continued, looking at me. "Your wedding ring is waiting to be picked up from the jewelers, whenever I choose to get it. And my aunt Brenda is a florist; she would love to do the flowers—just call her." Lucas let out a long breath and grabbed me in his arms, kissing me energetically. It wasn't as gentle a kiss as he usually gave me, but it was just what the occasion called for. I kissed him back, with equal vigor, my heart singing a song, more beautiful than any Christmas carol.

I finally leaned away from Lucas and cocked my head to one side, smiling at him. "I've been thinking I must have taken this big apartment for some reason. It's plenty big enough for two people. There's lots of

ONCE AGAIN I FEAR

closet space, and room for all your other things. I have no doubt about that, after seeing that dinky place you live in. What do you think?"

"I felt at home in this apartment, the first time I came through the door. That sounds like a wonderful idea to me. At least you don't have your bedroom—soon to be our bedroom—done in pink, with frills and lace." Again, there was his mischievous smile.

"I think our bedroom will be just right for us, my darling." I kissed him quickly and laughed happily.

Dad sat grinning, a look of profound joy on his face.

Finally, Lucas said, "Isn't it time for Christmas dinner? I'm starved. And, I just thought, Stan, I've got to start practicing calling you 'Dad'. Come February fourteenth, that's what I'm going to call you. That'll be okay with my own father, because I call him 'Pops'"

Dad grinned and grabbed our hands, starting for the kitchen. "And, Lucas," he said, "I'll be very proud to call you 'Son'."

Printed in the United States
68840LVS00008B/10